DREAMS ENTANGLED

What Reviewers Say About Sophia Kell Hagin's Work

Whatever Gods May Be

"A riveting novel with a twist of romance, *Whatever Gods May Be* is a fun and exciting read, hard to put down."—*Midwest Book Review*

"*Whatever Gods May Be* by Sophia Kell Hagin is brilliant! This is one of the books that leaves you just wanting to say 'WOW!' Kell Hagin writes about war with a freshness that keeps the heat, the fear and the violence in the front of your mind as you are turning the pages, glued to the action. There is nowhere to hide in this book, it is full on."
—*Lesbian Review*

"There are twists and turns throughout the book and to give any one of them in a review would be a disservice to the reader. Suffice it to say that each twist and each turn is believable and will keep the reader turning pages as fast as she can. Kudos to BSB for departing from their norm and publishing this book. This book deserves a wide audience, if for no other reason than to say to lesbian publishers, your readers want more than what is being served up to them now. This book is a start."
—*Lambda Literary Review*

"*Whatever Gods May Be* is an exceptionally fine first novel. Jamie Gwynmorgan, its heroine, grabs the reader by the heart in the first few pages, and never lets go. With great character development and an exciting plot, this is sure to be a novel considered for the GCLS award for Debut Author."—*Just About Write*

"This is a story about survival and resilience as a young soldier in the army, thrust into marine basic training, and then into war. The central character is wonderfully drawn by Hagin, and convincingly portrays the vulnerabilities a self doubting young woman, and the pressures and responsibilities she faces as more and more is asked of her. There is grit in the telling of events, and Hagin sets a blistering pace in the action, that at points I could hear the gunfire going off in my head."—*Lesbian Book Review*

"This physically and psychologically intense war novel has balls. The blood of battle courses through this novel's pages with an astonishing relentlessness; the harrowing experience of prolonged interrogation becomes horrifically riveting. This isn't a novel for the faint of heart. It is a novel for fans of straight-up war stories, with a dash of the supernatural on the side."—*Gay Calgary Magazine*

Shadows of Something Real

"This novel is a thriller, but also a romance, so much the sweeter for Jamie after all she's survived. Adele (Lily's sister and just as bad-ass as the rest of the family) is the emotionally open woman Jamie needs. Thankfully, all these women are humanized by their flaws. This book is chock-full of evil politicians and corporations, high-tech gadgetry and life-and-death struggles. Highly recommended, even to folks who don't tend toward massive woman crushes like me."—*To Be Read Reviews*

"Hagin has taken command of the words on the page and shown such a richness of language. ...It was another brilliant read, and I am waiting to see where her wonderful imagination will take us next." —*Lesbian Review*

Omnipotence Enough

"I think any lover of thrillers will enjoy *Omnipotence Enough*, but readers of the earlier books will feel a special investment in this last journey. Well done, Sophia Kell Hagin. I look forward to your future novels, for the adrenaline and compassion and all the future woman crushes sure to come."—*C-Spot Reviews*

"The personal narrative with Hagin's rich use of language has been my great love of all three books in the series. Jamie Gwymorgan is the thing that carries you through the work and she is one of those characters that you find yourself thinking about long after you have finished the book."—*Lesbian Review*

By the Author

Whatever Gods May Be

Shadows of Something Real

Omnipotence Enough

Not All a Dream

Dreams Entangled

DREAMS ENTANGLED

by
Sophia Kell Hagin

2025

DREAMS ENTANGLED

ISBN 13: 978-1-63679-892-9

This Trade Paperback Original Is Published By
Bold Strokes Books, Inc.
P.O. Box 249
Valley Falls, NY 12185

First Edition: September 2025

Credits
Editor: Cindy Cresap
Production Design: Susan Ramundo
Cover Design By Inkspiral Design

Dedication

for Susan

for *always*

If you wish to find the secrets of the universe,
think in terms of energy, frequency, and vibration.

—(attributed to) Nikola Tesla

Chapter One: Lurbegia

P irin Basamendi rarely made mistakes, but she had this time.
Why, she kept asking herself, had she handed over the ohskal, her amatchi's sacred lightning stone, to someone she'd only just met?

It started with Jessica, her childhood candy-shoplifting BFF, the first girl who ever brought her to orgasm, for years the only other lesbian in her orbit, still the smartest person she knew.

Pirin trusted Jessica Winter completely, unreservedly, told her (almost) everything. And now Jess trusted Frederika Peng, talked and talked about how Fred was "the real deal, *absolutely* the one," about Fred's quirky sense of humor, Fred's sexily subtle German accent, Fred's PhD, Fred's impressive geochemistry lab, Fred's even more impressive geochemistry expertise. "And good-looking too," noted delicately, blondly beautiful Jessica.

Not surprising, perhaps, that when Jess brought the good-looking real deal over to have a quick drink before all three of them went to Newburyport for that meet-my-new-girlfriend dinner, Fred immediately spotted the ohskal Pirin had forgotten to put away and marched straight over to it for a closer look. So, okay, no biggie—not until Fred took the ohskal out of its box *without even asking*.

"Well, this is handsome," she said, one eyebrow cambering as she held the ohskal up to the light. "Star quartz. Exceptionally clear." Then she turned the handaxe-sized stone to examine its other side. "Oh! An ammonite fossil—in pyrite, I'd say, given that dull-brass finish. Superbly preserved spiral. Easy to see all those Fibonacci-sequence details. With the quartz crystal growing off its backside. Where'd you get it? Ever had it tested?"

Inhaling slowly, Pirin shut her eyes against the sudden steam of *hmmph!* encircling her head and stiffened to restrain her temper and her mouth and her hands. Fred failed to see this because that would have required looking at something besides the ohskal. But Jessica noticed. She slid alongside Fred, gently took possession of the stone, picked up the wooden box from which Fred had plucked it, and handed both to Pirin with a plea in her apologetic smile.

"Mmm," Pirin heard herself hum, a useful sound that could mean almost anything, disguise almost anything. My own damn fault, she managed not to say, for leaving Amatchi's ohskal lying around in an open box where anyone can put their brazen paws all over it—paws that don't deserve to be warned about the ohskal's razor-sharp edges. She snugged the stone into its box's plush cloth folds before walking it over to the cabinet beneath her TV and stowing it out of sight. "No," she said, "it's never been tested."

Damn. Too curt. One glimpse at Jess's face mirrored how thoroughly her irritation had hardened the shadows darkening her own already angular features, the abundant eyebrows furrowing above near-black eyes gone ominous-dead just like always when something pissed her off. She knew it all added up to too much of the truth of her, a truth Jessica had seen often enough—too often maybe. But not Fred.

Relent, Basamendi, *relent.*

"We, uh, never played with it or anything, cuz it was my grandmother's." Pirin spoke almost softly. "She said it's come down through many generations. From, she used to say, before the beginning of time as we now conceive it."

"Any idea *where* that is?" Fred persisted, apparently oblivious of Jessica's glare.

With Jessica's eyes begging *please be nice, please*, Pirin inhaled again and smiled, first at Jess, next at Fred as her fingers raked her cropped, near-black hair, an old habit that usually helped soothe her pique. "I asked that once when I was a kid. My grandmother brought me over to our globe, spun it around, pointed at southeast Asia, and said 'Handik ihes egin genuen.'"

Jessica's eyes widened as she gazed up at Pirin. "Jeez, Pir, I've never heard that one before. What's it mean?"

"It means 'We fled from there.'"

"From southeast Asia, before the beginning of time," murmured Jessica. "I'd sure as hell like to hear *that* story…"

But Fred was still stuck on the ohskal itself. "Star quartz with pyrite isn't all that unusual," she declared. "But a pyrite ammonite fossil so well-preserved isn't quite so common."

Pirin nodded, even kept on smiling; she wasn't ready to relay what little she recalled of her amatchi's tales about who fled what—so sure, let's babble about the ohskal. "Well, it'll throw off quite bright colors, depending on the light."

"Really?" Fred glanced over at the ohskal-harboring cabinet. "I'd love to test it, get a look at its molecular structure."

And no worries, Fred assured her—the testing would be "non-destructive—no alterations to the specimen." Micro-CT scans, nano-CT scans, quick turnaround—just a week or three.

Another hum vibrated through Pirin's chest, the same meld of irritation and distrust. But she quashed it, and not just for Jessica's sake; she was also tempted.

Way. *Too.* Tempted.

She'd been curious about the ohskal for as long as she could remember. Then, when ninety-one-year-old Amatchi handed it to her one quiet evening, kissed her good night, and never woke up again, Pirin's grief flared into a desire to find answers to all the questions she'd neglected to ask.

Amatchi hadn't ever called the ohskal a star quartz, nor described its backside spiral as an ammonite fossil, but the gemologist Pirin showed it to did, then offered to buy it. She declined (the dude babbled way too much about "auras"). Instead she'd wait and hope some answers to her myriad questions might surface in the fullness of time.

Four years on, however, those questions lingered, as did Pirin's sense of nagging disappointment: The ohskal had never shown itself to her as anything but a damn rock.

In stark contrast, the damn rock had shown plenty to Amatchi as well as at least some of the grandmothers who preceded her. *This* ohskal, Amatchi indicated, was special—nothing like the traditional green or gray polished stone long reputed to keep your house safe from lightning if you plunked it narrow-side-up in the ground outside your door.

Certainly, Pirin never once saw Amatchi do anything like this with *her* ohskal. Instead, she scrunched an old steel axe-head into the dirt next to the back stoop alongside a bunch of lilies-of-the-valley, leaving a few inches of the sharp end sticking out. Kinda like a boot-scraper, Pirin always thought. So why, she'd asked, use an axe-head when you have an actual ohskal that, Amatchi had long implied, would be preferable to metal when it came to steering lightning?

Because, Amatchi explained, unlike any metal axe-head ever, *this* ohskal protected the woman whom it claimed, not the woman's etche—her house. Such a special ohskal manifested old-time "lurbegia"—deep-earth truth: ancient myth and magic that, for Pirin anyway, amounted to little more than corrupted history and wishful thinking contorting each other.

For Amatchi, however, "lurbegia" was neither myth nor magic. It offered a means to comprehend fundamental, underlying reality.

And if you happened to be Amatchi's granddaughter, it offered stories, too. Amatchi told and retold the ohskal's stories in ways so immediate and indelible that Pirin could envision the people in them, even sense the rhythms, if not the specifics, of the long, immensely dangerous journey they endured.

Pirin dubbed these yarns Amatchi's Favorite Fables—not unlike other families' stories of Santa Claus, she occasionally joked (but never in front of Amatchi): First, in your child-innocence, you believe it all, until you grasp how preposterous it is—yet it remains so appealing that you keep playing along and, if pressed, mumble something about the virtues of metaphor.

Of course, Amatchi saw the eye rolls and small frowny headshakes that quite eloquently expressed Pirin's unspoken skepticism. But she never wavered. "You are a child of your times," she once told Pirin with amused benevolence. "And your times, too, suffer from the rigid mindsets of fearful people."

The ohskal had always showed her things, Amatchi said. "Egunen batean ulertuko duzu," she then repeated—one day you will understand. And despite her old-world roots and increasing fragility, Amatchi could not be easily disdained. She was, right to the end, a deeply intelligent, astute, intuitive woman. Farsighted and wise in so many ineffable, unlikely ways that she attributed to her ohskal.

Still, when Pirin pushed for details about what the ohskal had communicated and how and when, Amatchi's responses stretched well beyond scientific reasoning. When Pirin pointed this out, Amatchi merely said "Zientziak bere mugak ditu." Science has its limits.

True enough. This, however, did not prevent Pirin from concluding that the power of the ohskal depended entirely on one's willingness to believe in the power of the ohskal.

Yet...

Yet in the four years since taking possession of that same rock, Pirin regularly remembered those sunny afternoons when Amatchi, ensconced in a comfortable chair near the south-facing windows in her room, lifted the ohskal to the sunlight, staring at it almost dreamily while the sun's rays refracted through its craggy array of hexagonal crystals to cast vivid streaks of colored, occasionally coiled light across the walls and across her face while she nodded and murmured.

As if she and the ohskal were in conversation. And then, within days, even hours, Amatchi would say or do something that could only be described as prescient. "How'd you do that?" Pirin once asked. "Does the ohskal tell you more than just old-time stories?"

Amatchi smiled and said something cryptic about dreams and insight, concluding with "Argi egokia denean"—when the light is right—before she winked and added "Aldi egokia denean." When the time is right.

Yeah, yeah, but a scabrous, sharp-edged chunk of rock able to protect chosen old women from lightning, show them ancient tales, make them preternaturally intuitive?

Before Pirin could embrace any of it, she'd have to see it *rationally* explained. Plus, of course, whatever was rationally explained would also have to be tested and verified. Not gonna hold my breath, Pirin thought. But, hey, scientists have a lo-o-o-ong way to go before they discover every damn thing everywhere, so Pirin had to acknowledge that maybe Amatchi's take on the ohskal was *not* entirely impossible.

So *what if* Jessica's pushy geochemist could spot something in the ohskal's see-through hexagons, in its crystals' helically-arranged atoms and trapped electrons? Something capable of reconciling those mythic links to lightning and "lurbegia" with the empirical world Pirin lived in. Because the ohskal was all she had left of Amatchi, and oh Basandere, how she missed that old woman still...

Upon being asked what various scans of the ohskal might reveal, Fred regaled Pirin with incomprehensible jargon which, when translated, came with too many squishy maybes and possiblys that added up to not a whole lot. But, Fred reminded her, this is always how it goes with scientific endeavor. "We talk about 'hypotheses' and 'experiments' for a reason. We won't learn anything about your specimen if we don't look."

Pirin didn't much like the way Fred kept describing Amatchi's sacred lightning stone as a "specimen," but once lubricated by several glasses of wine at the hip new restaurant on Water Street (where Fred happily paid for dinner), she agreed to *consider* allowing Jessica's geochemist to examine the damn rock. A few days later, after gazing at "the specimen" for an entire evening in fruitless hope it might somehow offer up a hint about how to proceed, she called Jessica.

"Okay," she said. "I'll do it. As long as it's only non-destructive testing, understood?"

"Great!" Jessica enthused. "I'm coming up to spend Sunday with my mum, so I can stop at your place Monday morning to pick it up and then give it to Fred as soon as she gets back from Germany."

When Pirin handed the ohskal to Jessica, she tamped down a thin, sharp trickle of apprehension, repeated the stuff about only non-destructive testing, then drove off to interview a couple of claimants involved in what her colleagues thought was a typically minor, one-off fraud scheme. By day's end, she'd uncovered a much larger organized scam, juicy enough to attract her boss's exuberant praise. Not even this, however, alleviated the strange queasiness that had gripped her all day. Nor did working out that evening on her elliptical till her legs trembled.

Likely nothing would've prevented the nightmare, either—the one about another geochemist who noticed the ohskal in Fred's lab: Micro-CT scanning and nano-CT scanning just wouldn't be enough, he insisted. Oh no, we need x-ray diffraction and x-ray fluorescence and nuclear magnetic resonance and optical microscopy and electron microprobe analysis—which meant making thin sections, grinding some of the specimen down to powder.

And Fred agreed. "She'll never know if we're careful about what we take," Fred told the other geochemist. "A little here, a little there…"

Pirin startled awake sweaty and shivering. Amatchi had always said the ohskal must *never* be cut up, *never* be heated, and on Amatchi's last night on this earth, as Pirin took the ohskal into her hands, she'd promised to always care for the sacred lightning stone, *always*. "Egunen batean ulertuko duzu," Amatchi whispered one more time, the last words she ever heard her grandmother speak. One day you will understand.

And now—*now* she had betrayed her promise…

"Jess!" Pirin yelled into her phone before she'd even rolled out of bed. "Have you still got it? Please tell me you still got it!"

To her credit, Jessica understood. "Change your mind, Basamendi?"

"Yes! Do you still have it?"

"As it happens, I do. Fred won't be back till next Monday."

"Esker Amari!" Pirin back-flopped onto her bed, suddenly out of breath.

"I remember that one. Means, um, 'Thanks to the Mothers,' right?"

"Right. Gold star for you, Winter. I want it back. Today."

"Okay." Jessica didn't sound surprised. "I left it at the office, but I'll bring it home tonight. I won't be back in the village till Sunday, so if you want it right away, feel free to come by my place after work."

"Yes. Done. When will you get home?"

"Let's say six. And bring wine in lieu of that gold star. I'm gonna need it cuz I'm not even at work yet and I already feel like shit."

CHAPTER TWO: THOSE FIFTY WORDS

E ver since that terrifying Wednesday, Gracie blamed the damn rock—the one she brought home when the office got shut down and everyone was told to work remotely till further notice.

Since she wasn't into rocks, she'd glanced only briefly at the raggedy, lopsided gush of clear crystal spears she'd agreed to look after till her work buddy Jessica could reclaim it. That would have to wait, however: Jessica was stuck in the hospital struggling to breathe.

For the record, Gracie had nearly forgotten to take the rock with her. She'd been focused on Jessica's "important stuff—my laptop an' 'specially the silver flash drive in the righthand drawer."

Understandable: In her muddled state just before she collapsed, Jessica had unintentionally obliterated a passel of unsaved document revisions, and somehow the silver flash drive contained the only surviving copies. The "wood box with the sparkly stone inside" was an afterthought. "No big deal," Jessica had taken the trouble to explain from the ER between tea-kettle wheezes while Gracie rummaged through the drawer in question. "Just, y'know, it's not mine an' I promised...t' take...extra special...."

Gracie didn't remember if Jessica ever finished that sentence. But she did remember spotting the little oakwood box and briefly checking inside—yep, a "sparkly stone"—before putting the box in the canvas bag with the rest of Jessica's hurriedly collected office stuff, and, once home, uploading everything on the flash drive to the Institute's cloud where Jessica could eventually deal with it.

The oakwood box ended up forgotten on the desk in her bedroom's gloomiest corner until the next day when, after a morning working at said desk, Gracie took a break, and, noticing the box's intricately carved decoration (way more interesting than what it held), picked it up before ambling to the overstuffed chair next to her living room's only window to enjoy the view of the expansive park across the street.

There she nibbled her lunch, pleased to have just learned that at least Jessica was no sicker. Pleased, too, that for the rest of the day, while the Institute finalized various work-from-home protocols, she'd been freed from further online meetings. Freed from inevitably noticing her own insipid onscreen image and wishing that everything about her didn't look so…beige.

As Gracie gazed out her living room window at the park, she was—well, not exactly happy, but at least comfortable. Relaxed. That's when, out of curiosity, she opened the oakwood box again, gingerly lifted the stone to the light streaming in the window, which refracted slightly through those clear crystal spears…

It was a beautiful day.

Until it wasn't.

In a matter of seconds on that unseasonably warm, seemingly innocent Wednesday, the sun disappeared behind ominous dark clouds and a rush of wind-thunder-rain—lots of it all at once—inundated the park. The scene was biblically cinematic and Gracie was enthralled.

Then lightning lit up her world. She watched a single bolt in the roiling sky above the park split into three—a vast, electrified trident plunging down from the blackened heavens. All three of the trident's tines struck simultaneously. One gouged the middle of the park's soccer field, another cleaved a mid-sized oak across the street, the third attacked the utility pole twenty feet from her third-floor window—together inciting a single immense *BOOM!* that shook the ground, the building, the window, and every cell in Grace Gwyllt Olwyn's body.

Shook her right out of the chair, too, maybe out of time itself: From the middle of her living room, she watched mesmerized as a thin spear of ghostly, pale-blue electricity streaked horizontally from the utility pole through the open window to touch the "sparkly stone" she couldn't remember leaving on the windowsill. This instantly provoked violent pulses of blinding, headache-inducing light that burst into whirling spirals of every color imaginable.

Maybe she screamed. Her head hurt that much.

Just as instantly, the pale-blue thread of lightning withdrew, taking its impossibly intense lightshow with it. Moments later, the storm and her headache evaporated. Moments after that, the sun returned.

Gracie required a bit longer to shake off enough of her astonishment and fear to grasp that she'd come through unscathed and could risk inching back toward the window.

Still perched on the windowsill, the rock appeared entirely normal, just as crystal clear as before. It wasn't even hot (Gracie touched it— *very* carefully—to make sure).

Outside, a few people had already ventured forth to examine the scorched gash in the park's soccer field and the scattered debris from the eviscerated oak, while a downed live wire from the stricken utility pole sparked and whipped across the sidewalk and into the street, halting traffic. Just as the police arrived to cordon off the area, Gracie realized the power was out. She also noticed a small frayed hole in her window's screen where, she assumed, the pale-blue lightning bolt had entered and exited.

Also, whenever she closed her eyes for longer than a normal blink, behind her eyelids she saw savagely bright light whirls alive with every color she'd ever seen or imagined. A heartbeat later, her head throbbed painfully for a few minutes in cadence with the erupting light.

This bizarre effect lasted all day before subsiding with nightfall, and Gracie dared to hope for a quiet, mundane evening, which was exactly what she got.

But then everything changed—because of the dream. At least that's what she believed, and she hasn't encountered a damn thing since to persuade her otherwise.

Back when she was in college, Gracie often had dreams that were indistinguishable from ordinary waking life. Many mornings, she'd rouse recalling details of conversations she'd later discover had never happened. So she learned to wait for those she dreamed about to offer up a sign that the conversations she thought she'd had were real; at least half the time she'd figure out that no, it really had all been just a dream.

This latest just-a-dream, at least, was different. It gave itself away while it was happening, which made it worth writing down afterward:

⚡ I stood at the edge of a robust nighttime campfire around which a group of women quietly chatted. Although I could make out individual voices, I didn't recognize the language they spoke.

There were maybe twenty of them, all wearing simple handmade clothes of undyed, coarse-knit hemp or wool; they sat cross-legged knee to knee, the nearest of them with their backs to me. Over on the opposite side of the fire, I spotted an empty space and wondered if I was supposed to sit there.

No, I concluded—I'm just an observer.

That's when I realized I was dreaming.

Which prompted a question: Was I *actually* there, dream-present in their world? Or was I, y'know, "at the movies"?

"Oh, you're here all right," someone behind me said as a hand rested on my shoulder. "And you have a job to do."

A woman's voice, low and commanding. As I turned, the hand on my shoulder tightened its grip. Eyes front, it insisted—and I complied. So I barely glimpsed the figure in a full-length, face-obscuring hooded robe.

"Watch now," she said as the soft lilt of campfire conversation subsided, leaving only the crackling sounds of burning wood. "Watch and remember."

On the far side of the fire, a human form—also in a full-length, face-obscuring hooded robe—stepped out of the darkness and joined the circle amidst the respectfully murmured greetings of the seated women. Lithe, long-fingered hands, bronze in the firelight, slid back the hood to reveal an older woman's benevolent, smiling face.

Then this older woman said something I couldn't quite hear (and likely wouldn't have understood) while she stared at me. At me alone.

Except she didn't.

Every single other person around that campfire had been spoken to, stared at by this woman just as I had, and at precisely the same moment. I knew this with unmitigated certainty, though I have no idea *how* I knew. Not until—

"You," I muttered, pivoting to the hooded figure who continued to stand behind me, whose hand remained firm on my shoulder. "You did that, didn't you?"

"Watch," she told me again. "And remember."

I still couldn't see her shadowed face, not really, and this annoyed me. I wanted to grab the hood and fling it back, wanted to yell how-dare-you-order-me-around! But her eyes, blazing darkly from beneath the hood, stopped me, shut me down completely.

She didn't say another word, but I heard her anyway: "Damn. You need training, Gracie. This will take longer than I'd hoped."

Then those smoldering eyes directed my gaze back to the campfire, to the woman who'd emerged from the night and was beginning to speak. Again I complied, and as I watched I comprehended what I heard.

⚡ When Gracie woke up, she remembered none of the woman's words. Those details were lost to pain just like the lightning headache, this time persisting for about ten minutes before it abruptly ceased.

Headache aside, Gracie certainly found the experience intriguing; in her whole life, she'd had only one other lucid dream. Yet she just couldn't remember what the woman at the campfire said.

No time to dwell on a dream, though. Soon enough, Gracie's boss's head would pop onscreen; a mere phone conversation, while "adequate," just didn't sufficiently replicate the "invaluable" experience of face-to-face office interactions, especially now that actual face-to-face anything had been indefinitely suspended. So it would have to be screentime—what Gracie thought of (with a wince) as "beigetime."

She already knew what he wanted: "results"—in the form of colorful charts and graphs as cartoonish as she could make them, because "the raw data's boring as hell and nobody cares about why this crosstab instead of that crosstab." She'd already run the data through the appropriate scripts and algorithms, even developed the report's outline—but she was behind on her cartoon production.

As she shuffled out of bed with cartoons on the brain, she spotted something scribbled on the pad of paper she always kept on her bedside table. The writing was childlike, primitive:

⚡ I am Ansosho Eletun who travels the Seas' waves to many Lands so that I may sing the Tales of the Mothers and impart the insights born of the Motherworld's Resonant Rhythms.

I sing this Tale, but one of many, with reverence and joy.

Remember my song. Remember and reclaim

⚡ For just a second, Gracie's stomach corkscrewed, her breathing halted. A wave of nebulous fear rolled through her.

That name—Ansosho Eletun...yes, that was the hooded woman from her dream who stared at her from across the campfire. Also, she recognized her own scrawl, even though it seemed to have been written by her left hand.

Yet she was sure she'd slept the night through—so when could she have written down anything...?

Oh god, she realized, I won't be able to control this—

She would damn well try, though.

She peered at those fifty words. They did make some sort of stilted, archaic sense. But what were the Tales of the Mothers? What were the Motherworld's Resonant Rhythms?

After a mercifully quick meeting with her boss, she undertook a futile hour of internet digging using a variety of search engines and search terms related to dreams—and didn't find a single relevant digital crumb.

"What'd you expect?" Gracie grumbled after stomping away from the computer in frustration. "It was just a dream. And hell, dreams aren't supposed to make sense."

Dreams fade quickly, too, if you let them. By the time she brewed a pot of coffee and ate some granola, she'd moved on.

Chapter Three: Too many.
And not nearly enough.

S hit!" Pirin bellowed. "*SHIT!!*" In swift succession, two coffee mugs exploded against the wall behind the bistro table and chairs near the large glass sliders that opened to her deck. At least the mugs were empty, though table and chairs were now thoroughly sprinkled with ceramic shards.

"Uh-oh. Was that about Jessica? Or are *you*—?"

Startled, Pirin pivoted toward the sound just as her mother peeked into her kitchen. "No no, Ama, I'm fine," she said, attempting to sound normal. "And Fred says Jess is still in the ICU but no worse."

Pirin gritted her teeth. How the *hell* had she missed the electronic ping signaling a presence at the foot of the back stairs leading to her sanctum above the garage? She'd installed that sensor to prevent exactly this sort of moment...

"No worse." Sasiama Basamendi visibly exhaled. "And none of us sick yet. Plenty to be grateful for..." But the worry in her hushed voice hadn't abated, and Pirin knew it wasn't just because they were only six days into their fourteen-day quarantine.

Shaking her head, Pirin apologized. She'd managed to bundle three stupids into a single idiotic temper tantrum. First she lost control of herself, then she made a damn mess that would take way too long to clean up, and mostly—*mostly*—she hadn't ensured she was alone, so her mother had witnessed that unnerving, too-familiar fury and no doubt understood it for what it really was: boundless.

Sasiama had knocked, of course. Sasiama Basamendi—Sama to her friends and her husband (but not her children unless they were feeling sassy)—always knocked, always waited to be invited across the threshold. This sacrosanct family protocol could be ditched only for an emergency. Or fear of an unfolding emergency—like when something loudly shatters while someone's screeching profanities.

"Anyway, I come bearing snail mail." Sama's careful smile didn't entirely wipe the concern from her face as she placed a couple of envelopes on the counter next to the kitchen sink before glancing toward the coffee mugs' remains. "So, uh, are you okay?"

"Yeah. Just work crap," Pirin fudged. "They want us doing interviews and every other damn thing from home for the foreseeable. Word is the governor's gonna declare a state of emergency tomorrow, so the company powers-that-be say no more field stuff. Means, basically, that we've all become desk investigators." She sighed melodramatically. "At least we'll still get paid as field investigators. For now, anyway."

Sama accepted it all. Pirin could see that, though she also noticed a thin crease between her mother's graying eyebrows—sure sign that the apprehension her outburst spawned had not entirely dissipated. Time to boost the distraction quotient. "How 'bout I bring over my tchistor and potato ragout for dinner tonight?"

"Really? You have the time?"

"Well, today's pretty much a write-off while the IT people deploy new work-from-home stuff. So yeah, today anyway I have the time. Plus I already have the ingredients. No problem making plenty enough for all of us."

At last, Sama genuinely smiled. "Okay, sweetie, you're on. See you at, uh—?"

"I'll bring everything across at six thirty."

Pirin made the ragout first, even before she cleaned up after her hissy fit, hoping that while she stirred her slow-simmering specialty she'd be able to calm down and do some clear, orderly thinking. But no-o-o-o—like an overexcited electron jolted out of its atomic orbital, her mind arbitrarily ricocheted from one fret to another.

Starting with how desperately ill Jessica was, even on day seven in the ICU, and the very real possibility that Jess might die—notwithstanding the tremulous optimism coming from both Jess's mother and Fred, who kept repeating that Jess was stable, not on a ventilator, not yet.

How Jess caught the virus remained a mystery. Fred was feeling crappy but no worse than a typical head cold, while Jess's mum was fine, as were Pirin and her parents and her sister Esti and her two nieces. So far anyway. Only upon completing the two-week quarantine could Esti and the kids return home. *If* everyone remained healthy. In the meantime, they'd be staying right next door while Esti's husband brought over groceries to leave on the back stoop.

And now an official state of emergency, which meant a statewide stay-at-home order with its cavalcade of disruption, nuisance, and hassle.

Like closure of the martial arts studio where for years Pirin typically spent a couple of evenings a week nurturing her abilities not just to fight and defend herself but to stay balanced and aware in body and mind no matter how stymied or threatened or angry she got. Even a brief loss of these workout-and-spar nights and the après socializing with her group of close-knit, like-minded women was beyond depressing.

Then there were the recycle projects.

At the very least her recycles would have to be redesigned, if not put on indefinite hold—including the latest one she'd been planning. This prospect left Pirin deeply frustrated; years ago, those recycles became her raison d'être. They were how she controlled her incalculable rage, why she decided all the way back in college to find a job in what's probably the world's most humdrum industry.

Because humdrum or not, she'd concluded that even an entry-level position (like the claims adjuster slot she managed to score at the start of the so-called "great recession") would provide access to the databases that mattered—those private, restricted, often absurdly pricey hoards of detailed information on nearly everybody.

To be clear, Pirin didn't give a hoot about "nearly everybody." But she cared ferociously about a certain subset of "nearly everybody": people she'd pinpointed because she or someone she completely trusted had seen or heard or suffered what they did.

So how many had there been since that first one all those years ago?

Too many. And not nearly enough.

Certainly no one had come close to stopping her, not least because no one—*not one living soul*—knew anything about Pirin Basamendi's recycle projects. This was a consummate accomplishment, one that increasingly sophisticated surveillance, communications, and pattern recognition technologies were making more and more difficult.

No matter. She would not forsake recycling.

Of course, she saw no profit from it, which was deliberate: Her recycles were most emphatically *not* about making money, though she'd occasionally collect an anonymous "fee" from the targeted to cover such infrastructure costs as software, server maintenance, dark web hosting subscriptions, and burner phones.

Yet after almost twelve years working at what did make her money—first the claims side, then the fraud investigation side of the insurance industry—Pirin had to admit it: She was bored. And she was struggling to get unbored, a possibility she'd never taken seriously way back when she started.

She'd moved from auto to property, from carrier claims adjusting to independent claims adjusting, where she made a lot more money and used the stretches of time between assignments to bag experience in penetration testing, drone piloting, and mobile surveillance. She'd even set up a couple of side businesses, one as a pentesting consultant, the other as a federally-licensed drone operator, and had grown a small list of commercial clients.

The good money, though, came from independent catastrophic claims adjusting, which was great—till the except-fors started piling on and weighing her down. *Except for* the out-of-town stints lasting for too many uninterrupted weeks in dismally crappy, occasionally dangerous motel rooms. *Except for* how her lengthy absences starved one coulda-been-serious relationship and stillbirthed two others. *Except for* when she returned home mere weeks before her amatchi died.

After Amatchi left this world, Pirin took all the pentesting and drone-piloting gigs she could get. But to pay the other two-thirds of her bills, she soon accepted a job with a carrier—this time on the bottom rung of the firm's investigative unit because, apparently, someone Important decided they needed at least one investigator who was under fifty and of the female persuasion.

Initially, the old fart ex-cops she worked with—and for—fobbed off all the crappy stuff on her and made too many snide remarks about "somebody" being on the rag. After peppering her first eighteen months with ripostes about gravity and shrinkage, she gained a bit of begrudging sufferance. It helped, too, that she was an ace interviewer, had that federal drone pilot license, knew more about cyber-insurance risks and hygiene controls than the rest of them put together, and ranked second in the unit for closed substantiated fraud investigations.

But nope. Still not enough. Even though there was much to like about life as a claims fraud investigator, she hated those days stuck in the office with "the guys" under largely pointless one-size-fits-all digital surveillance—keystrokes recorded, app and browser usage tracked, screen content intermittently grabbed—to ensure everyone stayed "productive," which actually cornered her into being less productive.

Perpetually restless, Pirin preferred field interviews and inspections (especially when she got to pilot a drone), even preferred offsite meetings with lawyers and law enforcement officers. Hell, despite their doltish tendencies, lawyers and LEOs had (unwittingly) taught her plenty over the years.

And at least the drives from appointment to appointment gave her a chance to plan her next recycle and brainstorm ways to outmaneuver the company's asinine monitoring software. Also, her employer was willing to pay for the courses necessary for acquiring those all-important—and often pricy—cyber credentials.

Indeed, her pile of credentials had grown sufficiently that maybe it was almost time to consider a career in penetration testing with drone work on the side; done right, this could make more room for recycles, for sparring at the studio, for whatever else would keep her boredom at bay.

But now, dammit, this pandemic was forcing a complete reassessment of her job and certainly her recycle risk. One of her preferred IP spoofing techniques, for instance, might become rather tricky; would she get hassled while wardriving during a stay-at-home emergency when virtually no one was supposed to be on the road?

So yeah, okay, Pirin told herself as she looked around her eleven-hundred square-foot space, better this than getting stuck in the company's soul-sucking hive of ridiculously monitored cubicles breathing that virus-laden *used* air while enduring perpetual male preening and bullshitting. Though not nearly better enough.

And what would happen if her sister decided to embrace their mother's suggestion and move back to Etche Basamendi for the duration, or even permanently, with two young kids and a husband exhibiting signs of drift?

Also, wait a fucking minute—*who* the hell ended up with Amatchi's ohskal after Jess collapsed?

"And *how* the hell," Pirin growled at her burbling tchistor and potato ragout, "do I retrieve it during a pan-fucking-demic?"

All these currents of anxiety swirled chaotically around each other, simmering with Pirin's ragout, tightening her jaw, twisting her gut. Nothing new about that; she regularly had to scrape herself off whatever ceiling she stood under. But this time was different. This time was worse.

Maybe it was because she feared the ohskal would never be more for her than just a damn rock. What if she simply didn't have, could never have, whatever the ohskal needed or wanted or expected—and none of Fred's geochemical shenanigans would ever have made any difference?

Maybe it was because the longer Pirin stirred the ragout the more she worried about Jess, who'd been part of her life since she was five years old. Pirin dreaded the prospect of living in a world deprived of Jessica Winter.

Or maybe...

Maybe it was because that very morning she'd woken from a disturbingly realistic dream about Ayesha, who told her to move on, you've fulfilled the promise you should never have made, find your own life now. "It's been long enough, Pir—let me go," Ayesha had whispered right before kissing her and then dissolving into the morning light.

Somehow that kiss seemed like a final goodbye.

Chapter Four: Know this true

F ive days. Just five days till it happened again—this time while Gracie was scrambling to get a new, last-minute research project under control. The project's survey data, her boss announced very late on an exceptionally tedious Monday afternoon, was already sitting in a chaotic digital heap, "and super-methodical you," he cooed, "are exactly who we need to find the gold nuggets buried in there."

After a ten-minute browse, Gracie grimaced. The digital heap held only fool's gold, she pointed out as politely as possible. No matter: Promises had been made to the Institute's board members, "and we need those nuggets yesterday." Do the best you can, she was told, and hurry.

Next day, at roughly nine uninterrupted hours in, she must have fallen asleep at her desk—and for more than a few minutes. She jerked awake, yanked reluctantly from the fading sounds of women singing to grasp that her computer and both its screens had automatically powered down from lack of use, that the sun had set, and that her head hurt. When she closed her eyes again and massaged her right temple, an image of Ansosho Eletun briefly shimmered behind her eyelids.

Oh. Another dream.

And yeah, she thought, she should write this one down, too. But damn, that headache. And besides, how do you write down what someone sang in a language you can't fathom? Especially if that voice sounds like several voices at once, sometimes several harmonies, all of them hauntingly, hypnotically beautiful.

Even after she unaccountably picked up on some of this sung story, all she recalled was a single refrain, now an earworm: "before the beginning of time as you now conceive it"…

So okay, Gracie decided, maybe this whatever-is-going-on-here would leave her alone if she scribbled down what little else she remembered:

⚡ Look to the Mothers, who remind us that neither Death nor Life can overwhelm the Balance; together they make the Balance, each defining the other in Rhythm as they dance.

⚡ Only later did she see the atavistic scrawls on the inner pages of the pad of paper where she'd written project coding notes. She was looking at the same crude handwriting—*her own handwriting*—that had turned her stomach days earlier when she'd first encountered it.

Once more, her stomach three-sixtied: She had no memory of this stuff either. But she understood that the dream it recorded was merely an introduction:

⚡ The prophecies of the old Mothers were coming true day by day: Skies roiled, Winds roused, Seas rose, Mountains ruptured, men raged. Upon the wilding Winds came storms more fierce than ever the Tales told of, and all manner of creatures—rooted, winged, limbed, and limbless too—were lost to relentless floods and frenzied firebolts, to cataclysmic earth tremors and once-innocent Mountains now mercilessly spewing molten rock and poisonous clouds.

Again and again, sacred Rhythm places drowned or burned, destroying many Communities, dispersing their survivors. Travelers found desolation where once shelter and celebration welcomed them.

Early in the turmoil, those Communities fortuned by circumstance provided succor to the casualties. But turmoil persisted and, as the cycles of the Sun and Moon encircled generations, one by one, Communities were overtaken—if not by turmoil's survivors or their hostile descendants, then by the burdens of defending against them.

As the weight of these burdens disrupted the Mothers' Balance, too many lingering Communities succumbed, and a new, volatile order slowly unfolded: Each person should claim privately for themselves the means to survive, and anyone who failed in this effort did not deserve survival.

Eventually, this new order acquired a name: Privation.

Amidst Privation's dogged thrusts, male descendants of those first brothers and sons who had helped their Mothers' Communities jealously took what little endured unto themselves.

Though lacking ageless Analakinak wisdom, from the remnants of the Mothers' Communities these men forged Privation's several dominions, which repudiated Rhythm and Resonance in favor of acquiring more for each dominion by taking from others.

Soon enough, what the men of Privation claimed for themselves included the very people from whom they took all that could be taken, people whose labor they coerced for their own gain with threats of pain and death.

Such organized duress powered new forms of sustenance: large-scale gathering and fostering of foodstuffs, coordinated removal of materials from the Mothers' Earth to forge tools and implements for trade, for coercion, for enslavement, for vanity...

But rarely did the men of Privation share such bounties. Thus rivalry evolved into hostility, and conflict between Privation dominions grew unceasing.

As possession alone became the touchstone by which individuals judged the worth of themselves and others, Privation men were trained from infancy to fight, while Privation women learned from infancy to encourage this fighting.

With passage of time, the Mothers' Balance vanished. Few could sense Rhythm. Too many came to dread the dark and almost all accepted Privation as inevitable and everlasting, best for them and their children, on whom they could bestow all that was taken from others less powerful than they.

Hence, as the cycles of the Sun and Moon encircled generations, the Mothers and the Land were wrenched apart. No longer did peoples move with the seasons across the Motherworld to feed on her generous, ever-changing bounty and contribute to it in return; they remained trapped by Privation in a single place with but a few seeds, subject to the covetous demands of their enslavers.

This violated the ancient Mothers' Rhythm—for enslaved Land, enslaved people will soon enough be made barren by their enslavement.

Yet know this true…

A few dared to resist, inspired perhaps by fragments of stories about Resonating with the Mothers' Rhythm, or perhaps by rumors about those bold enough to become outlaws, or perhaps by their dreams.

And a few others who persevered in hidden places sustained understanding of the Mothers' Rhythm and Resonance and Balance through sacred Analakinak knowledge. In their time they spiraled leftward, hated and hounded for their supposed superstitions.

Isolated and alone, each few unaware of the other few, they abided nonetheless…

 Damn.

As Gracie read, she could hear Ansosho Eletun's voices, could even match melodies to the words she'd written down. Another memory surfaced, too—of the hooded woman, behind her still, demanding that she record it all correctly. "Just like you hear it, Gracie. *Pay attention.*" And for the second time she noticed that her scribbled words made a kind of peculiar sense.

Which wouldn't have bothered her quite so much if she'd been able to recall actually writing down anything. But who else was there?

She remembered a British news report about how some weird dude managed to sneak in and out of a woman's attic for months without ever being noticed, occasionally even creeping down late at night to grab food from the woman's refrigerator…

Well, behind the kneewalls in Gracie's garret there *was* space enough for a secret squatter—as long as he didn't need to stand up. But *seriously*? She'd lived there undisturbed for almost four years. No one had visited since before the lightning invasion. And she'd always been scrupulous about keeping her doors locked.

After pacing back and forth for too long (and carefully inspecting all the spaces behind those kneewalls), she accepted the obvious: She'd done something that resembled sleepwalking.

But is there even such a thing as sleep*writing?*

Actually, yes—though it's rare.

Internet postings recorded a few assertions of brief, unremembered, typically nonsensical sleep*texting*, but Gracie's favorite example came from 1916, when a schoolgirl assigned an essay woke one morning to perfectly sensible preparatory notes she'd written while asleep.

The girl had no memory of creating the notes, but with her teacher's permission she used them to produce an essay her teacher described as "considerably above the usual level of her work at that time."

Okay, then, at least Gracie wasn't the only person on the planet to truly sleepwrite. This knowledge didn't help her for long, however. Because she also learned that sleepwriting was regarded as a medical disorder—a parasomnia.

As in: Something is wrong with super-methodical you, Grace Gwyllt Olwyn.

❖

Please. All she really needed was a stretch of time when *nothing happened.*

But a mere twenty-four hours after Gracie found that second sleepwritten dispatch, she woke from yet another dream, and this time her recall was crisply, disturbingly detailed:

⚡ I was hopelessly lost at dusk in a murky tangle of clawing underbrush and vines beneath a canopy of tall trees. I gulped back the fear stuck in my throat as I wondered whether to walk up or down the slope I stood on. Like so many other lost souls, I chose down, hoping to find people.

After a long trudge, however, I was as confused and disoriented as ever. So: Should I use the very last of twilight to select a climbable tree in which to wait for dawn?

That's when I noticed a distant glow through the woods to my left. Hoping I'd spotted somebody's campfire where I could get help, I blundered toward it.

As the glow grew larger, brighter, I heard human voices—male mostly, laughing mostly. Soon I heard women's voices, too, whimpering rather than laughing. A shiver prickled up my spine, but I didn't stop.

Not until I reached the edge of a clearing: Yes, a large, blazing fire with people around it. Wary, crouching low behind a broadleafed bush, I counted seven men, three women.

The ponchos the men wore draped to their knees but cinched at the waist, revealing their obviously enthusiastic erections. The three women, meanwhile, stood naked and trembling, each clutching a rope tied around her neck as one or more of the men held the other end and maliciously yanked.

The sight paralyzed me. I had no means to help the women, didn't know where to run—and surely these men could hear my heart's raucous, hysterical *what-the-fuck!?* slamming against my ribs.

That's when something on my left rustled. Of its own volition, my head snapped toward the almost-sound—and there she was, barely visible in the shadows, our shoulders already touching.

Her eyes sparking, she signaled me to silence with two fingers pressed softly against my lips, and I heard her voice, though she spoke no words.

"Stay down. Stay silent. Do not move from here until those men are dead."

Dead?!

"Better seven dead rapists than three dead women."

Dead?!

I must have blinked; how else to explain that quite suddenly she was gone. Just...gone.

A moment later, one of the men howled loudly as he arched his back before falling flat on his face without further sound or movement. Another blink and a second man crumpled, then a third. All three had arrows sticking out of them.

Only when the fourth man went down did I infer the *how* of what I was seeing: archers attacking their targets from several directions.

After the sixth man fell, *she* appeared again—at the opposite side of the clearing, a bow in her right hand, an axe in her left—and I understood: In less than a damn minute, this woman alone had launched every one of those arrows, each deadly accurate, each from a different spot just outside the clearing.

How?, I wondered as the last man still alive screamed at her in a language I didn't understand, though his meaning was unmistakable:

How *dare* you, cunt!

Grinning from some fifteen feet away, she replied by whipping her axe at him. The weapon sliced down the center of his chest and buried itself in his gut. By the time he fell backward he was both completely dead and completely blood-covered—and *she* was already using a shiny black handheld blade to slice away the ropes around the women's necks. Then she pointed them toward their escape.

As the three women ran off, *she* stepped from dead male body to dead male body using the same handheld blade to extract her arrows before wiping blood from them on the target's poncho and returning them to the quiver slung over her shoulder. Finally, she pulled her axe from the seventh man's chest and wiped it, too, before turning to gaze at me, still crouched and silent where she'd left me—and now, of course, beyond freaked.

All I could do was gawk at her, this hypnotically, rivetingly animate force with gleaming black eyes and reckless, undulating hair, naked like the three women she'd saved. Sinewy and strong and agile, she moved with exquisite grace, and in my whole life I'd never seen anything like her raw sexual power as she put two fingers to her lips before extending her hand toward me, palm up.

Immediately, the fire behind her erupted savagely, backlighting her, throwing her shadow into the darkness where I squatted as frenzied fire exploded out of her eyes.

I curled forward and covered my face, expecting to feel the scorch of that fire. But no, there was only cool silence.

When I looked up again, the sky had begun to gray slightly with the dawn's arrival, the fire had shrunk to embers, and *she* had vanished.

Very carefully, I stood, as befuddled as ever.

I inhaled.

I exhaled.

A hand gripped my shoulder.

"What are you doing here?" demanded a voice coming from behind me, a woman's voice I'd heard before. "You shouldn't be here."

Suspecting who I'd see, I pivoted, reached for the hood covering the speaker's head, and flung it back before I could be stopped.

And I recognized her. "*You?*"

The woman standing behind me, hand on my shoulder, had also stood behind me in not one but *two* other dreams presided over by Ansosho Eletun. And now—*now* this woman whose hood I'd just thrown back was none other than...Ansosho Eletun.

"God*dammit!*" I yelled. "You're *both* of you? *How* can you be *both* of you?!"

Ansosho Eletun smiled benevolently. As usual. "I don't expect you to understand."

"Good. Cuz I sure as hell *don't* understand!" I sorely wanted to slap that lingering smile off Ansosho Eletun's face. "How can you be two people at the same time? A-An' also—" I waved a jittery hand at the remains of the fire and the bodies strewn around it. "—What the fuck is *that?*"

"Extirpation of rapists is among the harsher imperatives of defying this particular Privation, which, as you might guess, is foundering."

Whereupon I began to implode. "No. Just no. I cannot do this."

Ansosho Eletun shrugged. "You've done this already. You, Gracie, and no one else. At least you'll understand some of the nuances of this Privation, since you inhabit another foundering Privation yourself. Perhaps that's why you've found your way to Kaldi so soon."

"*What?*" I shouted. "Found my way to—?"

Ansosho Eletun gently placed a finger across my lips. "Listen to me. *Listen*, Gracie. Many Privations have defiled the Balance and the Mothers' Rhythms, as is happening in your time. The Mothers remind us, however, that just as each Privation has a beginning, so too each must end, subsumed in the Cycle that never ceases its inexorable whorl through time."

This got my attention. "The Cycle that never ceases?"

Ansosho Eletun nodded. "Eventually each Privation's urge to dominate and enslave is defeated as the Balance restores the Mothers' essential freedoms—to go where you wish, to refuse what does not suit, to choose with whom you associate. The Communities of those who embrace these freedoms are transformed—but be warned: Rarely do such transformations occur benignly, for those who benefit from Privation do not willingly forsake their power."

I shook my head. "Just leave me alone, Ansosho Eletun."

"Call me Eletun. 'Ansosho' is an honorific, quite unnecessary."

"*Jeezus!* You've decided we're fucking *friends* now?"

"I didn't bring you here, Gracie. You did that as you became entangled. An impressive feat, really, since you accomplished it unknowingly. But you'll need my help to comprehend what's happening to you and how to adjust as you wind through the layers of moments. Because time works rather differently here. So please: Pay attention whenever you happen upon spirals." Eletun smiled again. "Right now, though, best you wake up."

Gracie had never thought of herself as crazy, but this dream and sleepwriting stuff was, yes, *crazy*. With a certainty she had no hope of logically justifying, she blamed the damn rock.

But try telling that to a medical professional. Nope, hopeless. Just one wayward step from getting ensnared in a quagmire of shabby medical theorizing and hit-or-miss "treatment"—that seat-of-the-doctor's-pants cobble of drugs and psychotherapy to "manage" the "condition."

Ugh. She'd rather endure the "illness" than what passed for a "remedy." And she'd rather endure this "illness" in private, thank you. Better that no one—*not one living soul*—ever knows anything about it. If she's crazy, she'll do closet crazy.

So okay, Gracie, you suffer from parasomnia—specifically, sleepwriting with a hefty side of weird dreams. Now what?

Exploring parasomnia "etiology" got her nowhere. Modern medicine remains clueless about what causes sleepwalking and, by extension, sleepwriting. That left Gracie with correlations—when certain attributes of two or more entities tend to vary in tandem. As in they dance together. But the fact that they dance together didn't tell her squat about *why* they dance together.

Besides, when it came to sleepwalking/sleepwriting, Gracie encountered way too many correlations. Some were easy to eliminate: not a child, not feverish, not magnesium deficient, not obviously schizophrenic, not slowly dying of Parkinson's disease, not taking antidepressants, anticonvulsants, antihistamines, or antibiotics.

But she probably consumed too much coffee (stimulant) and had been known to occasionally party on down (alcohol). Also, while she'd never been pregnant and was unendingly grateful to not want men or need birth control, she did menstruate (hormones).

Then there was that universal—stress. Did Gracie's approach to life cause more stress or less? She preferred, for instance, to handle complex problems by systematically thinking them through before actually doing anything.

Still, admittedly, her twenty-ninth birthday *had* unsettled her. Who cares, she'd tried to convince herself—until she understood what it truly meant: that her twenty-ninth year was over, done, gone, and she'd begun traipsing through her *thirtieth* year—cue mild OMG, the kind that makes your eyebrows sweat (hysteria? panic?).

What's more, by the time she experienced that second bout of sleepwriting, she'd spent upwards of six (stressful?) months living alone and, more recently, working alone—not even a cat for company after Sir Reynolds decamped for D.C. last year with her sort-of ex, Naomi ("sort-of ex" because theirs had been pretty much a "sort-of" relationship to begin with).

At least the working at home alone part she liked—so far, anyway. Beat the mix of perfume, fart-smells, and noise that dominated the Institute's overcrowded open office.

Yet, like scurvy, working at home alone reopened old wounds.

Even before The Divorce, breezily announced on her fourteenth birthday, Gracie had clashed with the person who started out as Mum but had mutated into That Damn Woman. Clashed right through what turned out to be their final quarrel. At least, Gracie told herself, she'd hear no more harangues about "making better choices"—code for why the hell does *my* daughter have to be a lesbian? And her sister? Hell, her sister seemed to have forgotten she existed.

So, apparently, had the so-called "friends" she'd found after Naomi skedaddled.

Her "sort-of ex" left plenty behind (clothes, furniture, even a functional laptop), but took what truly mattered—the cat and a bunch of pricey outfits jammed into two large antique steamer trunks. In retrospect, Gracie recognized the truth those trunks revealed: Naomi was always ready to bounce into a better offer. Once again on her own, Gracie attempted to bounce, too, hanging out with new people. Single people. And for about six months she did okay. Till the pandemic discovery that her new "friends" were way too much like Naomi.

"This is *so* boring—let's meet up in, y'know, *three* dimensions," ringleader Tory whined at their first online get-together. Gracie reminded the images on her screen that she hadn't caught the virus yet and intended to keep it that way. I'll be staying home, she told them.

Of course, they took turns mouthing all the right words—"Oh yeah, that's *so* responsible of you." Until Tory's next attempt at persuasion: "We'd be *reee-yul* careful. I'll put markers on my living room floor to keep us six feet apart. We could do martinis, cheddar-stuffed pretzels…"

Yeah, well, Gracie *did* get it. At the outset, like them, she thought: How bad can it really be? Then Jessica collapsed at the office right in front of her. She was the one who caught Jess, kept that lovely, brilliant head from slamming against the floor.

Nine days later she saw on Instagram that Tory had caught the virus and was quite ill, as was Tory's new squeeze. At least Gracie's quarantine had been uneventful so far. Two days to go, temp at ninety-eight point six, not gasping yet…

No surprise, though, that all this wrecked Gracie's sleep—and yessiree, sleep deprivation is definitely correlated with sleepwalking/sleepwriting.

"Don't forget those damn headaches either," she reminded the bathroom mirror when she interrupted her compulsive (neurotic?) pacing for a quick chat with the only person with whom she was completely at ease. Migraine headaches, after all, are considered a frequent sleepwalking/sleepwriting dance partner (comorbidity) and who the hell knows why.

"Not that you're necessarily having migraines," she assured the frowny face in front of her. "Might be a developing pattern though, huh? Crappy sleep. Dream. Headache. And then you find the weird left-handed whatever-the-fuck-that-written-shit-is."

She looked sad and a little frazzled, that face in the mirror now in its thirtieth year. Thinner, too—pudge mostly gone, cheekbones downright discernable—and pale enough to make mousy almost-brown hair seem distinctly darker than it used to be. "You need a haircut," she griped before hurrying off to find and answer her phone.

"Jess?" she guessed after an unrecognizably husky voice eked out a hey-how-are-ya.

"Yeah," Jessica managed. "The…one an'…only. H-How's tricks, Gracie?"

"Screw that, Jess. How the hell are *you?*"

"Still kickin'."

"Home yet?"

"Tomorrow. Maybe."

"Need your laptop? Anything else? I can—"

"Nah. I'm…good for now," Jessica wheezed, sounding wretched. "Fred's feeling much better…gonna take…care o' me." After a long, tight cough, she continued. "'Member that…wood box…with the stone…in my desk…that I…asked you…to take…home with you?"

"God, yes. Damn thing got hit by lightning right in front of me."

"Really?"

Shit. Gracie had been scrupulous about not saying anything about lightning or damn rocks to anyone; otherwise, they'd no doubt conclude that Gracie Olwyn had been spending too much time alone in her garret, forever diddling numbers on her computer, and now the lonely lezzy who'd always been, y'know, a tad off-kilter was full-on hallucinating.

Certainly she hadn't intended to say anything to Jess; the words burbled out on their own—something the lonely lezzy regretted and hoped Jess would forget, so let's move on to…"I can bring over your laptop and the stone to your place whenever you—"

"Better not. Can't work yet…an' I might…still be contagious… even now. Be a while…'fore we share air…with anyone." Jessica paused to drag in a couple of ragged breaths and then managed to convey that the woman who actually owned the stone wanted it back. "Okay if I give Pirin…your number? So she can…get in touch?"

Gracie agreed immediately. The sooner she got the damn rock out of her life, the better.

CHAPTER FIVE: LIKE STARS DURING DAYLIGHT

Pirin stood in the middle of her living room holding her phone, number memorized, thumbs poised—but her thumbs refused to move.

An entire hour since Jess had given her the name and number of the woman who had Amatchi's ohskal. Yet with every attempt at making the call, Jess's passing comment echoed—and stopped her cold.

"Gracie said…it got…hit by lightning…right in front of her."

The instant Pirin heard "hit by lightning," her reality shattered as violently as the coffee mugs she'd recently heaved at her wall.

NO!

Immediately her *NO!* deepened into a continuous low buzz of objection. Pirin found herself yanked back, back—to Amatchi's story about a long ago relative, a reputed sorgin who saw the ohskal get hit by lightning.

"This has never happened to me," Amatchi admitted in a tone that sounded, even to eleven-year-old Pirin, almost like regret. "But after it happened to my great-grandmother—the one you're named after—she was never the same. For the rest of her life she saw things no one else did. Because the ohskal had claimed her."

"Does that mean the ohskal hasn't claimed you?" Pirin asked.

"Ah, well," Amatchi replied, "I have been claimed. But not like that."

"So there's more than one way?"

"There are many ways. As many ways as there are stars in the sky, even though these ways are often invisible, like stars during daylight."

Cool answer, Pirin thought even back then. Nonetheless, as a sixth grader she'd reached the age when existential Doubt dawns, when old people, even those one genuinely loves, begin to shift from venerable to a bit too old-fashioned to take seriously because they simply *don't get it*. No surprise that this was also when Jessica declared Jesus was an illusion ("I bet he never existed at all!"), the apostles were scam artists, and the Bible was propaganda designed to keep women enslaved.

For Pirin, then, a magic rock able to pull lightning out of the sky and a bastard carpenter able to walk on (unfrozen) water seemed equally implausible.

But now...

Now Pirin wanted—needed—to hear every detail about what happened to Someone Else in the presence of *her* ohskal. Jess had nothing more to offer on the matter, however, or even means to draw a comfortable breath, much less engage in extended conversation.

On to Plan B.

Thus Pirin prepared for a typical interview: Gather all possible data about the interviewee and her circumstances, work up detailed questions ahead of time, memorize them, then develop an interview strategy designed to suss out state of mind, motivation, vulnerabilities, and, most of all, deception.

For two hours, Pirin poked through the digitally documented life of Grace Gwyllt Olwyn, consulting several of the myriad databases she accessed almost every day on the job—no matter that she lacked any legitimate reason to pry into the woman's life. Like her recycle activities, this was an offense for which she could be fired as well as arrested and prosecuted. *If* she got caught.

Pirin worked hard to avoid that, fastidiously adhering to plenty of rules about LNT—Leave No Trace—though in truth leaving a trace of something was too often unavoidable. She did better obliterating any trail that might lead back to her, thanks to the likes of virtual private networks, the TOR browser, IP spoofing, MAC spoofing, and an evergrowing variety of hacking techniques.

But when it came to Grace Gwyllt Olwyn, all her poking around turned out to be a waste of time.

Every detail about the woman pointed to banality: single, healthy, bachelor's degree in economics, nonreligious, no political party affiliation, little-used Instagram account, a renter living alone on the working-class side of a well-heeled suburb, no school or car or credit card debt, small savings, a steady job almost as boring as Pirin's own, no criminal record. The most "suspect" thing about the woman was her occasional habit of making diminutive donations to climate change activists.

As Pirin developed her Plan B interview questions, she could at last exhale, and the low buzz abated. Because, she decided, Grace Gwyllt Olwyn wasn't anybody special at all.

No, the ohskal had *not* claimed Someone Else. Hell, what happened didn't even count as a coincidence; it was *not* a surprising concurrence of events that, despite lacking any apparent causal connection, seemed meaningfully related.

"The damn cause was *me*," Pirin grumped at the drivers license photo of Grace Gwyllt Olwyn on her computer screen. "*I'm* the only reason you ended up anywhere near the ohskal, the only reason you were the one who saw it struck by lightning."

As soon as she spotted *that* number on her phone, Gracie answered the call without bothering about the usual formalities expected of a first-time conversation with a complete stranger: "So when're you gonna come get your rock?"

This was greeted with a longish moment of (probably surprised) silence—then, "Uhh, well, I'm stuck in quarantine through Sunday, so assuming I stay healthy, anytime after that. Except this coming Tuesday, the seventeenth. I'm getting dicked around about a court appearance—on, then off, then who knows? So if it really ends up on again, I'm stuck in court on Tues—"

"You pick it—Pirin, right? You pick it, Pirin, cuz I'm always here. But sooner is better. Much better. Your damn rock is making me crazy."

"Really?" Pirin exhaled audibly, as if this news sucked the air from her lungs. "I-I'd like to—I mean, can you tell me what you mean by crazy? How's the—?"

"Is that the price of getting this thing outta here? Having to talk about it?"

Gracie hadn't quite grasped how much anger she'd pent up until it filled this new silence. Not even her mild embarrassment while Pirin's (stunned? affronted?) hush continued could get her to fill the void. Instead she waited, suddenly, uncharacteristically stubborn: Hey, Pirin, it's *your* damn rock, plus so far I've managed, miraculously, not to indulge in a single swear word, not out loud anyway, so c'mon, *you* do the damn talking.

"What happened?" Pirin eventually asked, her voice low-soft and perhaps worried, too. "Jess said the ohskal was hit by lightning."

"Oh-skahl, huh? Assuming you mean the rock, then yes. It got hit by lightning. Right the fuck in front of me. Like six feet from where I was standing."

"And—?"

"And come get your rock before anything else happens. This Monday works for me. Say nine a.m.? We can meet outside. At the bench in the park right across the street from my apartment."

Pirin readily agreed, her tone determinedly solicitous as she confirmed Gracie's address. She even offered to bring coffee.

"You're on," Gracie responded, grateful that Pirin couldn't see her blushing as she recognized her own rudeness. "High-test, cream, no sugar. And, um, sorry for my assholery. I promise to behave on Monday."

For a whole sixteen hours, Gracie enjoyed a heady sense of emancipation: *Finally* the damn rock would be out of her life, which would no doubt bring an end to the bizarre episodes of sleepwriting and otherworldly dreams. Life would return to normal. Boring maybe, but predictable and please please please, *sane.*

Then came Sunday morning.

Gracie woke groggy, her forehead pounding, even though she'd slept for an uninterrupted eight hours. Or so she thought—right up till she found several new pages of her own scrawl on the floor next to her bed.

At first she thought that no dream had preceded this latest round of sleepwriting. But even before she got out of bed, she remembered a hazy *something.* Arguably she should have written it down—but that would've meant acknowledging another damn rock dream.

Anyway, she didn't remember much. Besides, the vague sense that this wasn't the first time she'd had the dream, or some version of it, repelled her.

Yet fragments of the dream lingered—beclouded splinters of nonsense about being a little kid tossed by huge ocean waves onto a wide sandy beach where she walked and walked until a girl like her, small and alone, came running toward her.

Her recollection of what the little girl whispered was much more distinct: "I am hiding from the Lotus Man, who wants to hurt me. But he cannot see you, so if you hold my hand he will not be able to see me either and I can escape him. Then someday we will meet again."

And, Gracie remembered, in *this* last dream, unlike all its previous iterations, Gracie took the girl's hand.

"I need coffee," Gracie announced—to herself, to the little girl on the beach, to no one at all. *"Now."*

Three cups and one shower later, she finally persuaded herself to read what her sleeping left-handed self had scribed sometime in the night—and damn if a glint of recall didn't oh-so-briefly flicker: "You require some further context, Gracie—so *pay attention.*" Eletun's voice, Eletun's words. Eletun's smile.

And damn again: There was no denying that a coherent story had begun to materialize—whether she wanted it to or not:

⚡ As Privation molded Kaldi, whose name means "pinnacle of time"—that which inevitably brings the living unto death—, so did a great Firemountain form Analergin, child of AmaBildun destined to become Analergin Segubansi, "powerful diviner whose hand renews life."

Though this Firemountain lay like a stepping stone into the vast Near Western Sea at the frontier edge of the great plain Sundaselai where Privation ruled, it was spared from Privation thanks to rising waters that, over many Suncycles, had taken her low outer rim and sequestered her.

Yet even that did not prevent hungry Privation gangs from trying to subjugate Firemountain Subendi and enslave her inhabitants—not until it awakened to rip and shatter the ground as fiery lava and clouds of superheated ash exploded skyward from a lopsided new crater where once her nippled center rose.

Like a monster that never slept, the molten rock snaked down Subendi's broad eastern face, boiling the surrounding Sea and sending thick plumes of acrid smoke on the Winds to choke the peoples of

Sundaselai, who soon came to believe that no one could possibly endure on such a dangerous Firemountain.

Yet a few did survive in Subendi's wet, fog-laden western forests, untouched by the streams of lava and the poisonous smokes oozing from the Firemountain island's eastern side.

Beyond Privation awareness, in carefully chosen caves, Subendi's Mothers sheltered from the frequent barrages of Lightning, from the angry Seastorms, from the flaring Sun that seared plant and animant alike. Unseen by hungry Privation eyes peering into the fog from beyond the island's foreboding, deadly rings of sharp reefs, the Mothers built new, well-disguised commonhouses, too.

Having mastered and memorized clandestine routes through the formidable reefs, they took to Sea in sleek outriggers to gather fish and, occasionally, to travel far off—always in secret—so a Chosen young woman might gather male-seed and return carrying a child of fresh malestock.

Small and self-sufficient, bolstered by their deep knowledge and clever tools, protected by both constant mists and the island's reefs, the Subendi Mothers' Communities moved through their precincts with the seasons, tending and gathering, exchanging and sharing with all the other Communities, together helping the Land renew as the Land helped them live.

Hence the creatures of Subendi thrived in dynamic, mutual beneficence even as the rapacious gaze of Privation beheld only charred scrub clinging ever-threatened to the relentlessly fiery, death-spewing Firemountain.

Shielded from the fevers of Privation, the Communities of Subendi became the last haven for the Sublimities. Even after more than a hundred generations of Privation, the Communities had preserved much of the Mothers' Rhythms: All of Subendi's women and most of her men were embraced by at least one Sublimity, and many by two or more, as in the old times.

Into this fearsome era a young Subendi fish-gatherer called AmaBildun birthed the infant who would become Analergin Segubansi, while at nearly the same moment Kaldi emerged among the Privation-tortured northwestern marshes of the Sundaselai hinterlands.

Like so many in that abject place, Kaldi's mother and grandmother were enslaved by their deep debt-obligation. They paid toward their debt by collecting lotus stems from the turbid marshes, then rolling and twisting the stems' fibers into thread used for weaving lotus silk garments that clothed the majesties of Privation dominions.

Harsh and difficult, this work commanded all their days and too many of their nights. They were always tired, always hungry, and yet their debt-obligation never diminished. Even so, for Suncycle upon Suncycle Kaldi's mother and grandmother—and indeed little Kaldi, too—produced the lotus silk thread required of them in order to remain in the enslaver's flimsy shelter and eat the scanty food the enslaver deigned to provide.

But then swamp sickness took Kaldi's grandmother, leaving Kaldi with only her mother, who did not have strength enough to meet the debt obligations of herself and Kaldi as well as those still due from her dead grandmother.

Desperate to ease her mother's burdens, Kaldi secretly mastered the art of crafting flatbow and arrows and arrowheads, becoming an accomplished hunter of small creatures, although such hunting was forbidden. But this was not enough, and inevitably other transgressions followed.

At first these passed unnoticed: an extra handful of rice grabbed unseen from the enslaver's basket, a missing flatbread, diminished quantities of lotus thread because Kaldi spent too much marsh time hunting rather than collecting lotus stems. Then one day the enslaver caught Kaldi's mother taking several forestfowl eggs and beat her; Kaldi responded by attacking him—and drawing blood.

Kaldi and her mother ran away rather than endure the official Privation punishments, which included lashings and imprisonment—and, of course, permanent separation; Privation judgment would make certain they never saw each other again.

Thereafter they lived as outlaws, surviving in the ever-shifting margins between frontier Privation settlements and the wilderness beyond. They were not alone, but neither could they trust those they encountered. Alliances were brief and unreliable; more than once they were robbed, more than once Kaldi ravaged those who sought to harm them.

Slowly, word of Kaldi spread across those western Privation margins, then seeped into Privation settlements, into Privation fears, into Privation hopes. We have few details now of these long-ago stories—only that they tell of Kaldi, even while yet a child, nourishing the innocent and liberating the enslaved and destroying the guilty.

Kaldi had become a necessary legend, held dear by those who suffered most under the yoke of Privation brutality. Tales of her sleight and her power exceeded anything she had done or even considered doing, reached places she had never been.

Some said she was a small child, new upon Mother Earth. Others claimed she was a very old hag, responsible for every calamity to afflict Privation's privileged for the last twenty generations. But the most oft-repeated stories portrayed a strong, grimly beautiful young woman who came from beyond time itself and whose mere gaze instantly struck her enemies dead.

"Kaldi is everywhere," the saying went, "yet nowhere to be found."

Whispers of her even wafted all the way to Subendi, carried on the lips of Privation refugees encountered by the island's Travelers. Likewise, rumors of Subendi the Sanctuary had long been spreading slowly, surreptitiously across the tortured great plain of Sundaselai all the way to the opulent eastern ports—despite Privation's unceasing attempts to quash them.

Yet, believing the Firemountain would continue to protect them, the undaunted Mothers of Subendi—descended of Alama who lived and thrived well before Privation invented itself—never allowed their attentions to be taken from each season's newborns, always cause for celebration.

As was the custom, the Mothers immediately sought omens of each newborn's gifts of Rhythm, those first signs of Sublimity and the first hints of how a child determines her name.

For AmaBildun's progeny, though, too many Mooncycles passed without any signs of Rhythm, and AmaBildun worried—until, in the darkness preceding one dawn, the child disappeared from her place in the high southwestern Community. Worried searchers found her a half-morning later splashing and babbling unharmed in the Sea.

After the child was set safely upon the fine, dark sand, three porpoises—affinitates of Travelers—were seen withdrawing to the open waters. This AmaBildun understood as Rhythm at last appearing: The child, she believed, was destined to be a Traveler.

Only Grandmother AmaSaba noticed more: Having discovered a remarkably long Lightning stone in the beach sand, the little one excitedly pointed it at the clear southwestern Sky while chattering at a solitary black bird spiraling high above them. Might AmaBildun's child also be a Weatherer?

AmaSaba was doubtful; as best she could determine with her own considerable Weathering skills, the child's chattering and gesturing portended nothing.

Then, less than a Mooncycle later, a delirious Seastorm whirled out of the southwest.

Know this true:

In another time, a Sublime Weatherer might have sensed the Seastorm's approach, understood the warnings of the birds, prepared the Communities. But this was Privation, when fear blinded even Subendiak Sublimity, when distraction disrupted even Subendiak Resonance.

And so this Seastorm burst unheralded upon Subendi nearly two Mooncycles before the usual onset of the wet monsoon. Its furious Wind shredded the island's forests, flooded her lowlands, flattened her Communities' commonhouses, and caught a small boat of fish-gatherers unprepared offshore. Neither the boat nor its occupants—AmaBildun among them—were ever seen again.

⚡ And yes, Grace Gwyllt Olwyn, it seems you really are out of your friggin' mind. But let's not tell anyone just yet, okay?

CHAPTER SIX: I MIGHT SURPRISE YOU

A lmost anytime Pirin spotted a way to kill two birds with one stone, she went for it. In her experience, the extra foresight and planning this required tended to pay off: She'd save time, duck pointless hassle, outmaneuver some moronic corporate bullshit, slip in a side gig, occasionally even take care of multiple recycles with a single slick move.

So when she realized her trip to pick up the ohskal could also nudge along her latest, pandemic-threatened recycle, she didn't hesitate.

Like most of her two-fer plans, this one's "first draft" emerged nearly fully formed. Not exactly easy-peasy, but certainly doable with a little luck. Which is to say, a little *more* luck, since it had been by luck alone that, months earlier, she'd ended up with the suspicious property insurance claim that started it all.

And a startling start it was:

When Pirin arrived at Andreas Nelumbo's office to interview him, his need to dominate by looming over her and insisting on an extended bone crush of a handshake caused him to forget about what had been animating his laptop screen. Which was why, just before he remembered to click it off, Pirin caught a glimpse not of the screen itself but its reflection in his office window where she saw a paused video image of two freshly pubescent girls with budding breasts, heavy makeup, legs spread wide to the camera, eyelids fluttering with fear.

Her heartbeat spiked at the sight, but she'd long since learned to keep even that kind of alarm from showing. It helped, too, that Nelumbo assumed she was merely another neophyte claims adjuster sent to confirm a few details.

So she played along and played up being intimidated by this smooth-talking big shot with his own investment firm, nervously setting up her smartphone's voice recorder, then dutifully checking boxes on a form as she clumsily read off questions.

Given Bonecrusher Nelumbo's breezy, grinning arrogance during the interview, she knew he bought her act. Indeed, he relaxed so completely that he occasionally contradicted himself when she asked different versions of the same question. By roughly halfway through the interview, Bonecrusher had unwittingly acknowledged two no-no's: including prior damage in his current property claim and significantly exaggerating the extent of the damage.

Early on, of course, Pirin's real focus had shifted to searching for something she'd long ago learned was likely scribbled on a nearby scrap of paper, if only she could spot it and read it without attracting attention: the username and password that would grant access to his laptop.

After pushing the interview as far as she could without provoking suspicion, though, she'd seen nothing. Normally, at this point she'd be all smiles, visibly relaxing as she slowly packed up (often while "forgetting" to turn off her voice recorder), easing into the conversational informality that tended to lure interviewees into becoming more talkative—and more revelatory.

This time, though, Pirin added one more move: As she rose to leave, she reached across Bonecrusher's desk to bear his handshake again—the price of getting near enough for one last close look at that laptop.

And she saw it: a long series of tiny letters, numbers, and symbols on a small strip of paper taped just below the laptop's keyboard, preceded by the username "EvoraDude." Given the length of the password, she'd likely spotted the laptop's administrator credentials. Skewed almost upside down, tough for someone less experienced to take in (and memorize) without giving themselves away—and exactly what she'd hoped to find.

Of course, Bonecrusher's claim was rejected, his policy terminated, and his name added to a widely-shared database of the dubious, thus ending the matter for her company.

But *not* for Pirin Basamendi. Not after she'd discovered those admin credentials. Couple more dance steps and she'd be able to check out everything on that machine, including the child porn she'd glimpsed. Just as soon as she could get to the machine itself.

Fortunately, she didn't need to possess Bonecrusher's laptop, only access it. Months ago, however, logistical challenges led her to put this off—but times had changed. Bigly. *If* Bonecrusher had taken the machine home with him once the statewide stay-at-home order closed so many offices, including his, she had a shot.

A quick swing through the search engine that tracks devices connected to the internet revealed what she hoped: Yes, Bonecrusher's laptop *was* linked to the Wi-Fi router IP address associated with the Nelumbo residence. She also discovered the IP and MAC addresses of all the other digital devices in his house, right down to every last Wi-Fi-linked camera and smartphone.

Next step: Acquire Bonecrusher's Wi-Fi router password. Once she had that, she could access his laptop as long as it remained linked to the Nelumbo Wi-Fi router. Getting the Wi-Fi password, though, involved a hack which could be quite difficult and time-consuming— *unless* he was as sloppy about the Wi-Fi network at his house as he was about the images that entertained him at his office.

Worth giving sloppy the first crack. This meant Pirin would have to position herself and her equipment within roughly a hundred feet of the Wi-Fi router in Bonecrusher's house. In a hoity-toity neighborhood where you better damn well have a solid excuse even in normal times if you lingered more than a few minutes. Now she'd be outright loitering during a stay-at-home state of emergency.

And retrieving the ohskal from Grace Gwyllt Olwyn, who lived barely more than a mile from Bonecrusher's place, provided the perfect cover. Thus Pirin's two-fer plan was born: Before picking up the ohskal, let's add a quicky targeted wardrive.

So: She'd set up her wardriving rig in the car she rented, placing her (disguised) directional antenna on the dashboard, then pretend to get lost due to a GPS fail. This would account for why she'd pull onto a side street and "just happen" to stop within about seventy feet of Bonecrusher's abode, where she'd spread an old-school paper map across the steering wheel and act like she was studying it to regain her bearings.

Her paper map would (literally) cover what she was really up to— hacking Bonecrusher's Wi-Fi router password, then spoofing his router into temporarily accepting her wardriving rig as a legitimate device on his local network.

Once surreptitiously "in," she'd use Bonecrusher's credentials to access his laptop, download her virtual machine onto it, add a network interface, alter its IP address, and run *the* command to install the covert gateway that would enable her to access the laptop from anywhere on earth. After which she'd (mostly) ensure LNT by turning off the virtual machine, then deleting it and its related files.

The challenge: Doing all this *fast*.

And what would she accomplish with this from-anywhere access to Bonecrusher's laptop and network granted by her exploit? Anything she wanted. All undetected. And all at a leisurely pace from the comfort of her home office forty miles away.

For starters, she'd track his network traffic to extract more login credentials, which she'd use to slip several covert apps into Bonecrusher's compute environment. These would log keystrokes, scoop up every byte of data traffic, capture every file on every linked device. She'd also install another covert gateway on his home automation hub to harvest everything picked up by his cameras and microphones. And all of it would be encrypted, compressed, and exfiltrated to her dark web cloud servers, then encrypted again before being sent to her own server.

Once "home," she'd sift through it both manually and with her Spotter app, an audio-visual recording platform able to tag the faces and voices as well as written and spoken words and phrases she selected. Any of which—all of which—she could send on to, well, whomever she wanted, whenever she wanted.

Based on the practice drills she'd run and, as always, assuming a measure of luck, the effort to get into Bonecrusher's Wi-Fi router should take no more than fifteen minutes. Then she'd zip-a-dee-doo-dah outta there to meet up with Grace Gwyllt Olwyn.

As for the nervous voice mail from her long-ago-lover and now-buddy Roz worrying about whether tomorrow's trial was happening or not? That could wait. True, the defendant was violent and unpredictable, but he was also home-confined with a GPS ankle monitor. She'd return Roz's call in a couple of hours while she drove back home.

The morning was notably sunny and warm for mid-March. Traffic had cooperated and her acting-lost timing was perfect as she took the wrong exit off of Route 2, then fumbled to Clifton Road before wandering onto Fletcher Drive where Bonecrusher lived in neo-Tudor extravagance.

And yes, he *did* turn out to be sloppy at home: He used his phone number as his Wi-Fi router password, and since she already knew his phone number, in mere seconds she'd penetrated his network.

After that, she accomplished everything she'd hoped to and got her rig concealed again within nine and a half minutes. A good thing, too: Eight and a half minutes was all it took to attract the interest of some older guy across the street glowering from a driveway in front of a house twice the size of Bonecrusher's.

Okay, Pirin told herself as she slowly drove away—nosy neighbor notwithstanding, that seemed to go okay.

Though the black motorcycle with its black-clad rider, which appeared behind her even before she exited Fletcher Drive, *did* concern her. Was he following her? Should she spare Grace Gwyllt Olwyn whatever dangers she may or may not have attracted?

Pirin decided to not yet decide by winding erratically through the town's center to the coffee shop she'd picked out beforehand. If motorcycle dude followed her—and yes, she'd be looking for him— she'd scrap her meeting and retrieve the ohskal another day.

But she needn't have worried. By the time she returned to her car after buying two coffees, extra hot, and a half-dozen doughnuts, motorcycle and rider had vanished.

Waverly Road was a well-traveled through street, but when Gracie saw a silver sedan approach her building a few minutes before the appointed hour, she got itchy—because she damn well knew who was driving, though she didn't understand why she knew. Or why the vehicle struck her as out of character, especially given that she'd never met Pirin Basamendi and quite sincerely wished she didn't have to.

The silver sedan behaved exactly as she expected when it rounded the corner and halted on the side street next to her building. Moving from her living room to her kitchen, she kept an eye on it anyway, compelled by curiosity about who would appear.

A lean woman, tallish, in well-worn jeans and a khaki field jacket, that's who.

While the woman ran her fingers through thick waves of cropped black hair before reaching back to grab two covered cups and a paper bag, Gracie got even itchier: Oh yes, this woman certainly was a stranger—but even from a third-floor window she seemed unplaceably familiar.

Gracie watched the woman cross Waverly Road to the park, walk straight to the bench where they'd agreed to meet, put down the cups and the bag, then perch next to them. On time and in the right place, which left Gracie simultaneously impressed and irritated. But not, as she'd hoped, relieved. Maybe later, she told herself while she donned her own jacket and grabbed the oakwood box—once the damn rock was finally out of her life.

When she opened the door to her building's front porch, the woman stood and watched her walk to the street, cross it, and enter the park.

Damn you, Pirin Basamendi, you've already checked me out...

Then Gracie got closer—and saw what might best be described as the essence of taut, unsmiling intensity. Not just lean, but muscled lean. Slightly taller than Gracie anticipated; too black-eyed fierce to be considered beautiful, yet almost sort of handsome. Also, inexplicably, hot as hell.

"Pirin?" A rhetorical question, of course, which garnered a silent nod. Gracie placed the box on the nearest edge of the bench before stepping away again to assure the governor's mandated six feet between them as Pirin came closer to pick it up with one gloved hand, open it with the other, then close it again.

Yeah, yeah, your rock's in there, Gracie didn't say—so hot or not, feel free to go now, departing smile entirely optional.

But Pirin didn't move anything except her impenetrable eyes, which, after flicking down to check out her precious stone, resumed their squinty stare at Gracie.

Why oh why, Gracie wondered, did she recognize those eyes? Who the *hell* was Pirin Basamendi? *And* why *the hell am I not walking away yet?*

"Seems innocent enough, doesn't it?" she ventured instead while Pirin stuffed the box into a jacket pocket.

"Just a damn rock really." Pirin leaned forward to push one of the cups and the bag toward Gracie before picking up the other cup and taking a giant step backward. At last, she smiled, transforming her face from fierce to almost impish. "High-test, cream, no sugar. Still hot, I hope. Oh, and doughnuts."

"Thank you."

Well, Gracie told herself—she *had* long since surpassed her rude quotient with this woman, who was, after all, a friend of Jessica's. Besides, how else would she find out where and when they'd met? Which bar? What party?

So she stretched to pick up the coffee. One sip, maybe two, ignore the doughnuts, and then she'd remember the moment buried in their mutual past, be done with it, excuse herself with some crap about an online meeting, and—"Oh wow, you brought the *good* stuff."

"The doughnuts aren't bad, either. Had one on my way over." Pirin attempted another smile. "I confess I'm hoping you'll talk to me for a few minutes about what happened to you with the ohs—the damn rock."

This, in Gracie's view, was not fair at all; Pirin's smile made her even hotter. It also made Gracie curiouser and curiouser: When had their lives intersected? Where?

"Can we walk around instead of standing here?" Gracie asked. "I could use the exercise." As they strolled the perimeter of the park, Gracie described that strange Wednesday, how the sky darkened and churned, how three prongs of lightning burst out of the clouds, how the nearest one spawned a horizontal blue filament that reached out and touched the stone for just a second—

"It moved horizontally?"

Gracie nodded. "And its touch lit up the stone. An explosion of light. All kinds of colors pulsing. Vivid. Blinding. Violent, really. Gave me a wicked headache. And then—" Gracie shook her head; no, stop, don't mention the crazy stuff...

"What?"

Gracie kept shaking her head. No...

"Please tell me."

Gracie lifted her eyes to meet Pirin's. She rubbed the side of the coffee cup across her forehead. "You're gonna think I'm nuts. God knows, I probably am nuts."

"Please, Gracie." What was it about the sound of Pirin's voice, low and soft and urgent as she spoke Gracie's name like she'd surrendered something? "*Please*. Tell me what happened."

Maybe the time had come for Gracie to surrender, too. "After the stone lit up, after that horrible headache...then, in the night, the dreams and, uh—the dreams started."

Pirin halted as if she'd slammed into an invisible wall. "Dreams?"

Gracie had turned when Pirin stopped walking and cringed when she saw Pirin's face, which had gone pale and agape. Now that she'd blurted out her belief that this woman's chunk of rock and the lightning and these goddamn dreams were somehow connected—well, it sounded ridiculous, impossible. Beyond overwrought. And to think she'd very nearly said something about sleepwriting...

"N-No, I'm sorry, I'm sorry," Gracie sputtered, lowering her head. "It's so tempting to assume links that aren't really—"

"You don't sound nuts to me. Not one friggin' bit." Pirin's voice had gone raspy, almost a whisper, and difficult to hear from six-plus feet away. "Please tell me the rest. I, um—I might surprise you."

Gracie looked up from the worn, browned grass at the edge of the park's soccer field, noticed what appeared to be the beginnings of tears in Pirin's eyes—and then shuddered: Two men were advancing on them *fast*. Skinheads, Gracie thought, and scowling angry by the look of them.

"Oh *shit!*" she gasped. "Behind you, Pirin!"

What happened next went down much faster than Gracie could comprehend it. Pirin spun around to face the men—and her instantly impassive, not-surprised expression wrenched Gracie right out of the moment, out of time. Pirin said nothing as she quickly moved toward the men—one long bring-it stride, then another, and they responded eagerly, the larger guy head on, the other arcing rightward to trap Pirin between them.

A few heartbeats later, Gracie was already videorecording with her phone when the larger man snarled at Pirin "Don't go to court tomorrow, bitch!"

"Why not?" Pirin retorted.

In reply, Larger Guy barreled straight at Pirin with so much momentum that when she ducked to avoid his lunge, his swastika-tattooed fist missed her head and he whooshed forward, losing his balance.

"Hey, Siri, call nine-one-one!" Gracie shouted at her smartwatch (last year's something-to-hide birthday present from Naomi) hoping that maybe a 911 call would be enough to send the goons packing.

No such luck.

Oh dear god, Pirin, they're gonna kill you—and me too probably, Gracie thought as Smaller Guy began to inch sideways toward her even before Larger Guy regained his balance. Yet it didn't occur to her to run; she watched it all from a bubble of peculiar calm—like the way she felt in those dreams with Ansosho Eletun's hand on her shoulder—and so she held her phone at eye level, trying to keep it steady, steady…

Gracie's video showed Pirin rocketing into still off-balance Larger Guy with a close-in flurry of fists and elbows, pounding his kidneys, his throat, his jaw, his gut while she also mercilessly, repeatedly kneed his groin before so savagely slamming the heel of her palm into the underside of his nose that the sound of it crunching just as his head snapped brutally backward was clearly audible.

The man yelped and folded, but right before his legs gave out Pirin sidestepped to grab his arm, twisting it behind him and upward until it popped loudly, which forced him to bend hard forward. Her long legs wide apart, leaning back to counter the centrifugal force of his body, Pirin swung him like a baseball bat head-first into Smaller Guy, who'd belatedly begun to charge at her. Both men collapsed, Smaller Guy trapped stunned and breathless beneath Larger Guy.

This was when the 911 operator answered Gracie's call and Gracie began attempting reply, which wasn't easy.

Not least because Pirin hadn't finished yet. She thumped one booted foot heavily on semi-conscious Larger Guy's back as he lay moaning atop the smaller attacker. "Shush, Big Dick," she muttered while she patted him down with cautious but speedy efficiency. This yielded a handgun, which she pulled out of his pocket and held pointed at the ground, ready to use. "How 'bout you, *Little* Dick?" she asked the trapped smaller man. "Carrying?"

"Fuck you, cunt."

Pirin's hand—the one holding the handgun—twitched. "Trust me, *Little* Dick—you do *not* want to tempt me."

He blanched. "Jacket. Left side."

Pirin moved her foot, and a good measure of her bodyweight, onto the ornate Byzantine cross etched along Little Dick's left forearm while she retrieved his weapon, which she slid across the grass away from both attackers before she stepped back. Was she offering these men a chance to bolt?

Little Dick thought so.

"They called the cops, bruh!" he wheezed as he tried to wriggle out from under Big Dick, who didn't rouse much at the news. "Gedda fuck *up!*"

Pirin pointed the weapon she held at his face. "Stay, Little Dick. I might get nervous if you move."

Little Dick went almost still, except for his hands. "We didn't mean nothin' by it," he whined.

"Sure you did, and now you're trying to fuck with me. Not a good idea." Pirin wiggled the weapon. "Cuz, y'know, *oops.* I wanna see your hands. Palms down. Fingers spread. And you do not move again. Not one fuckin' millimeter."

Little Dick grunted another profanity, but he obeyed her.

"Tell me how you know him," Pirin demanded right after pulling out her phone to video the manpile.

"Who?"

The gun in Pirin's hand shimmied as she hissed "*Vee*-chor-go."

"Y-You mean Veech? Veech Farkas?"

"Yes, I mean Veech Farkas. Must be quite the favor you owe him."

"Shit. Wasn't my idea an'—an' I said we shouldn't go through with it. We just—we owed him. A-An' this was s'posed to clean the slate."

"So who's the dude on the black bike?"

"Oh *man*, you saw him?"

"Hard to miss him. You and your buddies got in pretty deep with this one."

Two cops had arrived by then, just in time to prevent Pirin from learning more about Motorcycle Dude. At the sight of Pirin holding a handgun, they unholstered their own weapons and loudly ordered her to step backward away from her two attackers and place the handgun on the grass, which she did. "All yours," she said, carefully opening her jacket to show she carried no weapon of her own.

The cops made Pirin spread-eagle anyway, which spurred Gracie to scamper alongside them breathlessly describing what she'd just witnessed, beginning with "They attacked us! I can show you!" Shortly after the cops watched her phone video, Pirin was standing again, the thugs were face down in handcuffs, two more cops had shown up, and the one with three stripes on his jacket sleeves buttonholed Pirin.

"What the hell happened here?" he wanted to know.

He wasn't the only one.

Gracie realized she was gawking at Pirin, but she didn't care. How the hell was this woman so unscathed, so—so *poised?*

The strange calm that had overtaken Gracie during the attack had given way to a high-frequency shiver radiating from her solar plexus to her fingertips. She waited for her shiver to amplify, like when you narrowly avoid a terrible automobile accident and afterward you're trembling and hyperventilating and freaked…the…fuck…out.

But no, her shiver slowly subsided. It had all happened so unimaginably fast. Like maybe it hadn't really happened at all.

CHAPTER SEVEN: HOT DARK AND DANGEROUS

The whole time Pirin dealt with the cops, she was studying Gracie.

Well, more like she resumed studying Gracie. Other than her brief encounter with the two thugs, she'd been hyper-focused on Gracie ever since 8:59 a.m., when the door to 193 Waverly Road opened and, to Pirin's immense surprise, out came this woman who embodied... lightness.

Gracie's lightness seemed to lift her as she moved across the street and into the park, like gravity had granted her a discount. It animated her as sunlight shimmered off her sandy hair, off the unassuming symmetry of her gentle, ingenuous face. And those eyes—Pirin tried not to stare into Gracie's luminous, probing blue eyes. Tried and failed, because when Gracie looked at you, you were *seen*—and, to Pirin's astonishment, being seen by Grace Gwyllt Olwyn was exhilarating.

So much for an "interview strategy." One glance from Gracie and Pirin had no strategy about an interview or anything else.

As her senses were claimed by their conversation, Pirin began to understand: Gracie was one of the smart ones and had been paying a price for that, mostly in currencies of quiet, uncomplaining disillusionment and loneliness. For Gracie, Pirin suspected, life had so far been rather disappointing. Too many times and for far too long, Gracie had asked: The point of all this is *what* exactly? And a truly satisfactory answer remained elusive.

Watching Gracie, Pirin found herself pondering: What if it really *wasn't* so peculiar that the ohskal showed itself to such a person—a stranger, someone who seemed the utter opposite of Pirin herself?

Maybe the ohskal's most recent rendezvous with lightning simply meant that Amatchi's sacred lightning stone had at last, after generations, found its way home. To Gracie. No matter that Gracie wanted nothing to do with it.

All of which would require extensive thinking about.

First, however, Pirin needed to clean up the mess she should've seen coming and could've prevented if she hadn't so egregiously underestimated Farkas's anger and desperation—and reach. Starting with her ex and now old-buddy Roz, who had to be under threat, too. Which no doubt accounted for Roz's three voice mails and two texts, all received in the last five minutes.

"Please bear with me," Pirin said to the police sergeant as she reclaimed her phone after he finished watching her video of Little Dick admitting his connection to Farkas. "This'll help explain." He agreed—as long as she put her phone conversation on speaker.

"Roz, you okay?"

"Oh god, Pir, I *knew* it. What happened?"

"Couple goons tried to jump me, but they were pretty clunky and I'm fine. What about you and—?"

"We're good. Where I sleep is plenty secure, and Farkas's ex is at a safe house till the trial's over."

"Good. The guys who came after me are in custody and the police here know Farkas instigated it. But there's a third guy still out there. On a black motorcycle. Don't know if he'll try anything by himself…"

"Who can say? Took me till about ten minutes ago to confirm that Farkas really has reneged on the plea deal. I think he stalled for as long as possible so he'd have—"

"—A chance to catch us off guard, take us out. No witnesses left to corroborate the videos. Case dismissed."

"Heh. Not dismissed yet. His trial tomorrow is a firm go, and his ex and I will be there with bells on."

"So will I, Roz. Eight a.m. sharp."

"Just so you know: Besides trying to contact you, I asked Judy to have her patrol units keep an eye on your house. Cuz Farkas's guys probably followed you from there, right? Which means Farkas knows where you live."

"Shit." Pirin's stomach somersaulted; of course she'd been followed all the way from home. *Why the hell* hadn't she realized that already? "You talked to my mother? Are they okay?"

"Oh yeah, they're all fine so I saw no point in worrying them. Just said I was trying to reach you. Though I expect your mother has her suspicions."

"Thanks, Roz." Pirin squeezed her eyes shut. "*Bas*andere, I have been *so* stupid. So much for GPS ankle monitors, huh? Dude just calls in favors from his mama's couch."

Roz's tired exhale was audible. "We'll both be testifying tomorrow. Probably a one-day trial. But if somebody Farkas sent after you is still at large, he probably already knows they blew it. And he's got almost twenty-four hours to try again."

"Mmm. On the other hand, if he learns his minions got busted and babbled his name, he might back off."

"Either way, his ex is ducking till it's over and you should, too. I can get you somewhere safe tonight."

"Nah, I'll be fine."

"Please think about it, Pirin."

Having heard the whole conversation, both Gracie and the police sergeant were waiting expectantly as Pirin clicked off the call. "Roz Marin," she explained. "An old friend who runs a domestic violence shelter in the Merrimack Valley…"

"Yeah." The sergeant was nodding. "Heard the name. And that dude Farkas, I ran him—Suffolk County corrections officer no less. Your friend's probably right about laying low till his trial's over." He handed Pirin back her ID case, which included her company identification card. "But how the hell does an insurance fraud investigator end up involved in a mess like this?"

"I'm an occasional volunteer at Roz's shelter. When she's short-staffed, I'll sometimes go with her or one of her people when they accompany a client at risk of confrontation with her abuser. Tends to be about picking up the client's stuff from where the abuser lives too, which we try to do as fast as possible when he's not there. They bring me along cuz I'm good at quick-lugging bags of clothes and kids' toys. And mostly nothing happens."

The sergeant indulged in a crooked smile. "But not that time with Farkas, huh?"

"No." Pirin tried not to grimace; they were gonna make her talk about this, weren't they? "Not that time." Maybe if she just kept her head down…

"Jeezus, Pirin," Gracie blurted. "What happened?"

Pirin sighed. "Roz and I were with his ex, who has custody of their kid and had already gotten an abuse prevention order on him. She'd bugged out of their place since his mother owns it, so we'd gone back to pick up the usual, clothes and a few toys, while Farkas was supposedly at work. But he showed up spouting threats and crap about his 'rights.' Then he moved on her. Had his hands around her throat, throttling her, not letting go, screaming he was gonna kill her. I believed him, so I felt like I had to try to intervene. Physically."

"Yeah." The sergeant suppressed a smirk. "Says here CO Farkas ended up with a concussion, cracked ribs, broken wrist, bruised testicles—"

"He didn't wanna stop, so, uh…" Pirin shrugged.

"So," the sergeant continued, reading from a small tablet screen, "I see here he racked up two felony charges—DV assault and attempted murder—plus two other garden-variety assault charges, suspension without pay, revocation of his license to carry. Damn. Those two felonies—this guy's potentially looking at a hefty sentence. Must have a pretty decent lawyer to swing the bail conditions he got."

"I figured home confinement and that GPS ankle bracelet would do it." Pirin slumped. "Shoulda guessed that someone whose name translates to, literally, 'snarling wolf' would need to be in a cage. I just didn't think dark enough—that he's doing shit with former inmates. Those guys *are* former inmates, aren't they?"

"We'll know pretty soon," the sergeant replied, one finger pressed to his earbud. "A little birdie tells me they're already chatting away, looking for whatever deal they can make. You didn't hear this from me, but good odds Farkas'll be charged with felony number three—intimidation of a witness."

Gracie returned to her apartment alone, her mind roiling.

Roiling as in *What the fuck just happened?!*

Roiling as in *I hope I never see her again* how soon can I see her again *what if she never wants to see me again* if I see her again she'll bug me to talk about those dreams *and that sleepwriting* oh god oh god oh god *what do I do now?*

While Pirin was still caught up with the cops, she'd walked away with a quick nod and an understated call-me gesture, uncomfortably aware that Pirin's gaze never left her as she departed the park, crossed the street, and entered her building. At least, Gracie determinedly told herself upon closing the door behind her, *I never have to think about that damn rock again. No more sleepwriting, no more Eletun dreams, no more Kaldi dreams—*

Whoa.

No...more...Kaldi...dreams...

Suddenly Gracie couldn't swallow. Her heart thundered in her chest, in her ears. "Omigod!" she rasped aloud. "That's it!"

In cadence with her climb to her third-floor garret, she tried denial...no...no...no...no... But by the time she entered her apartment and carefully locked herself inside, the noes had failed: She'd met Pirin Basamendi before, all right—in a dream, when Pirin went by different name and lived in a different time.

Gracie wanted to curl up in a ball and sleep it all away. Except she didn't have a clue how to ensure dreamless sleep—and besides, a glance out the living room windows showed Pirin still out there in the park. No, dammit, she would not stand there staring at Hot Dark and Dangerous.

C'mon, Gracie, here's where we say (again) thank god it's over. And then we light up a joint. Say it now, Gracie. Now. And stop thinking about Hot Dark and Dangerous.

Now, Gracie. Now.

Because, Gracie told herself as she marched into her bedroom to her weed drawer, *it's finished. The damn rock is gone. Pirin is gone. With a little luck the damn dreams are gone. Write off the day, get high...*

Gracie was opening the weed drawer when her phone rang.

"I, uh, wanna thank you for, uh, sticking around through that." Pirin cleared her throat. "You kept it from getting really nasty."

"*Me?*" Gracie's quick laugh puffed out her nose. "Ha! I stood there like a useless fool while you—god, I've never seen anyone do what you did. It was—it was spectacular."

Pirin's voice stayed low, serious. "Wouldn't have gone down like that without you wielding your phone like a weapon. You never even flinched. That was impressive—and it discombobulated the bejeezus outta both of 'em. Which is why I'm not covered in bruises, or worse. A lot worse."

Gracie grinned but didn't know what to say.

"So, uhh…" Pirin stretched the sound into Gracie's silence. "I, um, just wanted to say thank you, and—and that's all really, I guess. Thank you for helping me. I, uh—I kinda think I'd prob'ly be under arrest but for you."

"Well, that would've been *outrageous!*"

"The price of shit like that going down in public. You're not righteous till the cops say you are."

"Good deeds are best done anonymously, huh?" Gracie murmured.

"Oh yeah."

Seconds passed, more seconds as Gracie grasped that Pirin wouldn't be pressing her to talk about the dreams—but she wasn't nearly ready to click off the call. "Where're you headed?" she finally asked.

"Home."

"Not gonna do what your friend Roz suggested?"

"Nope. Home." Pirin's voice had stiffened, but then—"Roz has Judy, who's a police captain, to cuddle up with. Hell, Judy takes a police cruiser home every night, so no one messes with Roz anymore. But Roz is right about my mother. She'll look out a window, see a cruiser once too often, and begin worrying."

"Have you talked to her yet?"

"Not yet. She's my next call."

Jeez, Gracie thought—you called me first. "Do you think that guy—?"

"—Farkas."

"Do you think he'll send anyone else after you?"

"Possibly, though it'd be a really stupid move even for him." Pirin paused. "The prosecutors have a strong case—solid witnesses, two videos—so I expect he'll be found guilty at trial. Unless he pleads out at the last minute. But even from a prison cell he can order a hit, y'know?"

"And you think he will."

"I do, actually. Maybe not right away. But eventually."

"So much for so-called 'justice.'"

"Justice is expensive," Pirin lamented. "Like organic food. Which means hardly anybody can afford it. Mostly we all go to bed hungry. The lucky among us manage to subsist on genetically modified mac-and-fake-cheese."

"You're hungry, aren't you?"

"Mmm. That doughnut was good, but kinda small. And I gave the rest to the cops in the park."

One more time, they both went quiet. A somewhat more comfortable quiet this time—until, to the horror of hesitant, closet-crazy Gracie, some Utterly Other Gracie blurted out the offer she was never supposed to make: "After all this hassle with Farkas's trial is over, if you still want me to, I'll tell you about those dreams."

CHAPTER EIGHT: *NOT ONE LIVING SOUL*

That *foul* prick!"
"At least it's over." Roz ran her hand affectionately up and down Pirin's back as they departed the waiting area outside the courtroom. "And now that he's gonna change his plea for real, we can finally relax for real."

Pirin sneered. "Sounds like his usual bullshit to me."

The defendant's scowl hadn't flagged for even a second during Pirin's testimony. Once more she found herself confronted by a male gaze combusting with that malevolent, wrath-filled how-*dare*-you!— and she no longer bothered about why.

She already knew why. It was always the same damn thing: This time 'round, it was Vicsorgó Farkas who'd been thoroughly humiliated for all the world to see *by a cunt*. He was a big dude—certainly way bigger than she was—and somehow she had flattened him in a matter of seconds. This he regarded as an atrocity.

Well, screw him. Screw that he, like all the others, wanted her, *needed* her to be afraid of him. Screw his 'roid rage when she wasn't.

Even as she described to the judge and the jury what he did and how she responded, she was assessing his how-*dare*-you! glare firsthand from a mere fifteen feet away. Of *course* she glared back unblinkingly cunt-proud as he sat hunched over the defendant's table, brow furrowed, eyes ablaze with menace.

And he made sure she noticed the stark red tattoo on his right forearm of, oh yeah, a snarling wolf, which he revealed when he unobtrusively shoved up his shirtsleeve while silently baring his teeth into (surprise!) a snarl. As far as Pirin was concerned, *that* was a threat.

"At least it's over," Roz repeated once they stepped outdoors into a chilly light drizzle that quickly glinted atop her rowdy mane of loose brown curls. "But I just don't get what he thought he was doing. The case against him has always been a slam-dunk, and if he'd taken the deal still on the table when he woke up yesterday, he'd have ducked the felony charges altogether and been out in less than a year."

Pirin shrugged. "I think he figured he'd walk away from *all* the charges, since he doesn't regard what he did as a 'real' crime like stealing another man's money. So, gambler that he is, he made a bet. And then tried to cheat."

Roz shook her head. "Now he'll do prison for sure, not a jail stint. And the only way he'll ever find his ex-wife is if she wants him to—and trust me, she does *not* want him to."

"But maybe it's not so much about his ex-wife anymore," Pirin said. "I got evil eye from him the whole time I was testifying. Plus he made sure I saw his wolf tat. And his snarl. Dude might as well have been screaming 'I will *get* you, bitch.'"

Roz's perennially tired face had clouded like the sky above them. "He wasn't that way when I... I mean yeah, he was obviously upset, but he avoided making eye contact with me. No tats in sight either."

Ah, Roz; despite fifteen years of working with victims of domestic violence, she maintained a remarkable idealism about the generic redeemability of the human male—an idealism Pirin didn't share. Now Pirin watched Roz's idealism strain a bit: "Oh," she murmured. "Oh shit. You think he intends to take another crack at *you*."

"Bingo," said Pirin. "Once he was arrested last night on the witness intimidation charge, he knew we'd testify today, knew he'd go down for assaulting his ex. So now he's got two reasons to fry my ass—revenge *and* squirming out of the intimidation charge. You bet I worry he'll try again."

A frown formed on Roz's face. "So he'll go after you and the guys who were supposed to scare you into silence?"

"Oh, I have no doubt Farkas's goons are on his shitlist. But what if there are others?"

"You think maybe your family—"

"Also that work buddy of Jessica Winter's—Gracie Olwyn. She not only saw it all, she made a video of it all and gave it to the cops. Which means she's a witness."

"Who'll have to testify to the veracity of her video if Farkas takes the case to trial." Roz groaned. "Thus qualifying her as someone he would want to silence."

Pirin nodded. "And probably sooner rather than later…"

Roz raised a hold-on-a-minute finger as she took a phone call during which she mostly said "Yes" and "Okay" and then, finally, "Thank you for letting me know."

"Good news, Pir," Roz said as they reached her car. "Farkas pled guilty to everything—even second-degree attempted murder. Signed and sealed a few minutes ago. What's more, he's already been sentenced because as of tomorrow jury trials have been suspended and courts statewide are pretty much closing their doors. He's already in a van heading to the Mass DOC Reception Facility."

"What'd he get?"

"Five to eight years in state prison, then five years' probation. Word is he's now brimming with mea culpas since any more shit'll see him sent to a maximum security facility."

"Wherever he ends up, he's getting off way too easy," Pirin grumbled. "Good behavior and he's out in two and a half years. *Two and a half!*" She paused. "What about the witness intimidation charge?"

"As far as I know," said Roz, "his not-guilty plea on that still stands. And since he's unlikely to get bail, he could've been stuck in the Middlesex County Jail till whenever jury trials resume. By pleading out today, in effect he's opted for prison, which any inmate'll tell you beats a county jail."

"Well, at least—"

Another call interrupted; for the best, given what Pirin almost said—*at least I'll have a few weeks to figure out how to shut him the fuck down.* No no no, that would reveal way too much to someone who'd already been suspecting too much for years.

As they waved goodbye, Pirin was grateful that she and Roz had driven to the courthouse separately. If they shared the forty-minute ride homeward, she might let something slip. What surprised her, frightened her, was how much she wanted to talk with another person about what was on her mind.

And in so many ways, Roz Marin was that person. Roz knew how to listen. She oozed sympathy. She was astute, inventive, determined, profoundly committed to women, with an optimism miraculously still mostly intact despite being tempered by real life. Indeed, Roz's optimism illuminated everything she did. That optimism even inspired Pirin to be a little in love with her once, and for three years they'd been together. Until…

Actually, there'd been a couple of untils.

Most problematic was Roz's blithe disregard for her own safety while dealing with predatory men who were aggressively hostile to anyone interfering with their "right" to do whatever they wanted to any women they pleased.

Also, Roz was curious. Too curious, at least about Pirin. Roz wanted to know all of it. All of *her*. In deal-breaking detail. That was a risk too far given Roz's propensity for noticing things: Coincidences, flukes, correlations that enticed too much speculation about causation…

Then there was Roz's deal-breaker: Either move in with me or I have to move on. Roz wasn't Ayesha, certainly—no one would ever come close to being Ayesha—yet Pirin had been inordinately tempted; Ayesha was gone and Pirin was lonely and Roz was kind, funny, loving, delightfully sexy (*and* a cunnilingus virtuosa).

At least they'd stayed close. Pirin regarded Roz as one of her best friends, (almost) right up there with Jessica.

Yet she decided not to mention Veech Farkas again. Even though brave, unflappable Roz had a way of calming her down, seducing her toward a brightness she rarely achieved without someone else's encouragement.

Who else but Roz could get her to admit that at least *in principle* people can genuinely change their ways? As Roz regularly reminded her, no one is born evil.

Driving home alone, Pirin wondered if Roz had a point: Had she overreacted to Veech Farkas's courtroom scowl?

Within seconds of allowing herself to ask that question, a black motorcycle steered audaciously close to her car, its black-clad rider turning his head toward her as he whooshed by way too fast, the two fingers of his gloved hand pointing first at his own eyes, hidden behind his black face shield, then at her.

And what was that on the side of his helmet, visible as he turned back to watch the road? Pirin got only the briefest of glimpses, but it sure as hell looked like a version of the exact same snarling wolf tattoo she'd just seen on Vicsorgó Farkas's forearm.

❖

"Is that all?" Gracie smiled. "After such a dramatic intro, I expected you to tell me something scary. Or at least unsettling."

"You're *not* unsettled?" Pirin allowed herself to exhale. "How can you not be unsettled?"

They'd agreed to communicate via a smartphone videocall, which wrecked any ability to sustain real eye contact. So Pirin watched slightly downcast eyes as Gracie answered her one question with two. "Maybe cuz the man's locked away in a cell? Cuz I didn't see his face or his tat? I suppose I've lived a sheltered life; I'm honestly not sure I know what 'rabidly murderous' looks like in real life."

"It looks scary. Unsettling." Pirin's voice descended half an octave into please-take-me-seriously territory. "And I'm really sorry. Cuz I should never have—have…"

"Oh please go on." Gracie looked straight at Pirin (which, Pirin grasped, meant she'd chosen to stare directly at her phone's tiny dot of a camera lens rather than at the face on her screen). "*What* should you never have—? Oh, wait—you want to apologize for what you *didn't* do, yes?"

Ouch. "I didn't notice those two assholes. Shoulda noticed, since they followed me for forty-five miles from my door to my mechanic's garage to your door. But I didn't. That's why you've been caught up in my crap."

"Yeah, it *is* kinda crappy, isn't it?" Gracie gazed out from Pirin's phone screen as her head cocked just slightly to one side. "Why," she asked, "do I have the feeling that you tend to attract certain kinds of crap?"

"Not on purpose."

"On the other hand, I'm betting you don't shy away from certain kinds of crap, either. The woman I saw out there in the park seemed awfully practiced at not shying away."

"Bugs me when men try to push me around."

"Do they usually end up under arrest like those guys did?" Gracie sounded almost amused.

"I wish."

"So they're generally not so egregious."

"Oh, they're plenty egregious. They just get away with it. Mostly."
Damn, Pirin thought—what the fuck is happening here? I need to
change the subject.

"Mostly? That sounds interesting…"

"It's boring, actually. Unlike those dreams of yours, I suspect."

"Oh. Yeah." Suddenly, Gracie's voice had grown hoarse—and
reluctant.

Pirin plunged into Gracie's silence as fast as she could. "Don't
know if you remember, but in the park you said that when the lightning
hit the ohskal, the stone, it produced 'violent spinning pulses of light'
that gave you a bad headache, and then—"

"—Then, later, came the dreams."

"If it's any consolation," Pirin offered, "you're not the only one. I
grew up hearing stories like that. My family has generations of stories
like that."

"Stories? Connecting the stone to dreaming, you mean?"

Pirin nodded. "Lots of women in my mother's family, the
Basamendis, had dreams because of the ohskal. According to my
amatchi, my grandmother, the ohskal communicates. She told me it
showed her things."

Gracie's blue eyes widened. "What things?"

"Like olden stories, myths I guess you'd say—but more than
that. What the ohskal showed her gave her a deep intuition, eerily
accurate. Amatchi would hold the ohskal up to the sunlight, and its
rays would scatter all over the room, all over her face. Beautiful, that
light. Mesmerizing. And then afterward—well, she knew things she
shouldn't be able to know. About what somebody was truly thinking or
wanted, even what was gonna happen. It was always mysterious. But it
was real. I can vouch for that."

"So more than just dreams."

"Oh yeah. Much more. Amatchi said the ohskal carries what
she called 'lurbegia,' which means fundamental, underlying reality.
Literally 'deep-earth truth.' She also said this ohskal was special. She
told me it protects the woman it claims."

Gracie stared blankly almost at Pirin, but she didn't speak.

"So, um," Pirin slowly continued, "I think maybe the ohskal
claimed you. Back when you saw the lightning."

"These—" Gracie's hand splayed across her chest and she seemed to gulp for air. "These dreams and stuff that've happened to me—you think it's about the stone."

"'Dreams *and stuff*'? What stuff?"

Gracie's head drooped and she didn't reply. I'll wait, Pirin thought—quietly, patiently, I'll just wai—

"Sleepwriting."

"Say what?"

Gracie flinched but carried on. "The 'and stuff' is sleepwriting."

"Never heard of it. Is it—?"

"Exactly what it sounds like. Quite rare, apparently. I have yet to remember doing it, but I know I did since, first off, no one else lives here, and besides, I recognize my handwriting, even though it looks like I wrote it with my left hand. And each time what I wrote is about the same people that show up in the dreams."

"Did you keep what you, uh, sleepwrote?"

"I did."

"Can I see it?"

At last, Gracie smiled again. Just a little and somewhat tremulously—but yes, Pirin saw a smile.

"I figured that if I managed to find the guts to tell you about this, then you'd want to look at everything."

Pirin nodded vigorously. "How many dreams have you—?"

"—Two. Long ones. Even though they freaked me out, I found myself writing them down as soon as I woke up. They were so different and I felt, I dunno—compelled, I guess. Also some fragments. They were harder to remember, so I didn't have much to write down. I'll email you everything, including the three sleepwritings. Seems like your stone wants to tell a story. Maybe now that it's home again it'll tell *you* the rest—in *your* dreams…"

CHAPTER NINE: SOMETHING REAL

After reading and rereading the attachments Gracie emailed, Pirin didn't sleep at all that night. Like a succession of exotic revenants wafting through a fitful fog of almost-memory, what Gracie had written was just a little too familiar…

And yeah, okay, maybe she shouldn't take any of it seriously. "I mean, *shit*," Pirin grumped at her bathroom mirror, "we're talking dreams and—and what's it called? Oh, right: parasomnia. Not exactly reliable."

No matter. She couldn't stop herself from reading it all yet again.

Gracie's first dream could've taken place anywhere, though Pirin thought the campfire and the women's coarse clothes hinted at a *when* that was very long ago, a notion Gracie's initial sleepwriting seemed to reinforce with its solemn references to Rhythm and Resonance and Tales of the Mothers.

What inspired Pirin's disconcerted doubletake, however, was "Ansosho Eletun."

This was not a name she'd ever heard before, yet its elements resembled words she knew: *antze*, meaning skill or talent; *oso*, whole, complete, entire; *ele*, word or talk or story; and *tun*, an archaic term for rhythmic drumming.

Nahhh, Pirin initially told herself, just a coincidence…

Yet the same thing happened with other names and places Gracie had recorded. "Analakinak" looked too much like a pluralized fusion of *anal*, an ancient word for ability or power, and *akin*, knowledge. "Sundaselai" reminded Pirin of *sunda*, meaning smell or stench, merged with *zelai*, prairie or plain.

And then—

Then she spotted "Subendi," which revived a neglected memory of her amatchi explaining how the other language of Etche Basamendi—Amatchi's own, native dialect—was only partly modern and shareable with others from the old country and the émigré communities on the western side of the Atlantic. The rest derived from "the ancient tongue," spoken only at home and perhaps (Amatchi could only surmise) by the few Basamendiak who clung on in the mountains of the old country, still tending their gardens and herds and telling the old tales.

Was "Subendi" a word from "the ancient tongue"? Pirin didn't know, couldn't know. But she recognized that it combined the word for fire—"su"—with an archaic version of the word for mountain—"bendi," a word she'd learned back when Amatchi had told her that the "original" Etche had once been named Basabendi...

"Not 'mendi' like our name now?" Pirin had asked.

"No," Amatchi replied, "long ago it was 'bendi.' But the ways people talk change over time."

"Like how we don't say things anymore the way Shakespeare did, or Beowulf."

"Bai—yes—like that, only more so. Our old words are much older than even Shakespeare or Beowulf."

"More than twelve hundred years?!" Pirin struggled with her incredulity. "Cuz that's how old Beowulf is." Her teacher had recently read some of the original Beowulf aloud in class, and at first she understood nothing of its Old English—until, all at once, her ear and her mind adapted and she understood everything.

Amatchi smiled. "Some of our ancient words are much older than twelve hundred years. Many times older..."

So what about other names Gracie had written down? At first, Pirin didn't recognize anything about them. Not until after midnight, during her sixth or eighth reading of Gracie's attachments, when a clouded memory floated to the front of her exhausted, fading consciousness—and spiked her adrenaline all over again.

The story she hazily recalled had been a kind of centerpiece around which Amatchi coiled many of those Favorite Fables that Pirin never quite took seriously. Like most tales, this one probably had a title, but she couldn't recall it. She did, however, remember one character in particular whose name, she realized around two in the morning, sounded an awful lot like Gracie's Analergin.

Amatchi's Anagin, by contrast, was all grown up and the brilliant skipper of what seemed to be a large ocean-going outrigger canoe crafted from a single enormous tree trunk and powered by what sounded like an impressively-sized crab-claw sail. Pirin was never sure how many people this vessel carried—at least a dozen, possibly twice that. It also had room for substantial cargoes of fresh water and food.

Back when Pirin first heard about Anagin, she paid little attention to the canoe's details; she was more interested in Anagin's remarkable ocean-spanning journey achieved with what sounded like magical navigation abilities. As told by Amatchi, Anagin not only understood and used the complex patterns of open ocean waves and swells to direct the journey but also "ulpirin."

"Like my name?" Pirin had asked.

"Yes, only in water," Amatchi responded. "'Ul' is an earlier version of—"

"—Of 'ur'—water?"

"Exactly. 'Ulpirin' are bolts of light that come from land and travel just beneath the ocean's surface. This is how Anagin could tell in which direction land was, and how distant, too, even when her canoe was very far out to sea."

Interesting, that story. But too fantastic for Pirin to take seriously—though later, learning to sail out in the Gulf of Maine reinvigorated her curiosity about Anagin's vessel and its journey. Especially when one of her instructors told her about crab-claw sails and Polynesian navigators and something called te lapa—documented light phenomena that seem to emanate from land and move in straight lines just beneath ocean surfaces.

Now Pirin wondered: Could Amatchi's Anagin and Gracie's Analergin be the same person?

"I damn well *hope* not!" Gracie didn't mean to actually speak the words, much less allow them to sound so ornery.

"Why?"

"Because—" Gracie scrunched her eyes closed, grateful that this time they were doing a simple, old-fashioned voice call and Pirin wouldn't see the flush she felt rising into her cheeks. "Because then it might—" She halted again. "God, Pirin, what if it's *real?*"

For a moment, Gracie heard only the sound of steady breathing. "What if it isn't?" Pirin finally countered. "Real, I mean."

"I—" Gracie strained for air. "I dunno."

"Mmm, let's see: *If* your dreams are mere dreams and your sleepwriting is mere parasomnia, *and if* the stories my grandmother claimed came from her ohskal are fairy tales made up by a frail old woman, *then* all the parallels between what you experienced and what my grandmother told me years ago—well, those're just coincidences, right?" Pirin made a sound too much like a chuckle. "And all else being equal, you don't strike me as someone especially comfortable with coincidences. Especially when they congregate."

"Shit."

"Ohh-kay." Pirin's voice rippled toward a tease. "So it's *shit* coincidence that your dreams and your sleepwriting started only after you brought the ohskal home and saw lightning zap it. *Shit* coincidence that—"

"Hey, *Pirin*," Gracie broke in testily, "while you're at it don't forget the shit coincidence about your name meaning 'lightning.' Woulda been nice if you'd mentioned *that* when we met."

"Didn't wanna scare you off. I, um—I figured we'd talk some first, and then I'd tell you. But before we got that far..."

"Yeah. We were interrupted by your stalkers. Just as well. Cuz finding out then that *you are lightning* probably *would've* scared me off."

Pirin laughed (a bit nervously, Gracie thought) but said nothing.

"Anyway," Gracie continued, "you're suggesting my dreams and this sleepwriting stuff point to something real..."

"Or maybe something that *was* real way back when."

"And this something that is or was real..." Gracie paused. Nope, said out loud, the notion was still just too damn wackadoodle (never mind that she'd privately, secretly believed it herself ever since that terrifying Wednesday). "You're saying this 'something real' got conveyed to me by your stone—your ohskal."

"By lightning making contact with the ohskal."

"That's—that's—"

"Implausible maybe." Pirin made a small, snorty sound. "But not impossible."

"You're saying lightning zapped this 'something real' from a damn *stone* into my brain? *How* is that possible?!"

"Well, for what it's worth, the 'stone' is mostly crystal quartz. Optically active and piezoelectric—but quartz is *an*isotropic, which means how it reacts to an external force like light depends on the direction of that force. Plus I'm told there might be pyrite in the ohskal, too, and pyrite sparks when—"

"So you're saying that because of the way the lightning hit the quartz crystal, my brain translated this 'something real'—which was originally articulated in some ancient language I don't know—into dreams and sleepwriting that I understood and wrote down in regular old American English?"

"Well, I have some thoughts about that, but they're, y'know... complicated."

"I'd like to hear those thoughts. In all their complexity." Gracie hesitated—until Utterly Other Gracie blurted "I wish we could have dinner together" even as Hesitant Gracie, not quite liberated from her crazy-closet, wanted to click off the call.

"Yeah. Me too." Pirin went quiet for a moment before her voice brightened. "We could try a screentime dinner. We could try it tonight."

Don't, Hesitant Gracie pleaded with the Utterly Other Gracie, stay away from her...

But a suddenly throbbing Utterly Other Gracie immediately assented to screentime dinner.

Thus, an hour before Pirin was due to call, Hesitant Gracie gulped down two glasses of Pinot Grigio from a bottle she couldn't remember opening while Utterly Other Gracie cobbled together an old supper-by-yourself standby: tuna salad sandwich, tabouli, potato chips.

A grinning Pirin called at 7:01 p.m. ("Uncool to show up early," she bumbled), her meal of obviously homemade chicken soup and a chunk of bread before her on an ornately tiled bistro table, along with (coincidentally?) a bottle of the same Pinot Grigio that Hesitant Gracie was already knocking back.

At Pirin's suggestion, they began their meal with a toast, and as Hesitant Gracie finished off the contents of her wine bottle, she surrendered to a what-the-hell blur.

Cuz hey, Pirin possessed the lightning stone now, right? Plus all her scribbles about the dreams and the sleepwriting, too, right? So if, as Pirin seemed to believe, the damn rock's "story" *was* something real… well, fine and fucking dandy—from now on it'd be "real" in Pirin's head, not hers.

No. Longer. My. Problem.

Right?

Besides, only moments after their toast, while she uncorked a second bottle of Pinot, Utterly Other Gracie had become thoroughly distracted. Not by Pirin's convoluted babbling about entanglement and wavefunction collapse and cognitive processes, all of which somehow apparently related to the damn rock, but because, in spite of herself, she couldn't stop imagining what it would feel like to kiss Pirin's magnificently inviting lips—not too thin, not too thick, and, in repose, surprisingly ready to impishly smile.

CHAPTER TEN: ZERO-CLICK

The sensation was new. Never before had Pirin wished she could forget about her recycles and concentrate on something else—on *someone* else.

Yet she didn't dare. Not now when she just couldn't know how long it would take for Vicsorgó Farkas to find a way to come after her and maybe Gracie, too.

The Commonwealth's Department of Corrections reception and classification center would be keeping him quarantined for at least a month. From there he'd likely be shipped to one of the medium security facilities where, after a few more weeks of new-inmate quarantine, he'd normally end up in gen pop, making friends, seeking ways to reach beyond the razor wire.

But these were not normal circumstances. The pandemic had forced the Commonwealth's prisons into a restrictive lockdown that was gumming up all their processes and protocols.

So—a little more time before the Veech Farkas threat level escalated. A little more time to anticipate him, foil him.

Pirin began by learning more about him. She already knew from a comment Roz made that he had a penchant for poker. Ah, gambling—often a good place to start when searching for someone's soft underbelly. To sniff out more, she used some of the synthetic credentials she'd long ago created to probe the usual proprietary databases for Veech's financial and credit history (not good), his employment history (meh), his arrest history (more than she expected albeit with surprisingly few consequences until just recently).

Three questions kept her on edge: How long before he got his sleazy hands on an illicit smartphone? How long after that before he arranged one or more contract killings? How to stop him?

Pirin didn't know. Not yet. But she had no doubt that smartphones would play a prominent role. And she had a lot to learn about smartphones.

❖

The morning after her screentime dinner with Pirin, Gracie swore she'd never drink anything alcoholic again. She'd fallen asleep contemplating Pirin, woke up contemplating Pirin.

Going for a walk didn't help. Binge-watching nineties TV shows didn't help. Eating chocolate ice cream (twice) didn't help.

"No," she groused aloud, "you cannot spend the whole of a fucking pandemic fantasizing about Hot Dark and Dangerous. Try being rational instead. Do something practical, like revamping your pathetic résumé since you're likely to get furloughed any day now."

This effort produced a nicely designed header on an otherwise blank document. Because one's résumé should target the type of job one seeks. But in all her life, Gracie had never been able to answer that question—*If you could make a living any way you wanted, what would it be?* The closest she ever got was *oh god no, not that.* Grace Gwyllt Olwyn seemed to embody a mathematical problem no algorithm could solve.

And with that dubious observation, she vaped herself to sleep.

She'd taken up bedtime cannabis vaping because her sort-of friend Tory had commented once that weed suppressed dream recollection—and it was ultra-fine with Gracie if she never ever again remembered a dream.

No such luck, however—though this was not immediately obvious.

Not until she floated to full consciousness and lay staring at the ceiling as she argued with herself about whether the brief yet unequivocally strange experience qualified as a dream—or had she really not slept at all? And should she write down what she remembered about whatever it was? Or maybe just ignore it, because *hey!* the damn rock is long gone and how fucking dare this shit start up *again!*

Utterly Other Gracie objected, of course, pointing out that regardless of what went down, it couldn't truly be called "awake" and, yes, Pirin needed to know all about it—every detail, no matter how visceral, how intimate. "You *promised*, Gracie."

Curiously, Hesitant Gracie recalled no such promise. Not one she'd made aloud, anyway. Even so, she started writing.

❖

"Just wanted to check..." Gracie didn't intend to sound conspiratorial, but she found herself holding her phone close and speaking low and fast. "You use a virtual private network, right?"

Pirin laughed. "A couple, actually. Which one depends on what I'm up to at any given moment. Oh, and hello to you, too."

Nope, no distractions yet. Gracie was on a mission. "Your VPNs also protect your email?"

Pirin's laugh now lilted through her hum. "Mmm-*hhmmm*."

"Remind me: Text and voice calls, too?"

"End-to-end encrypted. Far from perfect, but—"

"So like what I'm saying to you right now."

"Yep. Works pretty well as long as one's operating system isn't compromised."

"And if *I* send *you* an email?"

"Depends on the email service. The one I use most—you have that address—is end-to-end encrypted by a privacy-obsessed Swiss company." Then Pirin got serious. "What's up?"

"Just hadda make sure."

"Gracie, you've been speed-talking. What. Is. Going. On?"

"Well...ummm..."

"Whenever you're ready. I'll wait."

Time to own up, Gracie decided. "Had trouble sleeping last night, so I did a cleanout. More like a clean slate, I suppose. I, uh, used to be involved with someone—Naomi, who got recruited by this woman at a DC consulting outfit." And soon Gracie was describing Naomi's unceremonious departure.

"Seemed at first like she wasn't interested. But—well, one day I got this feeling I couldn't shake. So I came home early and found Naomi trying to ghost. Most of her stuff, including the cat, already gone. A breezy see-ya note on the kitchen counter. One last suitcase in hand. She jabbered about needing to 'try it out,' and I knew she meant more than just the job. Anyway, she left lotsa shit here, implied she'd come back for it—especially her loveseat. And also her laptop, which I think she intended to take but ended up so flustered she forgot it."

"God, Gracie, that's awful," Pirin exhaled loudly. "But honestly—Naomi is a fool. Has she come looking for her stuff now?"

"Uh-uh. Haven't heard a peep from her since she walked out the door almost seven months ago. So last night I finally decided to keep her loveseat and her little butler's table and stash everything else in the basement till I call a junk guy to take it away. But, um, before I added her laptop to the pile, I decided to try taking a peek inside. I'd noticed her entering her password a few times, and late last night I finally remembered it and went poking."

"You found something…"

"Mmm. What looks like a draft of an internal memo from the company that recruited her—maybe sent to impress her, persuade her. And they're—they're—"

"What?"

"Uh…" C'mon, do it now. Own up *now*…

"Gracie?"

"So, um, first of all, I understand why you're so upset about that guy Farkas." Gracie cleared her throat. "I mean, I get it now, that he's really dangerous, even from prison. So you have to do whatever you can to protect yourself from him. I understand that now cuz—well, I think maybe he's what the dream was really about."

"What dream?"

"Night before last. I dreamt about Kaldi."

For a moment, Pirin said nothing—then she spoke in a hush: "Another ohskal dream."

"I guess so. It started in my neighborhood and the other usual characters weren't in it, but Kaldi was. So I'm guessing there's some kinda connection to the ohskal. I wrote down what I remembered and I'll send it to you." Gracie paused for a deep breath. "But what I really called about is this stuff on Naomi's laptop."

"The files on her laptop have something to do with your dream?"

"I-I dunno. Maybe. Like the dream primed me for what I later found on the laptop. Hard to explain, but I woke up from that dream feeling like this Farkas dude really could have a bead on you. And then later, when I saw the stuff on Naomi's laptop, I thought it might help you to, y'know, protect yourself—even though I don't understand much of the details, especially the code—but I haven't told anybody about what I found, not one living soul, since I figured you'd wanna, y'know, uh…I just had this overwhelming sense that, uh…uh…"

"Slow down, Gracie, slow down."

Gracie groaned. "Sorry, Pirin…"

"Besides what you wrote about that dream, why don't you email me the laptop files, too? I'll check out all of it and get back to you."

❖

Pirin read Gracie's dream write-up first and found herself smiling—until she read the last sentence.

⚡ I was taking a walk around my neighborhood after dark, but the area's plenty safe so I wasn't the least bit afraid.

After a while, as the darkness began to ebb into light, I saw something I'd never noticed before: a surprisingly lush forest. How wonderful, I thought, to have an area that's so wild so close by, and I ventured into it a ways along a narrow but obviously well-used path.

Soon the path petered out and I didn't want to get lost, so I turned around, expecting to have no problem retracing my steps. But the path had disappeared and everything looked different.

I took a guess at which way was "back," but as I walked that way I began to sense that I was being watched. I didn't actually see anyone, but I got the willies and started to pick up my pace until I was outright running, quite sure that I was running *from* someone.

Finally, I crouched into underbrush to hide, convinced that this was the only thing that would save me.

Almost immediately, I heard a sound behind me and twisted toward it to find someone not more than three feet away. Young, naked, running for her life, she pounded right by me, gone as quickly as she appeared. I doubt she saw me at all.

But I recognized her—from other dreams. First one was when I was also lost in some strange woods and stumbled toward a fire in a clearing. The next time I saw her we were both much younger and I helped her hide from the Lotus Man by taking her hand. And here she was again: Kaldi.

I wanted to see where she was going so I chased after her—and soon I found myself moving faster than my legs could possibly carry me. I understood then that I wasn't with my body anymore.

But I didn't give that any real thought. I was focused instead on reaching Kaldi. Why was she running so hard? Was she in danger?

As I considered this, everything changed, like maybe what I thought *caused* everything to change—caused Kaldi to stop running and turn toward me and see me. That's when I became very aware of my solidity again, of being in my own body again.

That's also when Kaldi reached out to me, her hand extending to take mine. She'd stopped for me, jittery like a thoroughbred eager to run, *needing* to run.

So I grabbed her hand and began to run with her.

⚡   Those final words—*I grabbed her hand and began to run with her*—replayed in Pirin's head as she shifted to opening the first of several documents from Naomi's laptop that Gracie sent. One quick scan and she froze.

As in: She could not move. Not one muscle.

Because Gracie had discovered exactly what Pirin needed to contend with Veech Farkas. Discovered it, recognized its significance, told her about it, *sent it to her.*

As if Gracie understood everything.

But—

No. *Not* possible. Nobody knew anything about this part of Pirin's life. So *Gracie Olwyn* could not know anything about this part of Pirin's life. No. Fucking. Way.

Alone in her office, Pirin gripped the edges of her desk. *Shhh, calm down there's gotta be some sorta explanation…maybe it's not really what it seems, shhh…*

Minutes later (or, hell, maybe an hour later), Pirin inhaled deeply and began a deep dive into what Gracie sent.

Certainly, she'd heard the rumors. For several years running in fact—though she'd never gone searching since she hadn't needed anything so sophisticated. But now, right in front of her, was precisely what she *did* need: three documents carrying granular details of a genuine zero-click exploit aimed at smartphones.

Gracie had copied them from email attachments on Naomi's laptop and placed them in the body of a whole new email using a new account hosted by Pirin's preferred provider—"just to make sure this is all encrypted." Notably, these documents named no individuals, though they mentioned "the offsec dev team." And the company's name—Palasin Security LLC—was dropped twice in each document.

Pirin had heard of Palasin Security, a low-profile offensive security "consultancy" living off lucrative Department of Defense contracts. Perhaps the zero-click documents were part of a seduction by the woman recruiting Naomi. Whatever motivated their presence on Naomi's laptop, Pirin knew she was looking at one of the most dangerous and effective cyberattacks yet invented.

And they'd been sitting on Naomi's laptop for *seven months?* How? Nobody fucking *noticed?* No scenario Pirin could conjure spoke well for Palasin Security's own security.

Nonetheless, here these documents were with Pirin's widening eyes gawking at them. "Basandere," she whispered: To gain control of a target's smartphone she'd need only the phone's number. The target didn't have to respond at all. Indeed, the target would be oblivious.

Just send a text with, in this case, a faked GIF image that was actually a malicious PDF able to trigger a heap buffer overflow and remotely overwhelm the smartphone's built-in image programming library, thus crashing it and creating opportunity to automatically deploy a program that executes code with functionality the smartphone's designers never dreamed of.

Using only four logical operators, Pirin would have, in effect, an itty-bitty computer architecture all ready to be scripted. And with the right script, she could exploit logic bugs to foil the smartphone's ability to protect running programs, then move on to the smartphone's command and control server to eavesdrop on live voice and video calls, surveil the target and those around him by controlling the phone's microphone and camera—plus scoop up stored messages, emails, notes, photos, and videos as well as anything in the target's cloud storage.

"As long as no one turns off the smartphone—which will wipe the attack off the system—we'll be able to capture all the device's data," read a summary memo. "And as long as the smartphone isn't shoved into a cover that obscures what we can hear and see, we'll be able to keep listening and watching in real time."

Pirin was stunned. She'd spent lots of (rigorously anonymized) time in the more caliginous corners of the dark web, lurking, learning, scouting for tricks, techniques, exploits, and ideas to overhaul and redesign for use in her recycles. Certainly she was no script kiddie; having devoted years to teaching herself and honing an impressive skillset that she shared with no one, bragged about to no one, Pirin rolled her own with genuine mastery—and it had paid off. Repeatedly.

But *this*—

This, at the very least, justified her long-time instinct to maintain multiple smartphones; besides a company phone, she carried a "public" smartphone via which everyone she knew contacted her as well as "private" smartphone with an always-blocked number unknown to anyone which she used exclusively to remotely control her own systems and servers.

This also justified another instinct, which caused her to immediately buy two prepaid no-internet flip phones and overnight one to Gracie with an accompanying note:

Now I get why I'm so paranoid about privacy. Let's talk on dumbphones from now on. Call me whenever on the number in this phone's contact list—but be sure to smother all smartphone and tablet cameras and microphones when you do.

XOXOXO—P

Gracie had only just read Pirin's note and picked up the flip phone, which she nearly dropped at the unaccustomed sound of its ring. Then, as the thing clamored on, she wrapped her smartphone in a dishtowel and shoved it into a kitchen drawer before tentatively pressing what she hoped was the right flip phone button.

"Hello?"

"How'd you know?" Anxiety laced Pirin's subdued voice.

"That last dream...the way Kaldi showed up. Seemed like a warning," Gracie replied. "I guessed the rest."

The silence that followed stretched to (Gracie counted) ten seconds, twelve...until: "What'd you guess?"

Damn, Gracie thought, first you send that alarming email about deleting everything everywhere related to Naomi's laptop. Then you disappear—well, okay, maybe you were waiting till I received the flip phone you sent. But not even another email? And now you're grilling me? No "hey, you got the flip phone" or "gee, this stuff you sent could be useful" or "oh wow, seems like the ohskal dreams have struck again."

Fine, Gracie resolved—time to just *say* what I guessed: "That there's a significant part of your life you keep out of sight. Like an iceberg: A tenth is visible; the rest lurks below the waterline. And after a nudge from Kaldi, I guessed about some of that nine-tenths."

"Quite the metaphor, but it doesn't—"

"—Speak to the particulars of that nine-tenths." Gracie took a breath. "Seems to me you take risks. Dangerous, even reckless risks. I suspect you can't imagine *not* taking those risks, yet keeping your actions hidden suggests you don't dare trust anyone, you don't dare relax—ever. But you're getting tired. I'd say the iceberg's destabilizing and gravity's threatening to upend it, which'll expose what you've kept so hidden for so long. Maybe when you least expect it."

Silence again.

"You asked," Gracie said.

"H-How do you do that?" Pirin's question sounded more like a plea.

"Y'know—" Gracie inhaled again, slowly this time. "I don't think I've ever told anyone this before." She cleared her throat. "I get this sensation—like a soft, distant buzz—almost imperceptible. Then a hunch pops into my head: 'Oh, so *this* is what's happening' or 'Yep, *that's* the way it'll go down.'"

"How often?"

"Regularly enough, I suppose. Spent years shrugging it off. But every now and then, along comes a hunch that seems, um, more significant. And then I find out some version of the hunch *happened*. So I don't shrug those off anymore."

"Like the hunch that came along when you saw what was on Naomi's laptop."

"Yeah. I took one look at that and I damn well *knew* it would help you."

"So how do you think it works—your, uh, hunching?"

"Funny you should ask, cuz lately I've been wondering about that. I think maybe I'm picking up on some kind of energy—like a signal, which I experience as a buzzy almost-sound. I suspect I become aware of the hunch once my brain organizes what I've already sensed subliminally. And occasionally—more and more often lately—I can look back and recognize the process; otherwise it's just there, an indivisible whole."

"That's what happened when you caught Naomi trying to sneak away?" whispered Pirin, sounding like she'd seen a ghost.

"Yeah, I think so. And judging by the look on her face when she saw me, it scared the bejeezus out of her."

"Her loss," Pirin said—then, after a moment, "My gain."

"So I haven't scared the bejeezus out of you?"

"Yeah, you have." Pirin laughed softly. "But I think we should do another screentime dinner anyway."

"Feeling brave, huh?"

"Nah. It's just that I take dangerous, even reckless risks. And I *really* like being able to look at you."

"Okay, you're on, cuz I really like looking at you, too," said Gracie. "How 'bout Friday at seven? And I promise not to get drunk this time."

CHAPTER ELEVEN: MERELY THE CONDUIT

P irin called it the Gift.
Understandable: Thanks to the detailed insights and explanations that came along with this A-to-Z collection of design principles and code, she needed only days to wireframe her own unique zero-click exploit.

But given how far she had to go to get it ready for real-world deployment, she sure as hell didn't want to talk about it, not even on a flip phone, much less via smartphone-facilitated screentime. So at their second online dinner she diverted Gracie's inevitable curiosity by asking the first question—about working at the Institute.

Gracie responded with an I-get-it nod and performative cheeriness. "Yeah…well, it's the best job I've had so far. Not as much grunty data cleaning work. Plus once I analyze the data, I get to play with graphical toys." She paused to raise a glass of what looked like water. "Give it a few years, though, and an AI service'll do it better and cheaper. Assuming there's still an Institute by then."

This surprised Pirin, who was already thoroughly diverted by the sight of onscreen Gracie. "You think there *won't* be an Institute by then? Jess always said it helps fund valuable scientific research."

"Oh it does. Or did. In actual practice, the Institute markets the promise of involvement in sciencey stuff to well-heeled people who'll pay a bundle to 'participate' in field research in exotic places—a kind of adventure travel agency for rich would-be intellectuals. But the pandemic has devastated that business model. They're already talking furloughs."

"Shit. Will you—?"

"Look for another job? Very likely. Go back to my parents' place like at least half the people I know? Not an option. Mine split around the time I got breasts. Just after I finished college, my father had a fatal heart attack fucking his new girlfriend. Then my mother sold the house and moved to a senior complex in Florida where she immersed in new social aspirations, new friends. Plus lots of yoga and bitching—about my sexuality and my sister's mother-in-law. Then she caught the virus." Gracie's face turned away. "Now she's dead, too."

"Oh god, I'm so sorry."

Gracie turned back to stare at the camera lens—right into Pirin's eyes, it seemed—and shrugged. "It is what it is." Then she straightened her shoulders and launched a diversion of her own: "Am I right in assuming you get along pretty well with your parents?"

Thus began Pirin's attempt to spell out how a financially self-sufficient adult woman chooses to stay in the etche where she grew up—with not only her parents but her grandmother, too—until, at thirty, she moves forty feet away to an apartment over a newly-built garage. For years this explanation took much longer (circumlocutory excuses are like that), but eventually Pirin stopped squirming in the face of others' ill-disguised twitches of misgiving, the evenings that ended just a little too early. Because, hey, she is who she is.

Unlike others before her, though, Gracie seemed entirely unstartled. "So what I see behind you is your place over said garage?"

"Yep."

"Can I have a tour?"

After a half-hour frequently punctuated with versions of "Wait… show me that again," Gracie had questions, starting with "Where'd you get those wonderful oak pieces—the dressers and cabinets?"

"My father. He was a railroad guy, but besides my mother his real love has always been woodworking, especially furniture. Oak is his favorite. Mostly he gets it from the property."

"And the garage building itself—why do I keep thinking you designed it?"

Pirin blinked; no one except Jessica had ever guessed that. "I did actually. I wanted my own space. Dedicated office. A real workshop. And yeah, a bit of separation. No more waking up my mother when I come home late."

"So you weren't interested in, um—?"

"Oh, you mean—" Pirin tried not to look down, but couldn't stop herself. "Been a few 'almosts' after, uh—" She shook her head. "No serious commitment that stuck, though…" She tried to force her eyes back to her phone's screen, but they refused.

"What happened, Pirin?" Gracie asked in a hush.

"She died. Ayesha died."

"Ayesha…" Gracie repeated softly. "I'm so very sorry you lost her…"

Shaking her head, Pirin shrugged. "Long time ago."

"Next to your bed—is that a photo of her?"

Pirin could barely speak. "Yeah…I can't believe you spotted that."

"She's exquisite. Will you tell me about her someday?"

Pirin managed a silent nod, then a nearly inaudible whisper. "Someday…"

For a while, neither of them spoke. At last, Pirin said "After Ayesha was gone I didn't care where I lived. My mother and grandmother had rules about civility, about respecting privacy, and they let me be the sort of person who doesn't have to tell them everything. So I never felt cramped. It was easy to stay." Pirin smiled. "Till I got horny enough to want to have sex in my own bed instead of, um, elsewhere. The fam woulda been fine with whoever I brought home, but…"

"Too much of a crowd, huh? I bet running a before-and-after gauntlet like that kinda made your girlfriends cringe."

Pirin snickered. "Happened twice. Which is to say, once and never again with two different people. And yeah, it was cringy. So the idea of making love in my own bed in my own separate space, then waking up in the morning, having a quiet coffee with just her while we're looking out at the woods—I hadda try to make that real."

"Woods, huh? Sounds pretty nice."

"Yeah, this place—" Pirin glanced around her. "Almost six acres of woodland, another six of pasture leased to the dairy farmer in back for enough money to cover the property taxes—I love this place. With my grandmother's help, my parents bought it cheap like thirty years ago, after a nasty real estate crash. It's in the boonies at the edge of a faded mill town, but it was an opportunity they just couldn't refuse. And neither can I."

"Will you show it to me?" Gracie asked. "We could do a daytime screentime."

"I'd like that."

"Do I have to wait till you're done? Y'know…" One of Gracie's eyebrows hiked as she winked. "With the stuff you're not ready to talk about yet."

"Uh…"

"Say no more. You have to do your day job *and* carve out time to get a handle on 'the stuff.'"

"It'll take a few weeks, I think." Pirin lowered her head. "I-I'm sorry. It's just that—"

"I know. You have to do this. Right now. Which means laser-focusing on it." Gracie chuckled. "I bet you're damn good at laser-focusing."

"So I've been told. Please be patient with me, Gracie. Please."

The phone call—from a number Gracie didn't recognize—came too damn early. When she answered anyway, she heard a voice she didn't recognize.

"I bring news," the voice hoarsely announced. "I'm your new boss."

"Really?" Gracie stalled as she pondered: Who the hell *is* this? Male or female? Scam or legit?

"Till things get back to normal anyway. Or the Institute crashes and burns and we all get canned. Whichever comes first."

"Jessica? *Jess!* How're you doing? Are you really my—?"

"Yep. Meet the Institute's new director of communications."

"What about—?"

"He's strictly systems management and maintenance now. I lobbied for you on the grounds that you combine deep knowledge of our data with solid content creation skills—unsung and closeted but actually quite effective. So, time for you to come out. I've just emailed you the battle plan."

"Sounds ominous."

Jessica's laugh rasped irony—and congestion. "We gotta turn the ship radically—and fast. Toward online-as-much-as-possible: distance learning, webinars, local-engagement research with pandemic-aware ways for sponsors to engage." She paused to wheezily draw breath. "Obviously a whole new website. Keep us busy for several months. Longer if it works. Also—" Another grating breath. "Next week you'll officially be asked to 'volunteer' to accept part-time pay for full-time work—think semi-furlough—and I hope you'll agree…"

"Because the Institute is worth saving."

"Exactly."

Gracie said yes to all of it right there on the phone, even to what Jessica admitted would be a thirty percent pay cut. Because it beat any short-term alternative she could think of. It even had some virtues, like keeping her mind off Pirin Basamendi and whether the ohskal dreams were really returning. Besides, she relished the chance to work with Jessica Winter, the chance to do something kinda sorta creative.

For the next several days, she concentrated on adapting to her new job, which, she decided, would probably work out okay…for now…

But then, even before the week was out, came a morning when Gracie rattled awake with an overwhelming sense of foreboding. And there had been this raven.

"Omigod," she murmured. "Another one."

It had begun at Eletun's campfire with the same group of women listening to Eletun's story, which now featured a much-expanded cast of characters.

And oh the ambivalence! Because even if the ohskal dreams meant she was nuts, they *did* link her to Pirin, which made them valuable. Important. Besides, Gracie had to acknowledge, the dreams were fascinating, though she just couldn't accept that they emerged from her own meager imagination.

"Hell," she declared with only mildly wavering certainty, "that's why their *ohskal* dreams. I'm merely conduit."

Damn, how Gracie wanted to believe that—especially since this latest dream was a doozy, all of it recalled all at once, its details alive with colors and sounds and smells and movement. She got out of bed, booted up her computer, and began tapping:

⚡ I'd arrived late, and as I sat down Eletun nodded to me while she continued singing about this child—"progeny of AmaBildun"—who had scampered into a dense forest followed by one very worried grandmother.

"Is Rhythm dancing yet another omen?" sang Eletun.

I wish I could convey the effect of Eletun's song, its rhymed verses, its melodies vividly expressing the story's emotions rising, ebbing, whispering, crescendoing…

And don't ask me how I understood any of it. But I did.

Soon, Eletun sang, the child was out of sight, but grandmother AmaSaba tracked her tiny footprints, which eventually intersected with pawprints, large ones and small ones. AmaSaba followed these to an imposing rock outcrop and a large yellow-gray cat stretched out beneath it. Two kittens suckled at the cat's breasts—and, curled up unchallenged between the pair, AmaBildun's progeny suckled too.

As Eletun's audience emitted a single small gasp (of fear? delight? both?), I felt a hand rest on my shoulder, and instantly I knew—behind me sat the "other" Eletun. Without bothering to turn around, I waited for her reminder: "Just like you hear it, Gracie. Pay *attention*."

And I did try, but I bumbled what came next.

So all I can report is that grandmother AmaSaba watched the cat and her kittens lead the child back to "the high southwestern community," saw the felines nuzzle their goodbye before they faded into the forest.

This precipitated a meeting of Analakinak from all the Subendi Communities during which they examined the child and decided "such powerful endowment of Rhythm left untrained enticed danger upon them all." Thus the child who would become Analergin began accelerated training with new teachers.

One of them—AmaHeri, Subendi's Most Sublime Perceiver and Healer—was supposed to teach "the secrets of transforming the crystals, the essential truths of energies and vibration and balance, of Rhythm and Resonance." But to little Analergin, this old woman was mean and angry and to be avoided.

By contrast, the child adored AmaBidari, "a Weathering-skilled Sublime Traveler-Navigator accustomed to journeying across the Western Seas" who was a refugee from Sundaselai Privation. AmaBidari taught the child how to construct the outriggers so essential to Traveling afar and revealed "the Rhythms of Sky and Sea, the Rhythms of living things—limbed and rooted and winged, the serpents and swimmers, even the stone."

"Rhythm will always find you and invite your Resonance." AmaBidari told the one who would become Analergin.

Yet, Eletun warned us, "peril hovered and then lunged, for Analakinak had not yet been shown the whole measure of the gifts bestowed upon the only offspring of dead AmaBildun."

A soft hum rippled through Eletun's audience as they absorbed this, and I felt that hand on my shoulder tighten its grip...

Whereupon I was *her*—this child who would become Analergin—, still quite young but old enough to go pretty much wherever curiosity led.

She was—*I* was—on my way to visit Mother Cat when it happened.

About ten feet in front of me, I spotted a little ball of black. When I got close, it started to thrash and hiss and fan its tail. Then it went stiff and silent.

So I did as AmaBidari had taught about helping a baby raven: Pick it up and hold it so its wings are free, then raise and lower it in your hands to get it to flap its wings so it'll squawk and attract the attention of its family, which will come to its rescue.

Its family quickly responded, so I lifted the little raven into a tree's leafy branches, where it hung by one leg for a moment before righting itself.

"You'll be home soon, Bele," I told the chick as I moved away from the tree.

But almost immediately something nipped my hand, and when I jerked back from the sting I lost my balance. What happened next is a jumble.

I remember a creature—a serpent, I recall thinking as I fell, but it may have had wings. It came for me with a mouth opened so wide and large that it swallowed me whole—my hand first, then my entire arm, and then I was falling down into a blackness beyond time and place...

I must have closed my eyes, since I recall opening them to find myself with serpent *people*. They were black, everything around them was black—but their eyes gleamed. All the light of the world shone in their eyes. We would become friends, they said, once they'd transformed me into one of them. Then I'd be able to use their knowledge and power whenever I needed it.

What came next was grisly, but I was quite detached, felt no pain as they slowly pulled me apart and consumed me before vomiting me out, viscera and all, and putting me back together with a mixture of my own blood and their serpent-spit.

Then they were gone and I was back with my grandmother and my teachers and all the other people in my Community. I felt the Sun shining on me, but kept my eyes closed because I heard the Mothers arguing about me.

"My Senba has been tested by a serpent's potent poisons," I heard my amatchi insist. "We all know what that means."

"Yes, this child has survived because she has a Healer's gifts," said one of my teachers, the old mean one who was so important and wise. "Her instruction must be further hastened."

And then things got hazy…

When the dream sharpened again I was still the child who would become Analergin, though I could tell time had passed—and everyone, including me, was profoundly upset.

The Mothers were nervous, short-tempered. The men were around more—around too much, I thought. All "the young" were restless, and no wonder: They'd heard stories of people in other Communities injured, even dying in fights with bands of attacking Privation males.

But none of this was truly real—not until I saw my amatchi's body being carried home. That's when my dream intensified; the child's tears became my tears, her *NO!* was my *NO!*…

Amatchi lay so dreadfully still, covered in blood, the pain of death etched on her face. I kissed her one last time, but the face I kissed wasn't hers, not anymore.

After that, I woke crying every morning. Soon hatred claimed me and I imagined doing to every Privation man what had been done to my amatchi. Nor was I the only one.

I was within a few Mooncycles of my initiation, having been trained in several Sublimities—Tending-Gathering, of course, but also Perception, Weathering, Healing, Trancing-Taming, and Traveling-Navigating. But I'd lost all interest in acquiring these skills. Along with the other young ones, and especially my friend Otchani, instead I snuck into the forest to learn what I could of the art of killing men.

Otchani had already been initiated as an apprentice Traveler-Navigator—and as an apprentice Protector-Defender. He was

AmaBidari's son, as smart as his mother, and already an accomplished archer and spear thrower, skills he had begun to teach me. He was especially adept at inventing new weapons, including what he called "lehere," which combined sulfur powder, small stones, and dried leaves stuffed into a bamboo shaft with a line of cordage sticking out.

When Otchani touched the cordage to a flame and threw the bamboo shaft skyward, it burst apart in midair with a bright, loud flash that propelled the stones it contained into nearby tree trunks, frightening everyone.

The lehere explosion also attracted my mean teacher, AmaHeri, who commanded us to disperse. I knew I would obey her—but not before telling her what I truly thought.

"You cannot bear to face the warnings of your energies," I shouted. "But I hear their waves! We all hear their waves!"

The old woman glared at me for only a moment before her gaze followed a white-faced owl winging up into the canopy toward the Firemountain's peak. Silently, she turned away from me to follow the bird. And I knew as I watched her that something had forever changed.

This Eletun's song confirmed; she'd been singing the whole time I'd been swept "into" the child, and she was singing still: "Not long after that day, AmaBidari came to the child with a revelation: Sacred, precious Subendi would be forsaken."

Eletun's audience caught its collective breath.

"*Forsaken?!*" one horrified woman whispered.

Eletun nodded. "The Mothers of Subendi sought to save their children."

The Mothers believed an overwhelming Privation onslaught would follow the end of the next wet monsoon, Eletun explained. So they sent three vessels of Travelers across the Western Seas to find new sanctuary. Meanwhile, Subendiak waiting for the Travelers to return would prepare for departure, constructing more outriggers and sails, gathering seeds, fashioning utensils and tools.

Yet not even this upheaval, Eletun emphasized, caused the Mothers to neglect scrupulously timed Subendiak obligations to Rhythm.

Hence AmaBildun's progeny, as yet nameless, would enter the solitude of the Breach where she would relinquish her child's eyes and consciousness so that she might discover her True Name. Only then could she undergo initiation into any of the Sublimities.

For the child, who did not yet know she would become Analergin, the prospect of the Breach—"that still point around which Rhythm dances"—was frightening.

Even worse, AmaHeri, the mean old teacher, was the one who led her—blindfolded and bound and encircled by the deep, hypnotic drumbeat of the Naming—down into its pungent dankness where AmaHeri's voice boomed "You shall behold your True Name in the fullness of time..."

After that she heard no sound, saw no colors, sensed no motion.

So she waited—

And waited—for a noise, a bump, something to hint at her Name. But nothing happened.

Well, not quite nothing. She was getting angry—at the nothing.

"Violating the silence of the Breach at long last," Eletun sang while turning to gaze at me, "this child who was no longer a child railed at the pain in her bound arms, at the fire burning low in her belly..."

And once more I merged with her, this child who was no longer a child...

Drops of water had started splatting fitfully onto my face from somewhere above me that, infuriatingly, I couldn't see. Other than my own grunting and gasping, that splatting was the only sound I heard in the brutal, empty quiet of the Breach.

By then I'd concluded that nobody would be coming to help me no matter how much I yelled or whimpered. And screw trying to "discover" my True Name. All I wanted to "discover" was how to undo the ropes keeping my wrists tied behind my back. Then I'd yank off the wretched blindfold, dig my way out of the hole that sour old woman stuck me in, and breathe fresh air again, revel in sunlight again, find something to eat.

And, oh yeah, somewhere along the way I'd make up a goddamn name to satisfy the rest of the old women who took all this tradition shit so bloody seriously.

I'd tried their way.

Got taken (twice) to both of Subendi's "secret" caves—the one way up the mountain where Sublime Perceivers gather chunks of blackglass and clear quartz—and the other much scarier cave just above the Firemountain's magma chamber where I watched the Sublimes use the constant flow of molten lava, accessible through a gap in the cave's floor, to melt quartz into see-through glass without burning themselves alive.

I listened to endless babble about "vibration" and "balance" and "Rhythm" and "Resonance" and blah blah blah...

Don't give up, I told myself. Breathe faster. Breathe slower. Try thumping out a beat. Try humming. Stretch out. Curl up. Make clicky mouth noises. Swear. Doze. Think, dammit—*think!*

I'd resorted to begging. I'd wailed. Dear Mother, how I'd wailed.

Nope, nothing.

How long had I been like this? How many forevers?

In desperation, for lack of any other ideas, I succumbed to my body's unstoppable writhing and started moving to the beat of—well, I'm not sure.

Anyway, it worked, at least inasmuch as I began to almost enjoy the squeezing-tensing-rocking motion that claimed my hips, my glutes, my abs, my twat.

"Would you like me to show you how to undo your bindings?"

I didn't *hear* this question. I *felt* it as a subtle pulsing.

For a startled moment I stopped wriggling. The pulsing immediately began to fade.

"Don't go," I pleaded, wriggling again. "Yes, yes, I would like you to show me how to undo my bindings."

"You must speak your Name silently, to yourself," explained the pulse, "before you speak it aloud to anyone else."

"But I don't know my Name."

"I do. I have known your Name ever since you saved me from The Lotus Man."

"Tell me."

"I will show you."

And then I felt a touch, very light, caressing. Like hands, I thought—female hands, and by touch alone they taught my hands how to crimp and twist their way to freedom.

And then I saw her, even though I remained blindfolded. She was older than when she ran from the Lotus Man, and she had become, to me, profoundly beautiful—blazing black eyes, skin that reminded me of light brown ochre, wild black hair. Her warm, sweet scent enveloped me, and she smiled before she kissed me full on my lips, long and slow and reluctant to stop.

While her kiss took me to the verge of orgasm, she stretched herself alongside me, wrapping me around her touch, around the nearly imperceptible hum that emanated from her, entangling my squirming hunger into hers. And as I climaxed I heard my name.

"Kaldi," I said to her, "stay with me. Travel west with me and my people."

"Not now," she replied. "Our time has not come yet."

"But how will you find me?"

She smiled and again kissed me full on my lips, long and slow and reluctant to stop as her warm, sweet Kaldi scent transformed the pungent air in the Breach. "You will come for me, Analergin. You will feel me Resonating within you—after…"

"After?"

"When you leave the Breach," Kaldi whispered, "your raven will confirm what you already sense: Tomorrow night, or perhaps the following morning, Subendi will wake in fury. First she will spew a flaming rain. Then she will heave and burst apart, and the liquid fire rising from within her will boil the Sea and destroy all who are near."

CHAPTER TWELVE: RISK IT?

W hat are you afraid of, Gracie?"
The voice, so unmistakable and *so* unwelcomed, came from close behind her. But she didn't turn around, hoping if she ignored the question the voice might shut up—a foolish notion given that she was standing in a doorway she didn't recognize peering out at...what? Clouds maybe?

"Perhaps you fear what you're dreaming might be true."

Gracie sighed. "I *fear* being unable to distinguish between me and Analergin, between Pirin and Kaldi. I *fear* losing any sense of the boundaries of reality."

"You are not—"

"Save the bullshit, Eletun. Where I come from dreams reflect your own life back at you. They digest the day's information, synthesize memories, deal with unconscious desires and wishes, simulate real-life experiences, anticipate future threats." Gracie turned to face Eletun's irritatingly beatific smile. "Pretty straightforward, *really*."

"You are not crazy." Eletun reached a hand to Gracie's cheek to gently wipe away a tear. "But you *are* unusual."

"And *you* are a figment of—"

"—Of your own life reflecting back at you while you digest the day's information and synthesize your memories and deal with your unconscious desires, yada yada—all with a generous helping of metaphor, of course."

Gracie shook her head. "Metaphor or not, you're an *unhelpful* figment, okay? And my fervent desire is that you just fucking disappear."

Eletun's smile broadened into a grin. "We're only just getting started. Our story has a long way to go yet."

"*Our* story? You mean this ohskal dream stuff? So I was right about the damn rock?"

Eletun nodded. "And, despite all her distractions, Pirin will want to know everything, Gracie. Every detail the ohskal bestows upon you."

"Wait—" Gracie suddenly felt dizzy. "You know about Pirin?"

"Certainly. I suspect you don't quite recall—you were rather tipsy at the time—but Pirin nailed it when she mentioned entanglement. Actually, the two of you have become entangled not only with each other but also with—"

"—With you and the women around your campfire."

"More than that. Resonance—an essential aspect of Rhythm—has drawn you to my campfire so I can help you understand some of the ways you and Pirin are entangled with Analergin and Kaldi."

"But these dreams have nothing to do with me or Pirin. They're about a long time ago—" Gracie faltered, suddenly apprehensive. "Aren't they?"

Eletun laughed softly. "Across immense expanses of time and space, repetitive periodic vibrations—Rhythms—envelope us all. Sometimes we sync up with these Rhythms, become entrained by them, riff on them, which is what Resonance is about. Most people in your era struggle to recognize this, preferring 'coincidence' or 'fate.' Occasionally, though, along comes a Rhythm that enables us to glimpse beyond what we're trained to perceive. You'll understand soon enough—assuming I can persuade you to keep paying attention."

"Uh-uh, can't. I have a huge amount of work to do. A gazillion deadlines. No time."

"Time?" Eletun laughed again. "As I've told you, Gracie, time works rather differently here. The memories and experiences and anticipations that comprise your sense of the passage of time are formed from a continuous flow of many tiny observations of 'now'—like snapshots—but here your snapshots can get reshuffled somewhat, which upends your sense of episodic context. All in a good cause, of course. So let's proceed, shall we?"

"No, Eletun, *don't!*"

❖

Curiously, each ohskal dream invariably delivered unto Gracie a really good night's sleep. No waking up at three or four in the morning having to pee. No nightmare-induced sweating or whimpering like when she was a kid. No morning fatigue—despite the dreams' epic, vividly detailed realism. Even the effort of chronicling these dreams, though sometimes only half-remembered, felt oddly refreshing afterward when she reviewed what she'd recorded.

Of course Gracie would have to write down this latest one too before starting her workday. She'd promised Pirin, after all:

⚡ Lightning pierced the ominously dark clouds rising over Firemountain Subendi's center even as the Mothers' departing outriggers threaded the narrow secret channel through the island's treacherous reefs.

Each navigated by a Sublime Traveler and filled to its limit with people, with containers of seed and food and water, with living plants and creatures, with raw blackglass, with tools for navigating and gathering and defense, the vessels moved sleekly toward the day's last light.

Once upon the open Sea, the outriggers quickly picked up speed thanks to the recent surrender of the wet monsoon to unseasonably strong northeast Winds. By dawn the island had slipped below the eastern horizon, too distant to be seen—but Subendiak witnessed her end nonetheless.

First a column of smoke billowed behind them, soon followed by cracks and groans of faraway rending. Mere moments later a vastly larger fire-spewing plume spread smoke across the entire eastern horizon, blotting out the sun, darkening the day.

Almost immediately, an apocalyptic cloud of eruption rolled across the Sea toward the outriggers with terrifying velocity. From ancestral experience the people aboard knew they had but heartbeats to protect their hearing from the fast-approaching wave of Windshock and little time after that to shelter from falling ash.

Analergin, who served as apprentice Weatherer on the outrigger captained by AmaBidari, was comparatively novice at Sea, her experience limited to offshore fishing and rapt attention to Subendi Travelers' exhaustive reports of sailing to distant places. Yet one glance at AmaBidari's face told her that no one from any of the Subendi Communities had ever seen anything so calamitous.

At least the outriggers were in sufficiently deep water that the huge Seawaves spawned by the Firemountain's tumult would not harm them. Low and almost invisible on the water's surface, these immense undulations would certainly devastate Lands near and far as they inevitably surged ashore. "But out here we are safe from such powerful Hinhandiak," assured Otchani, who served as the vessel's Defender, "and perhaps even from Privation."

Analergin nodded, having already noticed that none of the Privation's many heavily armed ships had given them chase. This first stage of their escape, anyway, had succeeded. But there was no celebration aboard AmaBidari's outrigger, only mourning: Subendi was gone.

"Where are we heading?" Analergin asked, desperate for distraction. During her few earlier Sea journeys, she had learned only generalities about ocean Winds and Seacurrents and how these are affected by the seasons. Now her instruction began in earnest.

She was taught the moods of the air upon the water—when to let the Wind push the outrigger hard on its vigorous breezes, when to ease the sail in anticipation of a potentially capsizing gust.

She grew adept at shunting the mast so the outrigger's shelter always stayed windward regardless of their direction of travel, quickly becoming skilled at lowering the sail, carrying the short mast beyond the canoe's midline toward the "new" bow at the other end of the hull, and re-stepping the mast there.

She also learned how all manner of Rhythmic events cause ocean swells and Seawaves—the Wind mostly, but also the pull of Sun and Moon and Seacurrents, the vibrations of energy from earthtremors and erupting Firemountains.

Analergin was shown how those swells and Seawaves form detectable patterns of reflection and refraction in the open Sea as they move around and between obstacles like Seacurrents and bodies of Land and the Seabottom's Mountains and valleys far below them. She learned to hunker in the dark on the canoe's hull to sense the Seawaves' Rhythms and watch for the uniquely patterned bolts of light emitted from Lands both close and far away.

And through it all she watched the Wind drive vast billows of dense smoke and cloud from Subendi further and further south of their westward tack while she cast nets for fish and used the smoke-dimmed

Sunlight to distill fresh water into containers made on Subendi of Firemountain glass.

"Uncommonly high Wind," AmaBidari observed on the eighth day, noting that never in all her years Traveling had she seen such a steady, energetic northeast blow for so long so early in the season. More quickly than they dared hope, this Wind had carried them away from Sundaselai Privation.

Already they were nearing Hulartali, the great peninsula halfway between what had once been Subendi and their destination at the far end of the Far Western Sea. Why then, Analergin wondered, did such a worried frown burden AmaBidari's face?

⚡ "Hey, Eletun, it's all written down now," Gracie called out. She'd been unusually alert during this write-up and was in the mood for sex or, failing that, a fight. "Come take a look any *fucking* time, old woman. Maybe then you can give it a *fucking* rest for a while, okay? Maybe go mess around with someone *fucking* else for a *fucking* change. Oh-*kay?*"

By the next morning, Eletun appeared to have replied. Awakened by the sound of a loud crack, Gracie found herself alone. And dry. And grateful to be in her own bed. When she stood up, though, she briefly struggled to balance on what seemed like a swaying floor.

Then she heard a woman's voice, maybe from her kitchen, maybe from much farther away: "Write it down, Gracie. Write it down *now*."

So she did:

⚡ Damn. I get seasick on boats. *Really* seasick. I've tried—and failed—to tough it out; once I even signed myself up for a two-week sailing vacation in the Bahamas (anything for love, right?), which I aborted after what still ranks as the most miserable four days of my life.

So what the hell was I doing in Analergin's head out in the middle of some ocean, god knows where, no land in sight?

The descriptions I'd heard about these "canoes" didn't come close to preparing me for the vessel on which I found myself, which was unlike anything I'd ever experienced. Its (very strangely shaped) sail flared out on two booms connected to a stubby mast plunked onto what was, essentially, a huge carved-out tree trunk that sat *very* low in the water. Hell, both the dugout and its counterbalancing float were mostly *under* the water.

Despite being some fifty feet long with impressive storage space, it all seemed alarmingly flimsy and very crowded. AmaBidari had assigned everyone a space in the windward-side half-shelter built over the bracings that connected the tree trunk and the much smaller float, but no way could all twenty of us comfortably fit in there at the same time.

Analergin had been at Sea on this almost-underwater log long enough to have learned her way around, but she (rightfully) regarded herself as a novice. And she knew that, in a vernacular closer to mine than hers, the shit was about to hit the fan.

Eleven days at Sea now. The Wind blew furiously—and it was turning, starting to come at us from the southwest, the direction of the supposedly finished wet monsoon. So we began to sail north toward refuge, but on the thirteenth day a tempest loomed behind us, its unseasonable fury overtaking us even as we sighted Land. Soon we were fighting for our lives.

Up to that point, I'd been able to see several Subendi outrigger canoes sailing with us; now they heaved in and out of a savage, demented Sea's abyssal troughs. As several canoes slipped from sight in search of safe anchorage behind a sheltering promontory, I watched helpless while another—the largest in the Subendi fleet, which carried AmaHeri—was thrown onto ragged coastal rocks and splintered apart.

Meanwhile, AmaBidari fought to control our own outrigger's main steering blade amidst thrashing waves and howling Wind while Otchani worked the smaller steering blade on the float. Together they navigated us away from the threatening rocks—but then the windward boom loudly snapped, sweeping the sail into the Sea.

I moved to help several people who'd been whisked overboard, but AmaBidari screamed at me to stay put, and I obeyed. Through the day and into the night we battled to keep our damaged canoe intact.

By Sun's next rise, only the large main log remained. AmaBidari, Otchani, and five others besides me clung to it exhausted and thirsty. We had, at least, managed to retrieve several containers and fishing lines, but we were drifting helplessly eastward—back toward Sundaselai.

For two days we drifted beneath a scorching Sun. On the third day, the Sky brought rain, which we collected in our containers while the lines we dipped into the water manifested a few small fish. For the first time since the storm, we drank water and ate and slept.

I woke to a Moon just past fullness amid Stars glittering through dancing red auroras.

"AmaBidari," I asked, "where do you think we are?"

"Not where we want to be," she replied. "Soon will we face Privation, and we must prepare."

The night's peaceful beauty eased her words, but I shivered with fear while Otchani growled.

"Your fears are warranted," AmaBidari told us gently. I was beside her as we hunkered in the dugout, so she embraced me, but she spoke to us all. "The people of Privation are driven by dread as well as envy, and this makes them cruel and violent." Her words came softly yet carried great force. "I do not wish to be among them again. But understand: You can survive them, and you can escape them."

AmaBidari the Sublime Traveler who had herself suffered the blows of Privation answered anxious questions, proffered advice and reassurances. And as the southwest Wind persisted, we slipped once more into sleep.

The fourth day after the storm brought only mild swells. But the smokes of Subendi's eruption caused the eastern horizon to dawn redder than the day before. As we were driven closer and closer to Privation, we began to watch for signs of Land—with our backs to the Wind.

Too late, AmaBidari sensed the rogue Seawave looming incomprehensibly high behind us and shouted warning. In an instant, our log lurched upward and over and all of us spilled into a Sea suddenly far below us. We had opportunity for one last breath before we were submerged.

Deep underwater, I tried to resist confusion and the inevitability of drowning, tried to let my body float of its own accord. At last, I sensed myself ascending and kicked, kicked until I pierced the water's surface to gulp air.

Around me, raggedy rolling Seawaves seemed to have taken everything, everyone. I was alone but for black wings gliding high above me.

Just before panic took me, I spotted a broken piece of log—remnant of our canoe—and, a moment later, a body surfaced face down to my left. I'd begun to swim toward it when scrambling arms pierced the water in front of me, followed by AmaBidari's head, blood streaming across her eyes.

I grabbed her, kept her face out of the water, and after what seemed a very long time, reached the log remnant. That's when Otchani found us. And together the three of us drifted ever closer to Privation.

⚡ Three dreams now, all of them continuing Eletun's strange narrative. Three dreams Pirin knew nothing about.

So why not just email the write-ups to her, Gracie?

Maybe because you're miffed by the silence which, for days, had replaced Pirin's texts hinting solid momentum on her "project." Maybe because, flip phone notwithstanding, you're worried she's just not that into you. So you're doing what you always do—shrug and walk away (cuz hey, no way I'm chasing somebody who doesn't want me).

Or maybe Eletun's right. Maybe you're afraid—of what the dreams reveal about who Pirin really is, about who *you* really are.

C'mon, Gracie, what'll it be? Shrug and walk? Or risk it?

Fingers twitching on her flip phone's pain-in-the-ass T9 keypad, she chose:

fyi- analergin in trouble, kaldi disappeared, woke up this a.m. with sea legs -check email for attached write-ups- hope you're making progress, feel free to beta me when you're ready -g

CHAPTER THIRTEEN: SOME FUCKING TECHNOLOGY

The groveling apologies came first. "I get like that sometimes. Obsessively preoccupied." Pirin paused, hoping to be reprieved, but was greeted with silence. "I really am sorry, Gracie. I shoulda—"

"Oh, that voice." Gracie chuckled. "Stop, please stop. You're *way* too good. Now I feel guilty for poking you."

"Don't. I needed to be poked."

"I guess we're even, then. Cuz *I* needed to not be alone with this ohskal dream shit. It's doing a number on me."

"I can see why. These aren't even my dreams and they're doing a number on *me*. They seem so...*real*."

"Do you still think they're like the stuff your grandmother talked about?"

"Well, they're moving beyond anything I recall Amatchi telling me, but they're consistent with her stories—right down to coming off as being from a very long time ago. Makes me wonder: Do you have any idea about *where* this is happening?"

"I've been thinking about that. Seems like two places—and times. There's Eletun's campfire—always at night, in a forest clearing, no lights or buildings. Also, the women's clothes are all similar—simple, plain, definitely *not* contemporary. But the story Eletun sings—that strikes me as much older. An oral tradition, I'm guessing. Also, of course, it's happening somewhere warm. Tropical. And volcanic."

"Do you mind if I show your write-ups to my mother? She might know things, recall things from Amatchi's stories that were lost on me."

"In principle, I don't mind. But I worry your mother'll decide I'm a lunatic. Schizophrenic or something. These dreams are different, Pirin. Often I *know* I'm dreaming, so they're lucid—except I can't control what happens. First I'm at Eletun's campfire, then I'm swept against my will into this farfetched story she sings, one episode after another. Who the hell dreams like that?"

"Even if you're the only one ever, I still think you're dreaming something real—moments from another time and place that actually happened and somehow have been recorded or conveyed or what-the-fuck-ever into the ohskal, then bounced around your living room and into your brain by that streak of lightning. And not so farfetched, either. I mean, these days quartz crystal—like the ohskal—gets used for bulk holographic storage. As we speak, a satellite's circling the earth with a copy of Isaac Asimov's *Foundation* series stored in a memory crystal the size of a coin."

"I dunno, Pirin. The people in these dreams are—well, clearly not primitive, but their lives are simple, basic. No cars, no planes, no machine guns, not a smartphone in sight. I can't see them running around doing holography."

"Don't be so sure. You recorded how Analergin learned 'the secrets of transforming the crystals' when she was still on Subendi, remember? What if they had *solar-powered* lasers? In theory anyway, *that* technology *would* be possible for them."

"Seriously? Solar-powered lasers?"

"Oh yeah. The modern precursors came along about thirty years ago. Parabolic mirrors and sapphire 'light funnels' were used to concentrate the sun's rays into a beam eighty-four thousand times brighter than sunlight. And your write-ups have plenty of hints about Subendiak interest in crystals. Plus these days researchers are finding indications that thousands of years ago people were a lot more 'advanced' than twentieth-century 'experts' could accept."

"God, Pirin, I'd like to believe that. But it seems, well, fantastical."

"But *not* impossible. Just because they lived a long time ago doesn't make them unsophisticated. For all we know, they *could* have had solar-powered lasers. Could've had some version of optogenetics, too. Not to mention different priorities than the jackasses now running things. Maybe they focused on healing instead of fighting. Maybe they understood the limits of the planet's ability to support homo sapiens.

Could be these people were capable of creating and using technologies we wouldn't recognize even if we smacked right into them."

Grace went quiet for a long moment. "I'm not sure my little write-ups convey how surpassingly vivid these dreams are," she finally said. "How graphically, granularly lifelike they are. I've watched people die in these dreams, tasted blood in these dreams, felt pain and profound grief in these dreams. That's some fucking technology."

"What can I say? Eletun seems to have skills we peons don't understand." Pirin laughed softly. "And yeah, your dreams *are* different. *You* are different."

"Eletun called me 'unusual.'"

"How very perceptive of her."

Seconds and more seconds passed before Gracie spoke again. "Okay. Feel free to show the write-ups to your mom. And when you do, be sure to tell her your ideas about possible Subendiak technology. So at least we'll end up in the looney bin together."

"Just remember, Gracie—your suggestion," Pirin murmured to herself precisely seventy-two days after she first examined the documents Gracie found on Naomi's laptop. With that, she pressed ENTER on her keyboard, launching the first in-the-wild deployment of her zero-click exploit. She did this in the wee hours, just like she planned for her real targets.

By morning she knew her exploit worked: She woke at her desk to Gracie's slightly off-key version of "Zip-a-Dee-Doo-Dah" while one of her three screens careened through Gracie's apartment before settling onto a skewed view of a sleek black coffee maker.

"Ha!" Pirin snickered. "You've been waiting for me, haven't you, Grace Gwyllt Olwyn?"

For the rest of the morning, Gracie veered from singing to brief work conversations to chattering like a tour guide—until her smartphone's sound and video disappeared. Into a pocket, Pirin figured. Good opportunity to take a shower and get something to eat.

When Pirin returned to her office, Gracie's still-live smartphone screen displayed something new—a view of a pad of paper with six neatly handwritten words:

Don't forget to visit his mother

Only after twice reading those six words did Pirin grasp that Gracie was, yet again, a step ahead of her.

Even so, she stuck with her initial zero-click targets—Veech Farkas's lawyer and the two thugs who'd attacked her in the Belmont park—since their phone numbers were so easily fetched from police and court records. Within minutes she'd set up real-time key-, voice-, and video-loggers on all three devices, and her Spotter app was retrieving selected words, phrases, and faces while her command-and-control server collected contact lists, texts, emails, image libraries, and voice messages.

No surprise that Farkas's lawyer was careful about what he kept on his phone—definitely nothing that incriminated Vicsorgó Farkas or anyone else. But Pirin did discover the name and phone number of Farkas's correctional program officer, who became her fourth zero-click target. This led her to the man's DOC classification system login credentials, and some good news: The pandemic was still thoroughly gumming up—and slowing down—DOC processes.

Meaning Farkas had only just been transferred to his prison "home," Norfolk Correctional. Soon enough, however, he'd be making new friends in medium-security gen pop. So Pirin began digging into Norfolk Correctional's procedures, schedules, and staff and inmate deets.

Fortunately, she'd long since penetrated the Commonwealth's Office of Public Safety and Security and achieved surreptitious at-will access to all the Commonwealth's law enforcement entities, including Norfolk Correctional. Drilling through the layers would take time, of course, but at least she could see the route.

Meanwhile, she listened to recordings of the two goons who'd jumped her in the park yammering away on their smartphones—because, Pirin was unsurprised to hear, they were scared shitless. But not of Veech Farkas, who'd snared them into intimidating the witnesses who testified against him. Their fear was reserved for the Boss, who, Pirin soon learned, was Farkas's boss, too—and who hadn't known about, much less okayed, Farkas's witness-tampering.

And then came the kicker: The Boss was a Whiting.

Whoa.

A *Whiting?*

Pirin wasn't at all political except in that abstract way of women who despise the pointless burdens of ubiquitous patriarchy—but even she had heard of the three Whiting brothers: Brian, the apparently legitimate hedge fund manager; James, the quite popular congressman; and oh-so-handsome Billy, the conspicuously rakish, high-fashion, high-tipping "retail entrepreneur" with a shady streetlord rep. Then there was Cleary, their obscenely wealthy father, retired in name only.

The Whitings made a big deal of their "independence" from each other and the imperious founder of their black market feast, a stance respected by the media but not by rampant LEO rumor, which held that "the old man's OG, and the boys all show up at his manse every Sunday for dinner and marching orders."

Pirin had no actual evidence (yet), but she was pretty sure that "the Boss" was Billy Whiting or possibly one of his senior lieutenants. So her digging continued, especially since she still didn't know if someone had smuggled Farkas a phone.

Which was why, several days after her first zero-click deployment, Pirin decided to take Gracie's advice and "visit" Mother Farkas, whose phone number was easy to find.

So—five zero-click deployments now. And likely plenty more to come, because Pirin's version of zero-click worked beautifully.

CHAPTER FOURTEEN: SO CLOSE...

Damn.
She should be feeling better now, right? Admittedly, an eviscerated salary—but enough to get by (barely), and her job had never been more interesting. A bunch of mercifully dreamless nights, too—all in a row. And now that zero-click had been unleashed, her conversations with Pirin had begun to loosen up. She'd even allowed herself to get all jokey and mumble a quick I-think-I-might-be-falling-in-love-with-you—and received a husky, hasty me-too response.

Pirin had comparatively more to say about her zero-click deployments and the software used to filter everything zero-click collected. "I've never done anything like this," she kept repeating. Soon Gracie understood that Pirin's family knew nothing about any of it—and Pirin was determined to keep it that way.

"A clandestine recycle," Gracie teased her.

Pirin's chilly reply sent a shiver through Gracie: "Recycling is *always* clandestine."

Then there was the camera stuff. Right after her courtroom face-to-face with Veech Farkas, Pirin had decided to "radically upgrade" the standalone wildlife cameras sprinkled through the Basamendi property's woodland using something called PTZ surveillance cameras.

"The land behind the etche rises in elevation some thirty, forty feet," Pirin explained. "Once the oak leaves fall, it's too easy to be watched by strangers with good binoculars."

"Is there a road behind your property?" asked Gracie.

"Not close. Quarter mile off, on the other side of our dairy farmer neighbor's fields. Quite private, actually, since hardly anyone's ever out there. But if somebody *did* want to reconnoiter or sneak in from that side, we'd never know."

"Has that happened?"

"Dunno. But sure as hell it won't going forward," Pirin had declared with obvious satisfaction, "cuz the new cams—a dozen altogether—cover the entire perimeter of the woods around the etche. All five-point-eight-nine acres. The cams feed into a network video server with 'intelligent' software that records and integrates their video in real time. And it's a breeze to search. Won't be anything happening now without me knowing."

Fort Basamendi, Gracie decided not to say.

She appreciated Pirin's willingness to share such details, yet too much remained frustratingly beyond her reach. Masturbation has serious limits, she was discovering as she imagined Pirin's touch, Pirin's scent, Pirin's kisses…

She blamed the pandemic—how it had swept her into an involuntary, no-end-in-sight solitary confinement. Even so, having at last admitted to herself that she disliked living alone, she resisted talking about it; how could she broach the topic without sounding neurotically whiny?

Pirin knew anyway. "How do we ever figure out if we're a fit unless we can be in the same room together? In the same bed together?" she asked.

"A rhetorical question, I presume," Gracie replied dejectedly.

"Abso-fucking-lutely *not!* And I have a plan: Just to make sure we go in healthy, we do two weeks of no face-to-face contact with anyone else—I mean *nobody at all*—and then you move in with me."

"I see you haven't given up on dangerous, reckless risks. What about your fami—?"

"I predict they'll be welcoming. But if they don't like it, they can stay in their place and we'll stay in ours."

"So you haven't said anything."

"I will—by phone—as soon as *you* say yes."

"You do realize that if it all goes south you could be stuck with me for much longer than you want."

"And vice versa. But I'm not worried."

"Damn, Pirin. You should be." Gracie sighed. "I. Am. A. Hot. Mess."

"I'll risk it. Any reason we shouldn't start the countdown right now?"

"I guess not." Gracie paused to give Pirin another chance to back out, but all she heard on her little flip phone was Pirin waiting. "Okay then. Count me in."

"So that's a yes?"

"Yes."

"Excellent. I'm setting my timer as we speak. Two weeks starting…*now*."

❖

That first evening, Pirin called to wish Gracie a good night. "One down, thirteen to go," she said. By morning, Gracie suspected she might be in for a long two weeks.

"Had another ohskal dream," she told Pirin.

"Write it down yet?"

"Seems like I didn't really have a choice." Then Gracie offered up what she regarded as possibly her last secret. "With this one, something took over. My hands on the keyboard had a life of their own. Half the time I didn't even know what my fingers typed till I saw it on the screen." Yet what Gracie found on her screen was exactly what she remembered:

⚡ I found myself splayed on something jaggedy-rough, damp, almost cold. The air was so humid I had trouble breathing. I was desperately thirsty, too—even more than I was hungry, and I was very hungry.

And very scared.

Scared of opening my eyes as I listened for sounds of people. Scared when I sensed no footfalls, no voices. Scared as I finally risked looking around. Then startled at what I saw in the dim light:

Granite.

I was in a cavern, half of it naturally-eroded rock etched with ancient fissures, the rest more recently chopped away. My hand could just reach the natural side where a thin veil of water oozed from the fissures onto a small pile of sandy debris at my fingertips.

I seemed to be at one end of a claustrophobic J-shaped space; what I could see comprised maybe fifty square feet and arched upward to about six feet high. The scant light and rancid air seemed to seep in from the other, curved end of the J, beyond my line of sight where, I imagined, there must also be an exit.

And damn, I was over it. Sympathetic to her predicament or not, I hated the prospect of yet another Analergin ride-along...

"Okay then, you can watch instead. Like one of your movies."

I knew the voice, of course, and didn't appreciate the amusement bubbling through it. "How 'bout I just wake up?"

"In a bit."

"Aw c'mon, Eletun, gimme a br—"

But Eletun's "movie" had already begun, initially with her speaking, which soon became a hypnotic chant, then song...and, since it's impossible to resist Eletun's singing, away I went...

Analergin lay naked and alone, unable to recall how she came to this cave-place or who snared her ankle in metal and attached it on a chain to the spike driven into the rocky ground next to her. She tried to stand but lost her balance. Just rising to her hands and knees made her dizzy and nauseous.

Lying back down, she closed her eyes—and found her mind closed, too, chained like her ankle to thoughts and hopes dead-ending in what used to be, what could never be again: images of Subendi, of Amatchi, of AmaBidari's body on some strange beach, of the moment Otchani fell, speared as he saved her life.

All dead.

AmaBidari's last words echoed... "Remember us, Analergin. Remember and reclaim."

It all seemed so long ago. Perhaps she had been chained in this awful place for Mooncycles, Suncycles even. What, then, should she remember now, awake at last but captive, helpless—and on her way to dying, judging by her urgent thirst, her desperate hunger, her attenuated arms and trembling legs? What could she possibly reclaim now?

"You can touch the rock beneath you, Analergin," whispered someone she could not see. "Spread out on the ground...slow your breathing...let your hands and feet sense Mother Earth's messages."

So she did. But she sensed nothing. And then she fell asleep.

Upon waking, she immediately noticed what had not been there before: a jug of water, a bowl with some foul Sundaselai gruel, and an empty bucket (for her excrement, she concluded from the smell). She gulped the water and food, lay back, and fell asleep again.

Thus it was for some unknown time, during which the cave-place alternated between dim gloom and unmitigated darkness while Analergin, still chained, did what she could to strengthen herself:

Stiffen her prone body while repeatedly arcing her back off the ground. Picture herself stuck in thick mud, then tense arms, legs, belly, and back muscles against its imaginary suctioning force. Yank on that metal spike—to no avail, sadly, though she noticed a tiny, zippy tremoring in the spike whenever she held onto it.

Slowly, her body gained much-needed strength, and one day she was able to stand. Soon she could shuffle around a bit. Next she tried something like a push-up, then another...

The only other relief from endless cave-place tedium came from the jumpy, muttering Sundaselai woman who irregularly showed up to replace the empty jug and bowl with full ones and swap the full bucket for an empty one.

Just once, Analergin tried to speak to this woman, who gaped at her horrified before whacking her with the empty excrement bucket. After that, whenever the woman entered Analergin cowered around the metal spike at the back of the cave-place, hoping what appeared to be her servile terror would mollify the woman, first step toward the woman's indifference, the woman's carelessness.

Ah, but escape was impossible as long as her ankle remained shackled and chained to the floor—and innumerable attempts had taught her that no amount of pulling on the strangely tremoring spike would liberate her.

If Analergin had not been so distraught, she might have pondered the significance of that tremoring. Instead she exhausted herself yanking, then lay in the least uncomfortable spot on the ground to rest.

How long, then, before she noticed? The moment came when she'd resumed her yanking, one hand around the spike, and happened to set her other hand and both feet flat on the rocky cave-place floor. And there it was: The same tremor in the spike was also tickling her feet as well as the flattened palm and especially the fingertips of her other hand.

Soon she discovered that if she lay flat holding the spike but gave up yanking on it to simply attend to this tremoring, her hands and feet and sometimes even her backside would perceive more—a parade of distinct quivers, flutters, rumbles.

What could these sensations mean? Were they real? Or had Analergin's fear conspired with the bleak monotony of the cave-place to spawn apparitions?

She had no answer. But whatever this was—phantasm? reality?—happened *every time* she held the spike while she flattened her other hand and her feet on the rock beneath her. After a while, she picked up on something else: The quivers, flutters, and rumbles exhibited patterns.

They were dancing.

⚡ After Gracie sent the write-up to Pirin, she didn't expect to hear the flip phone ring until nightfall, but Pirin called again at lunchtime sounding downright chirpy. "I don't mean to change the subject, because what's happening to Analergin is pretty damn intense—but I have good news."

"Lemme guess. Farkas somehow got his own phone—a smartphone, right?—and called his mama. So now you have his new number."

Pirin snorted. "I still don't understand how you do that—but yeah, exactly. Now I'm chasing down everyone he contacts. And also how he got his grubby paws on an illegal phone so damn fast."

"Seems the snarling wolf has some well-placed friends."

"Yeah, he does." Pirin exhaled loudly. "And from Mama Farkas's comments I know for certain that some of them are Whitings."

"Who're the—? Wait—not those brothers, the famous ones…?"

"Yep, *those* Whitings. Turns out Veech Farkas's older brother Ezra works for Cleary Whiting. All in the family, since Mama Farkas is Cleary's first cousin."

"Cleary Whiting." Gracie paused. "Isn't that the old man?"

"Yes, ma'am. Making the Farkas brothers second cousins to Cleary's illustrious sons."

"So how come the richy-rich Whitings' second cousin works—*worked*—as a corrections officer in a county jail? Something's wrong with that picture."

"Curious, isn't it? Maybe second cousins don't figure very high in the Whiting pantheon." Pirin cleared her throat. "*Or…*"

"Ha! You have a theory, don't you?"

"According to my database prowls, Ezra Farkas has worked for Cleary Whiting upwards of twenty years. He's one of Cleary's key guys, fixer and chief courier between the supposedly hyper-legit philanthropist old man and youngest son Billy, who took over the old man's OG rackets—drugs, loan sharking, extortion, money laundering, gunrunning, and, more recently, gambling, sex trafficking, and crypto. My take: Billy wanted a pipeline to his guys in county lockup, so he got Ezra to snag a CO job for Veech. Just speculation, but it could explain a lot."

"And Ezra's a pretty effective way to separate the Whitings' black market rackets and their legal, tax-paying stuff," Gracie mused. "Well, for the people actually named Whiting, anyway. Still in the family, with all the tugs and obligations of family. Yet a Farkas is expendable should things ever deteriorate."

"Pretty nice flow of unreported income for Veech to fund his addictions, too," Pirin added. "Besides his Ducati, Veech has two more—poker and a handgun collection."

"Jeezus!" Gracie's stomach cramped. "The guy who wants you dead is into *handguns?*"

"He's locked up tight, Gracie. It's his 'friends' I gotta be prepared for. And I am. Mostly."

Gracie tried to sound encouraging, but for the rest of their conversation, she kept hearing echoes of "Mostly."

That night, Gracie couldn't sleep. Whenever she closed her eyes, she saw someone sneaking up on Pirin with one of Veech Farkas's handguns. This, however, did not stop Eletun, who eventually showed up and thrust Gracie back into the cave-place:

⚡ When I arrived, Analergin was lying flat on her back, having once more tried yanking on the spike and given up, and though her fingers still touched it, her body and her will had gone limp.

Figments, she'd concluded.

Seeking sleep, she'd just closed her eyes—only to be jolted alert by a heavy clunk and the appearance in the cave-place of the miserable Sundaselai woman, who exchanged the jugs and bowls and buckets with clumsy, inattentive clattering.

From within Analergin, who'd curled defensively against the cave-place wall, one hand clutching the immovable spike, I sneak-watched the Sundaselai woman shuffle out again, exiting with a thud (the door to the cave-place slamming shut, I still imagined, though, of course, I couldn't see it).

Next would come the funereal hush of this space cut off from the world by thick granite and what I suspected was a stout, noise-suppressing wooden door.

Instead, though, I picked up more sounds—notably the Sundaselai woman's low grumbles about the stink of the primitive's shit, her sneers of dark delight at having spat in the primitive's gruel—none of which I should have been able to hear.

Yet hear them I did, with undiminished clarity.

And even as the Sundaselai woman moved further away from the cave-place, I easily made out every word she muttered to herself. As if I was moving right alongside her.

I also heard an odd noise I struggled to identify—until Analergin's agitated mind calmed enough to contemplate possibilities. That's when I finally "saw" what I'd been "hearing": the Sundaselai woman pushing a cart up a rough incline, causing the cart's cargo of jugs, bowls, and shitbuckets to erratically thunk.

But when I let go the spike and sat up, it all evaporated.

Oh.

Figments after all.

Out of (Analergin's) habit, I ran my fingers along the spike again anyway. No tremoring this time, no quivers, tingles, or flutters—instead, the "sounds" and "images" from before immediately resumed where they'd left off.

Wait.

What?

So I did it all again.

When I kept my feet and hands flat against the cave-place floor, I sensed the now-familiar mix of high-frequency vibrations—slight, brief sensations before the "sounds" of the Sundaselai woman's cart returned, as did a somewhat washed-out "image" fringed in blurry black.

But when I *also* gripped the metal spike, I sensed no vibrations. Instead, I instantly "heard" and "saw" the Sundaselai woman and her cart—with full audio and visual clarity.

The spike seemed to be functioning as a perception amplifier, like a blind person's cane.

I kept on experimenting.

As long as my hand held the metal spike, I could "hear" the softest approaching footfall, tune into conversations—including hushed, whispered ones—occurring outside the cave-place. I even picked up sounds of people out there breathing and, curiously, an occasional small but distinctive metal-on-metal pattern that began with a light clanking and finished with dissonant, high-pitched scrape.

But was it *real?*

Possibly.

This I concluded after several occasions when I recognized the "sounds" of the Sundaselai woman approaching well before she reached the cave-place door and banged around getting it open. After a while, in a vague, black-fringed way, I could "see" her and others who occasionally were out there, too.

Or so it seemed.

But *how?*

Ah, well…

As Eletun pointed out, the Mothers of Subendi understood that *everything*, including sound and light and matter, is actually energy. Vibrational energy.

"Sound," for instance, constitutes a small subset of frequencies—oscillating vibrations—that we're able to perceive with our ears, while certain frequencies below our hearing threshold can be *felt*, like the rumble in your chest when someone plays the lowest note on a large pipe organ.

Yet what I experienced in the cave-place seemed different. It also seemed to have a limit. The vibrations Analergin (and I along with her) experienced as sound and even sight didn't extend beyond the area just outside the cave-place.

So: A long way to go—and only *possibly* real.

Indeed, Analergin might be hallucinating—and I along with her. Sensory deprivation will do that. Or maybe the Sundaselai woman brought her drugged food, drugged water. Perhaps someone had whacked her too hard on the head. Or grief and disorientation had driven her insane…

Yet if these sensations *were* real, it could mean that Analergin had transformed vibration sensed through mechanoreception and maybe nociception into audio and visual neural signals—in effect, a form of synesthesia.

Lying on the rough rock of the cave-place floor, Analergin (and I along with her) recalled the Seawaves she'd sensed on AmaBidari's outrigger that showed her where even faraway Lands were, thanks to the ways ocean currents and submerged Land form wave patterns. And yes, in those moments, in an ineffable way, she really was "seeing" those Lands…

Tremors, quivers, tingles, flutters; immense, rolling Seawaves— oscillating vibration by any other name.

Rhythm by any other name.

At last I understood: *This* is Sublimity.

And Sublimity, especially Sublimity associated with Perception and Healing, was what Analergin desperately needed—abilities that, despite her training, she'd never had a chance to hone before Subendi exploded out from under her.

I thought of AmaBidari's final plea: Remember and reclaim.

What Analergin remembered first (and I along with her) took her back to Subendi and that aspect of Sublime Perception centered on simple craft, made Sublime only by virtue of its secrecy: forming clear quartz crystal or melted sand into disks that, once properly ground, could focus sunlight to induce flame and, correctly combined, make viewed objects appear closer. Easy, at least compared to the vastly more nuanced *hard* part of any Sublimity.

As Analergin remembered, I began to truly comprehend: Sublimity requires more than perceiving and understanding energy as vibrational frequencies, as Rhythm…

Sublimity demands an ability to achieve Resonance.

It's a two-step: First you find your way to your own inherent, natural vibrational frequency—your own Rhythm. Then you learn to synchronize, to Resonate, with another's Rhythm—like dancing, only you're hooking up with a Rhythm that's much more subtle. And once you've hooked up, you're able to perceive oscillating vibrations, Rhythms, beyond what a human being typically apprehends *and* recognize what they signify.

Analergin recalled almost nothing about how to do this. Mostly, her remembering dredged up only the fearsome demeanor of AmaHeri, a woman she'd avoided as much as possible.

Chained to the cave-place floor, Analergin (and I along with her) resorted to what sounded like prayer but actually was a Rhythm-invoking chant: "Alama, I now begin anew. Alama, please help me… please help me…"

Gradually, as the cave-place skulked between murk and black, fragments of AmaHeri's lessons whispered out of memory and coalesced...

"Listen to your heartbeat while you slow your breathing, and let breath and heartbeat find each other. They want to, so let them. Once you feel the Rhythm of this, sway with it, stay with it, stay until this Rhythm, which is *your* Rhythm, dances with the Rhythm of the Motherworld..."

Disappointment surged through Analergin (and me). Nothing new here! She'd heard it all before, attempted it many times on Subendi—and mostly just fell asleep. Or snuck away to climb a tree.

But alone in the cave-place, she had nothing to lose. And everything to lose. With Analergin, I wrapped my hand around the metal spike, flattened my feet and the palm of my other hand on the granite beneath me, snugged my shoulder blades against the hard, unfriendly rock, then closed my eyes and tried to slow my breathing, slow, slow—and... nothing.

For a long time—days perhaps, Mooncycles perhaps—nothing.

Remember and reclaim...what AmaBidari had taught about sensing the Seacurrents to learn where Land is—which direction, how far...about feeling oscillations and using them to navigate...about perceiving Rhythm.

But no. Nothing.

I opened my eyes to...nothing.

I closed my eyes again.

Nothing except the thin streak of wet heat as tears slid down the sides of my face.

And then—

That metal-on-metal clanking again, and the dissonant scrape, and I heard someone moan. It came from out there, I was sure—from the other side of the unseen cave-place door. I kept my eyes closed and "listened."

"No," pleaded a whimpering male voice.

Then I "saw" a hand poking a small L-shaped metal stick into a hole at one end of a slot slicing across a small rectangular metal box linked on its shorter side to a length of chain; the box's longer side attached to a semi-circular metal ring shackling a hairy human ankle.

I squeezed my eyes shut—then opened them to stare at what was around *my* ankle: the same shackle, with a "lock" that I realized was, basically, a simple slidebolt controlled with a small, removeable L-shaped "key."

So simple—but frustratingly effective, since I had *nothing* remotely skinny enough to serve as a small L-shaped key.

Only a few granite stones and chips were within my reach, all too large. As I chose what seemed like the best candidate, I wondered: Would Analergin even live long enough to grate a granite shard into a two-inch long, eighth-inch thick, L-shaped key?—assuming that the "key" I'd seen was even real.

At least Analergin had some brief experience grinding crystals back on Subendi. Now the best she could do was make a paste of water using the sand washed out of the fissures in the cave-place wall, glob this paste between her selected chunk of rock and the granite beside her, and rub, rub, rub…

Whenever Analergin (and I with her) took breaks to relieve her aching hands, she spread out flat on her back—and lost what little survived of her sense of time.

So I have no notion of how much of it passed before Analergin truly understood that she no longer perceived quivers and tingles and flutters. Instead, at a whole new level of detail and specificity, she *heard* sounds. And she *saw*.

Beginning with the cave-place door that, of course, neither Analergin's eyes nor mine could actually behold. No matter—I "saw" it. Made of thick wood, windowless, I saw the inside first, then the outside, kept carefully barricaded with a heavy wood brace set into even heavier metal brackets while four- or five-inch slits above and beneath the door allowed in wisps of light and air.

Next I "saw" an inclined passageway with raggedy, human-hewn rock walls that became brighter as I moved upward past other heavy wood doors toward light. Above me, on the other side of all that granite, I "saw" a large building made of wood (ha! the cave-place was a deep cellar). And ahead of me I "saw" outside.

I "saw" an unclouded blue Sky!

A single bird circling high overhead swooped low, sunlight glinting brightly off its beautiful black wings.

Bele!

Analergin needed no convincing: The baby raven from so long ago on Subendi had survived and grown up.

When Bele again ascended, Analergin ascended too, and I along with her.

It was breathtaking, exhilarating! I could see what Bele saw, feel Bele's swoops and turns as she flew over the structure erected atop the cave-place, which stood in the middle of a densely-built settlement with narrow serpentine pathways.

From Bele's perspective, Analergin (and I with her) studied the settlement, how its pathways intersected, how to travel them to the nearby Sea.

This "journey" ended when the Sundaselai woman noisily arrived at the cave-place carting jugs and bowls and shitbuckets. Curled cowering against the back wall, hiding the residue of her granite grinding, Analergin (and I along with her) wondered: Do I dare trust what I've just "seen"?

As the Sundaselai woman departed, a voice whispered "Only by believing what you cannot prove will you ever know anything." Analergin felt a hand caress her cheek as a scent she recognized, warm and sweet, wafted close. "So the question is: What do you believe?"

She (and I along with her) had glimpsed an exit from the cave-place, glimpsed the settlement around it, glimpsed how close she was to the Sea. Glimpsed her only hope.

"I believe what I must," Analergin whispered.

And so she kept on grinding. Until finally, *finally*, her bloodied fingers held a small L-shaped granite stick that just fit the hole in the slot running across the box attached to that vile shackle.

And so she tried to slide open the bolt...

On the third attempt, perhaps the fourth, she succeeded.

Liberated at last, Analergin curled into the customary cringe at the back of the cave-place when the Sundaselai woman, bored and oblivious as usual, next unbarred the door, entered, and as usual turned her back to the prisoner.

Analergin rose up and lunged, easily clamping a hand over the woman's mouth, pulling and twisting her onto the ground, shoving a thick wad of tunic into the scream for which the woman had already drawn breath.

The sudden movement made Analergin (and me) dizzy, but holding the woman down, shackling her ankle, and locking it with the granite stick was easy, as was using more of the woman's tunic to tie her wrists behind her. Killing her would grant more margin for escape and the world would be burdened with one less malevolent human— but Analergin had seen that kind of death...

So she left the woman alive and ran.

On trembling legs she (and I with her) quickly traversed the passageway outside the cave-place into a dark lane, already aware that her Sublime Perception had been remarkably accurate.

But way too soon came a shriek—from the cave-place. The Sundaselai woman had somehow at least partly released herself.

Nor was fortune done turning adverse: I'd been seen by a nearby male who was already approaching; when he heard the woman's howls he came after me shouting alarm. He was quickly joined by others.

I sprinted into a narrower, darker passageway with pursuers mere steps behind me. Striving to recall what I'd seen from above of the settlement's pathways, I ducked and dodged. And it worked; although I lost my bearings, the shouting grew more distant. I'd eluded the men hunting me.

Winded, I paused for breath in an alley, looking to the clear night Sky to regain a sense of direction, then slipped from shadow to shadow toward the Sea. Analergin's Sublime Perception, I was realizing, had its limits: My flights with Bele turned out to be somewhat distorted, maybe like the way bats "see" via what amounts to ultrasound, or what happens in dreams.

Yet it was true enough, despite its slants and twists and blurry black fringe, and I was so close to the Sea I could smell it. Then I could hear it, too. And at last, there it was before me in the dark, blocked only by a lighted concourse and a small wharf beyond.

So close...

But even as I looked at the water, the whoops of the men hunting me grew closer. Behind me a light appeared at the far end of the constricted lane where I hid, near enough that I heard the gruntings of the men as they advanced, not yet aware of my presence. Before me on the wider, well-lit track—the only other way I could go—others were an arm's reach away.

Trapped.

Alama, I mutely begged as I waited for the men on the avenue to pass, please help me...

And for a heartbeat Alama seemed to respond: The men on the wider track were trotting right on by.

Then one of them noticed the light in the lane where I was hiding and stopped. At the moment he would have seen me I sprang at him, pushing him hard into his companion as I dashed for the water. I managed a couple of steps before another man grabbed me, then another.

I turned on them, kicking one as fiercely as I could in his genitals, another in his gut. As the two of them slumped groaning to the ground, I kept on running, a small gang of men only steps behind me.

So close...

The wharf and the boat and the dark water that could hide me were only a few yards ahead. I ran with all my strength, heard my own feet pounding on the wooden wharf as I ran for my life.

I was so, *so* close...

A sharp, fiery sensation jolted my right thigh, but I didn't stop. A few steps later, though, my leg gave way and I fell.

I tried to crawl across the wharf and tumble into the water below; they would never find me once the water had me, and if drowning was my fate, then so be it. Better than Privation rape and slavery. My arms were pulling me, pulling me over the wharf's edge, so close—but they caught me and dragged me back, roaring their rage, kicking me and kicking and kicking.

All during that forever while I was trying to kick back and block their blows, I heard a wild, frenzied scream above the commotion, sounding failure and fear and, to Analergin's everlasting credit, resistance too—and as my consciousness faded I comprehended that the scream came from both of us.

⚡

Chapter Fifteen: Cunned

Pirin had scarcely finished reading the latest dream write-ups when her flip phone rang. Gracie's tentative, near-whisper greeting sent a faint tremor down her spine.

"You okay? You don't sound okay."

"Might be nothing…"

"Tell me."

"Just talked to Naomi—"

"*The* Naomi?"

"Yep. She's on her way over to pick up all the crap she left here last year. Thing is, she's bringing along a couple guys who work at her company."

"All the way from DC?"

"I guess. No big deal—theoretically. Except for this tone in her voice, this tension. Like she's nervous. Or even scared."

"Of the two guys with her?"

"Maybe. I do wonder. She called out of the blue a few minutes ago, very rushed, insisting they had to get her stuff today, right now. They'll be here soon—a-and, uh…"

"What? What're you leaving out?"

"Damn, Pirin. And you squawk about how well *I* read *you*." Gracie cleared her throat. "Okay, confession time: Back when I snooped the laptop Naomi left here, I didn't want her to know—so before I even booted it up, I disconnected internet and Wi-Fi. Also deleted the laptop's logs after I copied the zero-click documents. But then I started worrying since the zero-click stuff came from that defense contractor, Palasin

Security. Like, what if they someday audit employee communications and eventually make their way to Naomi's old laptop?"

"Mmm. And if they did serious forensics on the laptop's hard drive, they'd very probably discover, log deletions or no, that someone had accessed it months after Naomi left it at your place." Pirin paused. "What'd you do to the laptop, Gracie?"

"It has an SSD."

A solid state drive, from which it's pretty much impossible to truly erase data. Pirin groaned at this worst of all possible news. "Of course it does."

"So I, uh, removed the battery, submerged the whole laptop in very salty water, and left it for several days till the water mostly evaporated. Then I put the battery back in and turned it on." Gracie snorted. "After the damn thing finished sparking and smoking, I dunked it again in salty water for another few days, drained it, and stuck it in the bottom box of Naomi's stuff down in the basement while it was still kinda wet. That was almost three months ago."

Pirin laughed. "Oh yeah, excellent odds you royally fried everything. Doubtful anybody'll recover any data, certainly nothing reliable, especially if the SSD was hardware-encrypted. I'd say your deniability is intact." Then she asked "Got your smartphone handy?"

"Lemme pull it out from its hidey hole."

"No, Gracie, wait. Let's assume Palasin has zero-clicked your smartphone and compromised it. So when you retrieve it, we stick to our protocol—say nothing, shut it off, wait about a minute, then turn it back on. After that, I'm gonna send you *my* zero-click again, so give it a minute to load, then set up the phone like you're charging it, but make sure the camera's positioned with a good view of where you think Naomi and her posse will be—like your living room maybe—and let the screen go dark. And hide your flip phone now. I'll do the rest."

"Thanks, that kinda makes me feel better."

Gracie disconnected the flip phone call, and when Pirin next heard her voice, it came through her smartphone. "Okay, all done."

"Good...and yeah. I got your camera's view. Right to your front door and—"

"Oh shit, Pirin, they're here," said Gracie upon glancing out her living room window. "I see Naomi getting out of a rent-a-van. Wish me luck," she whispered. And then she was talking to people Pirin couldn't see. "Please," she called out from her living room window, "don't forget to mask up."

Having already muted her own microphone, Pirin knew Gracie couldn't hear her muttering about the (uncomfortably high) odds that, yeah, Palasin *had* hacked Gracie's smartphone—and then hacked the phone numbers in Gracie's list of contacts. Including Pirin's so-called "public" smartphone number.

"Gonna do more than wish you luck, Gracie."

Nor, of course, could Gracie see what Pirin did next: retrieve her other smartphone, the "private" one reserved for remote communication with the systems dedicated to her recycles, then turn the phone off and back on again (cuz hey, ya never know).

A few app taps later, still muttering, Pirin had commenced the first field test of a new upgrade linking her private smartphone to her zero-click control server. The urge to berate herself ("Why the hell didn't I do this a week ago?") would have to wait.

By the time she had her SUV reversing out of the garage, her public smartphone had been shut off and secured in a Faraday pouch buried deep in a pants pocket while her dashboard-mounted private smartphone screen displayed Gracie's empty living room. A few minutes later, Pirin watched Gracie appear onscreen followed by a woman and two men, all of them masked.

"So you're Naomi," Pirin scowled at the slickly just-so figure who cast her eyes around Gracie's space without seeming to register the innocuous presence of Gracie's apparently recharging smartphone. Naomi looked anxious—perhaps because the men trailed her just a little too closely before roaming the living room like overeager dogs determined to sniff everything.

As the men disappeared out of camera view with Naomi wandering after them, Gracie gave chase. "Wrong way, fellas," she declared tensely from somewhere off-camera. "None of Naomi's stuff is in there anymore. Only her loveseat and the butler's table out in the living room are still up here." Gracie managed to relax her tone. "The rest is down in the basement. The boxes under the stairs marked 'Naomi.' Can't miss 'em."

After a moment, Pirin's view through Gracie's smartphone camera showed Naomi reappearing, but not the men. Then came Gracie's off-camera voice again, now way too edgy: "So both of you please get the hell out of my bedroom. And leave my masks alone."

Soon the two men reappeared and followed Naomi out the front door, Gracie right behind them. "Basement stairs are around back," Gracie was explaining as her voice faded.

Almost like everything would be okay.

Which Pirin didn't believe, not for a nanosecond.

"Fuck!" she growled. Reaching Gracie's place would take upwards of half an hour—assuming she continued to get away with barrel-assing much too fast down Route 495 to Route 3 to Route 2 and into Belmont.

Then, about fifteen minutes from Gracie's place, Pirin's remote access link went down, and no amount of tinkering-while-driving-way-too-fast fixed it.

"*FUCK!*" Pirin roared—because just before the link failed, she'd heard Gracie urging her visitors to hurry Naomi's furniture out of her living room, whereupon one of the men snapped "Fuck you, bitch." The situation was deteriorating.

This tempted Pirin to 911 the cops to Gracie's place. But might doing so reveal that, yes indeed, somebody *had* found Palasin's zero-click documents and was now using a similar exploit against them?

Possibly.

Too possibly.

So Pirin drove even faster, arriving eight minutes later at Gracie's—to a quiet scene, no rent-a-van in sight, and the building's main door ominously ajar.

"Gracie!" she yelled, already out of her SUV and running.

No answer.

Once inside, Pirin called out again but heard no response as she took the stairs three at a time to the second-floor landing, where she found the door to Gracie's third-floor apartment wide open.

Heartrate soaring, mind reeling *not again not again please not again*, Pirin scrambled to the third floor and quickly spotted Gracie sitting near the landing, legs splayed before her, mask pulled down, a wall keeping her upright. Her fixed eyes stared straight ahead and for an agonizing moment Pirin thought she was dead.

"Gracie," she pleaded, sliding to her knees, stroking Gracie's face.

The touch brought Gracie back; she blinked, grimaced, then blinked again before her eyes found Pirin's face.

"Pirin…hi," she whispered, eyes closing again.

"They're gone, right?" Pirin asked, glancing around the empty living room.

"Fuckin' prick...stole...other two masks...you sent me," Gracie lamented before she grimaced again and squeezed her eyes shut. "Damn," she objected, "too bright. Makes my head hurt...even more."

At least Gracie seemed aware and reasonably articulate. But *something* had happened, something not good. "They hurt you," Pirin seethed.

"Sorry." Gracie opened her eyes once more. "Tried to stop him." She sighed, eyes fluttering shut. "But...he slammed me...'gainst the wall...an' my head...whacked my head..."

A concussion. Pirin pulled out her public phone to initiate a consult—with her mother, who as a nurse knew a thing or two about concussions. But even before she could turn on the phone, Gracie yanked her arm. "Gotta get up...r-right now."

Pirin helped her to her feet and kept her upright as she stumbled erratically across the living room to the kitchen sink and vomited into it. She would have collapsed then, but Pirin caught her, cradling her as they both folded to the floor.

"I'm really glad you're here," Gracie murmured as her eyes closed again.

Rousing amidst a thick red snaking fog, Gracie was unsure of where or when or who. Was this yet another dream? Had she returned to Analergin's world?

Or—?

No, she decided, not dead. Yet nothing seemed real...

"You could open your eyes. That might give you a hint."

She knew that voice, but her head throbbed and the mere thought of opening her eyes intensified her nausea.

Mmm, might be better to just hang here a bit.

"Fair enough," agreed Eletun. "I invite you instead to listen... listen..." Whereupon Eletun's lilting melody picked up the familiar refrain that continued her story, though now what she sang tended to echo...

"Reluctantly did Analergin awaken…awaken amidst a thick red snaking fog, and she understood that she was still alive…still alive. Yet nothing…nothing seemed real. Death, she surmised, was near…near…

"So Analergin waited…waited while the snaking red fog grew denser, redder, closer…closer, and extremely painful.

"Thus was a fuller awareness forced…forced upon her, and gradually she recognized that she lay flat on her back on a rough, cool-damp, steep incline. Nearby something was burning…burning. She tasted blood…blood. She was sweating but she shivered…shivered.

"Finally, her body convulsed violently, scattering…scattering and shriveling this still-feeble…feeble awareness, which she had no desire…no desire to retrieve. Yet she did not recede entirely: A vague, vacillating murmur seduced her away…away from the red fog…

"Surrounding her, she realized, were the mumbles and whispers of people. Of women…women…

"This inspired Analergin to open her eyes…open her eyes, yet something had sealed them shut. She tried to move her arms but found them flung…above…above her head, and torrents of pain surged… surged through her shoulders.

"With great…great effort her hand found her face…face, found the crusty blood that covered her eyes and clawed it away…away.

"Thus she beheld a woman who studied her with tired, wary eyes…wary eyes devoid of the Privation rancor…rancor to which she had become much accustomed. The woman's mouth moved, and she heard a voice…a voice distinct from the others.

"'Yes…Yes, this is the primitive we heard about.' The woman's words, distilled through Analergin's haze, sounded aloof…spoken not to her…not to her but to others. 'What…What did they call her?' Curiosity had begun to subvert the woman's detachment. 'Oh yes… Ersean—between life and death…Ersean…between life…and death… death…'

"'She is not the one…not the one you hoped for, Sineusi,' said another woman. 'So we should do nothing…nothing. Sineusi…Sineusi, she is only a primitive…primitive.'

"'She is barely more than a child!' Sineusi objected. 'And what they have done to her is worse…worse than anything they ever did to any of us. Will you make me defend her…?'"

❖

Accompanied by a relentless thudding in her head, Gracie drifted from one gray, amorphous realm to another, each interrupted by brief, too-bright vignettes of awareness:

Pirin talking urgently to someone on a phone...

Eletun singing in rhythm to a rumbly rocking motion, singing "If I simply lie here...lie here, soon this will be over and I...I will fade... away...away..."

Pirin talking, talking while half-carrying her down a gazillion stairs...

Pirin patiently explaining about bringing her home "cuz you shouldn't be alone for a while"...

When was it that the white noise finally whooshed through Gracie's reluctance, whooshed until she opened her eyes to find herself in a speeding vehicle? The gray realms began to recede, and then Pirin was helping her out of an SUV that seemed ridiculously high off the ground. Gracie found she could walk okay—no longer so dizzy, the brazen brightness slightly diminished.

"A hospital?" Gracie asked upon finally noticing the large red brick building with immense white letters announcing its purpose. "Why are we—?"

"We're gonna get your head checked out," Pirin answered calmly while she masked up. "Let's put on your mask, too. And you'll also need your patience. This'll take a while."

Later Gracie learned it took nine-and-a-half hours, most of which involved waiting. She didn't mind at all since she got to nestle her throbbing head into Pirin's shoulder. Intermittently, she was queried and poked and trundled from one scan to another—all because, as far as she could determine, she'd acknowledged losing time after "that asshole man" slammed her into her living room wall. Well then, it had been decided (by whom Gracie wasn't sure), you must have lost consciousness, perhaps long enough to warrant serious medical evaluation.

With a diagnosis of no fractures and no bleeding plus a scheduled follow-up appointment, they returned to Pirin's SUV, at last able to pull off their face masks. The sun had nearly set and somehow the SUV had returned to earth sufficiently that Gracie managed to climb into it without help.

"A short ride this time," Pirin assured her. "Fifteen minutes, give or take."

"Your place? Do I remember that right?"

"Yep. So we can keep an eye on you." Pirin smiled. "That's my excuse, anyway."

"I-I don't have any clothes. Not even a toothbru—"

"No worries. I packed a bag for you. Clothes, underwear, laptop, tablet, both your phones. And your toothbrush. Anything else you want I'll go back for tomorrow."

"Hasn't been two weeks yet."

"Eleven days. I'll risk it if you will."

"Do I have a choice?"

"Do you *want* a choice?"

"No," Gracie said—but this was only half true. She'd been worried about the implications of that impulsive "yes" ever since she'd agreed to move in with Pirin—and had considered stalling for more time, not least because…

Other than that first rudely interrupted encounter, her time with Pirin had been exclusively virtual. Never shared a meal in the same room or spent a night in the same bed much less kissed each other. She hadn't even known what Pirin smelled like.

From her (tiny) phone screen she'd gleaned that Pirin's place wasn't much larger than her own rather crowded-for-two apartment, which had only (sort of, briefly) worked out because both she and Naomi went off to their respective offices for ten hours a day—no longer an option amidst a pandemic that didn't look like it would be ending anytime soon.

Also, what would Pirin's family, buzzing around a mere forty feet away, think of this interloper making far too big a deal about a bunch of weird dreams?

And then there was Jessica. How would her new boss react to her moving in with the woman Jessica referred to as "my best friend ever"?

Ah yes, Hesitant Gracie at her doubtful best, blinding headache be damned. Fair enough, those doubts—but how the hell else, countered Utterly Other Gracie, am I supposed to attempt a relationship, even a casual one, when we're all supposed to be holed up in our goddamn bubbles, limited to e-relationships? Oh, got no answer? Well, here's one: Merge bubbles.

About ten minutes from the hospital, Pirin exited the highway onto a classically unkempt New England country road. Nearly there, Gracie concluded. She reached across the center console for Pirin's arm. "Please, can you pull over for a minute?"

"Are you okay?" an alarmed Pirin asked as she yanked the vehicle off the road. "What's wrong?"

"I-I just need to—" Gracie unbuckled her seat belt before extending her hand to Pirin's cheek and leaning close. "I need to know."

Her mouth found Pirin's, parted lips tingling while Pirin's scent, delicately warm and creamy-sweet, filled her nostrils and sent a galvanic flow of exhilaration rollicking from her nipples, now at full attention, down her chest, through her belly, melting down, down to ignite her. She may have moaned as she pursued what her mouth had begged for, what Pirin, too, seemed to beg for, her lips and tongue exploring, tasting…

Ooooh, Gracie thought, now I understand what it means to cun…

When at last they separated, Pirin sat motionless but for her conspicuously rapid breathing, her head flung back against the headrest. Finally, she turned toward Gracie and asked "Did you find out?"

Gracie exhaled and re-buckled her seat belt. "I did." In spades, she thought with a grin, maybe hearts too—and made no attempt to hide the electric wriggle claiming her. "Thank you."

"That's it? That's all you're gonna say?"

"Well, I do have a question."

"Which is?"

"How can you be sure that you, um—?" Gracie halted, her eyes completing her question before she looked away.

Pirin chuckled. "Won't regret this by the end of next week?"

Gracie nodded without meeting Pirin's gaze—because what if she'd read the moment all wrong?

"I can't. Be sure, that is. But I have faith. Especially now."

"Because I kissed you?"

"Mmm. That too."

Maybe, Gracie mulled hopefully, I'm not the only one who cunned.

CHAPTER SIXTEEN: YOU *WERE* WARNED

Daylight was quickly receding by the time Pirin turned into the driveway of a classic cedar-shingled two-story house; off to one side and nearly behind it sat a separate three-bay garage. At first glance, the place seemed quite old, but its exterior chimneys, slightly oversized windows, and siting somewhat further from the road than a typical New England antique all hinted more recent origins.

Pirin didn't stop the vehicle until she'd parked it in the middle bay of the garage, its headlights revealing a workbench littered with what looked like propellers and machine parts.

"What's all that?" Gracie asked.

"Newly arrived drone parts mostly. Haven't shifted them over to the workshop yet."

Gracie couldn't understand why the sight of drone parts should overwhelm her, but it did. "Sorry," she mumbled when Pirin appeared at the passenger-side door, opened it, and reached across her to release her seat belt. "Sorry," she said again when Pirin gently urged her out of the vehicle, around it, and through a doorway leading to what looked like the longest stairway she'd ever seen.

"Almost there," Pirin encouraged her.

Even as Gracie trudged up those stairs, the world had gone blurry and black-fringed...the landing at the top...the firmly shut door on the left...windows and furniture off to the right...the bathroom beyond where she managed unaided to pee and drink a little water...then the close-by bedroom where she traded her tired clothes for her favorite nightshirt (how did Pirin know to pack *this?*)...and the bed, oh god yes the bed scented so sweetly of Pirin, inviting her to dissolve into sleep...

❖

Pirin did *not* spend the night on the living room sofa as her mother twice suggested. Too little, too late since she'd driven with Gracie all that time, neither of them masked. And besides, Grace Gwyllt Olwyn was in her bed at last. Deep in sleep—but, Esker Amari, *in her bed*.

So once Pirin finally joined Gracie there, she cuddled up close, studying Gracie between her own fitful mini-sleeps, daintily stroking Gracie's hair, kissing Gracie's forehead. She woke Gracie twice ("Can you tell me your full name?," "When's your birthday?") and lay back relieved that even concussed and drowsy, Gracie's brain seemed to work fine.

Too soon after the sun rose, she gave up on getting more shut-eye. Time to take a close look at whatever Gracie's phone screen had captured during Naomi's "raid."

Basandere. Gracie's phone had captured plenty, including an unobstructed view of Naomi's beefy goon sneering "fuckin' dyke cunt" as he smashed Gracie hard into her living room wall just before he yanked down his mask, which obviously irritated the hell out of him.

Within an hour of watching that video, thanks to Palasin Security's surprisingly ill-protected personnel files, Pirin knew the dude's name, phone number, where he lived, employee ID number, personal email address, place of birth, favorite food as a child, and mother's maiden name. She'd been contemplating how best to take him down—and should Naomi go down with him?—when she decided to check on Gracie again and found those blue eyes opened and gazing out the bedroom windows.

Suddenly tongue-tied, she managed only a soft "Good morning." After all, she'd shared her bed with only one other woman in the four years she'd occupied her sanctum and it hadn't ended well.

Gracie looked up at her and smiled. "Wow. You really did it. I half expected to wake up in Belmont."

"No way. You were attacked. And concussed." Tongue untied, Pirin continued. "I found out who that prick is, too, and—hey!" Pirin had spotted her public smartphone. "So *this* is where I left it." She clicked the phone open. "That's odd. I don't remember recording anyth—" She threw a glance at Gracie. "Nine minutes and nineteen seconds, starting at six fifty-one this morning."

Pirin took a moment to turn the phone off, then back on again before she pressed PLAY. A voice—unquestionably Gracie's, sounding hoarse and a little sluggish—said in a near-whisper: "I heard a woman speaking—"

Pirin pressed STOP, one eyebrow flitting upward. "Another ohskal dream."

"So it seems," Gracie muttered, and Pirin pressed PLAY again:

⚡ I'd heard her voice before, but I didn't dare open my eyes. That man might be nearby, and if I open my eyes he'll hurt me again.

"Dominion Almighty," this woman lamented, "what have they done to you?"

Someone grasped the back of my neck and lifted my head; water washed over my lips. Water. I *needed* water. I tried to swallow it.

"Enough for now," the woman soothed after a moment. "Rest a bit. There will be more."

Where is he?

I waited for the cruel male voice that had taunted me for so long, but when only the woman spoke, I finally peeked. A weary face, shadowed eyes. Before I could speak, I saw the bowl she held. Steam wafted from it. She gestured me to sip, and soon after I did I slid away from the pain into the solace of sleep.

I woke to an argument underway around me. The woman who'd cared for me—the others called her Sineusi—was now defending me.

The argument appeared to end in a draw, and as silence ensued I registered that I still lay on my back, but I'd been moved to a more level place, onto an almost-soft material that seemed also to cover me. I sensed pain's presence, but now it lay beside me rather than inside me.

Carefully, I turned my head leftward. No more than an arm's length away loomed a smooth, milky-colored rock wall thinly streaked with brown. "A cave?" I tried to ask.

"Many caves, Ersean," Sineusi replied. "You are in the Prison Caves of Ilchullo."

Then she proffered a small bowl of stewed roots and greens, which I gratefully ate. I had almost succumbed to sleep again when a low, rolling rumble shook the ground and echoed along the cave's walls, scaring me nearly upright.

Sineusi's hand calmed me. "Every other day they load the pulley cart with ingots and also charcoal to fuel the forges," she explained.

"After they lower it down here, we dump out the cart and the cave trembles."

I looked to my right. Through a cloud of dust I beheld a huge, jaggedly conical pitcave, its lopsided opening to the sky notably smaller than its inverted-bowl interior. I'd been placed in a kind of naturally eroded grotto, but most of the pitcave had been chopped out by humans, leaving ragged gray-white sides that gleamed when the meager streams of sunlight touched them, then went menacingly dark whenever the sun retreated.

Scattered across the pitcave were small rock-built structures, each harboring a smoldering fire that sent smoke slithering upward to the opening high above us.

"Welcome to Ilchullo's copperforge pitcave." Sineusi's tone exuded contempt and fear. "Legend holds that the first prisoners dug here for the building stone. Then they found copper, and the pitcave grew large like you see it from all they took out. After the copper was gone, they condemned female prisoners to build forges from the leftover stone, and now we heat and hammer ingots of copper-tin into tools, mostly for the prisoners in the mining caves."

I struggled not to vomit as I watched several dirty, too-thin women in crude tunics carry baskets of charcoal and metal blocks to the forges. In that moment I would have attempted anything to escape, yet I could do little more than lift my head.

Sineusi read my thoughts. "They make us send up our dead on their pulley cart," she said, "but if you are alive, the only way out is through the network of tunnels that connects all the pitcaves. Though I have never seen anyone leave here that way. The guards open the tunnel doors only to throw in new prisoners."

"Doors?"

Sineusi pointed toward one of the pitcave's gloomier recesses. "The inner door, made of forged metal bars, has a lock that opens only with a small tool. The outer door of thick wood and metal is barred on the outside."

For the first time, I wondered how long I had been in Privation hands. "The Firemountain that burst into the Sky. How long ago?" I asked.

"The great eruption near Kampar—on an island called..." Sineusi shook her head.

"Subendi."

"Subendi," Sineusi repeated, her demeanor tensing. "Lava burst into the Sky at dawn and for days rained down on the great gathering of ships before the island consumed itself. And the Seawaves...so immense, they swept away everything." Sineusi averted her eyes. "So much death. No water, no food, no shelter. Two Mooncycles afterward, I was seized for stealing rice. Twelve Mooncycles have passed since that day. And I do not know if my Senba is alive or dead."

I watched the smoke-hazed figures of gaunt, tunic-clad women shuffling across a shaft of sunlight at the far end of the pitcave while dissonant clanging from the forges resounded around me. I had been captive in Sundaselai for more than a Suncycle. And now I would be one of its many, many slaves.

⚡

❖

"Yeah. I remember that dream." Gracie's voice was subdued. "And the woman in it."

"Sineusi," said Pirin, her voice wavering.

Gracie defied an urge to shrug—as in: You *were* warned—before she replied. "I wish I could tell you I recall picking up your phone. Or saying any of the stuff it recorded. But I can't."

"Your words, though." Pirin eyed her phone.

"Oh yes. My words. My dream." Gracie sighed. "Guess I do sleeptalking now too, huh?"

"Sineusi..." Pirin repeated absently. "Means 'to believe.'"

"Does it?" Before Gracie could say anything else, she heard knocking, and instantly Pirin called out "Come on in, Ama."

"Oh god," Gracie muttered, reminding herself that she could always go back to Belmont as she put on the mask Pirin handed her.

This thought was interrupted by the sight of a masked Sama Basamendi, almost as lean as her daughter though not as tall, wearing a loose blue linen shirt, light jeans, and moccasins. Her darkly flashing eyes hinted her smile while her graying hair loosely pulled to the nape of her neck gave away her age.

Even before Sama spoke, Gracie had to resist blurting "Oh! It's *you!*"

When Sama asked how she was feeling, she squelched her shock long enough to mumble "Doing much better now"—but didn't dare say another word for fear of giving away her astonishment. Mask or no, when Gracie first beheld Sama Basamendi, she wondered if she'd been whisked back into Eletun's Tale—because for just an instant she'd have sworn she was looking at Sineusi. Gracie closed her eyes and rubbed them. An illusion, surely, thanks to Sama's mask and the damn concussion.

"You're a bit pale," Sama noted as she perched on the edge of the bed. "When was the last time you ate something? Or drank anything?"

Gracie blinked. "Um…"

Sama glanced up at her daughter, who humphed "She only just woke up."

Smiling, Sama stood and ruffled Pirin's already disheveled hair before turning back to Gracie. "Can you do scrambled eggs, bacon, toast, maybe some OJ?"

Gracie nodded.

"Coming right up." And with that Sama trotted off.

No, Gracie concluded, neither Pirin nor Sama had noticed anything. In the nick of time, she'd caught the crazy, still way too alive and well (and indulged by Utterly Other Gracie).

But she was freaking: She'd been in Belmont the first time she'd encountered Sineusi. (That *was* a dream, right?) And the second Sineusi dream went down hours before Sama showed up. *Before*, dammit!

So…*what the fuck?*

Gracie decided to contemplate her ill-formed question in solitude.

Her resolve was tested during breakfast, however, which on this pleasantly breezy late-June Saturday was served outside on Pirin's deck, large enough that they could remain six feet apart and maskless while she and Pirin chowed down and Sama nibbled bacon.

Gracie's first full-face look at Sama changed nothing. Yep, still a Sineusi seem-alike.

So Gracie took refuge in talking too much about anything other than what she couldn't stop thinking about. She effusively complimented Sama's cooking, admired the circular patio in the meadow behind the garage with its spiraling granite pattern amidst a riot of wildflowers, marveled at the mini-forest of oak and pine rising behind all those flowers. And then…

Then Sama gave away why she'd lingered through breakfast. "Pirin mentioned," she said casually, "that you've heard an interesting word in a dream."

"I was asking Ama about the history of 'Alama,'" interjected Pirin diffidently, like she was seeking Gracie's permission. We can shut this down right now if you want, her eyes offered—just shake your head.

Gracie looked at Pirin's apprehensive face—wow, you haven't talked to your mum about this yet even though I told you it'd be okay to tell her?

Smiling, Gracie took the plunge. "It's more than just a word, Ms. Basamendi. And more than one dream."

"Oh, call me Sama, please." The woman's easy grin made Gracie realize she'd never seen Sineusi smile. "The dream—dreams—they're recent, yes?"

Gracie nodded. "Ongoing, in fact. I seem to be dreaming somebody's life story."

"W-We call them ohskal dreams," Pirin added uneasily.

Sama's eyebrows levitated, her eyes snapping from Gracie to Pirin. "Ohskal? As in—?"

"Yes, ma'am," said Pirin, straightening herself, readying herself. "As in Amatchi's ohskal. Best we can determine, it all started with a lightning strike." Whereupon Pirin confessed: "I wanted to know more about the ohskal so, I—I'm sorry, I gave it to a geochemist for testing. Gracie is how I got it back before the geochemist could, uh… Sorry. Shoulda told you."

Sama's head dipped slightly, her face expressionless while her narrowing eyes locked onto Pirin's: Yes, you most definitely should have told me.

No wonder Pirin left out anything extraneous, like the geochemist being Jessica Winter's girlfriend or getting attacked by two thugs in the park the day she met Gracie to retrieve the ohskal or Veech Farkas or zero-click. Seated the required six feet away from Gracie and her mother, Pirin slowly relaxed as she talked on—sensing, Gracie suspected, Sama's rising interest in the dreams along with a begrudging willingness to forgive what had been a significant overstep.

Quite unobtrusively, Pirin had rested her hand on the table next to her while her eyes flicked between Gracie and a folder Gracie hadn't noticed before lying beneath her increasingly twitchy fingers.

Oh, Gracie realized, printouts of all my dream write-ups.

Nodding at Pirin, she said, "Open sesame."

Gracie could see Pirin's broad shoulders release the last of her tension as she picked up the folder and handed it to her mother, all while making it sound like Gracie should be awarded a medal or at least a standing ovation. Good time to scoot off for a shower, because Sama was counting pages. Next would come the reading.

One protracted shower later, Gracie learned (to her amazement, since it never once occurred to *her* to count) that she'd produced three sleepwritings, ten dream write-ups—a couple of them quite lengthy—and, just last night, a voice recording.

"So," Sama summed up when they reconvened, "on what I'll bet is an unprecedented scale, we have a charismatic narrator leading you through a series of mythically rich episodic dreams—and even some sleepwritings and 'sleeprecordings'—about the same crew, mostly in chronological order. Dreams that, Pirin explained, are sort-of lucid and so vivid that you've been able to recall them in great detail, though you don't always have clear memories of the experience of recording them. Plus you suspect it's not over yet."

Gracie lowered her shaking head while she laughed softly. "And somehow, after all that, your daughter tells me I'm *not* crazy."

Smiling, Sama raised her hands in mock protest. "When I get asked 'How old are you?' I often tend to reply 'Depends on who's counting.' I see 'Am I crazy?' as like that: Depends on who's asking. If you're asking me, I'd have to admit I might be crazy too, because I recognize what you're dreaming. It's a very, *very* old origin story. Though, frankly, your write-ups include much more detail than I've ever come across before."

Jeez. Not anywhere near as bad as Gracie had feared. And Pirin looked okay, a little revved even.

"The so-called experts say that dreams are, y'know, self-generated," Gracie began. "So our brains can synthesize memories, integrate experiences, cope with fears and trauma and unconscious desires, stuff like that. But," she continued, "these ohskal dreams are different, totally unlike any dreams I've ever had. Besides their cohesion, they also have this extraordinary clarity and detail."

Sama's eyes flared slightly as she nodded, an invitation to tell her more, Gracie decided.

So Gracie did—to a point. "I wake up thinking what I've dreamed is real. Because it *feels* every bit as real as my waking life. Even right now, my memories of the dreams are like the rest of my memories. And it all started only after I saw that thin blue thread of lightning touch the ohskal and pop this very powerful light all over the room, all over me. At least it *seemed* like the lightning caused the burst of light." She paused, her eyes meeting Sama's. "Do you think that could happen? And could it cause dreams?"

"Wish I knew," Sama replied.

"If lightning making contact with the ohskal *did* cause the burst of light—well, that raises some questions," said Pirin. "Like, did it happen naturally, say when lightning hit a defect in a crystal? Or could the ohskal have been intentionally jiggered to behave like that?"

"Feels awfully convenient, doesn't it?" Gracie shrugged. "Sure lets me off the hook crazy-wise. But it sounds *so* farfetched. Could be the dreams I'm having are just, well, the dreams I'm having, and all the rest—the lightning, the burst of light from the ohskal—was just a grand coincidence. Random. Unrelated."

Sama's head moved minimally back and forth in quiet objection. "Not so simple, Gracie. These dreams of yours have real meaning beyond your experience and understanding, right down to an intricately mythic story and strong hints of an actual language—a version of a language I recognize, as it happens."

"As for the ohskal, it can't tell us a whole lot, either," Pirin added. "Any sort of tests we might do now—even just subjecting it to various frequencies of light—could alter its current state. Means we'll never know the condition it was in before the lightning hit it."

Gracie laughed. "So it all adds up to a resounding maybe."

Sama laughed, too. "Yeah, I suppose it does. But I gotta say, 'maybe' can be pretty rich territory."

Chapter Seventeen: Show me

Pirin suggested it, and Gracie quickly agreed: Yes, for now let's stay "sorta quarantined." She really liked Sama, who was wonderfully, generously embracing even from six feet away—but Gracie wasn't nearly ready to engage the rest of the fam, at least not all at once, given that it included not only Pirin's father but also, thanks to the pandemic, Pirin's sister, two nieces, and a semi-present brother-in-law.

Thus began Gracie's "period of relative rest."

"What does that even mean—'relative rest'?" she asked Pirin. Again.

"It means no going back to work till Tuesday at the earliest, and only then with frequent breaks. No screens. No heavy lifting, physically or mentally. Acetaminophen as needed. It's all about not worsening your symptoms—especially that headache—or triggering new ones. So you take naps, wander around aimlessly, kiss me whenever you want."

Standing in the doorway to Pirin's office—the room tucked behind that door off to the left at the top of the stairs—Gracie grinned. Despite her intractable headache, that last part sounded promising.

Still at her desk, Pirin had yet to look up from the three monitors which seemed to so enthrall her. The Great Veech Farkas Takedown probably. And an opportunity.

Gracie tiptoed from the doorway to Pirin's chair and leaned in to kiss Pirin's neck just before she swung Pirin's chair around to face her. Both hands holding the chair's armrests, Gracie renewed her kisses, smooching her way from Pirin's jaw to Pirin's lips. Ah yes, even more intoxicating, that scent, those lips.

"I believe I'll do just fine with relative rest," she declared, swinging Pirin's chair back around to face the monitors. Retracing her steps, she halted. "Besides kissing you whenever I feel like, can I wander around on that path out back?"

"Uh, sure. It's longer than it looks, though. Once past the patio and the wildflowers, it loops through the woods, comes out right behind the etche. You'll find several little side paths, too."

"Sounds interesting. And how 'bout—?"

"No screens, no reading for at least three days." Pirin clamped her gaze onto Gracie. "And no matter how many times and how many ways you sneak up to it, the answer stays the same."

"Damn." Gracie turned toward the living room. "Jessica's gonna freak. We have deadlines. Gotta-be-done-yesterday deadlines."

"Jess'll understand. You'll see when she gets here."

"Here?"

"In about an hour. We're calling it afternoon tea on the deck."

"You talked to Jessica…" When the hell, Gracie wondered, could Pirin have talked to—?

And then Pirin was right behind her, arms enfolding her, that already-familiar sweet breath warm on her neck. "It'll work out," Pirin said, undulating slowly into Gracie, inspiring her to sync with the swaying contours of Pirin's compact breasts and those sleek hips and that magnificent mons that Gracie was already venerating, sight unseen, as it nestled into her—a perfect, spectacularly fervid fit. "Trust me."

Pirin nuzzled into Gracie's shoulder as they swayed together, both quickly entraining to the eager pulse of their newly discovered rhythm.

"I do believe you're changing the subject," Gracie declared.

Pirin's kiss didn't miss a beat. "I'm trying."

Jessica was more than understanding. "I've become a big believer in the healing benefits of relaxation," she declared soon after easing into one of Pirin's deck chairs. "So I've done some juggling, which'll give us margin. And time for you to recover."

Gracie had brought her phone out to the deck, expecting to check her calendar and rearrange the several meetings scheduled for the upcoming week—but Jessica waved that off. "I've already pushed it all to later." She winked at Pirin. "No doubt you'll be busting ass, Basamendi—but you, Gracie, have nothing to worry about for at least the next couple of weeks."

Ah, relief. "My throbbing head thanks you, Jess," Gracie said while Pirin flashed a told-ya grin.

The limits of that relief soon became evident, however, and as Gracie began to feel increasingly sluggish, Pirin noticed. "Surrender, Gracie," she said quietly. "You don't look so good. Why not go in and lie down for a while?"

"Yeah," Gracie agreed. "I think I will."

So much for exploring this new environment—the paths in the woods out back, where to stash her clothes and set up her laptop. Instead, the sledgehammering in her head kept her on the sofa, eyes closed beneath a folded towel to reduce the vehement glare.

Gracie didn't expect to fall asleep, didn't think she *had* fallen asleep. Not until she woke up remembering yet another dream. She contemplated sneaking off to attempt keying it all into her laptop—until she saw her smartphone on the coffee table next to her and realized that Pirin and Jess, still chatting away out on the deck, wouldn't spot her picking it up and talking to it:

⚡ At least, as I joined Eletun's campfire, my head didn't hurt. Not at all—even though Eletun sang of Analergin enduring the excruciating depths of Ilchullo cruelty.

She described how, every morning, the enslavers required the women in the copperforge pitcave to line up within their sight and, one after another, yell out "Here!" to prove they were still alive. At the copperforge pitcave, thirty-six shouts meant thirty-six live prisoners whom the enslavers didn't bother to identify individually.

The prisoners "paid" for their foodstuffs and other essentials by meeting a quota. Failure diminished both the quantity and quality of a pitcave's provisions. So Ilchullo's comparatively few enslavers tracked how much food was lowered into a pitcave on the pulley cart—but not water, since freshwater streams trickled, and during the wet monsoon poured, through every pitcave.

Rumor, passed from one brief generation of copperforge pitcave prisoners to the next, held that the other pitcaves—those devoted to mining and smelting—were even worse. For Ilchullo's prisoners, the differences between the caves were measured in how long one could survive in them. Many succumbed in less than a Suncycle, most in less than two, victims of some combination of abuse, despair, malnutrition, exhaustion, disease.

The high mortality of Ilchullo's prisoners did not threaten the wealth it generated, however; for every dead prisoner, two more arrived in chains.

Unlike most male prisoners, who were enslaved in the mining and smelting pitcaves, females worked both in pitcaves—producing tools, utensils, baskets, tunics, sleeping mats, where contact with the enslavers was minimal—and "up there" where they burned wood into charcoal and dispensed whatever might be needed in the pitcaves, which meant withstanding the enslavers' vicious moment-to-moment supervision.

Grim as the copperforge pitcave was and despite what Sineusi had told her, Analergin did not at first grasp what every other prisoner in Ilchullo understood: No prisoner *ever* came out of a pitcave alive. Although we don't know when she first accepted this terrible truth as she watched fear and suffering drive the women around her to brutalize each other, we do know that there had never been Taming at Ilchullo.

Yet Taming kindled between Sineusi and Analergin.

Besides ensuring that Analergin had food, Sineusi acquired a dead prisoner's tunic and foot coverings to protect her from the forges' sparks, found a sleeping mat to help warm her chilled, emaciated body. Nightmare after wracking nightmare, Sineusi wiped away Analergin's sweat and stroked her quaking body back to fitful sleep. Sineusi's soothing voice filled her forlorn world, its soft persistence finally eliciting a glance or a nod or a murmured thanks.

Despite horror continuing to drench her dreams, all she remembered upon waking was a man's face, jeering, contemptuous, always imposing humiliation and pain, its rough, hirsute features leering so close that she could feel the heat of his fetid breath. So she retreated—from other people, from her memories, from life itself.

Sineusi understood and continued to shield Analergin, contributing both her own share to the pitcave's quota and much of Analergin's as well. What she could not complete herself she induced from some of the other women with pleas, coercion, whatever was necessary.

At last came the day when the first signs of Taming's power appeared: Analergin stood unaided during the enslavers' morning prisoner count and called out "Here" without prompting when her turn came. She had seemed incognizant of this Ilchullo ritual only the day before.

"Ersean! You must be mending," Sineusi said.

"I am ready to work," Analergin replied. "If you keep doing my share, I will have killed you."

⚡

❖

"Basandere—*another one!*" Pirin's surprise pulled Gracie out of a what seemed to be some sort of reverie.

"Uhh…" Startled all the way awake, Gracie blinked at the ceiling, then at Pirin. "I, um—I must've fallen asleep again." She pushed herself upright. "What the hell. That's two now since I came in here to flake out. Two. In one afternoon."

"Two *dreams*, you mean?" Pirin tried to keep her face neutral, but this was downright surreal. "Like, back to back right here while you've been on the sofa?"

"Yeah, the voice memo I assume you've just listened to plus another one, which I've just woken up from. Wanna listen while I record it?"

Pirin nodded, silently handed Gracie her phone, and watched as Gracie closed her eyes and began to speak, slowly at first before gradually slipping into the same soothing chant Pirin had heard on the earlier recordings. She's gone to a different world, Pirin thought—or maybe she's bringing that world into this one:

⚡ I started out distinct from Analergin and tried to stay that way, but I was inexorably pulled until I was back in that wretched prison cave…

During my first real day of work while I stood next to Sineusi over the unyielding heat of the forge, I fainted only once. Couldn't raise my left arm above my shoulder or put full weight on my right leg, but I began to learn anyway—how to pound the hot red metal into the shapes of bowls and tools like pickaxes, hammers, chisels, awls.

Soon I was strong enough to contribute my full share to the pitcave's quota. But Sineusi was weakening. Without more rest, I realized, this woman who'd saved me would die like the three prisoners whose naked bodies I'd already watched being hauled up from the pitcave in the pulley cart.

So I sought ways to relieve some of Sineusi's burden, though I didn't say anything about what I was trying to do. Actually, I barely spoke to anyone, which bothered Sineusi.

"Ersean," she whispered one night as the pitcave went a little cooler with the darkness and we huddled next to each other on our mats. "You must talk. Words will help you remember."

"There is nothing to remember," I insisted.

"Not your mother?" she asked. "Not your home?"

"My people are dead and my home is gone forever."

"All the more reason to remember."

No—silence had become my refuge. Silence kept me from that amorphous, bulging red-fog terror I couldn't bear to confront because then I'd know, I'd *feel* what happened to me. What they did to me.

Better to work—even if every moment I worked in the pitcave was an act of surrender to my enslavement.

Better to work because my labor was also an act of rebellion: When I did some of Sineusi's work too then I was resisting Ilchullo, defying Ilchullo. The more I worked, the longer we would live.

Sineusi kept pestering, though—until the morning I harshly shoved her away from me, which I regretted immediately, even before I saw the flash of surprise in those tired eyes. All through that interminable day at the forge I avoided Sineusi's glances and couldn't keep my hands from shaking with a shame so great that I considered exiling myself to another cranny in the pitcave.

But when the long day finished, I returned to my place next to Sineusi's mat; our shared grotto seemed like the last refuge in all the Motherworld. I curled up tight trying to make myself as small as possible and beseeched the Mothers for help, for forgiveness.

"You did not eat tonight, Ersean," Sineusi said softly as she placed a bowl of food in front of me. "This is not good."

Unable to meet Sineusi's gaze, I ignored the food.

"Ersean," she gentled, delicately raising my chin with her finger until our eyes met. "I will not die here. Your love keeps me living."

That's when I lost it. "Sineusi, I am so *so* sorry," I managed to say through my sobs. "Can you forgive me?"

She held me until, finally, her voice and her touch calmed me. And then I asked her to tell me about her senba.

"Oh, I so miss my brave, brave girl."

Sineusi's wistful stories were of a child's curiosity and eagerness to help. How her senba would gather small fallen branches for their fire. How her senba knew before anyone else when rain was coming. How her senba always found safe shelter when they had to hide from Privation patrols. How her senba screamed when Sineusi was caught and taken away: "I will find you, Amatchi! I will find you and we *will* be free again!"

We slept entwined that night, Sineusi and I, and I woke to the slim light of dawn in the pitcave, a distant voice whispering, "Remember. Remember and reclaim…"

And so I started to remember. My mind became animated with sounds and images from my past. As those memories showed me all that I had been, I became someone *truly* beginning to heal. The next time Sineusi called me Ersean, I told her "I am between life and death no longer. I am Analergin."

Sineusi responded with genuine joy, and her celebratory laughter—tempered by the need to not attract *them*—was noticed by the other women. Why, they demanded, would anyone here laugh like that? Sineusi told them my name and insisted I recount a memory I'd shared with her in the night.

So I whispered it to them…

"My mother was lost too soon after weaning me, and—ugh!—I hated the horrible mush fed the weaned ones. One day I decided to look for my mother's breast in the forest, and before long I stumbled into a hole left by a tree ripped away by the Seastorm that also took my mother.

"Soon I heard one of the Mothers who was searching for me. But I did not want to be taken back and fed that mush, so I hid in the hole and stayed very, very still. The Mother looking for me never noticed me or even the hole. And then I fell asleep.

"When I woke the hole was gone. Someone was carrying me. I saw a cat's fur and jouncing green forest and sky: I was in the cat's mouth. She was a very large cat, but I was not afraid since I felt no pain and did not know that cats eat babies. I thought we were playing, so I stroked her fur.

"After a while, she put me on the ground and laid down on her side. Two kittens I had not seen before scampered right to her breasts. She had so many breasts! I thought she might have my mother's breast, so I crawled over to one of them and suckled. It tasted wonderful!

"The cat let me suckle that day and on many days afterward. She became, for me, Mother Cat—though I have wondered since if I was supposed to be dinner the day she found me."

While Sineusi smiled and the women muffled their amusement to avoid the enslavers' attention, I understood that my simple tale had somehow changed our grim lives.

⚡ Pirin didn't realize she'd been claimed by the rhythm of Gracie's voice until silence jolted her. Which was okay—now they could talk about this latest dream, right?

Wrong: The effort seemed to have exhausted Gracie, whose eyes remained closed, whose deep, unhurried breathing confirmed that within seconds of finishing her recording she'd slipped once more into sleep.

This, Pirin reminded herself only slightly nervously, was to be expected. So she'd let Gracie snooze while she—well, she could take her pick: Focus on the paying job she'd been giving short shrift for too many weeks, do the hell-bent workout on the elliptical in the office that her body begged for, review what her zero-click deployments had collected on Veech, finish cleaning her drones, resume the long-neglected care and feeding of her Bonecrusher recycle—

Nope: Alarmed at how much Gracie needed sleep, Pirin called her mother. Sama managed to calm her down, explaining that concussion recovery can be like that. Let Gracie sleep and keep watch, Sama said. So Pirin brought her work laptop into the living room and camped out next to Gracie, who slept like a perfectly normal person while she churned through the fraud case reports she'd dodged for too long.

But after Gracie roused to use the bathroom, she went to the bedroom and was soon asleep *again*.

When Pirin woke early Sunday morning, Gracie seemed not to have moved at all in the night. Then Pirin noticed her phone, clutched in her hand: Sometime in the wee hours, she must have picked it up.

Gingerly, Pirin slithered the device from between Gracie's fingers without waking her—and, yes, there it was—a new voice memo recorded around three a.m.

"You talked to this thing for *eighteen minutes*? How? How the *hell* didn't I hear you?" Even Pirin's high-pitched whisper didn't stir Gracie. Nor did the sounds of the recording when Pirin poked PLAY:

⚡ The women of the copperforge pitcave insisted on hearing the Tale of Mother Cat again and again. Each time Analergin told it she added detail, shifted emphasis, grew more expressive as she found new ways to make her audience smile and sometimes even laugh.

After a while, the Tale of Mother Cat carried an unmistakable Rhythm of its own which, eventually, the women of the copperforge pitcave shared, a kind of whispered chant, and in their sharing they strengthened the Tale's Rhythm until it entrained them all.

At first Analergin did not recognize the effects of this entrainment on herself. Too accustomed to a prisoner's impotence, she feared she was succumbing to illness, illusion. Delusion.

Yet there was no denying that when Analergin sustained the Tale's Rhythm with her lilting hum, her hands became unusually warm. And not only that; when she massaged her battered leg and shoulder with those warm hands, her limbs felt better and, in time, became appreciably stronger.

Might she also help make others feel better, become stronger?

Certainly she would try—especially with Sineusi, whose lifeforce was too quickly ebbing. And yes, her touch did help restore some of the strength Sineusi so desperately needed.

This was noticed, and soon others approached her, haggard and hushed in their despair. She gave what she could, sometimes able to help in small ways. But it was not nearly enough. Often she knew simply by looking into a woman's eyes that she could do nothing. Too many had been wasting away for too long; they died because they no longer had strength for anything else.

Even so, the women's faith remained steadfast: First Sineusi and then the others began to call her Analergin Segubansi—powerful diviner whose hand renews life.

"No," Analergin told them, "I have no power. I renew nothing."

Yet know this true: Each time Analergin hummed her Tale's Rhythm she was roused once more to yearn for freedom, despite the immense gap between the release she envisioned and the exhausting effort of surviving in the copperforge pitcave.

Worst were those bleak wet-monsoon days of malevolent Winds spinning ceaseless rain down upon the women to mock their relentless oppression, days when no sunlight glinted across the pitcave's walls.

On those days, Analergin stared at the listless rock so different than the granite of the first Privation cave that imprisoned her. Alternately despondent and defiant, knowing a secret lurked in the rough stone surrounding her, she'd begun to sense a pathway, an exit from Ilchullo. But where?

Night after night, to the Mothers she sent her appeals for insight as she drifted into sleep warmed by Sineusi's embrace, only to awaken into a new day as crushed by hunger and failure as ever.

Until the night she dreamed of the pitcave lush with green vegetation and ripened fruit, of the women smiling and comfortable on their mats, lavished with food. This dream returned several times before she grasped its message: Food, and the aspirations it nourishes, must come first—*before* freedom.

But how might she obtain more food while imprisoned in a pitcave, enfeebled by enslavers who were quite successfully working her to death?

Through each debilitating day she found herself battling an impulse to succumb to hopelessness, to simply stop and lie down and die.

Then one morning she looked up—and kept on looking. Usually just a quick glance at the sky above the pitcave opening left her deeply dispirited because that opening was so out of reach; even the sun's strongest rays only briefly lit a slivered path across the pitcave floor.

But on this day, as Analergin beheld a blue, cloudless sky, she noticed something dark trace a slow, purposeful, widening coil high above the cave opening. Bele perhaps, whose freedom she so somberly envied.

That night, wide awake in the dark of the pitcave, she imagined herself bathed in a bright, vast light. She floated in it, laughed in it as Bele flew overhead. She slipped into sleep imagining that light twinkling and dancing on the pitcave's walls, alive and intelligent and playful.

In the next morning's twilight, even before she opened her eyes, Analergin understood she had awakened before anyone else—and sensed that everything had changed: Crisper air, Sineusi's breathing had eased, and she knew the women around her would have more comfort from their rest. When at last the others woke, they moved to an ethereal cadence she had never sensed before.

As the women began nurturing the fires of their forges, Analergin watched how the first rays of sunlight teased the pitcave's upper walls. All through the day, she watched sunlight glitter and flash off the rough, uneven rock, sometimes with momentary brilliance.

By day's end she had seen it—and wondered why she had failed to see it before.

The next day, she stole time from forge-work and spent it gathering what soil she could find in the pitcave to spread over an area near the stream that supplied their water—a spot the enslavers couldn't see either from above or from the tunnel doorway. She deposited the collected soil along with ashes from the pitcave's forges, then added the women's feces, which she had persuaded them to heat in the forge fires.

"Dominion Almighty, it *stinks!*" Sineusi complained to a chorus of agreement.

"The heat of the fires purifies it," explained Analergin. "And once purified, it makes the soil much richer."

This is when Sineusi grasped what Analergin was trying to do. Together they mixed soil, ash, charcoal, manure, and even their menses for what Analergin called a Tending where she planted seeds of soybean, cabbage, and water spinach set aside from her own scant food allotment.

The other women said little, but they looked upon Analergin with pity and vast disappointment, having concluded that the pitcave had deformed her mind. No one believed anything would grow on a dark, rocky pitcave floor a hundred hands below ground.

Despondency overtook the women—until the first shoots of soybean appeared, which beget grudging curiosity. Several days later, as other shoots emerged, the women sorted into two camps: a few cautiously hopeful, encouraged by Sineusi; the rest hostilely skeptical, led by one named Jarrai, the copperforge pitcave's longest surviving prisoner, who grumbled that scraggly, inedible grasses had occasionally tried to grow in that place—and had always failed.

"These plantings will succeed," Analergin responded as she gazed up at the pitcave walls. "Especially if we make a few changes."

She insisted that a forge be moved about two reaches, claiming damage to her Tending from its light-blocking smoke. The cautiously hopeful did what Analergin wanted, though the rest stopped speaking to her. Only when the shoots took recognizable shape—yes, they were real soy and cabbage and water spinach plantings—did the skeptical women relent.

Yet jealousy rather than joy replaced their doubt and anger. Most assumed Analergin would keep the soybeans and cabbage and water spinach for herself. Led by Jarrai, some of them were ready to take possession of the Tending. They were stopped by Sineusi, who nearly killed one of the skeptics and who was in turn stopped by Analergin's demand for peace.

How, the women wanted to know, could such things grow in the darkness of a pitcave? Would Analergin share her secret? Would she share her food?

"This Tending is for all of us," she told them.

Then she explained quite precisely how the shimmering, crystalline rock of the pitcave walls reflected the sun's rays onto the Tending.

"The reflected light is weaker, so growing is slower down here and what grows will be less robust—but thanks to how we have encouraged the soil, these plants can grow well enough. And we can make the sunlight somewhat stronger, too, if we chisel the rock—" She pointed upward. "—There. And also there. If we do that and keep our Tending well-watered, each of us will have a bit more to eat."

Soon everyone in the pitcave participated—even Jarrai, who was longest reluctant. While most of the women labored at their forges through the arduous days, a few permitted Analergin to climb their backs and furtively hew the pitcave walls to better steer sunlight onto the Tending. Others carved more space at the Tending's margins, scraped the entire pitcave floor clean of soil, transported and mixed in more ash, charcoal, manure, and menses.

The cabbage ripened first. In a little more than a Mooncycle, the women were able to pick a few cabbage leaves even as the plants continued to grow. Soon the water spinach, then the soybeans followed. The greens' seeds, they agreed, would be set aside to plant another growth. Meanwhile, every woman in the copperforge pitcave ate of cabbage and water spinach and soybeans, each one enjoying a small helping of the bounty of Analergin's insight.

Only those who have felt grievous hunger burn their bellies yet could not find strength to lift a hand to sustenance, only those who have looked helplessly into the hollowed, dulling eyes of someone loved and beyond saving even with the greatest banquet—only those can truly comprehend what Analergin's Tending meant.

Eventually, four times during each Mooncycle, the women in the copperforge pitcave celebrated a modest extra meal thanks to what they were able to gather from their Tending—no more than a few swallows, yet those few swallows sparked life amidst overwhelming death, nourished hope, powered defiance.

No longer did the women cheat or harm each other. In their acceptance of another ethic, they deposed Ilchullo's cruel cynicism in favor of trust and love and loyalty.

And as they gained fortitude from their few swallows and from each other, the women began to exploit the enslavers' complacence: The tools they forged to meet their quota became just slightly smaller, the chains and hoops and nails just a bit thinner. From the embezzled copper-tin they fashioned their own secret tools and extra implements to feed into the quota on days when someone was sick or caring for the Tending instead of working a forge.

Thus were sown the first seeds of the New Motherworld.

⚡ "Dreams within dreams. What's that about?" Pirin asked when Gracie finally did wake up.

"No clue. I just try to say what I remember before the heaviness comes back. Everything's so cumbersome, so dulled."

Everything, Gracie noted, except the ohskal dreams, which kept on coming with a clarity that shimmered and echoed through Gracie's voice recordings. The written ohskal dreams had been interesting, fascinating even, but the ones Gracie dictated—something about them riveted Pirin.

On Monday morning, Gracie recorded another one. Pirin discovered it around midday but refrained from asking aloud the question that now haunted her—What the hell is happening here?—as she clicked it up:

⚡ Sineusi believed the food from the Tending saved a number of women in its first few Mooncycles, and she believed she was one of them. Only four had died instead of the usual seven or eight. For this, Sineusi was intensely grateful, but she also worried.

"Analergin Segubansi, what if they notice?" she asked one day as they worked their forge. "We no longer give them enough dead."

Analergin had not considered this; her efforts had been devoted to bringing Taming into the pitcave, to sparking hope. Now a knot of foreboding tightened in her chest.

"Will they come in here to inspect?"

Sineusi had no answer.

Analergin shut her eyes against a rising dread. Might the enslavers discover the Tending and kill them all? Would that depraved man enter the copperforge pitcave seeking her for his perversions?

What should she do? What *could* she do?

Perhaps not accidentally, the slight breeze that suddenly brushed the air around her carried the hint of a whisper... "You *know* what to do, Analergin..."

But did she?

Through the Mooncycles during which she attempted to revive in herself what the Subendi Mothers called the Sublimities, she had divulged this effort to no one, not even Sineusi, though she did gradually reveal her rehabilitated Weathering skills, since such an aptitude served the Tending well.

The women had quickly become accustomed to asking what the next day would bring from the Sky, yet Analergin hesitated to show them more as she regained her abilities. She had learned how utterly such skills as Sublime Perception frightened the peoples of Privation, even those Privation victimized.

But had the time come to reveal more?

She'd remembered and reclaimed the way she once escaped the granite cave-place (albeit not for long), and though the copperforge pitcave had been hacked out of a very different sort of rock, she nevertheless sought spots where she might best sense those certain subtle vibrations from the world beyond it.

Perhaps not accidentally, that spot turned out to be where she slept, next to Sineusi.

The rest of the copperforge pitcave women watched her but said nothing when she rolled up her mat to lay on the bare pitcave ground, hands and feet flat, eyes closed, breathing slowed. They pretended to ignore her when she forged a copper-tin spike and pounded it deep into a cleft in the ground next to where her mat had been, then resumed lying on the ground, now gripping her spike...

Analergin told no one when at last her hands and feet sensed something initially faint, chaotic. She waited and waited, calming herself...then, at last, came a parade of tiny tremors—yes, quivers, tingles, and flutters, but also deeper, lower-frequency vibrations, too.

It had begun...

There was no "first time" she "heard" the flowing waters of nearby Rivers, the rush of Wind sweeping over hills, through forests, into pitcaves. These Perceptions simply became gradually present. Eventually she "heard" human voices, though at first the words were unintelligible. As they became clearer, she realized she was "hearing" the enslavers at the pitcave rim above them.

Yet even this was not enough. To grasp the scope of Ilchullo, to understand the landscape around the prison and what escape routes might hide within it, she needed to "see."

Once more, Analergin closed her eyes. Once more she implored... Please, Alama, show me, show me.

⚡ Pirin blinked at the too-familiar word. She'd seen it at least half a dozen times in Gracie's write-ups, heard it in Gracie's recordings, and now here it was again: *Alama*, syncope of "ahal," meaning power, ability, and "ama"—mother.

How does this English-only-speaking stranger from Belmont via Wayland, whose people floated over from Wales a hundred and fifty years ago, come up with words like "Alama"? Words like "Amatchi" and "Subendi" and...?

Even in her debilitated state Gracie seemed to understand Pirin's worry. Yet she had no explanation. "The only times I feel anywhere near normal is when I'm dreaming. More like hyper-normal, really. I'm alert and aware in these dreams. Everything's wonderfully clear and crisp and I'm all there. Instead of being here, I guess."

Then she apologized.

Then she ate a piece of toast and went back to bed.

Chapter Eighteen: When the time is right

Several dreams now that Gracie had somehow recorded when Pirin was out of earshot. But how? Pirin had stayed close by, listened intently for Gracie's voice. Consciously or not, had Gracie found—maybe even chosen—moments when Pirin was busy elsewhere?

Listening once again to the rhythm of Gracie's voice, husky and slow, Pirin grasped how it had a sneaky way of stretching the ordinary almost beyond recognition while simultaneously epitomizing it. The effect was unsettling; Pirin had begun to question where the edges of possibility lay.

Come Tuesday morning, a groggy Gracie pointed to her phone as she stumbled out of bed and headed for the bathroom. "'Nother one," she mumbled. "Getting intense."

Pirin hesitated for only a moment before clicking up Gracie's newest entry:

⚡ That's the thing about dreams. They shift of their own accord. So there I was one more time seated at Eletun's campfire just as someone worriedly asked "But Analergin found help, yes?"

"Indeed," Eletun responded, smiling at the round of shushing from her audience. "From Bele, who followed Analergin to Ilchullo. And when at last Analergin achieved Resonance with Bele's Rhythm, her Sublime Perception rose with Bele high into the air."

I watched the women around the campfire nod and murmur their anticipation while they waited for Eletun to continue. Eletun said nothing, however. She was at it *again*: Staring hard at me—and I knew what she was about to do.

I shook my head, opened my mouth to object…

Too late, as usual—and suddenly I was soaring skyward, reveling with Analergin in the movement, the light, the beautiful vast expanse all around me as Bele slowly spiraled.

I looked where Analergin looked: down. This was my first view of Ilchullo, from far above the copperforge pitcave, and it robbed me of breath, depleting my horrified gasp. Analergin recalled nothing of her arrival at this appalling place, and the women's sparse descriptions hadn't prepared either of us for its vast size.

Ilchullo's perimeter—at least five miles around, I'd say, marked by a rough stone and earth rampart about fifteen feet high—encompassed part of a north-south ridge of tropical savanna overlooking the confluence of a large, lazy south-flowing River roughly half a mile to its east and a smaller tributary a quarter mile to its north.

Among the ridge's minor knolls and shallow vales I saw numerous dark, roundish holes. A couple of seconds passed before I understood: Each hole was a pitcave opening. A few were wider and shallower than the others, and especially smoky; after a moment I understood: these pits produced charcoal.

Grimy prisoners trudged along dirt paths snaking between the openings, some carrying, others pulling or pushing loads while enslavers prodded and berated them, often with whips. I also noticed several ramps leading down to smaller vertical openings that seemed to have doors—these, I concluded, were entrances to the tunnel network connecting all the pitcaves.

Despite its size, Ilchullo had only one way in and out—an imposingly fortified north-facing portal that commanded a view of the tributary just before it met the larger River to the east. North of this sole gate I spotted a wharf and realized from a foggy fragment of Analergin's memory that this was where Ilchullo's prisoners arrived by boat before being marched up a bluff to the prison.

Nope, can't go north.

Eastward from Ilchullo's ridge, those above ground could see a broad flood plain stretching for miles beyond the far side of the larger River. To the south stood a small settlement, likely where Ilchullo's enslavers lived.

Scratch east and south.

To the west, however, I saw our salvation—and our profound challenge: Small stands of shrub dotted a few miles of dense, rolling grassland gradually populated with more and larger trees as it rose in elevation. Then, about ten miles off, thickly forested hills ascended to much higher, starkly foreboding peaks with plenty of places to hide. Mountains really, without a single sign of human activity.

The trick: reaching those forested hills undiscovered.

I retreated then from Analergin's Sublime Perception. And no wonder: She was overrun again by tangled memories of beatings, of *that* face twisted in ruthless laughter at her agony. *That* face haunted her, renewing the nightmares Sineusi's touch had driven away, threatening once more to steal her sleep and infest her waking.

I tried to escape her, but I could not. For what seemed like days afterward, as Analergin fought for breath because she dreaded another look at Ilchullo, so did I. No matter that, unlike her, I knew I was safe in Pirin's sanctum.

At least I *thought* so. But actually I couldn't be sure of, well, of anything much. For a period that lacked beginning or end, I didn't experience time—or waking—like a regular person. I seemed instead to be slipping in and out of Analergin's awful existence…

Except sometimes I was awake.

Maybe.

Then, during one Ilchullo afternoon rest period, Analergin (and I along with her) glanced skyward as Bele's black wings caught her eye; she steadied her breathing and, a heartbeat later, she was high above the prison gazing down at it.

This time a mist shrouded the land, a mist she'd never sensed from the depths of the pitcave, and she heard a woman's voice—a voice we both recognized—whisper "The time has come. The time is *now*."

⚡ Pirin took the dream's last sentence seriously. It was, she believed, a warning.

She'd always fretted about how Gracie might react upon learning her darker truths. Should she—*could* she—keep those truths hidden, a collection of eternally unrevealed secrets? She'd been ducking this question, hoping to find an obvious answer "aldi egokia denean." When the time is right.

Now Pirin could see into that unavoidable sometime ahead when her secrets would demand she lie to Gracie. And for the first time, she knew she would refuse. Because of these moments when Gracie hid nothing and risked everything, she would refuse to lie.

And then what?

Would Gracie stay? Would Gracie be able to bear the sight of an entirely truthful Pirin Basamendi?

At least, Pirin reminded herself, she still had some time. Those dark truths could wait where she'd stashed them. For a while yet anyway she could relish the experience of having another human being right there with her twenty-four seven—albeit a very sleepy human being whose dreams kept on coming:

⚡ The sun was close to setting as I walked a path through a forest—maybe the woodland behind Pirin's place, I thought, and I was juiced at the chance to finally explore it. But as I walked on the sky began darkening into night and I got skittish, which was when I saw a campfire.

And I just knew it was Eletun's. A few seconds later I came upon the usual band of women already settled around it.

Okay then, another dream. But hey, maybe this time I'd be able to decline the offer and wake myself up. Please, Eletun, just this once…

"I do give you credit for being stubborn," she said from behind me as she placed her hand on my shoulder—and immediately I was again "with" Analergin.

Can't say how much time had passed, but I noticed that her Sublime Perception had evolved: She no longer needed to sync up with Bele's Rhythm to "see" and "hear" the broader, subtler vibrational frequencies—what Analergin called Resonances—generated by the world around her. She now entrained directly with these frequencies.

Even so, she understood too well that whatever Privation peoples did not understand they generally tried to destroy. So the women still knew nothing about her using Sublime Perception to spy on Ilchullo's enslavers.

This changed unexpectedly (for me, anyway) after Analergin had "returned" from monitoring a clutch of enslavers at the pitcave rim. Standing at her forge, gazing at the hammer in her hand, she had an epiphany.

Could it really be *so* simple?

"The enslavers are afraid of us," she told Sineusi.

Nearby, Jarrai overheard and gaped in disbelief. "Afraid of *us?*"

"Have you ever wondered why there are *two* doors between the pitcave and the tunnel rather than only one?" Analergin asked quietly, awed by her own belated comprehension. "Why whenever they unbar those doors there are never fewer than four enslavers, all of them armored and carrying weapons? Why they always command us to lie flat on the ground before they shove new prisoners in here?"

"They enjoy making us grovel," growled Jarrai.

"They make us grovel because all these pickaxes and hammers and chisels and shovels we make—these are not merely mining tools." Analergin lifted the hammer she held. "These are—"

"—Weapons," Sineusi declared, her eyes sparking. "In *our* hands."

"Exactly," Analergin responded. "And this terrifies the enslavers."

"They do not act afraid," Jarrai snarled as she approached Analergin.

Sineusi stepped in front of Jarrai, but she spoke to Analergin. "How do you know this?"

Don't risk it, I implored—prevaricate. But Analergin did not.

"I can 'hear' what they say," she said. "I can 'see' what they do."

"From here." Jarrai's tone had flattened. "You can see them from here."

"Yes," Analergin replied.

Jarrai squinted her doubt. "When you lie down and hold that spike you insisted on beating into the ground?"

"Yes. I Perceive with the most clarity then, though sometimes I can sense even from—"

"—From where you stand right now?" Jarrai demanded.

"Perhaps." Analergin closed her eyes. "I can try."

Jarrai moved away, as though something dangerous in Analergin might be contagious, but Sineusi stayed put. This Analergin couldn't see, but she knew (and I along with her). She lowered her head and hummed very softly, the vibration in her throat tingling through her lips and her nose. The women went mute, as did Analergin a few seconds later. She stood unmoving, statue-still. And stood. And stood.

And because I stood with her, Perceived with her, I was aware of her silent chant urging the women to return to their forges lest the pitcave's extended quiet attract the attention of the enslavers above. I was also aware that Analergin had no idea what she was doing or what might come of it; hers was an act of pure, blind instinct.

An instinct that proved breathtakingly true.

One by one, all the women but Jarrai, Sineusi, and Analergin herself drifted back to their forges and resumed the pitcave's cacophonous work. Some long minutes later, Analergin lifted her head and opened her eyes.

"Listen," she said to Sineusi and Jarrai. "The others have made a Rhythm." And indeed, the women's tool-hammering at the forges, initially jarringly random, had entrained to a single distinct cadence. "The secret to all of this lurks in the Rhythms we share."

Jarrai closed in on Analergin. "But did you—?"

Smiling, Analergin lifted her gaze to the pitcave opening far above them. "Our quieted forges *did* attract the enslavers' attention. Fortunately, the others returned to their tasks quickly enough, so by the time I withdrew, all but two enslavers had dispersed. Those two are still near the pulley cart frame, complaining. The enslavers complain a great deal."

I had "inhabited" Analergin long enough to fear how Jarrai might respond to this revelation. For a long moment she said nothing. She simply stared.

Then Sineusi nodded.

Another moment passed and, incredibly, Jarrai also nodded.

I don't know how the rest of the women understood what had happened, but they did, and without abandoning their new Rhythm, nods and murmurs of agreement looped around the forges: They, too, believed Analergin Segubansi.

That they did not pummel her dead on the spot signaled the depth of their desperation. Certainly, every one of them grasped that their meager Tending could never sustain them indefinitely.

What the women of the copperforge pitcave needed was freedom. *Real* freedom—which meant finding a way out of Ilchullo.

But how?

Analergin did not know. So much had been taken from her by Privation, by Ilchullo and its enslavers. She'd begun, however, to remember and reclaim the threads of what she'd lost. Starting with the Sublimity she'd just inadvertently revisited.

She'd done it once before. Long ago, back on Subendi when she was very young, she'd fooled the Mothers and only later learned that this was what Subendiak called Trancing. Later, the fearsome AmaHeri had undertaken her training in this Sublimity—only to declare her performance disappointing before stalking away. Shortly after that the island blew up.

Now Analergin vowed to teach herself Trancing.

Eager to help, the women in the pitcave granted her occasional relief from forge-work, and soon Analergin envisioned how she must proceed:

First, use Sublime Perception to locate an enslaver and identify his basic Rhythm.

Next, generate a Rhythm close enough to the enslaver's that *his* Rhythm gradually entrains to it.

After that, carefully alter this entraining Rhythm's frequency— typically by gradually slowing it down—to induce the enslaver into Trance (*aha*, I thought: dissociated disinhibition!).

Finally, introduce Resonances—harmonically-related frequencies—that insinuate directives to the enslaver, who will act on them unawares.

That, anyway, was Analergin's strategy.

The initial two steps were comparatively straightforward, since so many elements of human physiology, like pulse and breathing and heartbeat and muscles and brainwaves, can't help but be seduced into Rhythmic entrainment.

Alas, the rest turned out to be much more problematic.

Analergin tried. And tried.

And got nowhere.

Perhaps if the other women helped her...

So she explained it all to them as best she could explain any Sublimity to Privation people, taught them to consciously synchronize their metal-pounding at the forges and then ease it into the slower, Trance-inducing Rhythm she needed. Led by Sineusi and Jarrai, the women generated what sounded to me like a three-beats-per second metallic percussion.

At first Analergin's efforts had no effect. Her multiple attempts failed again and again, which condensed the increasingly panicky women into a mob, more and more fevered, the menace of their intensifying belligerence manifest in suspicious glares and muttered epithets.

But once-skeptical Jarrai now had stalwart faith in Analergin. She helped the others resist their fear, persuaded them to keep pounding out Analergin's Rhythm. And slowly, long habituated to apathy and carelessness, the enslavers succumbed to the shrewd commands Analergin implanted into their routines via her Resonances.

Analergin's first command led to more provisions unconsciously piled onto the pulley cart and lowered into the copperforge pitcave.

After a half-Mooncycle of noticeably fuller pulley carts, the women's rancor evaporated and they venerated Analergin. They had witnessed her master seduction in its most exalted form, as much psychological as physical, as much timing as focused Intent, as much cadent sound as sleight of mind.

This prodigious achievement also produced discoveries:

Every enslaver she "encountered" despised Ilchullo almost as much as its prisoners did. Soon she realized how little she needed to do. Their quest for relief led the enslavers to nearly constantly inebriate (as well as gamble and indulge in casual cruelty toward prisoners). For instance, those overseeing Ilchullo's huge perimeter and numerous aboveground paths at night did so only intermittently; most of the time they were asleep.

Given how patently dissociated and disinhibited Ilchullo's enslavers already were and how deep their indifference ran, Analergin's three-beats-per second Rhythm combined with their near-constant intoxication made them spectacularly easy to Trance into near-torpor.

Yet after several Mooncycles of daily probing, and despite "encounters" with numerous Ilchullo enslavers, she had yet to discern *him*, the man who'd so relished abusing her. This brought no relief, however: She was quite certain he remained at Ilchullo, and the prospect of facing him petrified her.

Despite her fear, she did her best to maintain her daily Trancing of the low-rank enslavers watching over the copperforge pitcave and patrolling Ilchullo's perimeter and tunnels. The effort exhausted her; Sublime Trancing required not merely Perception of extremely subtle vibrations beyond the scope of human sight and hearing, but also dynamic manipulation of these vibrations in exceedingly nuanced ways.

"Sineusi," Analergin whispered one night to the woman who stroked her throbbing head and sought for her a calm beyond words, "I will not have strength for this much longer."

"So the time has come?" asked Sineusi.

"Yes," Analergin whispered. Grateful that Sineusi didn't ask anything else—for she had no plan, no solution—she exhaled quietly as Sineusi's breath warmed the nape of her neck, and soon she slipped into a translucent sleep. In her dreams, she and AmaBidari and Otchani danced through Ilchullo's network of tunnels, opening the doors to all the pitcaves, and the prisoners ran free...

Before the first gray light of the next morning, she was awake, her scheme completely formed.

And she began to speak openly to the others of escape.

⚡ "Yeah," Pirin whispered to herself as Gracie's last sentence echoed. "Being some asshole's prey really sucks."

Unlike Analergin, though, Pirin could keep track of the man so eager to harm her. Now all she had to do was wait for him to signal his next move. She worried, of course: What if he didn't signal anything, at least not via smartphone? That would leave her clueless, flailing.

Thus while Gracie slept on, Pirin diligently monitored Veech Farkas's smartphone. And came to wonder: Was it a good thing or a bad thing that the strains of a pandemic-necessitated prison lockdown were spinning the snarling wolf into full-tilt stir-crazy?

He devoted much of his phone time to bugging his mother for the number of this or that "old friend," which the woman dutifully produced. These Pirin immediately zero-clicked and added to her lengthening to-be-investigated list. Almost as immediately, she fed every Farkas-related number she zero-clicked into her Spotter app. Theoretically, this could liberate her from having to live-monitor Farkas's conversations.

But as Gracie's sleepfest continued, Pirin hunkered in the office, listening in more and more often to get a sense of the dude—his lingo, his plans, vulnerabilities, prejudices. His patterns.

Hardly a surprise, then, that somewhere in there Gracie recorded another ohskal dream:

⚡ "I cannot see what you see," Sineusi said to Analergin. "But I know that you have seen a way."

Analergin lowered her head but did not speak.

"Tell us," Jarrai entreated her while others whispered encouragement.

Analergin began with a safe subject: the weather. "I see that the wet monsoon will recede early this year, so the Rivers will be full and flowing fast even as the land in the Mountains' rainshadow on the western frontier is drying."

"Ah, the western frontier," murmured one of the women. "High grass on the savanna, easier to hide. Easier to move around the bogs once the rain retreats."

Analergin nodded; this woman knew the terrain. "Yes, Mardul—precisely."

"But if we escape to the west, they will catch us before nightfall," worried a woman called Honsoli.

"I agree," said Analergin. "So we must misdirect them."

"How?" asked Sineusi.

"I do not remember much of arriving here," Analergin began, "but most of the rest of you do."

"Yes, yes," Jarrai interjected, impatient as always. "Up the River in chains on a boat we had to row against the current while the enslavers whipped us. Then bullied ashore, up that beastly bluff, into the holding pit just inside the gate where those drunks spent the night brutalizing us before sending us to our enslavement."

"This time, Jarrai," Analergin replied, "we will put that boat to better use." She raised a hand before Jarrai could speak again. "Let me tell you how."

Analergin divulged what Sublime Perception had shown her: that the boat brought new prisoners twice each Mooncycle, then waited overnight for the ore and smelted metals piled just inside the prison gate to be loaded aboard the next day and floated down the River toward the distant heart of Sundaselai.

"When the boat comes a Mooncycle from now, we make our escape," Analergin proposed. "The wet monsoon will be receding, *plus* a shadowed moon will darken the night sky sufficiently to hide us."

"So," noted Sineusi, "we have a Mooncycle to prepare."

Every woman assented.

They then memorized the maps of hiding places and locations of food and water sources to the west that Analergin had "seen" and sketched in charcoal on the pitcave floor. They set aside flint rocks to make fires; crafted tools for cutting, digging, and defense; made replicas of the key Analergin had "seen" that would open all the locks on Ilchullo's doors, including those to the tunnel ramps and the prison's single gate to the outside world.

Analergin had not yet revealed her entire plan, for she did not believe all the women would have strength and will to accompany her as far as her Intent was taking her. Perhaps some would join her. Perhaps none would. She could not know, but she could try to set them all free, she could try to give them all a chance and a choice.

When at last the dark, moonless night was upon them, they trembled, they wept, they hugged. They whispered to each other: Be brave.

⚡ Gracie had been sleeping almost constantly for five days. *Five.*

"I'm kinda freaking, Ama," Pirin said to her mother as she paced her deck. "Should I take her to—?"

Once more, though, Sama counseled waiting, since during those brief periods when Gracie was awake she was cogent and showed no signs of physical distress beyond exhaustion and a slowly-ebbing headache. Plus Gracie's voice memos indicated no cognitive impairment. Another twenty-four hours, they decided together. If Gracie still needs to sleep twenty-plus hours a day after tomorrow, they'll bring her to the neurologist who saw her right after she got whacked.

An hour or so later, Pirin noticed Gracie's phone on the coffee table in the living room with a yellow sticky note attached: "Eletun's still at it, keeping me on my toes, wearing me out. But I'm not so groggy now, will try to stay awake through dinner tonight." So, one more time, Pirin pressed PLAY:

⚡ I have no recollection of Eletun whooshing me into the pitcave, but she must have, because there I was "with" Analergin, whose Sublime Perception enabled me to "watch" the boat full of new prisoners approach Ilchullo's wharf. And I understood: one last chance to check everything one last time.

I'd already stuffed a flint grinder and some clear crystals into the pockets Sineusi had sewn onto my tunic—but, sadly, no blackglass. We had only the copper-tin blades and axes we'd secretly forged to aid our escape.

I'd told no one, not even Sineusi, about the dazzling, reckless Lightning-bolt Energy that had begun to charge the air around me even before the sun had risen. Said nothing about the voice—distinctly female, far away, anguished yet determined, a voice I'd heard before—calling "We *will* be free again!"

Tears filled my eyes as her words reverberated. Because at best only thirty-six of us would be free again; I'd been unable to conceive a plan that would liberate all the prisoners trapped in Ilchullo. Every scenario I'd played out ended with hundreds of dead people, and too many ended with every copperforge pitcave woman dead, too.

As it was, Trancing an enslaver to unbar the outer door between Ilchullo's labyrinthine network of tunnels and the copperforge pitcave had proved difficult. My first three attempts fizzled, and I was losing strength and hope. But Sineusi encouraged me to try again. And again.

The seventh time, I succeeded—but by then I was shaking so much I couldn't get the key I held to unlock the inner door. Mardul had to do it for me.

Sineusi carried one of the other keys we'd crafted so she could unlock the door at the end of the tunnel near the west ramp; Jarrai would use the third key to lock the tunnel door again after everyone had exited to disguise the fact that anyone had escaped that way. "The enslavers *must* believe," I'd told everyone, "that all of us crept toward the gate, opened it, and then ran north down the path and onto the boat."

I watched Sineusi and Mardul lead the women toward the west ramp, past the first of several soundly sleeping enslavers, patted Jarrai's back as she followed Honsoli, then barred the outer copperforge pitcave door again and began moving in the opposite direction.

One by one, I hoped, I prayed, all thirty-five of them would make it out of the tunnel, across the open expanse to Ilchullo's encircling rampart, and despite the darkness find the wooden ladder I'd managed to Trance an enslaver into forgetting in the high grass.

Then they'd climb the wall, lower themselves down its outer edge, and scramble into the protection of the reedy, shrubby savanna beyond. Jarrai would remember—please, Jarrai, *please* remember to ease the ladder back to the ground inside the wall so your route won't be discovered too soon.

Once everyone was outside the wall, Mardul would lead them to the clump of thick shrubs I'd "seen" on the far side of a small hill that would obscure Ilchullo's view of them. There they'd use their flints to light a couple of torches to see by, then follow Mardul and Sineusi westward toward steepening forest, toward the small River I'd "seen" descending out of the foreboding Mountain wilderness beyond the Privation frontier.

If they followed that River upstream all night before choosing a shelter in which to rest and hide, I'd be able to catch up with them by day's end.

But *so much* could go wrong…

I knew too well how frightened the women of the copperforge pitcave were, how unsure of their bearings, how high the likelihood that some of them would end up limping, or worse, as they stumbled toward freedom. I worried they'd be tempted—or forced—to leave someone behind. Someone easy to terrify or torture into revealing where they were heading.

Meanwhile, I'd have to execute my part of our plan unaided by any Sublimity: traverse the tunnels all the way to Ilchullo's sole gate, leaving a trail of small misleading signs of escape; once past the gate, move unseen down the bluff to Ilchullo's wharf and free the boat tied up there to drift east until it reached the southerly current of the larger River, which would take it southward.

I prayed to the Mothers that, come morning, the enslavers would believe we were all aboard the boat and pursue it. Prayed that by the time they found the vessel, they would believe, *please believe* we had abandoned it and dispersed somewhere well downstream.

I shivered at what I'd soon face, what scared me most as I approached Ilchullo's gate: the holding pit full of new prisoners.

Well before I saw it, I heard its horror: An enslaver's vicious laughter startled the air out of my lungs as a prisoner moaned; other enslavers joined in with crude taunts slurred by their drunkenness. For a searing moment, as I wondered whether *he* was there among the enslavers, belly spasms doubled me over. I could not move—not forward, not back.

Then I understood: I was being buffeted by more than the monstrous memories I'd tried so hard to bury; I was sensing *her*—that reckless Lightning-bolt Energy—sensing her enduring wave upon wave of torment at the hands of the enslavers.

Do not stop, she urged me, and her urging empowered me.

Crouching low, I shoved through my terror toward the lamplight rimming the holding pit. And there she was, suspended by her chained wrists off to one side away from the other prisoners, her face battered and bloody.

Tottering, swaying enslavers stood with their backs to me abusing her, so she alone saw me—but she gave no hint of my presence as I crept toward the unavoidable light. For a second our eyes fastened, and I knew: She'd been expecting me.

The rebellion burning in her eyes commanded the enslavers' brutal attention, challenging them to extinguish her fury even as her bloodied body twitched and shuddered. I heard her silent, clarion command:

Run! RUN!

So I sprinted through the lamplight to the safety of the darkness just inside the prison entrance.

Perhaps noticing movement even through his intoxication, one of the enslavers started to turn toward me. But the reckless Lightning-bolt Energy spit her blood into his face with tenacious accuracy, inspiring a roar of rage as he pounded her with his fists and then with a long wooden club.

And I—

I ran on unseen.

Then fortune graced me again: The guards at the prison's entrance portal had joined those savaging the new arrivals, and the commotion of their festivities obscured the ponderous gate's shrill whine as I opened it. Leaving it ajar, I moved northward beneath a moonless but starry, aurora-filled night sky that provided just enough light to guide me.

Still unseen, I ran the quarter-mile down the bluff to the empty, unoccupied boat. The sleeping enslavers guarding the dock where the boat was tied up didn't stir—not when I released the boat's lines and shoved it into the tributary's robust easterly current, not when I ducked westward from the wharf into Riverside underbrush.

Aided by starlight and auroras, praying to the Mothers that I'd avoid both human and nonhuman predators, I moved west through savanna toward an unfettered forest that became progressively denser until it jumbled into a wilderness where few Sundaselai people ever dared venture—even though it really wasn't all that far from Ilchullo.

And still my good fortune held: no Privation males, no crocodiles, no boars, no wolves…

But because I remained uncomfortably close to the prison, I'd planned to continue not only through what remained of the night but also through the day until I found the women of the copperforge pitcave.

Yet—

Yet the pull of the reckless Lightning-bolt Energy persisted. Alama! *She's still alive.*

Knowing I should press on and find the copperforge pitcave women as fast as possible, I hesitated anyway. *She's still alive!*

Breathe, I told myself as my hesitation tightened its grip and I plucked a banana tree leaf to fold into a water container I'd fill in a small nearby stream.

This was when I noticed a shallow rock shelter in the shadows above the stream, well-obscured by shrubbery. Plus it faced eastward— so any pursuers would be unlikely to sneak up on me without my knowing, especially if they carried torches.

I climbed up to the shelter to see if I was being pursued, keeping watch as I drank the water I'd gathered in my banana leaf, all the while asking: How can I leave her there *when she's still alive?*

But what of the copperforge pitcave women? Where were they? How much danger were they facing?

I closed my eyes and sought Sublime Perception, but to no avail. I was too anxious, too distracted. I drank again from my banana leaf container, attempted again to calm myself...

And perhaps the Mothers took pity on me, because that's when Sublime Perception at last showed me the now-fugitive copperforge pitcave women.

Like me, they had not trekked far enough from Ilchullo through the rugged, grasping forest. Unlike me, however, they hadn't yet stopped, even though one of them had died falling from a ledge, and some of the others were succumbing to fear and hopelessness.

"Just a little farther," Sineusi cajoled them, "we are still too close, too close"—and I wondered with a shiver if there was, in fact, such a thing as ever trekking far enough from Ilchullo.

Then I "saw" them find the spot to which I'd directed them—a stream swollen by monsoon rains into a small River.

Is this the right one? they debated.

Yes, I implored them from my rock shelter—follow that little River further upstream. Breathing, hoping, I implored them with what power and strength I could muster. I sent my pleases to each of them by name, to all of them together…please *please* follow that River…

Soon—too soon—Ilchullo's enslavers would discover our absence, discover that none of us had ever been on their boat. And then they'd come rampaging west just like they'd once come rampaging to Subendi. Only this time there'd be no Firemountain to stop them.

I opened my eyes, ready to depart the little shelter, and happened to glance at the glittered sky where the red auroras danced on and on.

That's when I "saw" something else: a vast, rugged Mountain place—colder than anywhere I'd ever been. So cold that sometimes rain fell from the sky in white flakes that weighed down the Mountains' unbounded forests of strange, beautiful trees.

Although it was very far away, Seas away, it beckoned me, this place; its Winds sang to me, its scents wafted around me, already showing me the way. And in that moment I knew that this place, this New Motherworld somewhere in the distant northwest, was where I must go. Even if I spent the rest of what life I had getting there.

First, however, I must truly escape Privation—and offer the copperforge pitcave women a chance to join me.

Yet…

Yet my Sublime Perception swung back through the early morning twilight to Ilchullo and refused to look away.

⚡

"Basandere!" Pirin had nearly shouted. Not on purpose. It was just that Gracie had also recorded *another* voice memo timestamped several hours after the one she'd just listened to:

⚡

The sun was just beginning to peek above the eastern horizon when Analergin's Sublime Perception finally enabled her to behold the moment when Ilchullo's enslavers noticed that the copperforge pitcave's prisoners had disappeared. From her rock shelter, she "saw" the enslavers waste time scurrying through the tunnel from pitcave to pitcave screaming their panic, feverishly seeking someone to blame.

She reveled as she Perceived the empty boat continuing to drift southward with the larger River's monsoon-swollen current while Ilchullo's commanders became convinced, just like she'd hoped, that the women had stolen it and taken it downstream. Reveled as the enslavers give frantic chase, shifting their attentions farther and farther downstream.

Reveled, too, that so far no one from Ilchullo had headed west in search of escaped prisoners. The possibility that anyone might travel that way was apparently beyond the enslavers' comprehension, since Ilchullo was a remote outpost on the Privation frontier and rare was the courage in Sundaselai to venture into the wilderness beyond it.

Reason enough to fear for the women from the copperforge pitcave: They were people of Sundaselai, ignorant of the Motherworld and her Rhythms, terrified of the wild into which they had fled.

So Analergin's body trembled with relief when her Sublime Perception revealed the women coming upon a shallow cave alongside the little River she'd directed them to and choosing to stop there and rest. If she left her rock shelter *and* kept a swift pace *and* was lucky enough to duck enslavers and predators, she'd reach them before the day's end.

Standing at the edge of the rock shelter, she "heard" a faint but impassioned whisper. "Yes, Analergin," urged the Lightning-bolt Energy, "lead them to freedom."

Still alive! *She's still alive!*

Soon Analergin's Sublime Perception "found" her—alone and blood-drenched in the empty copperforge pitcave. Ignored by frenzied enslavers busily rousting the rest of the prison to display their belated diligence, the dying Lightning-bolt Energy whispered "Better this than slavery."

The whisper echoed, ricocheted—and Analergin remembered. How had she failed to recognize that voice, that Resonance?

"*Kaldi!*"

Already on her feet, Analergin called in the old Subendi way: "I hear you, Kaldi. I am coming for you."

What, then, made her abruptly halt and look up?

High above in the already clouding Sky, something darted quickly downward: A white-faced owl had found prey.

"Use your Sublime Hands, Senba."

Bewildered, Analergin yanked her gaze to a figure standing perhaps five paces in front of her.

"AmaHeri?"

How many Suncycles had passed since she saw the mean old woman's outrigger fractured by furious Seawaves? AmaHeri might once have been Subendi's Most Sublime Perceiver and Healer, but AmaHeri was dead. *Isn't AmaHeri dead?* And besides, never once had the old woman called her Senba, a term of affection Mothers and Grandmothers reserve for their progeny.

Analergin squinched her eyes closed, expecting the apparition to vanish. But her eyes opened to AmaHeri's smile, AmaHeri's glowing hands extending toward her, palms upward.

"You must use your Sublime Hands to stop Kaldi's bleeding," AmaHeri said gently. "Do not doubt yourself. You are capable of Healing even from this distance."

These words seemed to slow time itself. Analergin tugged her eyes away from AmaHeri's shimmering presence to gaze at the palms of her own hands. Because she *did* doubt herself. Profoundly.

She had never been made even an initiate Healer. And no matter what the women of the copperforge pitcave believed when her touch brought them some small alleviation, she doubted she'd ever be a true Sublime Healer like AmaHeri, who had been renowned for Healing from afar.

When Analergin looked up from her hands, everything had changed. She was sitting cross-legged now, as was AmaHeri, their knees nearly touching. The old woman's body had become brighter, too, as had her luminous hands.

"To help Kaldi," she said, "you must unite with Kaldi, entangle with Kaldi until you and Kaldi become one."

Slowly, gently, AmaHeri's hands engaged Analergin's; first their fingers, then their palms joined, and the radiance in AmaHeri's hands enveloped Analergin's. "Close your eyes and turn your full Intent to Kaldi as you breathe with me, Senba, breathe with me..."

AmaHeri began to hum a slow cadence, and this hum became Analergin's hum. Their sound filled the rock shelter; Analergin felt it on her tingling lips, up her nose, through her head, into her chest as she spiraled slowly out of time itself...until...until she sensed the bleeding deep within Kaldi's body slowly wane and then cease.

"Yes, Senba, yes..." murmured AmaHeri. "Go to her now."

When Analergin opened her eyes, AmaHeri was gone.

As she hurried back to Ilchullo, Analergin worried about the copperforge pitcave women waiting for her next to the River. Would they sustain their new communion, keep safe in their cave through this day and then through the night when, according to their plan, they were to resume traveling west?

Once more, she implored them. Breathing, hoping, she called to them with all her power and strength. "Please wait for me…"

Long before she caught sight of the prison, an east wind carried its stench to Analergin's nostrils, and she shuddered. How she thought to retrieve Kaldi from the copperforge pitcave and escape yet again we can never know, for in all her tellings of this Tale of Kaldi's rescue, urged on by listeners ravenous for every detail, Analergin Segubansi never recounted her meditations. Thus many have wondered:

Could she have fomented the mists that convened around her as she rushed toward the pitcaves of Ilchullo—mists that swirled thicker and thicker over the Land, densing the air to protect her from the malevolence of Sundaselai Privation?

Could she have induced the wild cresting of erratic Rivercurrents to impale a boatload of pursuing enslavers on rocks hidden beneath the River's impatient flow so that nearly all of Ilchullo's other enslavers hurried to the cries for help, leaving the prison's pitcaves almost entirely unguarded?

"No," she said once, "these events I merely Perceived. But there was so much I did not sense, so much I could not see…"

⚡ Pirin wanted to reread Gracie's dream writings, listen again to Gracie's voice memos. All of them.

But just as she settled in at her desk and got started, a burst of new real-time Veech activity appeared on one of her screens. He was on his smartphone again.

For days, his texts and calls had been providing her with additional phone numbers to zero-click. The most interesting of these led her to still more smartphones and zero-clicks. Despite her Spotter app having become exponentially busier, though, she didn't yet have actual evidence that Veech Farkas intended her harm.

Even so, as the saying goes, absence of evidence is *not* evidence of absence. Which meant she couldn't afford *not* to learn what he might be up to.

So Pirin reluctantly set aside Gracie's dream writings and recordings to focus again on the snarling wolf's latest communications.

She'd already discovered that his "friends" nearly always "had to go" within seconds of answering his initial call and didn't pick up when he attempted contact again. Even brother Ezra, his only sibling, seemed to be ducking him; much of the interaction between them went through their frazzled mother.

However, the snarling wolf had a staunch ally in Ezra's son, eighteen-year-old Zach Farkas. Thrilled to have become keeper of Uncle Veech's Ducati ever since Veech got locked into an ankle monitor and confined to his mother's house, the kid communicated often with Veech—way more, Pirin suspected, than Ezra realized.

When she discovered images on Zach's now zero-clicked smartphone showing him astride Veech's bike in a helmet adorned with a too-familiar bright red snarling wolf decal, she figured she'd identified the gesturing dude on the black motorcycle who messed with her as she drove home from testifying at Veech's trial.

No accident, then, that when Ezra finally succumbed to his mother's pressure and agreed to talk to his brother, Pirin heard it live from the start:

"Shit, man," Veech mewled, "I'm on a smash here, an' they ain't endin' it anytime soon. I did Billy's biddin' in that hellhole, took risks for him for *fifteen fuckin' years*, bruh—an' now alls I'm askin' is you smooth it for me, y'know? Help me get her put in the hat ay-sap. C'mon Ez. 'S about gettin' some respect, y'know?"

"*Respect!*" Ezra hissed. "You embarrass the crap outta me an' Ma with Cleary—I mean, a *video* catchin' you whackin' your wife an' gettin' your balls busted by a damn *dyke?* Not even Billy can magic away that much stupid. You can thank Ma for your fuckin' *smart*phone, but it came outta *my* hide, smart*ass*. So you *already* owe me—an' *now* you're moanin' about *respect*, sniffin' for another fuckin' *favor?* Christ! Give it a goddamn rest. You're fuckin' lucky Billy's squad don't put *you* in the hat. No way they're gonna touch any o' your dumbass revenge shit."

That Wednesday afternoon exchange put Pirin on high alert. So she was listening again on Thursday morning when Veech called a number she hadn't seen before.

"Miss seein' y'at Zelda's back table, boy," rumbled a rich baritone. "How's it hangin' wicha Norfolk crew?"

"Not my crew," Veech griped.

"Sorry, gabacho—y'be keepin' y'ass innat whip, or we got nuthin' t'say. I know the whole joint's in lockdown, but unnerstand—y'got value *wich* 'em, but y'got *shit* wichout 'em. Not like before, boy. Now the *only* thing y'got t'trade is whatcha can tell me 'bout Billy Whiting's hustles. T'do that y'gotta be useful t'his lockup crew. Y'be our mole inside, Veech, we help ya out here."

"But—"

"Only offer I got, gabacho. Keep it cool an' take whatever BS Billy's boys dish out so we can get it regulated again. Y'on th' other side o' the c-wire now. So I be needin' a little somethin' extra from ya. T'reestablish trust 'fore we reestablish terms."

"I got *shit*, TJ," Veech groused, his voice pitching higher. "An' I can't get nuthin' 'long as I'm trapped in this bitchin' coffin alla fuckin' time!"

"'S why we gon' front ya, boy. Gedda runner slot f'ya in Billy's Norfolk squadbay."

"But Billy's really pissed at me an' his squad here knows it."

"Whatcha expect, man? Y'blew a real solid setup. An' f'the record, I'm not too happy wicha myself. Think I f'got that big-ass nut y'owin' us? Y'remember that nut, don'tcha, Veech? Ha! *Su-u-re* y'do. But hey, we be givin' y'a sweet chance t'pay it back. Wich interest, y'unnerstand."

"Jeezus, TJ, it wasn't my fault!"

"Damn well *was*, Veech. But we never messed y'up like we coulda. *We* pro-tec-ted y'ass."

"An' I really 'preciate that," Veech toadied. "*Really*. But now I—to fix it up I needa show 'em I can get payback, needa show 'em I can get someone waxed from in here—"

"Hol' on, boy. We can help, but all outta sight, man, unnerstand? Y'gotta *look* like y'pullin' respect like that y'own self."

"But—"

"Y'on convict time now, Veech. An' y'need convict cred, like what'll come from 'at runner job. After three runner deliveries—solid packages, y'unnerstand, *worth* somethin'—we see t'that little problem o' yours. An' just t'show how much I look forward t'your success, tell me who y'lookin' t'green-light."

"Pirin Basamendi."

"Never heard o' him."

"Her."

Silence reigned for a long moment. "Ohhh." TJ laughed heartily. "Y'mean the split-tail in that video y'starred in." TJ laughed again. "Needin' a fix o' revenge sugar, boy?" Then TJ's voice went low and, to Pirin's ear, unmistakably foreboding. "Patience. Meantime, no mouthin' off. We will let you know when the time is right."

CHAPTER NINETEEN: FOR EVER, FOR ALWAYS

Hyperaware of Gracie still asleep thirty feet away, Pirin leaned back in her chair and exhaled: knew it…knew it…fuckin' *knew* it…

Yes, she damn well *had* seen and understood Veech Farkas clearly that day in court. So should she wake Gracie to share her news—and the irrefutable evidence that, oh yes, Veech Farkas *is* actively looking for a way to kill her?

But what if Gracie suggests calling the cops? Cops who'd ask how do you know this man wants to harm you? Since you'd rather not mention your use of exotic, dubiously derived surveillance software, you're left with "Umm…I didn't like the way he looked at me in court."

So while Gracie snoozes, reexamine what you've dug up on Veech and find *something* to power a Veech Farkas recycle while there's still time to execute it before he executes you.

A bunch of data streams attracted Pirin's interest, but three paid off: where Veech Farkas spent his money (fifteen years of his ATM transactions); where he went (his car insurance history, which included location data collected by his vehicles' telematics); and where Veech played poker (expanded research on local gambling operations—who had licenses, who got hassled/accused/busted for illegal shit).

Hours later, she'd put together her Veech portrait:

More than a decade earlier, three or four times a week he took to parking his car either close to one of a handful of bars known for "private" cash poker games or near a pier from which a casino cruise was about to depart. And wherever he parked, within minutes he'd withdraw cash from a nearby ATM.

About seven years ago, he changed things up, no longer bothering with ATM withdrawals and visiting just one poker venue, a suburban sports bar called Zelda's. After further arcane and illicit database diving, Pirin determined that Zelda's was owned by someone named Tarrio Jacques Sunty.

A shit-scary dude, Tarrio Jacques Sunty. From various law enforcement databases, Pirin gleaned that he'd begun it all with offshore casino cruises before expanding into other cash-based ventures that put him in direct competition with, among others, Billy Whiting.

These same LEO databases indicated that, beginning about eight or nine years ago, an increasing chunk of this competition played out in the Commonwealth's jails and prisons, from which both Tarrio Jacques Sunty's and Billy Whiting's incarcerated captains easily commanded their respective street operations—while neither streetlord had ever himself been arrested, much less convicted of anything.

So what're the odds that TJ and Tarrio Jacques Sunty were one and the same?

Pirin reckoned that Veech Farkas had already been a Suffolk County CO doing Billy Whiting's bidding for some eight years when TJ recruited him, probably using a mix of ego-boosting, bribery, and blackmail.

"Gotcha," Pirin whispered as she squinted at one of the three monitors she'd filled with Spotter transcripts, database query results, spreadsheets, and videos.

"Farkas, I presume?"

Startled by the voice coming from behind her, Pirin looked up to find Gracie, whom she hadn't heard approaching, right behind her—and she thought: It begins…

When Gracie's eyes blinked opened in the middle of what turned out to be the first Thursday afternoon in July, she registered a vaulted pinewood ceiling sloping from high above her down to a row of three perfectly square windows placed above a span of built-in dressers on the wall opposite the bed cozying her.

Pirin's place, now much clearer and crisper than she remembered.

And then she began to remember more.

Not a dream exactly. Well, not an ohskal dream, anyway. She'd felt a high-frequency thrum coursing through her body, and just a second ago Eletun's voice was reminding her "Every Rhythm carries a message, Gracie."

"What message?"

Eletun smiled. "Warnings aren't always explicit."

Why the hell did this old woman insist on being so damn cryptic? Frustrated, Gracie looked away. Fine, she thought, I'll figure out better questions. When she turned back to Eletun, however, there *was* no Eletun.

She'd been left alone in an oddly foggy, formless world—but only briefly: The fog seemed to be swiftly lifting, and there she was in Pirin's refreshingly fog-free bedroom. Awake. That's when it clicked.

Warnings, Eletun had said.

Warnings point to *threats*.

Gracie gazed again at the vaulted wood ceiling above her. Pirin's ceiling. She ran her hands across the bedsheets faintly infused with Pirin's scent and the promise of—

Wait. Where *is* Pirin?

Gracie's belly clenched. Warnings…threats… What if—?

And right then Gracie was back. All the way back.

Getting out of bed took more effort than she anticipated but didn't slow her down, instead eliciting a mere grunt before she hurried across the living room toward Pirin's office—

And yeah, Pirin looked perfectly normal sitting there, engrossed in her screens, and probably everything's okay…

"Farkas, I presume?"

Whirling around in her chair, Pirin grinned her surprise. "Gracie! You're up! How're you—?"

"Waybetterthanks." Gracie gulped a breath. "You okay? I was worried."

"I'm fine. Just been in here, um…"

Salved by the consummate relief of seeing Pirin safe, Gracie smiled. And kept on smiling: The last time she'd approached Pirin's desk, those three screens—filled as before with spreadsheets and documents and videos—had been instantly flipped into images of spiraling galaxies. But not this time. This time she could see everything. Ah, she thought, it begins…

"What's wrong, Gracie? You look...kinda odd..." Pirin shrugged her confusion. "Another dream?"

"Just Eletun, actually. Right before I woke up she said 'Warnings aren't always explicit.' Another way of telling me to pay attention, I suppose. And what keeps yanking at my attention—what I can't stop thinking about—are those dreams of Analergin holding the metal spike and sensing these eensy vibrations that her brain translates into sounds and images."

Pirin nodded. "When I read about that, it reminded me of what blind people can do with their canes. Extended touch, I think it's called."

"There's something else, too. Even when I was dreaming that— *when it was happening to me, too*—the experience struck me as a kind of synesthesia."

"Synesthesia...Something about cross-sensory perception, right?"

Gracie nodded. "Documented all the hell over the place. Sensory deprivation can actually induce it. Lots of different kinds, too. I suspect what I experienced through Analergin *could* happen, probably *does* happen somewhere in *this* world."

"Including the part about using a metal spike?"

"Well, I have a whole other thought about that. How much of your schoolroom physics do you remember?"

Pirin's face scrunched. "Some. Try me."

"Okay, so like any object, a metal spike vibrates—creates an oscillating wave—at its natural frequency, right?"

"Yeah, that rings a bell." Pirin winked. "Let's see—an object's natural frequency, also called its resonance frequency, is based on both its length, which affects frequency wavelength, and on what it's made of, which affects the speed of the wave. And when you apply an external vibrational force—another oscillating wave—that happens to be a multiple of the object's natural frequency, the object will oscillate with more force as compared to what happens when you apply a frequency that's *not* a multiple of the object's natural frequency."

"Oh good, we're on the same page." Gracie nudged herself closer because Pirin smelled downright delicious. "So when Analergin's metal spike vibrating at its natural frequency encounters multiples of its natural frequency that are generated by various external vibrations—"

"That's when the metal spike achieves resonance with those other frequencies." Pirin's dark eyes flared. "Just like Eletun kept telling you in the dreams."

"Yeah, she did, huh? All that stuff about Rhythm and Resonance. When I first heard it I figured it was just myth devolved into wishful thinking. But now—I guess I'm finally seeing how it could be a real thing."

"Makes me wonder about resonance between you and Analergin." Pirin peered at Gracie. "Same natural frequency? One of you is a frequency multiple of the other?"

Gracie lowered her head. "I wonder the same thing, but from a different angle. I can't stop thinking about the dream when Analergin feels the threat of that man who tortured her, knowing he can come for her anytime he wants."

"So you're wondering…" On her feet now, Pirin eased Gracie into a hug. "Wondering about whether there's some sort of resonance or entanglement between what you're dreaming and—"

"—And what *we're* living."

"No way of knowing." Pirin kissed Gracie's neck. "For what it's worth, I think resonance and entanglement are pretty much the same—just depends on the scale. Newtonian classical or wavy quantum packets of energy probabilities conveniently collapsing into 'particles' when a human being perceives them. Guess that makes me an *as above, so below* kinda girl. Also, for what it's worth, I agree with Eletun. About warnings not always being explicit, I mean."

"Well, on the topic of inexplicit warnings, I've got more ohskal dreams for you."

"I, uh—" Lowering her head, Pirin started talking very fast. "I got a confession. I've been listening to your voice recordings all week, I just…"

Gracie nodded, smiling. "I was hoping you'd keep up with me."

"I just hadda know how you were doing, what was happening in your brain." Pirin stopped to gaze at her. "And I still can't figure out when the hell you did all that talking."

"Dunno," Gracie shrugged. "Whenever I woke up."

"Which seems to have been whenever I was somewhere else."

"In here, I bet—three-screening it."

Pirin actually looked a little sheepish then. "Guilty as charged."

"Well, I'm glad you've also been keeping up with Analergin's travails. Not sure you've heard the most recent, though—one last night, which I recorded in the bathroom so I wouldn't wake you, then another shortly before I came in here."

"Can I hear 'em?"

"Right now?" Gracie asked, surprised. "What about—?"

"Actually, Veech can wait for just a bit. When I show you what I've got, you'll understand. But after, okay?"

"All yours," Gracie said, handing over her phone:

⚡ Melded again, Analergin and I...

Hoping for strength, for concealing mists, I traveled back with her to Ilchullo much faster than she (and I) had lurched away from it. When the mists appeared so quickly, so formidably, I chose to believe Analergin would be formidable, too.

But when she saw him near the western ramp leading into Ilchullo's tunnels, a captain's arrogance smirking out of the heavy mist as he spotted her, all illusions of formidability dissolved. I even forgot that Analergin carried a metal blade and an axe in the rope-belt around her waist.

He was alone, some ten paces in front of her, and she recognized him immediately as he raised his cudgel high and opened his mouth to call for assistance. But then he lowered the weapon and laughed—a cold sound brittle with contempt—and I saw his decision etched into his sneer: He would need no help with something as pathetic as her.

"Left behind, cunt?" He snorted. "I shall make a fine example of *you*."

No, I thought along with Analergin as she stood paralyzed by the old terror squeezing her throat—*no, no*, this is *not* happening.

But there he was, marching toward me while I stood frozen, trapped in myself, gasping.

And then he backhanded me so hard that I tumbled yards away from him. Tasting blood, I stared up at him as he strode across the space his slap had put between us. And still I could not move.

He leaned over me, yanked me to my feet by my hair, hit me again. And again I went rolling across the ground. Once more he approached, this time kicking me onto my back as he pulled aside the tunic that covered his genitals. Even as he and his erecting penis straddled me, he just wasn't real.

Silently, I begged his image to retreat into the mists—until I remembered how Kaldi, chained and beaten in the prison holding pen, felt no fear of Ilchullo's persecutors, only immeasurable fury. And finally, *finally* past and present fused, wrenching memories too awful for awareness from their hiding places—and unleashing Analergin's rage.

He saw it, I think, because for just an instant he hesitated. Which was when he recognized her, the helpless primitive he'd taken so much pleasure in hurting.

"*You—!*" he snarled.

"Analergin!" she (and I along with her) growled back at him as her foot—and all her fury—slammed into his dangling testicles.

He fell backward, stunned and groaning and wheezing. I scrambled to my feet and stood over him while he thrashed in pain, his hands clutching his bruised gonads. Remember this, Analergin ordered both of us—how you did it, what it felt like, sounded like—so you never forget how to do it again. He tried to rise, so I (yes, *I*) kicked him a second time and then a third, and damn hard too, after which he didn't move or make a sound.

A quick glance around revealed no other enslavers. Not a single one. So I claimed the waterskin draped across the captain's shoulder, ran toward the west tunnel ramp, through the now wide-open tunnel door, all the way to the doors of the copperforge pitcave, still no enslavers in sight. I used the key still stashed in my pocket to enter—and found Kaldi in a bloodied, swollen, almost unconscious curl near the inner door.

Before this moment Analergin had seen Kaldi only in dreams and nascent Sublime Perception. But never once in the flesh. And now here she was. Mangled. Barely alive. Analergin wanted to hold her, heal her. Wanted to love her. To make love with her.

But we dared not linger in the copperforge pitcave one heartbeat longer than necessary. I filled the waterskin at the pitcave's stream and persuaded Kaldi conscious enough to drink from it before lifting her to her feet and helping her don foot coverings and one of the tunics we'd left behind. After refilling the waterskin, I draped her arm across my shoulders and we moved into the deserted tunnel.

Kaldi stopped me as I turned us toward the west ramp. "Wait. Use your key...help the others."

"That will slow us down."

"Will slow...*them* down...even more," Kaldi rasped.

Them...the enslavers, she meant. And she was right.

I wanted to ask her how she knew about the key, but we had no time for that. I propped her against the tunnel wall and unbarred the nearest pitcave's outer door.

The dreaded sound had some of the men within cowering; no doubt they expected the enslavers had come to beat them. I tossed the key through the thick metal bars of the inner door to the nearest man.

"Use it to open every door in this evil place," I said.

He picked up the key. "We heard of the escape," he whispered.

"As many doors as you can," I exhorted him. "The more prisoners you free, the likelier you are to get out of here for good."

By the time I retrieved Kaldi and we'd stumbled up the western ramp, the shouts of emancipated prisoners, who seemed to be moving toward the prison's entrance gate, echoed behind us.

Moments later I saw the captain near where I'd left him, now on one knee, fumbling for his cudgel. I readied Analergin's axe; no, this monster would *not* stop us.

But I needn't have worried: The sight of him inspired in Kaldi a savage otherworldly power. She wrenched herself away from me, seized the captain's cudgel, and swung it ferociously at his genitals just as he looked into her igniting eyes. I heard a devastating crunch; he yelped as his body shuddered with the sickening sigh of rupture, and then he crumpled into absolute stillness.

I understood immediately: He was dead. Thanks to Kaldi, he would never hurt anyone again.

We reached Ilchullo's western rampart close to where the women of the copperforge pitcave had made their ladder-assisted escape. I could have scaled the rampart unaided—but not Kaldi, despite her extraordinarily regenerating strength. So I'd begun searching the tall grass for the ladder I hoped remained somewhere nearby—just as commotion began to billow out of the tunnels behind us.

Kaldi's bruised, bloodied face managed a lopsided smile: A prison-wide escape had commenced. Then she pointed to the ground at her feet; she had found the ladder.

A swift scan around us showed neither enslavers nor any escaping prisoners coming our way. So I propped the ladder against the wall, pushed Kaldi while she pulled, followed her up, then shoved the ladder so it fell back again into the grass. Eventually, I knew, the enslavers would grasp the ladder's significance; I could only hope that by the time they did we'd be beyond catching.

Shrouded by mist, I helped Kaldi scramble as fast as she could down the outside of Ilchullo's wall and then we hurried toward the forest. We kept going for what I'm guessing were hours before she foundered. But we remained much too close to Ilchullo. With stamina I didn't know I had, I hoisted even more of Kaldi's weight across my shoulders and we hiked into increasingly dense forestland.

We didn't travel nearly as far as we needed to. But we were depleted and I was no longer sure of my bearings. To find out, I needed time to breathe, to focus into Rhythm and then attempt Sublime Perception.

So, despite our proximity to Ilchullo, we rested unsheltered on a hill. The site was well-hidden by trees and shrub, high enough that we'd notice whether anyone pursued us. I heard Analergin praying— *please Alama, please help me See…*

But she could not achieve the focused relaxation necessary for Sublime Perception. Her mind was convulsing, whirling weightless through the world as she closed her eyes and recalled again what Kaldi had done.

He was dead.

Analergin (and I along with her) did wonder whether she would have managed it herself. For all her practicing at war so long ago on Subendi, she'd never contemplated killing this man who grew aroused when she writhed under his whip and laughed as he raped her and then beat her yet again because her blood dared spatter onto his tunic. And upon facing him once more, she thought only of escaping him. But now…

Now he was dead.

Like water at last undammed, breath escaped me and I felt a small snap at the back of my neck. Involuntarily, Analergin (and I along with her) slid into a trembling collapse, grateful that the call of the New Motherworld somewhere out there far, far to the northwest, had not ceased.

We slept only briefly through the day's remnants, waking to a sun just arriving at the western horizon. Waking with sufficient calm that Analergin was able to kneel over Kaldi, hands heating as they moved in Resonance with Kaldi's body, sometimes just above her skin, sometimes gently massaging her.

Kaldi needed more time to rest, to rejuvenate—but soon enough pursuers would come west looking for us, and we had a long, long way to go.

We would walk through the coming night because we had no choice.

⚡

Beneath a heavily clouded sky devoid of moonlight or starlight or auroras, Analergin and Kaldi moved westward in silence, no torch to aid them. Nevertheless, somehow Kaldi saw that which Analergin could not—whatever was around them in the dark—and they moved swiftly.

Holding tight to Kaldi, Analergin muddled blindly through perhaps the blackest night she'd ever experienced wondering how Kaldi managed to see anything at all.

Her Sublime Perception had at last shown her where the women from the copperforge pitcave waited at the River farther west, even revealed the presence of a large wetland nearby stretching off to their south—but Analergin perceived it all via the black-fringed haze of Sublime Perception that left her worrying: *how* nearby? Would one more step put her in water up to her knees, her shoulders, her nose?

They had been walking a long time when, at precisely the same instant, both of them froze. Analergin did not know what prompted Kaldi to halt; her own stillness was response to a series of vibrations: creatures—including three human males, judging by their gaits—coming closer with every step.

"Are you strong enough to climb?" she whispered into Kaldi's ear as she tilted her head toward the cluster of large banana trees at the tips of her fingers, which they had been using to steer around the edge of the wetland. When she felt Kaldi's nod, she proffered the blade she carried, "so you can defend yourself," and boosted her companion into the closest tree before fumbling to its neighbor and climbing.

None too soon: Even as the vibrations persisted, Analergin spotted a small flicker of flame swaying closer, larger. Yes, three men—in a line, six or eight paces between them, the first one carrying the torch that barely lit their way.

Suddenly something splashed.

"Dominion Almighty!" protested the man in the middle, visible to Analergin only as an amorphous shadow. "I should never have believed you. Even escaped convicts know better than to pass through this filthy swamp—and now, thanks to you, I am in water up to my—"

"Quiet!" hissed the man behind him. "Do you hear that?"

"I hear nothing," complained the obviously irritated lead man with the torch, who now stood directly below Kaldi's tree.

"We should light another torch," said the last man in line. "We are being followed."

The lead man's torch swung around. "I see no light anywhere."

"What follows us is not human."

"Crocodile?" asked the now-nervous lead man. "Wolf? Cat?"

"Come back here with the torch," implored the man at the rear, his voice wavering. "You have the longblade. Whatever it is, *you* can ki—"

Another splash interrupted him just as the light of the torch disappeared and one of them screamed.

Unable to see much of anything, Analergin dared not move from her perch—though she sensed that perhaps Kaldi had. Thus for too many heartbeats she could only listen to the sounds of male grunts and loud splashes of water, followed by a single distinctly male shriek.

Then...silence—except for a strange, deep-in-her-chest vibration that drove Analergin to blindly drop from the tree, axe pulled from her waistband, ready for the worst.

"*Kaldi!*" she whispered desperately as her feet touched Mother Earth.

"Behind you, Analergin." Kaldi spoke very softly. "Beware the bodies when you turn 'round."

A half-step from where Analergin had landed, she made out a large lump, somehow blacker than the blackness around it. She blinked, blinked again before realizing the lump comprised two male bodies heaped over each other, smelling now of blood. "Did you—?"

"—I did. Your friend there—" Kaldi's shadowy hand pointed leftward. "—She killed the third one."

After another long moment, Analergin discerned what Kaldi pointed at: a very large cat no more than twelve paces away, on its haunches, one enormous paw resting possessively on the ripped-open chest of the third man. As she gazed into the cat's eyes, the strange, deep vibration she'd sensed subsided.

"She saved me," Kaldi murmured. "I am not yet ready for three at once."

I should be afraid, Analergin thought.

And then she understood.

"Oh, Daughter! I am so pleased to see that you survived," she said aloud as she took a step closer to the cat and bent down on one knee, her hand extended palm up. "My friend Kaldi and I thank you for helping us."

The cat's nose lifted and the creature leaned slightly forward to pick up Analergin's scent before emitting a deep, extended snort. This prompted a smile from Analergin before she joined her hands just below her chin and exhaled into a low hum. Then she rose, backstepped away from the cat with a final bow, and silently resumed walking westward with Kaldi.

When at last they came upon what Kaldi had begun calling Analergin's River, bloated with receding monsoon waters, a new day had begun to lighten the eastern sky. They paused just long enough to strip down and, as Analergin said, "wash away this Privation stench." And, of course, to allow Analergin's attempt at Sublimely Perceiving the location of the copperforge pitcave women.

"Still there," she told Kaldi excitedly after a time. "Still waiting. We have all this day to reach them, and the weather will not interfere."

"I will keep a good pace," promised Kaldi. After walking for a time, she asked "How do you know Daughter Cat?"

"Long ago, her Mother and I were friends."

"On Subendi."

Analergin nodded. "Mother Cat bore many children. Now I know her youngest found means to safety. I am keenly grateful she recognized me."

"Daughter Cat can live in these hills and the western Mountains more easily than we can," Kaldi mused. "Bounty hunters will chase us all the way to the western shore if necessary. Because Privation cannot tolerate what we have done."

"I am resolved to leave Privation far behind," replied Analergin. "Even the western shore is too close. I hope others will travel with me, but each must make her own decision about which is more dangerous— strange Lands or Privation."

"*Nowhere* along the shores of the Near Western Sea has escaped Privation," Kaldi said as she stared hard into Analergin's eyes. "Not entirely."

"Yes, my people have long understood Privation's reach. When we had to leave our Firemountain, the Mothers made plan to sail *beyond* the Near Western Sea. We were within sight of the great peninsula Hulartali, the Far Western Sea before us. But then came a powerful Seastorm..." Analergin shook her head. "I fear my people are gone forever."

"None survived?"

"I know of only me. And Daughter Cat. Perhaps also a small family of ravens and a few Resonances not yet dissipated..."

Kaldi frowned. "No one else?"

"I watched our largest outrigger sink, saw several others in peril..." Analergin squinched shut her eyes at the recollection. "Then the Winds destroyed the outrigger I sailed on and drove the debris I clung to all the way back to Privation shores. Only now do I understand why."

"Yes." Kaldi's frown transformed into a smile. "You had yet to find me."

Analergin smiled too. "For a supposed Sublime Perceiver, I am quite sightless. I did not recognize you."

Kaldi's kiss, full on Analergin's lips, lingered, its energy entwining them both. In all her life, Analergin had never known anything like its animating, exhilarating force, and when at last Kaldi's sweet, warm breath signaled the kiss's finish, Analergin wanted more. *Stay*, she wanted to plead, *stay...*

But they could not pause.

They continued upstream with Kaldi occasionally asking the sorts of questions that revealed a deep faith in Analergin—a faith as blind, Analergin concluded, as her own inability to see in the unrelieved blackness of a clouded, moonless night. A faith she must honor and cherish just as Kaldi honored and cherished her.

Sometime later Kaldi asked, "Will you go in search of others from Subendi?"

"I will always hope," Analergin admitted. "But I intend to search for the New Motherworld that Sublime Perception has shown me. A rich, beautiful Land"—she pointed northwestward—"that is very, very far away and free of Privation."

"Beyond Hulartali, then."

"Oh yes, well beyond even the Far Western Sea."

"How?"

"I will build an outrigger on the western shore and sail there."

Kaldi nodded, comprehending. "And Bele will help you know your New Motherworld when you see it. How many of the women do you think will join you?"

Analergin shrugged. "When we find them," she said, "I shall ask first if any wish to accompany me into the Mountains. Some may, others will not."

"And then?"

"Once across the Mountains, on the western shore, I shall tell those with me of my Intent, of the vessel I will build and sail to the New Motherworld. I shall invite them to join me, but also warn them that the journey will be immensely long and arduous, full of unknowns. I shall warn that the Sea is extremely dangerous—no caves for shelter during the terrible lightning storms, Waves as high as clifftops—and their captain is a novice. But I—" Analergin turned to face Kaldi. "I do hope that *you* will join me…"

Kaldi smiled and kissed Analergin again. "I have joined you already—for ever, for always."

Tears brimmed in Analergin's eyes. "We are together, then," she said, reaching for Kaldi with her hands, with her body throbbing into Kaldi's, with the kiss that started gentle and quickly filled her with fire. "For ever," she murmured against Kaldi's ardent, inviting lips. "For always."

All that day, Analergin and Kaldi followed the River into higher, drier land without finding any sign of other human beings, though they dodged a boar and noticed wolves in the distant north stalking a pod of elephants. They reached the women of the copperforge pitcave as another twilight began to dim the western Sky and all the women but one had crowded around a small fire.

Only Sineusi stood apart, watching nervously at the eastern edge of the shallow cave. Her eyes turned liquid bright when she saw Analergin approaching. Before she could speak, Analergin said "I have brought someone with me."

Bruised and limping, Kaldi stepped toward the firelight, causing Sineusi to gasp. The rest of the group had begun to clamor greeting, but the way Sineusi and Kaldi mutely beheld each other silenced their happy commotion.

Analergin looked first at Sineusi, then Kaldi. "Yes?" she asked them.

"Yes," they responded together, their eyes never leaving each other.

Sineusi reached across the small space and the painful years to help her daughter to a place near the fire.

"I feared you were dead, Ama," Kaldi said quietly.

"Oh my Senba," Sineusi responded softly, "I thought I had lost you forever."

And then they held each other and wept.

⚡

CHAPTER TWENTY:
GREATER THAN THE SUM OF OUR PARTS

Enough, Gracie decided.

"You *do* know you're staring at me again, right?"

"Sorry," Pirin mumbled, looking away—reluctantly, Gracie thought—before she placed Gracie's phone on the coffee table in front of her, removed her earbud, and rose from the sofa to pace the living room. "All these dreams…" She shook her head. "It's an incredible story you've—"

"Please don't say 'created.' I haven't created anything. I'm the person who's *recorded* someone else's story." Gracie sighed. "Eletun's story, I suppose. Certainly not mine. I'm merely the messenger."

"Well, messenger, it's friggin' weird how close it feels, how much I recognize. Like déjà vu." Pirin's face gnarled between smile and frown. "But talking about it with anyone besides you or Ama…"

Gracie laughed. "Welcome to my world." She followed Pirin to the sliding glass door overlooking the little forest at the back of the Basamendi property and wrapped an arm around Pirin's waist. "Most rational people would argue 'just coincidence.' Just coincidence the way my dreams resemble a myth familiar to you and your mother. Just coincidence these dreams are full of words unfamiliar to me, but you and your mother recognize them. Move on, folks, no cause and effect to see here, only a neurotic woman's search for patterns that aren't really there."

"Unless those patterns *are* really there," Pirin quietly countered. "Clearly, humans are pattern-recognition mavens; it's one of our basic survival tools. And I get that we tend to 'over-recognize' meaning, impose it where a probability analysis would favor random chance. But hey, *random chance* is a wilderness where meaning goes to hide. Current scientific understanding has plenty of gaps, plenty of unsolved puzzles. So maybe your dreamstory illustrates patterns or paradigms we haven't recognized as even possible—yet. Wouldn't be the first time."

"Sorry to keep harping on this. I just—I'm *not* a mystic, y'know? So I'm looking for a rational explanation."

Pirin inhaled slowly. "Seems to me there are *possible* rational explanations. Hints that invite hypotheses. Like the vibration stuff you experienced in some of the dreams." Then she leaned in. "Also, I really *really* wanna kiss you, if that's okay…"

Claimed again by that exquisitely warm, creamy-sweet Pirin-scent, Gracie's eyes refused to stay open, the nagging remnants of her headache fading as she hiked up on tiptoes. Their lips hovered close, closer, electric and hungry—until Gracie moaned into a sigh and Pirin plunged and oh yes, how wonderful that everything her body remembered of their first kiss in the car was true.

But there was so much more she needed to know, to feel. She took Pirin's hand and backed through the living room all the way to the bedroom, where she began working open what seemed an inordinately large number of buttons while she gently pulled Pirin toward the bed. "I want to taste you, Pirin Basamendi. Right. *Now*."

"So, um, you're feeling better."

"Oh yeah."

❖

"You sure, Gracie?"

She'd lost almost a whole week, she said as she maneuvered Pirin onto the bed, her blue eyes gleaming. "Almost a whole week passed out right next to you and I never really saw any of you. Or felt any of you. What a terrible waste."

I agree, Pirin didn't say as she got her first real look at Gracie's subtly toned swimmer's body, Gracie's small, firm, high-flying breasts (thankyoujesus!). The getting naked part remained something of a blur for Pirin, but a thrumming galvanic melt arched her pelvis up, up to shiver-sense the maze of light brown hair that guarded Gracie's Venusian mound (yes! pubes! thankyou*thankyou*jesus!).

By the time Gracie's crotch circled into hers, pumping out the rhythm of its tease, slow at first, then faster, then syncopating, Pirin's eyes had closed. Because damn, *damn*, she managed not to blurt out, I could come right now and…hey…wait…I haven't even immersed in Ayesha yet…

"Oh no you don't." Gracie chortled as she pulled herself away with a final shimmy. "Not so fast."

"Uhhh…" Please don't go, Pirin silently begged, *plea-ease*…

She needn't have worried. Their rhythm continued as Gracie smoothly slithered alongside her, one thigh angling around hers to tantalize her crotch while curious lips caressed her jaw and a nose obviously expert at titillating left earlobes launched a leisurely exploration and, oh yes, *yes*, she surrendered.

Thus began a slow, celebratory, full-bodied dance. Nibbling. Grinding. Hovering. Retreating. Thrusting. Diving.

Gracie talked the whole time—a soft, playful lilt—until her tongue became otherwise engaged and she insisted that Pirin pick up the slack.

Basandere—did this mean Gracie was a sexbed talker?

Not that Pirin objected to sex talk in principle; she just didn't *do* sex talk. She'd never been able to muster more than a grunt, a gasp, a low groan, a very occasional "yeah, like that."

"Quan…tum…mechan…ics…" Gracie murmured into Pirin's labia, then lifted her head. "Something about photons, right? Light in particle form."

"*What?*" squeaked Pirin as Gracie's tongue briefly introduced itself before withdrawing.

"Quantum," Gracie repeated. "Tell me."

"*WHY?*"

Gracie's tongue two-flicked her answer—"I'll wait"—eliciting a faint groan.

"Qua-Quantum…" Pirin panted. "A discretely quantized ph-physical magnitude."

"And?"

"Uh…uh…described…in terms of…of…"

"Of?"

"Prop-perties…"

"Like?"

"Uhhhh…"

Suddenly, Gracie's rhythm shifted—faster, slower, faster again—and then she retreated into labia kissing. "You were telling me about quantum properties…"

Seriously?? Pirin inhaled, ready to scream *STOP!* or maybe *GIMMEEEE!*—but she heard herself mumble "Polarization…frequency…angular momentum…other…stuff…*please*, Gracie…"

"Aw, c'mon, this is *fun!* What else?"

"Gra*cieee!*"

"What else?" Gracie repeated, her face still buried between Pirin's legs.

"Oh…my…god," gasped a breathless Pirin. "You're *dangerous!*"

Gracie flicked her tongue again, once for each syllable: "What…*else?*"

Now fully comprehending the bargain she didn't know she'd made, Pirin tried to play along, each syllable an immense challenge. "Quantum…systems…a-act like waves…when in motion…but…but then…act like particles w-when…*uhhh*…when there's a…a classical system…"

Pirin hoped that would be enough, but no. Gracie emerged asking "A classical system—like when people're watching, right?"

"Y-Yeah…"

"And then?"

"Th-then," Pirin stuttered, "th-the…quantum wavefunction c-collapses…"

Gracie surfaced again. "Ah, so that's when it randomly adopts just one of those possible quantum states."

"Uh *huhhhhh…*"

"And so it's all about waves, oscillating vibrations…" Gracie giggled into Pirin's pubes. "As above, so below. Got it."

"Uh *huhhhhh…*"

"See? Not so hard."

"Says…you…"

"I promise it gets better." And with that Gracie licked along the inner folds of Pirin's labia then circled, nipped, and circled some more before reintroducing *that* rhythm, generated now by a spinning, swinging, twirling, diving tongue.

Which came first? Pirin's guttural shout? Or her buck into a protracted orgasm that unfurled in layer after intensifying molten layer to leave her pulsating and lightheaded and breathless?

"Okay." Gracie had waited for Pirin's trembling body to calm before she hiked up and draped herself across Pirin's hip. "So while your twat calms down, tell me about entanglement."

"You gotta be kidding…"

Grinning, Gracie shook her head while her fingers crawled into the warm slick between Pirin's legs. "I have high hopes for entanglement." Her finger flicked. "Is that when a quantum system's particles can't be independently described?" Another flick.

"Uhhhhhhhhhh…"

This seemed to inspire Gracie to play upon said twat like a slide guitar—"Nah, you don't seem quite ready yet…"—even though Pirin's hips arced upward, carrying Gracie with them. "Soon though, I think." Gracie's fingers continued their slick strum. "C'mon, tell me," she purred. "Entanglement."

"Wh-when particles b-become…" gasped Pirin, who felt Gracie touch every cell in her body, "become…so perfectly correlated…they act…as an in-inseparable whole…even across large distances…prob'ly time, too." And then she erupted into orgasm again.

"Mmm…perfectly *correlated*…Tickle one and the other giggles."

Pirin's closed eyes snapped open. "What a good idea." She couldn't have told you (should you ever have asked) how she did it, but a heartbeat later Gracie was looking up at her shit-eating grin. "*My* turn, Grace Gwyllt Olwyn."

"But I'm not done yet," Gracie protested, trying to suppress a laugh.

"Damn right you're not."

Whereupon Pirin learned that Gracie enjoyed cunnilingus as much as she did.

"*This* might be entanglement, huh?" Gracie delicately twirled a finger around Pirin's left areola. "Between this here digit of mine and your—" She laughed as her finger stilled. "Ah, see? You've gone all puckery."

Pirin had been almost asleep. Well, she thought as her body jittered, best I know now: This woman is damn rambunctious. Damn *sexy* rambunctious. Abetting her involuntary squirm, she squeezed her glutes and pulled Gracie in for a lingering pillow talk kiss.

"Mmm," Pirin mumbled once they came up for air, *"that beat* of yours—*that* might be entanglement."

Stretched out next to Pirin, Gracie wriggled to that beat's rhythm. "Ha! *That body* of yours begs for entanglement," she quipped. "At least metaphorically."

"Actually," said Pirin, suddenly serious, "I think entanglement *has* happened to us. And I don't mean only metaphorically."

"You think we're *literally* quantum-entangled? As in we're connected..."

"Synchronized, correlated, entangled—even all the way down to the quantum level. Yes."

"So synchronized-correlated-entangled that we're—what exactly?"

"Well, let's start with your dreams, which seem to be synchronized-correlated-entangled with my amatchi's stories. What I used to call myths but now seem way more real than I ever appreciated."

Gracie switched her twirling finger to Pirin's right areola. "And how does that work?"

"Uhhhh..."

"C'mon, you're good at this now. Synchronized-correlated-entangled..."

"Umm...start with synchronization, which seems like entanglement at the macro scale. I mean, under the right circumstances almost everything can spontaneously synchronize..."

"The right circumstances..." murmured Gracie.

"Like what a clit does when a sexy woman plays with a connected nipple. Or when people dance. Pendulum clocks do it, our brains do it, even pure quantum systems do it." Pirin scooped up Gracie's roving fingers and kissed them. "Then there's phonons, which are about vibrational motion in a lattice of atoms or molecules. The lattice oscillates like a wave at a single frequency." Pirin turned to come nose to nose with Gracie. "*Like. In. A. Quartz. Crystal.*"

"The ohskal, which is mostly quartz crystals..."

"And therefore has a phonon thing going." Pirin winked. "Photons and phonons and electrons can entangle with each other. And they all exist in living things."

"Examples?"

"My favorite is birds. When a photon of sunlight hits a bird's retina, two unpaired electrons get released, then each electron spins to align itself with the earth's magnetic field, which is how birds know where to migrate. Same sort of thing might be happening with insects. Quantum behavior has also been shown in photosynthesis."

"How 'bout people?"

"Well, retinal neurons in our eyes perceive light—which is to say photons. Also, neurons in our brains emit biophotons, as many as a billion a second—so it's likely our brains do transmit light between neurons. And we know, of course, that light can carry complex messages."

"So maybe lightning entangled me with the ohskal? Or set off something in the ohskal that entangled me…"

"Well, lightning consists mostly of electrons—"

"Wait!" Gracie popped upright. "So lightning hits the ohskal, which maybe contains lattices of phonons that somehow carry the story that's been unfolding in my dreams. And this triggers entanglement between the lightning's flow of electrons and the ohskal's phonons, which in turn generate the photons that burst out of the ohskal and onto my retina." Gracie sighed. "Everything about this sounds so…"

"Mmm—unbelievable. But *maybe* that's only due to the fact that we're, y'know, stuck in a limited point of view. What you just suggested—that entanglement can happen across time as well as space—*has* been shown. Two quantum systems that never interacted with each other and also don't *simultaneously* interact with a common resource can be entangled when that common resource is first entangled with one of the quantum systems and then, *at a future time*, passes on the initial entanglement to a second quantum system."

Gracie looked like she couldn't decide whether to laugh or cry. "I get the feeling you're gonna tell me more about another point of view."

"Well, kinda…" Pirin chuckled, hoping it might be contagious. "Anytime anything's about dreams, point-of-view gets, um…"

"Upended."

"Back in the day, and possibly even still, the Iroquois believed in something called Ondinnonk—described as a secret desire of the soul that reveals itself in our dreams. Because for the Iroquois dreams are the language of the soul. When these secret desires aren't realized, the soul gets pissed off and the dreamer ends up unhappy or sick."

"The 'soul'…" Gracie murmured. "For a while now—like half my life—*my* point of view has been that, really truly, there's no such thing as a 'soul' with its own existence beyond the body. The so-called 'soul' is our mind, our brain—but we're desperate for separate since that duality feeds the illusion of life after death. Which, to me anyway, makes the 'soul' the centerpiece of extortionist religious bullshit."

"Yeah, I don't do dualism either. I see the 'soul' as that aspect of any living whole which is greater than the sum of its parts."

"I don't know what that means, Pirin."

"Physicists talk about quantum entanglement as the whole being greater than the sum of its parts because entangled particles no longer function as separate, individual components. They've become part of a next-level, irreducible single entity. My guess is that's what dreams do: give us glimpses of the irreducible whole that's greater than the sum of our parts. Where Ondinnonk is."

Gracie went quiet, nodding slightly. "I like that," she said finally, and then rose from the bed announcing "I think this irreducible whole's Ondinnonk is hungry. How 'bout I make us some dinner? I'm thinking hamburgers, home fries, and a fat-ass salad."

Pirin looked Gracie up and down. "Can we stay naked?"

"Hell yes!"

By Thursday evening, the Thursday morning when Gracie finally returned from what Pirin dubbed the Great Sleep seemed like a gazillion years ago.

Even so, Gracie wanted to know all about "gotcha."

"Ah," Pirin responded, "so you heard that. Whaddaya wanna know?"

"Everything."

"Okay. So I've learned a shitload about Veech Farkas over the last few days. The big news is that he really does wanna kill me. Got recordings of him saying so while he tried to recruit a hit man."

Gracie tried to suppress the wave of shock fear horror before it reached her face. "He's trying to do this from *prison?*"

"Yep."

And so Pirin led the way to the office where she laid it out on her three screens, window upon window of detail—database query results, image captures, audio recording highlights from her Spotter software.

"Remember the part about Veech being hooked up with Billy Whiting, who's his second cousin?" she began. "No surprise the Whitings and Veech's brother Ezra are bullshit at him for losing his corrections officer job. So zilch help from them. Next stop: this dude TJ, who years ago got him to rat out the Whitings. And I recorded it all."

"Jeezus. Are you telling me Veech Farkas *betrayed* his own brother?"

"Mmm-hmm. Among others."

"So who's this TJ?"

"A very nasty, violent prick. Young, smart, and after Billy Whiting's dirty little empire."

"Which you figured out *how?*"

"I decided to sift through my Veech data again looking for patterns," Pirin explained as she pointed to one of her screens. "Expanded from there."

Gracie leaned over Pirin's shoulder to study the screen. "Wow. Fifteen years back. ATM transactions. And that's, um, vehicle location data?"

"Which show—"

"Yeah, I see it. Time- and place-proximity of Veech's car to both cash withdrawals and gambling joints belonging to this guy Tarrio Jacques Sunty. TJ. And you think TJ manipulated Veech into turning on his brother and Billy Whiting by—?"

"—Exploiting Veech's poker addiction. I think TJ stoked Veech's resentments, let him win, then made sure he lost and ended up in debt." Pirin pointed at one of her screens. "*Then* TJ dangled a way out. Once a week for seven years, Veech showed up at this joint called Zelda's— owned by TJ. I figure that's when TJ paid him, gave him orders. Probably kept him gambling, too. So he'd stay in just the right amount of hock."

"So TJ owns Veech," Gracie mused. "And you can prove it."

"Thing is, TJ's agreed to take me out. Not an imminent threat, though."

"Why not?" Gracie demanded through gritted teeth.

Pirin smiled. "Because Veech has to ante up something worthwhile on Billy Whiting's operations *three times over* before TJ'll help him. And before *that* can happen, TJ needs to pull strings at Norfolk Correctional to get Veech a prison runner job in the unit that houses Billy's Norfolk crew. *Then* Veech has to smarm his way into the good graces of Billy guys, who don't trust him."

"You can bring down Veech Farkas right now, Pirin. You have the recording of him betraying Billy Whiting."

Pirin nodded. "Gotta figure out the how details, but the real question is when. I'm inclined to let it play out for a while. We have time—weeks at least, maybe months. So why not watch and wait? Cuz there's an opportunity here to bring down more than just Veech Farkas."

"How sure are you that TJ is Tarrio Jacques Sunty?"

"Let's say ninety-eight percent. The clincher was when I found Zelda's—the 'common resource' entangling Veech and TJ. Took me a while to uncover it, track down ownership. TJ's name is nowhere on the documents. He's all hidden behind LLCs and shit. But he's there all right. And I can prove that, too."

Gracie rested a hand on Pirin's shoulder. "So how do we find out who decides which prisoners at Norfolk Correctional get chosen to be runners?"

"Already working on it."

CHAPTER TWENTY-ONE: CAN I COME WITH YOU?

When Gracie woke that Friday morning after the Great Sleep, there were no dreams to remember; instead she was awash in an apprehension which quickly escalated into a how-fuckin'-dare-you *hmmph!* that bounced her out of bed.

Over morning coffee, Pirin urged calm. Again. "Norfolk Correctional's still in lockdown except for prisoners with kitchen and maintenance jobs. So jobless Veech Farkas remains stuck in his cell and the narrow tier outside his door. He can't get near Billy Whiting's guys, which means he's useless to TJ. Take it easy, Gracie. Take it easy and *breathe...*"

So Gracie did—or tried to anyway—and went about discovering her new normal now that she felt (mostly) like herself again.

First discovery: During the Great Sleep, Pirin had been busy with more than work and Veech Farkas data diving. She'd also set up a workspace for Gracie in her office. "Plenty of room for two in here, but if you don't like it..."

"This is for *me?*" she asked, genuinely thrilled as she approaching a two-piece oak corner desk situated alongside a bank of windows overlooking the wildflowers and the woodland. "I noticed this yesterday, but I—it's the best workspace *ever!*"

Then there was the Basamendi property and the other people who lived there.

The first time Gracie walked the woodland path with Pirin, she was enthralled. The main trail, kept broad enough for the family UTV "so we can cart around tools and wood," linked several other narrower side paths just wide enough so anyone walking them could dodge ticks. The woodland's acres were also dotted with those wildlife cameras Pirin had mentioned, most of which Gracie would've missed if they hadn't been pointed out. This really *is* a little enchanted forest, Gracie thought, deciding she'd stroll through it every day she could.

Thus she soon encountered Pirin's father, a friendly sixty-something fellow who stopped to introduce himself and welcome her as he hauled wood into his basement workshop. Pirin once described him as "the reason I know I'm not crazy," a comment Gracie had found mystifying—until she beheld the kindness in his eyes.

The following morning, as she again ventured across the meadow behind the garage toward the woodland, she met a child who proudly announced "I'm *four* now!" and then named every wildflower around them.

"Congratulations!" Gracie offered up her biggest smile. "How'd you learn so many flower names?"

The girl beamed. "My amatchi taught me."

My amatchi.

For a moment this disoriented Gracie. Had she slipped into some sort of waking version of an ohskal dream?

Reorientation arrived with the appearance of a woman pushing a trail stroller with an infant busy practicing heel kicks, which prompted an animated greeting from the four-year-old: "Ama! Look, Ama, fireweed!"

"Is it? Already?" replied a slightly fuller, prettier, auburn-haired version of Pirin who bent over the flower in question. "Yes, sweetie, you're right. What a great eye you have!" Then she turned to Gracie. "Welcome aboard! I'm Esti. I see you've already met Alaia. And here—" She tilted her head toward the stroller. "—We have Astiri."

Which meant that Alaia's amatchi must be Sama, right? And maybe this really *was* a waking ohskal dream…

Excellent, Pirin thought as she eyed Gracie. Going better than I dared hoped.

She'd worried because actually she hardly knew this smart, sexy, exquisitely numinous woman. Worried because her place was, perhaps, too small for more than one person despite her efforts to make it couple-capable. Worried because she couldn't quite see how it all would play out—just her and this woman whose epochal dreams defied explanation, whose gaze seemed to notice everything.

Their first week together certainly had been worrisome; Pirin had never dealt with concussion, and here was Gracie sleeping upwards of twenty hours a day. She loved lying next to Gracie, loved watching Gracie sleep—but by day three, she'd begun to worry that Gracie would keep on sleeping and dreaming forever...

Then *finally* Gracie woke, abruptly, completely. And with still more ohskal dream recordings, too, which reinforced Pirin's intensifying conviction that this smart, sexy, exquisitely numinous woman she hardly knew had tapped into something real that couldn't be explained by current paradigms of physics or time or medical science—not least because these were not just any dreams.

Pirin suspected that Gracie was chronicling Pirin's own genesis, reaching back countless generations. She hadn't actually said this aloud to (you guessed it) any other living soul, not even her ama—though her ama had sort of almost hinted a similar belief, despite how preposterous it sounded, and then refused to speculate further.

"I don't want to influence what's happening to Gracie any more than I already may have," Sama told Pirin. "Not even indirectly. Let's see where her dreams take her."

The person with whom to explore her suspicions would, therefore, be Gracie.

But, well—no.

As Gracie said so succinctly over breakfast coffee, "Only reason I'm the dreamer is that I was in the room when lightning touched the ohskal. Coulda been anybody. Or nobody."

"But it was *you*," Pirin objected. "Nobody else."

"Coincidence," Gracie grumped.

"*Meaningful* coincidence."

"Yeah yeah—*unus mundus*." Whereupon Gracie changed the subject with a piercing don't-make-me-hurt-you glare.

Gracie's staredown aside, she seemed to be settling in quite well at her desk in the office. Too well, perhaps. For several days, she'd spent hours hunched over her laptop, evidenced by how many more acetaminophen tablets she'd consumed.

When Pirin suggested she ease off, Gracie agreed. "Wasn't working the whole time—not at my job, anyway. Just sent Naomi the bitchiest email I've ever written in my life, along with that video file I asked you for, the one showing her pit bull slamming me into my living room wall. Told her the creep has cost me weeks of work and maybe I should make a police complaint. Or sue her ass off."

"Is this your way," Pirin asked, "of deploying chaff against Palasin in case they actually recover anything from Naomi's laptop?"

"Two for one, I guess, because I'm also pissed as hell at her. Those guys were *her* pit bulls. Her responsibility. So she can pay the fine."

"Think she'll offer you go-away money?"

"Yeah, I do. Unless Palasin fires her. We'll see." Gracie rose from her desk chair and took Pirin's hand, which she seemed to study intently. "In other news from another email, my landlord wants his apartment back. Not right away—he's willing to give me into the fall— but it means we, um, kinda have a deadline about deciding whether we're, y'know, compatible. Cuz if we're not…"

"Do you—?" A wave of consternation burned outward from the center of Pirin's chest. "I thought—" Her gaze got stuck on Gracie's hand holding hers, then on the floor as she tried to keep her face neutral. Tried and failed. "Have I fucked this up already? Cuzza Veech Farkas? Or—?"

"No no no!" Gracie grabbed Pirin's other hand and tightened her grip. "I don't want to go. I want to stay here. With you." She gently kneaded the hands she held. "I just thought I should give you an out. In case you, um…"

Pirin shook her head. "The last thing I want is an out."

"Same here."

Encouraged, Pirin escalated. "How soon can you move out of your apartment?"

"My landlord lives downstairs and wants to combine my unit with his, so he'd be happy to get rid of me yesterday."

"Great! Let's move you outta there, like, tomorrow!"

Laughing, Gracie nudged her forehead against Pirin's. "We're working tomorrow. Y'know, at our jobs?"

"Nothing I can't rearrange. How 'bout you?"

Gracie turned serious, conveyed by her forehead massaging Pirin's. "Are you sure? It's a big step."

Pirin lifted a hand to cup Gracie's face and kept her gaze on those blue eyes. "Truth, okay?" She inhaled deeply, exhaled slowly. "I'm scared shitless because you see me so damn clearly. Scared you won't like what you see. That what you see will drive you away forever. But there's something about the *way* you look at me, the *way* you see me…" Pirin tried to smile. "So I—I gotta try…"

❖

Moving Gracie's stuff from Belmont into Pirin's digs went smoothly, not least because there was little to move. The landlord made use of what Sama didn't want; the rest—including Gracie's clothes, her revered living room chair, and her books and computer gear—Pirin had anticipated and made room for.

Then came the matter of the rent. Gracie and Pirin had their first genuine argument about the rent, which Pirin didn't want Gracie to pay. At all.

"Of *course* I'm gonna pay you rent!" Gracie huffed. "I refuse to be a kept woman."

The squabble continued until Pirin proposed a compromise. "How 'bout a percentage of your take-home pay?" Eventually Gracie (reluctantly) agreed to twenty-five percent, though she insisted that thirty-three percent would be fairer.

They made peace by making love. This launched what Gracie referred to as Wicked Horny Week, a cannabis-enriched romp that encompassed Pirin's birthday. Except for an afternoon cake-and-ice cream family gathering on the deck, they spent at least half their waking hours horizontal, red-hot throbbing wet, and way too preoccupied to say much of anything. When they got vertical (naked but for aprons), Gracie discovered Pirin's tchistor and potato ragout while Pirin discovered Gracie's cranberry scones and walnut chocolate chip cookies.

Soon they began to form joint habits—taking turns at meal prep and cleanup and various household chores, like vacuuming, dusting, dragging garbage cans to the street, weed-whacking the woodland's paths. They established work rules, too: No interrupting to casually chat (or kiss or feel somebody up) during core working hours—"because," as Pirin put it, "if we stay laser-focused and get our shit done, the rest of the day is *ours*."

Once they realized they were both productivity freaks, they teamed up to achieve impressive efficiency during the weekly grocery shopping Pirin wanted to take on for all of the seven-sometimes-eight people in the two Basamendi households. "Least I can do," Gracie insisted as she also assumed the job of Grocery List Keeper, "since you won't let me pay my fair share."

So far so good, Gracie thought, in spite of a vague, nagging restlessness in her solar plexus. No more ohskal dreams (not yet anyway), but she often woke in the night and stayed that way unless she crept out to the living room to pace till fatigue engulfed her and she'd return to bed, at last able to sleep again.

If Pirin was aware of this, she gave no hint. She rose crack-of-dawn early—*way* before Gracie, who'd never been an early riser—rousing Gracie just enough to cop a good-morning cuddle-and-kiss prior to disappearing for some two hours anyway.

Gracie wasn't sure initially because she was too drowsy to quite register the pattern. Until she did. "Where do you go so early in the morning?" she eventually asked.

"I start with a quick scoot to the office to check out what Spotter's picked up. Then over to the etche to work out downstairs. Weights, the rowing machine. Back to the office after that. What I do next varies. No pentesting stuff at the moment, so I've been catching up on case reports. And sometimes I'll do an interview. This morning, though, I *finally* finished prepping the drones."

"Drones," Gracie repeated. She'd forgotten about Pirin's drones. "Right…"

"I'll be flying 'em out back later today to make sure they're behaving, cuz I accepted a mission for tomorrow. Just down the road, checking out the roof of a condo complex after yesterday's storm. No more than an hour of flight time, but flying's always fun *and* it'll boost the bank account a little."

"Can I come with you?"

"Oooh." Pirin grinned. "I'd *love* that."

CHAPTER TWENTY-TWO: ONLY A DREAM...

Pirin possessed three drones, but when it came to flying for business rather than kicks, she chose the newest one, a commercial-grade quadcopter called FourSoar that she'd agreed to beta-test for its developer and hoped to keep when the testing concluded.

"Gotta get in enough hours for them not to want their beta back," she explained to Gracie as she prepped FourSoar and its camera payload for the condo roof inspection job. Gracie, meanwhile, studied the machine's user manual.

Though such initiative struck Pirin as over-the-top, it contributed to Gracie's presence speed-evolving from along-just-for-the-hell-of-it to the more formal role of flight observer, eyes on the drone and its surrounds while Pirin piloted and took close-up photos and video of the large, convoluted condo roof. Quite endearing, the way Gracie embraced this task with almost childlike eagerness—and a really good sign too, thought Pirin, who was eager to establish common ground with Gracie beyond ohskal dreams, cunnilingus, and cranberry scones.

Gracie turned out to be a damn good observer, dashing around to maintain visual line of sight with the drone, alerting Pirin to a storm-damaged utility line, explaining their unusual behavior to curious condo owners, even helping Pirin avoid a fallen tree limb.

By mission's end, Gracie's blue eyes were alight. "Oh *yeah*," she proclaimed, "I gotta learn how to fly drones."

As they packed the little machine into its carrying case, Pirin noticed Gracie paying particular attention to the handheld ground control station, her fingers delicately moving over its dual joysticks and assorted buttons, its two antennas, its now-blank touchscreen that had come alive with the drone's camera view during the flight...

"Wanna try flying my trainer quadcopter when we get home?" Pirin asked—an instantly rhetorical question given that Gracie's squealy "*Yes!*" reverberated across the condominium complex parking lot as soon as Pirin got out the first three words.

An hour later, they'd set up the trainer on the granite patio behind the garage and completed the AbsolutelyNecessaryEverySingleTime pre-flight check.

"Okay, Gracie, I've backed down the stabilization on the controls, so you'll be doing almost *all* the flying manually," Pirin explained again. "Except if you feel like you're losing control, right? Then you just let go of everything and press the big red Return to Home button, and as soon as you press it the drone'll automatically come back to this very spot."

Squinting at the ground control station, Gracie listened, nodded, then resumed muttering what had become a kind of mantra: "Left joystick's throttle and yaw—" She moved the small stick forward, backward, then right and left. "Right joystick's pitch and roll—" She pushed the right joystick forward, backward, right, left. "And I'll be moving 'em both at the same time."

"Yep. Keep it slow at first. Small joystick movements. *Small*. And remember—" Pirin was about to repeat the usual reminder to novices about how when the drone and its camera point away from you, the controls are intuitive, but when you steer the drone back *toward* you, the controls invert, so when you move a joystick right, the drone approaching you goes left...

Before she could say more, though, the trainer's propellers whirred and the little quadcopter zipped upward. Fast. Pirin held her breath. *Way the* fuck *too fast!*

"Yeah!" Gracie hooted. "*Yeah!*"

The quad wobbled for a second or two as it lifted higher, higher, then steadied and zipped away from them for about fifty feet before it rolled right, reversed direction, leveled, and came speeding directly back at them. Oh shit, Pirin worried as the trainer whizzed closer, she's gonna slam it right into the garage—

But no—with maybe three feet to spare Gracie rolled the trainer again, banking it hard left this time while she pushed the throttle forward so the drone ascended dramatically before she began to execute a smooth figure-eight high above them. Thoroughly alarmed, heartbeat thumping wildly, Pirin pivoted to stare at Gracie, who couldn't possibly know what she was doing. Except maybe she did. Somehow.

"You've—" Pirin struggled to keep her voice low, calm. "You've just skipped about a gazillion lessons. I thought you said you've never done this before."

"That's right." Gracie beamed, her gaze shifting between the ground control station's screen and the drone circling above them. "I haven't."

Basandere, Pirin thought, you really *are* dangerous, Grace Gwyllt Olwyn.

Besides the small trainer quadcopter and the far more sophisticated FourSoar beta-test quad, Pirin also had a fixed-wing tricopter capable of vertical takeoff and landing. Acquired from "this dubious drone forum dude," it had been goosed into achieving, among other wonders, a two-hour flight time and a maximum forward speed of ninety miles per hour—and the first time Gracie saw it assembled and flying she fell in love with it.

A sleek gray carbon-fiber corker measuring fifty-two inches across and weighing in at slightly under three pounds, Pirin referred to it as "the tri." Gracie called it Dragonfly. It looked like a glider but for its tail propeller and two more frontward-extending rotatable props that enabled it to hover, then suddenly move at spectacular speeds in the most unexpected ways.

In love with it or not, Gracie was afraid to pilot the thing, not least due to its daunting ground control station. On its top screen, this dual-monitor marvel displayed live layered video from a gimbaled hi-def electro-optical/infrared camera and a micro LiDAR camera. The bottom screen, meanwhile, further boosted the pilot's situational awareness with imagery from multiple integrated wide-angle low-light navigation cameras overlayed with real-time telemetry from myriad operational sensors, including GPS and extensive detect-and-avoid automation.

Oh and don't forget the military-grade encrypted multiple low-latency transmission channels and the autonomous object tracking. Dragonfly even came with a directable spotlight. Its extensive automation meant one could plot a course and the drone would fly itself from takeoff to landing. Or it could be flown manually. Or semi-manually. Or, as Pirin put it, "whatever you damn well want."

Gracie damn well wanted it all.

If you'd asked her why, she wouldn't have been able to tell you a whole lot. She understood only that she was totally, unabashedly exhilarated as soon as she'd first moved the joysticks on the trainer's ground control station and the little machine began to defy gravity. More tiny moves of the joysticks and it took off, it turned. Just like she wanted it to. The experience was eerily reminiscent of "flying" with Bele the raven in the ohskal dreams. Except when she flew the drone, *she alone* was in control of where it went, how it went.

By the time that first training flight was over, Gracie already had a feel for the relationship—and the airwave-dependent timing—between drone and joysticks. She had no trouble staying oriented, either. Despite standing on the ground alternately looking at a digital screen and glancing skyward, she nearly instantly experienced the world as though she was *inside* the drone looking out. Likewise with FourSoar, which she successfully piloted a few days after flying the trainer.

But *Dragonfly*—jeez, Dragonfly was scary. In another league entirely.

So Gracie spent every spare moment with the tricopter's flight simulator software, part of Dubious Drone Forum Dude's impressively complete package of Dragonfly extras. Her hours on the flight simulator helped. Bigly. As did Pirin's patient, careful (and distractingly sexy) preflight coaching about calibrations and systems checks.

"You're a natural, Gracie." Pirin's compliment came with a gently suggestive nudge, simultaneously teasing and serious. "Sure as hell you don't need any flying tips from me."

Gracie returned the nudge, just as suggestively, she hoped—and with a gratitude she didn't disguise. "Thank you for letting me fly this one, Pir."

Grinning, Pirin bowed. It felt to Gracie like a vote of confidence.

Even so, her fingers jittered when she took her place at the edge of the patio and picked up Dragonfly's ground control station, wonderfully lightweight but as intimidating as ever even after two weeks of using it in simulated manual flights.

"Ready?" asked Pirin.

Gracie inhaled, exhaled. "Yeah. Ready."

As her thumbs and forefingers worked the joysticks and Dragonfly rose smoothly upward, she relaxed: Her fingers knew exactly what to do.

Dragonfly swooped wide left and climbed as it rounded the side of the garage before lifting higher and higher above the long driveway. By the time it reached the road, Gracie had gotten herself properly oriented (synchronized? correlated? entangled?), imagining herself into Dragonfly's cockpit as the machine traveled well above the trees along the Basamendi property line, its forward-facing camera scanning the landscape beneath her.

Just like she'd practiced on the simulator. Just like she damn well wanted. Her rapport with this remarkable two-piece machine had begun. That night brought her the best night's sleep she'd experienced since recovering from the concussion—plus an ohskal dream, too.

"So they're back?" asked Pirin, eyebrows lifting with ill-concealed excitement as soon as Gracie spoke that word: ohskal.

"One dream anyway."

"Did you—? Can I—?"

"—Yes, I did." Gracie laughed. "And yes, you can." Then she handed Pirin her tablet:

⚡ "Emegon—Good Women—as we now approach the moment that begins the journey so familiar to us," Eletun commenced while her audience again settled around the fire, "we truly know it for the first time."

Wait, I wanted to yell out, whaddaya mean *the moment that begins the journey?* And whaddaya mean *so familiar?* I don't know shit about any of this!

But before I could open my mouth, Eletun shot me the Look. So I kept quiet and Eletun continued: "We can at last appreciate why Analergin and Kaldi entangled as intimate partners for the rest of their lives, why they undertook their long, difficult journey during such treacherous times, and why they articulated the profound principles by which we still live and love each other. Yet there is a further matter…"

The women around the fire rustled and murmured.

"Hurrulgahsoa!" one of them called out.

"Yes, yes, the Sea Beyond," seconded several others. "How did—?"

"Stop!" I shouted—because no. *No!* If I lost the thread now I'd never figure out what these damn dreams meant. "Are you saying all this stuff about Analergin and Sineusi and Kaldi and Privation has been some kinda *prequel?* Well, goddammit, *I* never saw the original movie!"

Whereupon the women around the fire turned as one to gape while a smiling Eletun shook her lowered head. Omigod, I realized, they can hear me. *They can see me!* I've become part of whatever the hell this campfire thing is.

"We have many songs about this period, Gracie," Eletun acceded, "so let's see if we can fill you in a bit. Again." Then her gaze flicked from woman to woman around the fire. "Emegon, I ask for your assistance."

A brief buzz accompanied their near-unison nods even as some of them turned for a quick second (or third or fourth) glance at me.

"Excellent. Thank you." Eletun was grinning now. "So: How many of the women decided to climb into the Mountains with Analergin and Kaldi and Sineusi?"

"Twenty-one joined Analergin, Kaldi, and Sineusi," someone declared. "Seven chose to follow one of the River tributaries southwestward while five others lost nerve and turned back to Privation. We know nothing of their fates."

"Quite so, Eki—thank you." Eletun bowed her head in acknowledgement. "The Tales tell us that after Analergin and Kaldi reached them, the women departed their shelter by the River in daylight. Did any Privation bounty hunters find the twenty-four who journeyed into the Mountains?"

"Oh no," laughed a chorus of voices.

Eyeing me, a woman called Gwele explained. "Kaldi always walked last and hung back to make sure they were not seen or followed. One story describes Kaldi returning of an evening with blood-covered hands, but all she would say is what she always said…"

A soft chuckle rose from Eletun's audience as they recited together what I understood to be a familiar mantra: "'No one seeks us now, we are safe tonight.'"

"And after sixteen days crossing the Mountains," Eki added, "they reached the shore of the Near Western Sea—all twenty-four of them."

"What did they do when they arrived there?" asked Eletun.

"Gathered food for their first meal," said Eki. "This was especially difficult since the western shore had not much regenerated after suffering the Seawaves invoked by Subendi's eruption. Not even after five Suncycles."

"They also found a hillside cave to serve as their Lightning shelter, for they were on the stormy side of the Mountains where Lightning abounded in those days," noted someone called Kurruh. "And they chose where to construct their commonhouse. All on the first day."

"Also, Kaldi made a fire," offered a woman named Sagar. "They gathered 'round it and this is when Analergin told them she intended to build an outrigger canoe and sail to the New Motherworld. Not all rejoiced at this prospect, yet none complained."

"The next day they began working and learning," said Gwele. "Analergin taught a few of the women how to swim, and these soon taught the rest."

"And some foraged their food, always in double pairs so they might protect each other," added Kurruh, "while Sineusi laid out their first Tending and Analergin went in search of the proper tree for her canoe—a large ederorri. This is when Bele appeared again."

"Ah, Bele the raven," I murmured, imagining Bele and Analergin once again soaring over treetops.

"Yes, Analergin relied on Bele to show her many, many things," Sagar added with a glance that made me wonder if the woman had read my thoughts, or perhaps shared my dreams, "including which ederorri would best serve for the canoe Analergin intended to construct. And when Analergin returned with Bele to the hillside cave, the others had a meal prepared and they all took time to celebrate their freedom."

"They also celebrated Analergin's first sighting of the porpoises," said someone else, "and chose a name for their vessel, too."

"Indeed, Ametsa." Eletun bowed to Ametsa. "And that name was…?"

"'Bisiberria'—'The New Life,'" Ametsa replied. "Then, at last, while Jarrai and Mardul maintained watch and Sineusi guided the others at their tasks, Analergin and Kaldi went off by themselves and made love. And all the women felt it, their love. We feel it still. Every day. Every night."

A silence ensued. *That's it?* I wondered. That's all you're gonna tell me? Before anyone else spoke, I asked a question of my own: "How long did it take them to build Analergin's canoe?"

"Oh, many Mooncycles," Ametsa said. "It was nine reaches long, and to craft it the women had to learn almost *everything* from Analergin."

"She taught them so much," added Kurruh. "How to build small cone-shaped drinking water makers that used charcoal and Sunlight to remove salt from Seawater, how to craft tools like threading bones and fishing lines, how to find all they needed to journey across the Seas."

"Not just fish and edible plants to eat, either," Gwele pointed out. "Also flax, for its oil and its fiber to create bowstrings and raiment, too, so they might warm themselves during the cold nights on the Sea. Even before they felled the ederorri tree, they worked on crafting the floats and crossbeams and platforms and the windward shelter and the mast and booms and poles and rope and cordage, lots and lots of cordage."

"And while some formed the hull by carving and burning out the ederorri, others gathered and prepared the thornyleaves that would be lashed together into the canoe's great birdwings sail," said Eki.

"The Tales tell us the women worked together well," Sagar noted. "Analergin's leadership was firm but attentive and generous. In the pitcave and during their trek to the western shore, she had observed each woman's abilities and weaknesses, who created close friendships with whom. This knowledge she employed to strengthen their communion and commitment."

"Even before each woman sailed in Bisiberria during shakedowns," Kurruh elaborated, "Analergin suspected several would shrink from the impending journey. And she was right. Six women admitted they did not want to go to Sea. In those days, the Sky churned and Lightning struck much more often than now—more on Land than at Sea, of course, but on Land women sheltered in caves. Not at Sea, though, which made travel by Sea terribly dangerous."

"Yet the six wanted to learn all they could from Analergin and Sineusi and Kaldi, who knew how to 'live wild,'" added Sagar. "So they stayed to take care of the Tending and the commonhouse, where they continued to live after the others set sail. When at last Bisiberria departed, some of them wept as they waved from shore. After that, we know nothing of their fates."

"So no Privation bounty hunters ever found them?" I asked.

"Oh, Privation tried," replied Ametsa. "They came looking—by Land *and* by Sea. Kaldi, with Jarrai and Mardul and Honsoli, stopped those who approached by Land. The Tales say that not a single Privation bounty hunter who came over the Mountains survived to reveal the women's presence. As for Privation boats, two approached several Mooncycles apart—and both sailed by without finding anyone."

"Because," Eki added, "Analergin saw them coming."

"Yes, with the help of Sublime Perception and Bele and also her two-crystal shaft," said Gwele. "This gave the women time to hide. Analergin had taught them well how to hide."

"So Analergin, Kaldi, Sineusi, and fifteen others set to Sea in search of this—this New Motherworld?" I asked.

"Yes!" everyone replied in unison.

"The women were novices," Ametsa emphasized, "but under Analergin's direction they made a fine outrigger canoe and an excellent sail that, the Tales tell us, brought Bisiberria all the way to the Land touched by Hurrulgahsoa."

"The Sea Beyond, you mean." I searched the faces gazing at me. "Where *is* the Sea Beyond?"

"*That* is what we want to know," Ametsa said, turning expectantly to Eletun.

"And so you shall, Emegon," replied Eletun. "First, however, we must tell Gracie how many generations have passed since Bisiberria departed the western shore."

The women chorused "Twelve hundred generations."

"And how many more generations will pass before Gracie herself takes form in the world?"

For the first time, Eletun's audience hesitated as their murmurs rippled. Oh, I deduced, they're counting. When the murmurs subsided a few seconds later, Gwele spoke up. "Four hundred generations," she declared to a hum of agreement.

"Yes," Eletun concurred. "Quite so."

Pirin spoke in a hush. "Gracie, that's—that's a total of *sixteen hundred* generations!"

"And a generation is—what? Twenty years? Twenty-five?"

"Basandere!" Pirin shook her head like she was trying to rid it of cobwebs. "By that measure, the time when you're hanging out with Eletun and friends was eight to ten thousand years ago—and Analergin and Kaldi and Sineusi come from somewhere between thirty-two thousand and forty thousand years ago."

What could Gracie do but shrug? "Only a dream…"

CHAPTER TWENTY-THREE:
BEYOND VISUAL LINE OF SIGHT

Y ou wanna fly at *night?*" Pirin was incredulous. "That's totally illegal."

Gracie shook her head. "Not if I fly as a recreational pilot. And I'll keep Dragonfly over the property. Promise. Promise promise promise." She paused into a frown before her face brightened. "Plus I could cheat—turn off the ID stuff. Nav lights off too if you want. So no one'll know."

"*I'll* know." Pirin rubbed her face more in frustration than surprise. "You just wanna play with the infrared and LiDAR cameras in the dark. Tracking cars down East Broadway."

"*And* getting some photos and video of the full moon."

Ever since Gracie first flew the tri and proceeded to flounce beyond visual line of sight (allegedly) without realizing, she'd wanted more BVLOS drone piloting. Easily accomplished "by accident"—like every damn time she dipped the drone behind the tree line to fly low over the six-acre pasture at the northwest end of the property.

Now she was in pursuit of ultimate BVLOS: darkness. Flying the tri manually in first-person-view some three hundred feet above the property relying entirely on infrared, LiDAR, and luck for situational awareness. Without being able to see squat from the ground. While taking pretty pictures.

Was it irony that Pirin had no doubt Gracie would do a fine job? A spectacular job even; some three months after her first flight, Gracie was already an accomplished FPV drone pilot, had acquired her remote pilot certificate from the FAA, and along the way developed quite decent aerial photography and videography skills. She'd even used some of her own video in her job at the Institute, to Jessica's delight.

Still, in the *dark?*

"Aw c'mon," Gracie pleaded, "it's not really darkness when the moon's full…"

"It's raining. And foggy. And friggin' cold out."

"Weather's supposed to clear and warm up some by tomorrow night, just in time for the full moon. And besides, you said yourself that Dragonfly's better equipped for bee-vloss than—"

"—Yeah yeah, 'any military or commercial drone in its class.'"

"Be*cause*…" Gracie's come-hither gesture, accompanied by a sly grin, meant that until Pirin acquiesced she'd keep right on hithering.

Pirin sighed. The "illegal" argument had always been a lost cause. "Because," she recited in a singsong, eyes rolling, "Dubious Drone Forum Dude pilfered the tri's design specs and source code to use as a starting point for his own drone, which was way better than anything coming out of the DoD-funded companies that either fired him or refused to hire him—and yes I knew all that when I paid a fraction of what the tri's really worth, and yes I gave him cash so he could scurry off to Panama or wherever the fuck he's hiding." Pirin sighed again. "Satisfied?"

Gracie saccharine-smiled. "Almost." And kept on saccharine-smiling.

"Alright, dammit. Al*right*." Pirin raised her hands, palms outward, fingers spread. Acquiescence complete. "But don't you *dare* get caught."

Gracie did not get caught. Or crash the tri. Not on the clear, bright night of the full moon nor on any of the other three nights over the following week when she took the tri aloft again.

Pirin said okay to all of it because flying the tri distracted Gracie. By then, Pirin had been zero-clicking her way into the bowels of the Whiting organization—and Norfolk Correctional—for more than four months. While Gracie conquered BVLOS, Pirin was tracking dozens of smartphones, not quite overloading her Spotter app or her own ability to follow who was who, but nearly.

To keep up, Pirin had generated a detailed Whiting empire organizational chart that reflected Cleary Whiting's propensity for classic corporate titles: "vice presidents," "directors," "managers," "team members," plus "independent contractors"—lawyers, accountants, and such "advisors" as the occasional politician or cop or CO on the take. And, just as she hadn't divulged much to Gracie about significant past "events" in her own life, she'd defaulted into "not bothering" BVLOS-distracted Gracie with too many details about the Whitings.

Not until she figured out what to do with what she'd learned.

Trouble was, she hadn't figured out shit.

Now, the morning after the tricopter's fourth night flight, Pirin faced a new round of Gracie's questions about Veech, notably: Has he found a hit man yet?

Short answer: No.

But this time Gracie wanted specifics, the kind where one thing leads uncomfortably to another.

"Well," Pirin began as she sat with Gracie at the bistro table drinking coffee, "After six months, Veech has finally managed to contact Billy Whiting's Norfolk Correctional crew boss."

Gracie's eyes widened. "Smartphone?"

"Yep. So I zero-clicked it, put Spotter to work on it."

"How'd Billy's guy respond? To Veech, I mean."

"Followed the boss's orders—ignored Veech's text, then deleted it. Billy still thinks Veech is an asshole and doesn't trust him."

"What about...?" The frown on Gracie's face gave away the rest of her question.

"Norfolk Correctional's still locked down, so Veech is still stuck in his cell and his tier," Pirin assured her. "Judging by recent notations in his inmate record, Norfolk's administrators don't trust him either. So no runner job yet, and probably not anytime soon."

"*Yes!*" Gracie pumped a fist. "And what about TJ?"

Pirin shook her head. "TJ doesn't ever communicate with Veech using a smartphone."

"So no zero-clicking him."

"Nope. He's not taking Veech's voice calls, either, but does respond maybe a third of the time to Veech's texts, always with some version of 'you're not trying hard enough.'"

Gracie indulged in a long, slow exhale, then a tenuous smile. "Anytime you tell me Veech is still isolated and friendless, I breathe better."

"Mmm, well, he's not entirely friendless. There's his mama, who keeps his inmate account maxed. And he regularly whines on his phone to his nephew, Ezra's kid."

"Zach?"

"Yeah, Zach. Now nineteen and living in a college dorm in Worcester, but as enthralled by Uncle Veech as ever. Except for his mama and Zach, seems like Veech has given up on getting much from outside of Norfolk Correctional. Makes me suspect he's moving in the only other direction available to him: trying to make connections inside, on his cell tier. Connections beyond the reach of zero-click and the Spotter app."

"Connections," Gracie added bleakly, "that could eventually lead him to a hit man."

"Well, at least 'eventually' points to later rather than sooner." Pirin took a deep breath; time to tell Gracie the rest. "Which works out cuz, uh, I have other news."

Gracie's face darkened. "What?"

Pirin rose from the table and glanced toward the office. "Lemme show you."

A moment later, they were gazing at a screen that displayed Pirin's Whiting org chart. "Here," Pirin pointed. "These are—"

"Yeah, I see: Whiting 'independent contractors.' Quite a collection."

Pirin's finger rested on one line in particular. "This."

Gracie read: "Nucifera Financial Management."

"S-So, um," Pirin bumbled, "This is the outfit that does the final-stage laundering of the Whitings' dirty money—last step before brother Brian, the hedge fund Whiting, turns their millions into billions. Nucifera Financial Management is owned by this dude Andreas Nelumbo, a-and…umm…"

"What, Pirin? *What?*"

"I've met Nelumbo. Last year he submitted a bullshit claim that I was assigned to investigate. So I went to his office to interview him. He was so busy trying to break my bones with his testosterone-drenched handshake that he neglected his laptop screen, and I glimpsed its reflection in the office window just before he remembered to click it off. A paused video of two naked, scared, barely pubescent girls. Before I left, I managed to spot the laptop's password, and I, uh—I coulda called the cops, but, frankly, I had no faith in them caring enough to do shit…"

Gracie was staring now. Staring hard. "So you—" She squinted. "No, you didn't steal the laptop…" Her eyes squeezed shut for a second—"Oh"—before popping open again, bluer than ever. "You hacked into it, didn't you?"

Pirin winced. *How* does she do that? "On the day we first met. His place is close to—" Pirin blinked against her rising *ouch!* "So I did a little wardriving…"

"And those two thugs in the park? They caught you?"

Pirin shook her head. "Don't think so. That was about exactly what it looked like—Veech Farkas's compulsive hatred of women who refuse to submit to him. Bonecrusher—that's my nickname for Nelumbo cuz of his ridiculous handshake—Bonecrusher and his penchant for budding breasts was a whole other matter. My interview with him went down a month before I ever crossed paths with Veech Farkas."

"So…" Gracie snickered. "You're claiming coincidence."

"Yeah, I guess I am. But when I discovered the connection between Bonecrusher and the Whitings, it got me wondering how Bonecrusher came by those images. Then I found out that Billy Whiting's contribution to his daddy's empire includes more than the two glitzy gambling-and-entertainment palaces he's opened in the last few years. He's also hooked up with an 'independent contractor' named Ryle who operates the palaces' very lucrative 'custom leisure services' as a 'franchise.'"

Gracie grimaced. "Lemme guess: The Whitings' Chief Pedophile-Pimp."

"Exactly. Besides all the flavors of trad adult prostitution, Ryle offers everything the well-heeled pedophile could ever want. Underage anything. Videos are just the beginning. And no surprise that he keeps meticulous data on all his customers—including Bonecrusher. Very useful for extortion and blackmail. Plus Ryle's franchise status gives Billy deniability should anyone ever get caught doing anything, y'know, unpropitious."

After four-plus months of living with Pirin Basamendi 'round the clock, Gracie felt more at ease than she'd expected. And found herself *way* hornier than she'd expected. Which was saying something; prior experience had her concerned that her attraction to Pirin would do what all her previous attractions had done: fade too soon, then dully loiter while she vainly hoped for some kind of miraculous turnaround.

So yes, Pirin was different. Excitingly, sexily different.

For one thing, Pirin was still really fun to talk with. Pirin also liked to play in every sense of that tricksy word. There was a bonus, too: Pirin was great fun to look at.

Gracie kept discovering different parts of her. The intelligence in her eyes when she squinted. The quirky, slightly crooked smile. The breathtaking agility of her magnificently muscled legs, those robust shoulders, tuned biceps and lats and glutes. The intricate ways the flexors in her forearms danced when her fingers worked a keyboard. Combined with a temperament that commingled relaxed-and-easygoing with high-octane, take-no-shit ferocity, Pirin was a trip to watch, a trip to touch and kiss and lick and surrender to.

Nevertheless, Gracie knew she still had much to learn about Pirin Basamendi. Much that Pirin resisted showing her, despite what she saw roiling in those bottomless eyes, in words almost spoken but not quite. Why? *What the hell could be so awful?*

At night, lying in bed next to Pirin, she contemplated answers to that question—in the form of What Would I Do If [fill in the blank]…?

And yet Gracie didn't press. Pirin would reveal what she wanted when she wanted. Perhaps she'd already begun. Apparently Sama thought so. Jessica, too.

"I'm really grateful Pirin has someone to confide in," Sama told Gracie early on. "There's so much I don't hear because she doesn't want to worry me."

And then, during their most recent Tuesday morning screen meeting, Jessica commented "Y'know, I think of Pirin as indrawn. With you, though—it's like she's finally exhaling."

But maybe not exhaling voluntarily. Never mind that Pirin seemed to be showing her, leading her, inviting guesses and insights. Was she getting this wrong—or was Pirin riding a seesaw of ambivalence?

Gracie did wonder. Because there were these moments when she just *knew* what Pirin had done, was about to do, wanted to do. Moments of eerily striking clarity when she comprehended that which she had no "rational" way of comprehending. Rather like what she'd experienced in the ohskal dreams when Eletun thrust her "into" Analergin.

And so far at least, Grace Gwyllt Olwyn, it sure as hell seems like Pirin *wants* to be comprehended, her reticent mumbles and pauses notwithstanding. C'mon, Pirin damn well knows what's happening and *invited you to move in with her anyway.*

And now she's telling you about this creep who wants to kill her. About this obscenely wealthy, deeply corrupt family enterprise wreathed in vicious criminality. She's showing you stuff that, in the right hands, would bring the world down on their heads, and down on her and her family and you, too, if any of them ever discover what she's got.

And then—*then* she squints that squint of hers and you *know*: She will *not* let it go. You *know* she'll huddle in the office gathering data, sussing out patterns, planning some damn thing or other—all while doing the job that pays her a salary and garners kudos from her supervisor.

And when she emerges, she'll stretch as she strides into the living room to "synopsize" what she's been doing in ways that both avoid the underneath truth of her and nevertheless circle closer to it as you watch, alert for the details that spark your moment of clarity. And then you'll tell her what you've perceived, whereupon her head will drop into a nod, her raspy confession coming first in wavering mumbles, then a torrent. And this time, like every time she does that, you'll fall a little bit more in love with her.

CHAPTER TWENTY-FOUR:
A MOMENT THAT HASN'T YET OCCURRED

The thing about falling in love is that even when you want to it's scary. And when the woman you're falling for belongs to a mini-tribe with long-established (even ancient) habits and rituals—a mini-tribe that hangs out forty feet from where the two of you make love—things can get downright discombobulating. Downright vertiginous. And damn unnerving.

For Gracie, adapting to the Basamendi tribe would have been much harder but for Pirin's drones and Alaia. Every time Gracie went down to the patio to launch a flight, Alaia appeared, eager to "help." This was distracting at first, but how do you shoo away a smart, adorable four-year-old who really does make a good assistant?

So they became partners in crime, agreeing not to tell Auntie Pir when the "funny little plane" dipped out of sight below the trees or around the side of the garage. They did, however, decide to let Auntie Pir know about the "hurt" wildlife camera Alaia noticed along one of the narrow side paths near the southwestern edge of the property's woodland.

"Hurt?" asked a clearly dubious Pirin.

"Yes," Alaia answered firmly as Gracie, standing behind her, silently nodded. "Somebody got real mad at it, Auntie Pir."

"Okay." Pirin rose from her desk. "Can you show me?"

"It's Number Three," Alaia called as she bounded down the stairs to lead the way.

Alaia was right about all of it: Yes, the Number Three wildlife camera had been messed with—turned downward *very* carefully so that it still worked fine but its field of view covered only a small patch of ground, not the thirty-foot sweep Pirin had originally set up.

"Somebody got real mad at it all right," Pirin grumbled after Alaia scampered back to the etche for dinner. During their own evening meal, Gracie and Pirin figured out when the wildlife camera had been diddled, which took a while since the wildlife camera recordings had to be manually retrieved, uploaded to a computer, and reviewed by a person.

"Got it!" Pirin finally proclaimed while eating ice cream. "Happened late last night—two forty-seven. Can't see who did it, though. So now we unravel how this asshole got past the perimeter cams. Cuz we've got a serious point of failure somewhere."

Queue up search number two, a wearying *manual* examination of the automatically recorded and integrated perimeter cam video stored in the network server.

"I didn't realize last night was *so* foggy," Gracie said as she again studied a segment of slow-motioned video on one of Pirin's screens. "Ah. There." Her finger circled a portion of the screen's upper right quadrant. "See this kinda shadowy movement? Just slow enough to make it seem natural, but it's—I think it looks wrong…"

Gracie glanced up in time to witness Pirin's face go marble-hard expressionless, her black-eyed squinch locked on the screen, and her eyebrows, Gracie noticed incongruously, seemed to have thunder rolling through them.

We're being reconnoitered, Pirin thought—by somebody who's either dumbshit lucky or quite skilled. She'd have preferred the former but feared the latter, feared that the "hurt" Number Three wildlife camera signaled a scout's carefully planned point of entry.

Number Three was attached to an oak that stood mere feet from a section of the side path that ran very close to the low stone wall marking the southwest-facing property line—along what the fam called "the backside." Beyond the wall, only a few more feet away through thick underbrush, stood the neighboring farm's easy-to-breach wire fencing where, Pirin suspected, she'd discover some kind of mark—subtle but findable in the dark—enabling the scout to locate the spot again.

Basandere! This was about as discreet a point of entry as there was on the property—suggesting (to Pirin anyway) that even a scout who was just dumbshit lucky would likely have needed more than one try to discover it.

How many times, then, might this scout already have shown up on the perimeter cams, apparently innocuous, apparently innocent? She and Gracie searched earlier video to find out, and by their usual bedtime they'd identified the same guy walking along the road bordering the northeast-facing street side of the property—twice.

"Obviously no point in setting up alerts for regular ol' road traffic, and he knew that." Pirin scowled as she clicked up a different video. "But whaddaya bet—yeah, look. There's the same dude walking through the field in back trying to act like a farmhand. Let's see if he—shit!" Pirin rubbed her cheeks. "There. He's pausing along the backside near Number Three…"

"You think he sabotaged the wildlife camera?" Gracie asked. "Why one of those when it's the perimeter cams that—?"

"—Maybe he never noticed the perimeter cams. I did try to camouflage them. So he might think we've got only the standalone wildlife cams. Or he could be smart and clever and aware of the perimeter cams. Looks like he breached the backside only once, when the fog was ridiculously heavy, so he coulda worn heat-suppressing clothing to exploit how the fog messes with infrared detection. Bottom line, dumb or smart, he got by our perimeter cams last night."

"So how late're you gonna work on the calibrations?"

"Till I get this so-called 'intelligent' software to recognize 'kinda shadowy movement' for what it really is. And tomorrow I'm gonna check the neighbor's fenceposts along the backside. Especially near Number Three."

Gracie rested her hand on Pirin's skittish shoulder. "I could be wrong about 'kinda shadowy movement.'"

"I'll risk a buncha false positives," Pirin said adamantly. This is on Veech Farkas, she did not say; how fuckin' *dare* you mess with me, you deluded prick. And damn if right then she didn't sense Gracie startle ever so slightly. As though she'd said what she thought out loud.

Gracie nodded, a gesture Pirin felt more than saw. "Okay with you if I go prep Dragonfly?" Gracie asked. "I'd like to take it up tomorrow."

"Yeah, sounds good," murmured Pirin, already engrossed in her suddenly hyperactive screens.

"So, um...I'll check in on you later, Pir," Gracie said.

"Yeah, sounds good," Pirin murmured again. Or maybe she didn't. Either way, when she finally glanced up Gracie was gone.

❖

Eight in the morning—a comparatively early hour for Gracie—and the space next to her in bed was empty. Not unusual. Even so, this was hardly a typical Saturday morning. Thanks to the perimeter cam alert app on her smartphone, she knew nothing had happened overnight—but it might have. Also, she'd woken to a crisp and detailed recollection of another ohskal dream. Eletun had returned:

 Emegon, I shall now tell you how Bisiberria took the copperforge pitcave women all the way to the Land of the New Motherworld on the coast of the Sea Beyond. We begin with the day Analergin and seventeen others departed the western shore, which happened to coincide with the appearance of yet another Privation vessel.

Were the Privation people aboard this boat searching for them? This we cannot know. We do know that when they saw the tall birdwings sail of Analergin's outrigger canoe, they gave chase. But under Analergin's hand Bisiberria moved sleekly southwestward, soon leaving the much slower Privation vessel below the eastern horizon.

Although by then the women had often sailed aboard Bisiberria, they had never before ventured out of sight of Land, and some grew frightened. "How do you know where we are?" they demanded of Analergin. "How do you know where we go?"

Analergin replied that Bisiberria was on the fastest, most direct route to their first stopover: Hulartali, the immense peninsula separating the Near Western Sea from the Far Western Sea. "If we remain close to the coast," she told them, "we also remain close to danger—from both Privation bounty hunters and local pirate males. To understand where we are, I watch the Sun, the Stars, the Seawaves, and more besides. I will show you all I know."

In that moment, the women began to learn how the Seawaves around them respond to the pulls of Sun and Moon, to vibrations of earthtremors and erupting Firemountains; how they form patterns as they rebound among Seacurrents and the shape of the Seabottom and Landmasses; how Lands both near and distant emit streaks of underwater light; how all these unique patterns aid navigation since what they reveal is detectable even from very far away.

"No matter that a night may be cloudy," Analergin told them. "We know well enough where we are and where we are heading."

After steering Bisiberria south to avoid a late-season wet monsoon storm and its Lightning, Analergin exploited an invigorated northeasterly dry monsoon Wind and Seacurrent to bring Bisiberria to the south tip of Hulartali, where she hoped to rest, for she had slept little since departing the western shore.

Thanks to Bele's warning, Analergin knew that Hulartali had not recovered from the immense, obliterating Seawaves spawned by the great Subendi eruption—not even after more than six Suncycles. And indeed, the women found little worth foraging and no sign at all of humans.

Yet on Hulartali, Analergin's vision of the New Motherworld unfurled with fresh clarity, revealing that Bisiberria must continue west and north and west again—across not one but *three* further Seas.

Not all the women shared Analergin's vision, however. Seasickness and Seafear caused three to disembark on Hulartali and walk inland in search of the friendly people they believed would embrace them. Perhaps they survived, even thrived; the Mothers of Subendi had regarded Hulartali as somewhat more tolerant than the heart of Privation. But we know nothing of their fates.

We do know that the fifteen women who departed Hulartali aboard Bisiberria were surpassingly fearful of Privation's reach, and so they committed to Analergin's vision of a distant New Motherworld. Upon sailing west for three days accompanied by a family of porpoises, they next put to Land on a long, narrow island where Sublime Perception revealed areas less damaged by Subendi eruption Seawaves.

There they found rich fishing grounds offshore; on Land they discovered taro, coconut, several kinds of leafy vegetables and healing herbs—as well as thornyleaves for renewing their outrigger's birdwings sail. When at last Bisiberria departed the island, it was well-stocked for what would be its longest voyage yet.

Seawind and Seacurrent and clear Sky helped Analergin and her companions as they sailed west-northwest for most of the next Mooncycle, becoming increasingly expert at fish-gathering, which minimized consumption of the foodstuffs they carried aboard.

Whenever someone asked Analergin "How far before we next stand upon Land?" the answer was simply "Too far to measure with a woman's step"—until the night Kaldi whispered a question of her own: "Are you afraid, Analergin?"

"Yes," Analergin confessed. "Our next harbor is Bastegaleki, 'The Western Edge'—as far as Subendi Travelers ever journeyed. Once each Suncycle, people come to Bastegaleki from all the Lands around the Far Western Sea to gather fish and fruits and exchange male-seed. Sailing west from there means..." Analergin lowered her head and fell again into silence.

"Means you will be as lost as the rest of us." Kaldi placed her hand on Analergin's. "At least we will be lost together."

Several days later, Bisiberria approached a gray-yellow coast; soon more distant gray-brown Mountains became visible. Closer in, the women saw lines of rich green growth slithering down from the Mountains before converging into a thicker green swath that slowly gave way to a broad beach of blazing white sand.

Analergin's Sublime Perception had shown her that Bastegaleki had been little harmed by the Subendi eruption's Seawaves—but according to what the Seacurrents and Seawaves conveyed, just days earlier Mother Earth had tremored violently nearby, though this had deterred neither the fish nor the porpoises.

Analergin examined the shore through her two-crystal shaft and saw no people on the beach. Nor did she see any boats. Had Mother Earth's tremors driven off the people?

Or had pirate males—possibly even a fleet of especially acquisitive Privation invaders—already robbed, raped, killed, and left nothing but death?

Gazing at Bastegaleki's coastline, Analergin understood that something was wrong. She considered sailing on past the place—but after Bastegaleki they faced the most arduous stretch yet of their journey.

So she decided the lesser risk, despite its potential dangers, was to warily put ashore. They all needed the rest only Land could provide, and even if exchange was impossible, they could fish as well as gather fruits and, Analergin hoped, flax to be retted and dressed into linen, then spun and woven into the raiment so necessary for staving off the deepening cold they would encounter as they continued northward.

Analergin did not speak of the ever more powerful pull of the New Motherworld, nor of the strange urgency suddenly surrounding it, though Kaldi sensed her agitation even as Analergin said only "Here we will find what we need."

On Land, the women of Bisiberria came upon no one at all, not even after two days of beach fishing and fruit gathering. On day three they discovered flax fields but had yet to find any effects of tremors; Analergin concluded that these likely occurred even farther inland and had been strong enough to disperse any people who may have assembled.

But as some women began cutting flax stalks, Kaldi suddenly turned and dashed further into the green upland. Analergin understood immediately: Kaldi had sensed someone and was in pursuit.

Soon Kaldi returned with three people—two women, the younger one visibly pregnant, and a boy at the very beginning of his maturity. All three were too thin, too dirty, and very afraid. They spoke a language no one on Bisiberria understood, though eventually, after some food and drink and much improvised signing, Analergin and Kaldi learned at least some of their story.

The three were part of a group that had traveled to the area to exchange the boy's male-seed for blackglass, fish, and fruit. But the day after they arrived, Mother Earth shook violently, setting off a landslide that took their people. "Only we three lived, but we lost all we had," the older woman's hands signaled. Then her hands asked "May we join you?"

Analergin explained where Bisiberria was heading, yet the three were eager to come along and the copperforge pitcave women had no objection. So after more than a Mooncycle at Bastegaleki without anyone else appearing, Bisiberria ventured west, escorted by porpoises, carrying eighteen souls and filled with food, water—and flaxcloth that Sineusi and others stitched into raiment as Bisiberria sailed on.

On the third day at Sea, the porpoises departed as Bisiberria approached Land that rose up on their right and their left to form a long, narrow channel through which the outrigger sailed. "Like threading a stitching bone," Sineusi commented nervously while Analergin called out when to shunt the mast so Bisiberria might maintain its northwesterly direction in the face of northerly winds.

Thus Bisiberria entered a new Sea—Kaldi named it the Narrow Sea—that soon widened somewhat as they continued tacking northwestward. The two women they had picked up at Bastegaleki warned against approaching any eastern shore that appeared green. "Pirate males lurking there," they indicated, "will try to steal everything."

So Analergin steered Bisiberria right up the middle of the Narrow Sea. While the women gathered fish using their lines and gathered drinking water using their cone-shaped devices, Analergin spoke little and only rarely forsook the steering blade. She seemed to be in a hurry, as though something dangerous chased her.

This continued for more than half a Mooncycle, during which they endured no Seastorms, no Lightning, saw no signs of people on Land or Sea. When they approached what appeared to be a rugged promontory dividing this strange body of water, Analergin steered the outrigger leftward—onto a still narrower Sea that brought them even farther northwestward.

By the second day on this even narrower Sea, an already profoundly fatigued Analergin had become more and more distressed.

"Talk to me," Kaldi urged her as the Sun rose over low eastern hills on a shore that, to Kaldi, seemed much too close. "What roils you?"

For a long moment, Analergin said nothing. When at last she spoke, her voice grated with worry. "Everything tells me we are exactly where we are supposed to be." She made no attempt to hide the tears filling her eyes. "But soon after we pass those Mountains to our west, this Sea *ends*."

"And we can sail no further?" Kaldi asked, her voice betraying her alarm.

"The Land ahead is low-lying—a swamp many tens of thousands of reaches across—and it blocks our way," Analergin whispered. "Crossing it on foot will take at least a Mooncycle."

"We will have to abandon Bisiberria?"

"I fear so," Analergin replied. "How did I not See this, Kaldi? How did I fail so completely?"

Before Kaldi could reply, she felt a low, ominous vibration.

Earthtremor!

Analergin closed her eyes, already sensing the coming onslaught of violent convulsions pulsing upward from Mother Earth's depths toward the immense cliffs Bisiberria had sailed past only yesterday—and she knew...

By the time Analergin opened her eyes, Kaldi, too, had sensed what was about to happen. Their eyes locked. "Now I understand why you were in such a hurry," said Kaldi.

Just then, from the Narrow Sea behind them, came a series of rumbling jolts, cataclysms of wrenching, cracking.

Whereupon Analergin understood something more: She had *not* failed. Her Sublime Perception *had* shown her the right place—at a moment that had not yet occurred but was now about to.

"Seawaves!" Analergin yelled to Sineusi, who had just emerged from Bisiberria's shelter. "Rouse those who are sleeping, tie down all you can—especially the drinking-water cones. We have but heartbeats before the water rises high behind us! Everyone must find some strong part of Bisiberria and hold on tight."

In her next breath, she called Mardul, Jarrai, and Honsoli to lower the sail, then sent Kaldi to the windward float to take up the second steering blade, saying "One blade will not suffice. Lash yourself to a crossbeam and steer just as I do."

Analergin, too, lashed herself to a crossbeam and pointed Bisiberria northward while Mardul, Honsoli, and Jarrai pulled in the sail and secured it. "Alama," Analergin whispered while the waters in front of Bisiberria grew shallower and shallower, as though some great Sea-mouth behind them sought to greedily swallow every drop, "Alama, please help us."

Then it was upon them, an impossibly, monstrously huge mass of water rising, rising behind them, claiming the sky, lifting Bisiberria precipitously stern-first.

Even as Honsoli, Mardul, and Jarrai scrambled back toward the outstretched hands of those in the shelter, Analergin and Kaldi steered the outrigger leftward to angle down the mounding face of the immense earthtremor-spawned Seawave, struggling to keep Bisiberria from flipping end-over-end.

Carried along the front face of the vast and burgeoning surge of water, Bisiberria moved faster than it ever had, faster than Analergin believed anything or anyone ever could. To their left, to their right, the rugged Land raced by them; ahead, the water had disappeared and the wet sand and raw rock lay inconceivably far below them.

"Steer right, Kaldi!" Analergin bellowed, "Steer *right!*"—and the two worked to angle the vessel back toward the center of the ever-narrowing Sea, then left again, then right, left, right...until the huge Seawave carried Bisiberria past the flanking Mountains as it flowed farther and farther northward over a widening green lowland.

A long time later—neither Analergin nor Kaldi had any notion of how much later—the Seawave began to slow and smooth out, only to be caught from behind by a second Seawave that pulsed the outrigger northward again. This happened twice more before Bisiberria, intact and upright, still carrying eighteen people, came to rest on a wide, shallow expanse of choppy water.

Trembling as they clutched their steering blades, Analergin and Kaldi both collapsed in exhaustion—yet only for a moment before one, then the other scanned the wide Sea-horizon before them, the shore not far behind them, assorted plant debris floating around them.

"Which way now?" called Kaldi.

Analergin gazed Skyward, where a black bird circled high above them. Gliding on the streams of air high overhead, Bele had begun to slide westward, Analergin realized—but a Seacurrent was shoving the outrigger eastward. So she rolled onto her belly to seek sense of these new waters.

Larger than the Narrow Sea, she soon discerned, but smaller than either of the Western Seas, populated by all manner of islands, encircled by vast Lands whose Wind patterns erratically drove its Seawaves, ruled by a great gyre of a Seacurrent that generated numerous smaller eddies. Also cold. Very cold.

"We go with the Wind, Kaldi." Analergin stood and gazed Skyward again at gray, unfriendly clouds. "We must raise our sail and let the Wind take us westward while it remains amenable. I fear it will not be amenable for long."

⚡

Write-up finished, tablet in hand, Gracie padded toward the living room looking for Pirin. She wanted Pirin to read this one immediately and to ask: Was she crazy for feeling like Eletun's story was trying to tell her something?

For *eight months*, Eletun had been weaving this tale. And despite Pirin and her mother smiling benignly about it, Gracie knew the experience was, if not uniquely bizarre, then at least a rara avis. So rara that only in the internet's bullshit-laden Q&A websites did she find people who described experiencing an extended multi-dream narrative.

But but but…everybody dreams, right? And these dreams damn well meant *something*, right? So, Gracie, is this ohskal dream alerting you to a moment that hasn't yet occurred but is now about to?

Pirin sat in yesterday's clothes at the bistro table drinking coffee, surveying the woodland that rose behind the house and garage. Now that the property's many oaks had dropped their leaves, the view through the crowded jumble of bare branches nearly to the rear of the gently upsloping acreage revealed a low sun occasionally peeking through November's clouds.

"I know nothing happened last night," said Gracie. "So why do you look so—?"

"Found a deep gouge this morning in one of the neighbor's fenceposts along the backside. Quite fresh, right near Number Three." Pirin kept her eyes on the woods. "Surprise fuckin' surprise."

"Did you get any sleep at all?"

"Not really." At last, Pirin glanced up and did a doubletake at the sight of Gracie's face. "Oh." Her eyes slitted. "Another ohskal dream, huh? And it's got you…concerned."

"Yeah. Kinda." Gracie handed over her tablet. "Nothing obvious or explicit…"

"Of course not. Eletun doesn't work that way."

"But I…I dunno, Pir. Tell me what you think."

Pirin read the write-up slowly, carefully. "Mmm." Her stony expression didn't yield even after she put down the tablet. "Seems like a warning. About timing."

Well, Gracie thought, you *would* say that after staying up all night in anticipation of an attack that never happened. But her quick, silent nod attested her agreement. "Still figure it'll go down at night?"

"Likely."

"At least you don't have to work today. So you can take a nap."

"Maybe. Later." Pirin raised her coffee cup. "Here's hoping my calibrations work and the cams pick up him, or them, or who-the-fuck-ever, so we can..." She shrugged. "Y'know..."

"I don't actually. So we can *what?*"

"Protect ourselves."

"Or we could call the—"

"Only if we need their help removing a body."

"Jeezus, Pirin." Several times already, Gracie had broached the idea of calling the police, thus triggering their second genuine argument, which she lost hands down. Time to change the subject, she decided. "Eaten anything? I'm gonna make eggs and bacon and marmalade toast just like your ama's. Interested?"

Finally, *finally* Pirin almost-smiled, and for about an hour she almost reverted to what Gracie had come to think of as "normal."

Almost.

"Unlike the cops, I gotta take this seriously, Gracie. Cuz it's a real threat—and it's aimed not just at me but at all of us *because of me.*"

"So you think it's—"

"—Veech Farkas. Who the hell else? I've been really—" Pirin stopped herself, but Gracie sensed what she didn't say: Careful. *I've been really careful.*

What've you been really careful about, Pirin?

Gracie was about to ask, but Pirin wasn't done yet, and now her clenched, slamming fist paced her words. "Veech is the *only* person who's threatening my *life.* And if he's got some *dude* sniffing around here, then he's *aware* of my family." Pirin's grim expression darkened; for the first time, Gracie grasped—felt—the depths of her vehement, bottomless rage. "My *family*, Gracie. That is *so* not okay." She stood and took another moment to gaze out at the trees behind the garage, then hissed "*I do* not *like being prey.*"

Pirin would devote the rest of her day to defense: inspecting the property and its cameras (again), checking the new perimeter cam calibrations (again), reviewing whatever the Spotter app had picked up on Veech (again), napping briefly in the afternoon after cleaning her two handguns since she'd be up all night watching, waiting (again and again and again...).

Gracie understood: They would live like this until Pirin deemed the threat neutralized. And though she and Pirin had never explicitly discussed it, she resolved to respect what she knew Pirin wanted: Say nothing to the fam about the threat. My problem, insisted Pirin's stony silence, so *I* will deal with it.

But wait.

"What the hell makes you think *I'll* be able to sleep?" Gracie called out as she followed Pirin into the office. "I realized last night that I'm not down with the different perimeter alert zone sounds yet, so take me through it all one more time, okay? I need to be sure I recognize what I'm hearing as soon as I hear it. Also, I want you to let me take up Dragonfly again—yes, in the daytime. I'm still getting used to how it looks from up there now that all the leaves are down. You can watch the video later if you want. On the night shift."

CHAPTER TWENTY-FIVE: TWENTY-ONE MINUTES

H ow 'bout if we just call that cop friend of—"
"No, Gracie."

Pirin tried to keep the irritation out of her voice, but dammit, she refused to explain it all yet again—how the cops would take forever to show up, shrug some version of whaddaya-expect-*us*-to-do?, and even if they did stick around for a few hours in a patrol car out front, the bad guy(s) would just wait for them to doze off or finally piss off. No, Gracie—the quickest way to put an end to this bullshit is to let it play out. As in come and fucking get me. And besides, that so-called cop friend is merely an acquaintance, an old lover's new lover.

Gracie sighed rather melodramatically into the eloquence of what Pirin didn't say. "Another night in Bigfoot drag it is, then."

Pirin managed to add a small smile to her nod.

"So—got your IR night vision binoculars?" Gracie asked with the exaggerated patience of someone who's done this too many times already.

"On the strap around my neck."

"Smartphone charged, video server app linked and clicked up?"

"And easy to reach in my righthand pocket."

"Earbud in?"

"As promised."

"Flashlight?"

"Easy to reach in my lefthand pocket."

"The baseball bat again—really?"

"Really. It's right here, ready and willing."

"Yeah. Great." Gracie grimaced. "Jeezus, Pir, I wish you'd reconsider…"

"Also the Glock's cleaned, loaded," Pirin persevered, patting her right side. "Holstered right here inside my sweatshirt."

Slowly shaking her head, Gracie handed off a large bundle of material that looked like a combination of brown leaves and netting. "Ah, the glories of cosplay," she mumbled. "Too bad this is for real."

Hell's bells, Grace Gwyllt Olwyn, you are tenacious, Pirin thought as she donned what she always referred to as her nightstalker camouflage—pants first, then the jacket-hood-facenet combo. Designed to randomly break up and dissipate body heat so the wearer's silhouette would be notably less visible to infrared thermal detection, it had worked pretty well both times she'd used it to live-test her calibrations of the perimeter cams' IR detection capabilities.

Gracie sighed again as she fluffed the jacket's sleeves. "You're all set, Bigfoot." She lifted the facenet and pushed back the hood to plant a kiss on Pirin's cheek, then another lingering, please-don't-do-this kiss on Pirin's mouth. "Okay then," she said in defeat several long seconds later when it became obvious that Pirin would not relent, "I'll be in bed pretending to sleep."

"Act as if," Pirin replied, hoping she sounded cheery as she doused all the lights, then sat down at her desk to survey her three screens full of live videocam imagery. Like last night and the nights before that, she'd keep watching, keep waiting.

And waiting…

And waiting…

❖

"Fuck fuck fuck," Pirin muttered, sipping lukewarm coffee as she blearily pulled her gaze from one screen to the next and the next and back again. Deep into yet another night and zilch. Which surprised her; she figured whoever was after her would make a move during the new moon when the night sky was especially dark. Now, though, the moon had begun waxing again.

Fuck…fuck…*fuck*…

She'd tried for years to avoid just this sort of situation—perpetually full of dread about some asshole coming after her and those she loved, and she'd have no control, no way of anticipating when or how…

❖

On the second or, yeah, maybe the third ping, Pirin jerked awake, her eyes blinking into focus on the leftmost screen where she saw a green-hued figure moving along the neighbor's wire fence, approaching the backside property line.

One dude, right?

Only one. Bright as green-infrared day.

Could she really be that fucking lucky?

Pirin scanned her screens again, all of them…c'mon, *hurry*…and yes, thank you Alama, just one homo fucking sapien. She watched him sneak parallel with the fence and the low stone wall behind it—

Whaddaya bet he'll keep going for another four hundred feet or so, till he finds the gouge he carved into that fencepost close to Number Three…

Then whaddaya bet he slips across the fence, over the wall, a few giant steps to the path, which'll take him toward the garage and the etche…

Pirin had, of course, contemplated scenarios, what-ifs. Yet she could only guess at green guy's intentions. Just scouting? Or would he try to burn down the etche with everyone in it? Gut her with a k-bar? Shoot her dead?

As she grabbed the baseball bat off her desk, Pirin glanced over her screens one last time—yes, still just one green guy, still moving as expected. She left the lights off as she raced down the darkened stairs to the middle garage and its rear door that opened beneath the deck. She halted there to pull her smartphone from her pocket and locate green guy on the video server app linked to the perimeter cam feeds. Where the fuck is he now?

Where?

There. Still scooting along the neighbor's fence…

And then she was outside, her mind streaking ahead of her, seemingly ahead of time itself as she crouched low to scurry across the patio and the now desiccated field of wildflowers toward the trees, into the woods, hoping she'd pull off the surprise interception that depended on her moving quickly enough, quietly enough, invisibly enough.

The earlier blusters of rain had ebbed into clouds and puddles and layers of saturated oak leaves slicking the roads while temperatures had settled into see-your-breath chilly. Snugged against a bare maple roughly halfway to where she believed she'd rendezvous with green guy, Pirin pulled out her night vision binoculars to track him…

Yep, moving a bit slower now, from fencepost to fencepost through the darkness, feeling for the one with the gouge—his breach point.

At least she knew every path in her little woodland—every tree, every fallen branch and exposed root, every spot where the winds blew fallen leaves into unlikely piles, every camera location. And she knew she had enough time to reach the large oak where she needed to be.

The tree stood close to the low stone wall marking the backside property line, right next to the narrow side path Pirin figured green guy would use, and she waited behind it, baseball bat poised, ready for him to take fifteen, maybe twenty steps along the path until he was slightly past her. He'd be Intruder Dude by then, unequivocally trespassing, and she was ready to sneak up behind him to stop him, to cripple him so he'd never be able to threaten anyone ever again. Kill him if necessary, face the consequences if necessary…

It almost happened exactly like she wanted, like she dreaded.

Almost.

He crept past her as expected—following the handgun (with a silencer, no less) he held in both hands out in front of him, which she did not expect. When she emerged from behind the oak, bat raised, one breath away from swinging, she hesitated—because *shit!* He was facing the garage and the etche; if his weapon discharged when she whacked him, the bullet could kill someone in the garage, in the etche.

Hell, depending on its trajectory, that bullet could travel all the way to the house where Jessica grew up, the house where her mother still lived.

On to Plan B, which Pirin conceived and executed instantly, autonomically: She held the bat high with her left hand while she crouched down to pick up a stick with her right hand and loft it over Intruder Dude's head to his ten o'clock. This induced him to freeze as he aimed his weapon into the darkness toward the sound of the stick ricocheting through the trees on the far side of the path.

Both hands on the bat again, Pirin whistled, a quick mimic of a black-capped chickadee's high-pitched "see you" call, causing Intruder Dude to spin about-face, weapon-first.

He moved with surprising speed.

Already swinging her bat, Pirin realized too late that she'd screwed up both her timing and her velocity—and understood, also too late, that Intruder Dude would be pulling the trigger on his weapon while it was pointed at the center of her chest.

To a silent, desperate hyperchorus of shit*shit*SHIT!, she released the bat to complete its journey on its own while she dove for the ground, rolling onto her left side so she could reach for her Glock. How Intruder Dude's bullet missed her and instead struck the bat will forever remain a mystery because it happened too fast to comprehend.

What happened in the next instant, though, Pirin *did* comprehend because right then time itself shifted into extreme slow-motion. So slow that she caught sight of the explosive aftereffects of the bullet's contact with the bat's barrel, saw the bat's knob snap back at Intruder Dude and smash his weapon out of his hands, heard his howl of pain as he grabbed his left forearm and began running back the way he came.

From the ground, Pirin had a clear shot, and yes, she'd have taken it if she'd had more confidence that she'd actually strike her target. If she missed, though, *her* bullet could hit a cluster of houses a quarter mile away on the far side of East Broadway—assuming it didn't strike one of the neighbor farmer's cows first.

Even before she lowered the weapon, Gracie's voice blasted through her earbud. "Pirin! Are you okay?! *Pirin!*"

"Yeah. I'm okay."

"You're not moving. Did he shoot you?"

"Tried and missed." Pirin looked skyward but saw nothing. "Where is it?" she asked. "I don't see any lights."

"Dragonfly's dead-ass above you, about three hundred feet up. No lights. No ID transmission either."

"Saw the whole thing, didja?"

"I did. You sure he doesn't still have a gun?"

"Not the one he used to shoot at me. The bat knocked it out of his hand. Can you see him?"

"Oh yeah. He's running—well, kinda stumbling-running toward where East Broadway meets Merrimac. And, uh, I can see a heat source near the intersection, just off the road."

"That'll be the engine of whatever he drove in on. Try to follow him, Gracie. I wanna know who the hell he is."

"Yes ma'am!"

At last, Pirin stood. And promptly tripped. Yep, rattled. Damn fucking rattled. "Gracie?"

"Still here."

"Where are you?"

"Up on the deck."

"Does the cam-watching app on your phone show the same all-clear I see?"

Pirin could hear the little smile in Gracie's reply: "Yep. Just checked."

"Anybody awake in the etche?"

"Don't think so."

"Thank you, Alama. Thank you."

"Come back in now, okay?" Gracie pleaded.

"Gonna see if I can find his gun, some kinda semiautomatic. Prick put a silencer on it. So he meant business. Sure as hell don't wanna leave the thing out here for Alaia to find. Maybe I can locate what's left of the bat, too. Gimme a few to look arou—"

"Hey, he's getting on a motorcycle! Gotta focus now on following him, Pir. Hurry back."

The first thing Pirin realized as she returned to the garage was that Gracie was no longer standing on the deck. A quick peek into the third bay's workshop revealed that the tricopter had returned and been put in its case, its battery charging. Obviously, retrieving Intruder Dude's gun and her baseball bat (still in one piece despite having captured the bullet that deeply cleaved it) had taken longer than she figured.

Upstairs, Pirin found Gracie lying on the living room sofa, only a nightlight in the bathroom down the hall staving off complete darkness.

"Find what you were looking for?" Gracie asked, sitting upright.

Pirin nodded. "Finally. Perimeter still quiet?"

"Still quiet." Gracie stood, slouching slightly as she moved toward the office and its screens.

Following her, Pirin tensed. "How'd it go?"

Gracie didn't reply until she reached Pirin's desk and swiveled the desk chair, gesturing to the screens. "Have a seat," she said tonelessly. "You need to see this."

She then retreated to the lounge chair in the corner where she stretched out, her feet on the ottoman, one arm covering her eyes. Pirin's stomach cramped. "Okay…"

Initially, video from the tricopter's main camera showed the driveway in front of the garage receding as the machine lifted and swung around the building to rise over the woodland before moving south to hover above the greened image of Intruder Dude moving along the backside of the property just before breaching near Number Three. Pirin had to look harder for her own presence, difficult to discern when she was motionless, looking ghostly blurry-vague whenever she moved.

Next came a brief flurry of motion, the bright flash of the gun firing, the afterglow of the gun's heated barrel, then Intruder Dude frantically careening back toward the stone wall. No wonder Gracie worried she'd been shot.

Gracie kept her cool, though. And kept the tri well above the fleeing man—until he clambered onto a motorcycle, got it started, and drove toward East Broadway, by which point Gracie had brought the tri swooping very close to Intruder Dude's right side—likely the first moment he perceived its presence, judging by the panicky left turn he took rather than the right turn he'd begun to attempt.

Seconds later, Gracie had maneuvered the drone close in to the motorcycle's *left* side, twice forcing Intruder Dude to stay on East Broadway and enabling the tri's camera to catch a fine, clear view of the cycle's license plate.

"Slick, Gracie, very, *very* slick," Pirin murmured, pausing the video to scribble down the plate number.

"Please," Gracie said from the chair, her arm not moving. "Watch the whole thing first."

Something in her voice kept Pirin from challenging her. "Okay."

As soon as Pirin resumed the video, its tempo escalated wildly: With the tri right behind at about four feet off the ground, the motorcycle accelerated, causing it to fishtail on the wet, leaf-scattered pavement as it headed down the narrowing road toward the river. Despite the slippery conditions, though, Intruder Dude managed to keep the bike upright and soon even regained some speed. If he kept on going, the road would take him to a bridge crossing the Merrimack River, his best chance to outrun the drone.

Gracie, however, had other ideas. At the last intersection before the road reached the bridge, she steered the tri parallel with the motorcycle again, on its right side roughly at Intruder Dude's eye level, then surged ahead and suddenly veered left, forcing Intruder Dude into a skidding left turn onto the road that paralleled the river.

Gracie then arced the drone high, somehow threading its fifty-two-inch width between overhead tree branches and utility lines before lifting it out over the river while its tracker ensured that the tri's main camera followed Intruder Dude as he struggled to accelerate on the leaf-slicked old road's tight curves.

So, Pirin thought, this is where Gracie gives up the chase.

Instead, by the time Intruder Dude reached a relatively straight stretch and opened the throttle, Gracie had used the tricopter's impressive acceleration to position well ahead of him, swing across the wide-open expanse of a large lawn, and plunge down again to fly directly at the oncoming motorcycle.

The move took Pirin's breath away. Basandere, she's *attacking!*

Pirin watched motorcycle and rider race directly toward the tri's camera—and realized that Intruder Dude hadn't yet seen the drone. Not until Gracie briefly flicked on the tri's spotlight, now aimed right at him, causing him to swerve off the road across a small, unfenced embankment and take flight out over the river.

At speed.

While the tricopter rolled and climbed away from the spot, its tracker kept the main camera on green-hued Intruder Dude as he and his motorcycle Evel Knieveled into the water and disappeared a few seconds later. Pirin wondered: Would Gracie circle back to see if he surfaced?

No. The remainder of the video, its last three minutes, showed only the tri's half-mile return to base.

Twenty-one minutes, Pirin noted as she clicked off the video. Twenty-one minutes from the moment Gracie launched the tricopter till the moment it landed in the middle of the patio behind the garage.

CHAPTER TWENTY-SIX:
BY WHATEVER MEANS NECESSARY

This was a whole new realm for Utterly Other Gracie, so somberly confounding that it kept her flattened and numb on the office lounge chair. "You saw where he ended up." She spoke in a hoarse monotone, eyes closed. "Prob'ly didn't survive, huh?"

Seated on the edge of the ottoman, Pirin gently stroked Gracie's arm. "He wasn't very far from the riverbank, so if he let go of the handlebars and is a decent swimmer, he could've made it. But the video shows him holding on, not letting go. Also, the river's tidal where he went in and the tide was going out at the time. So—"

"Guess I should call the cops and own up before they come knocking—"

"No. Please don't."

"But—"

"No, Gracie. I doubt anyone'll come knocking."

"But—"

"Thanks to your prodigious drone camera skills, I was able to check out the license plate number on that motorcycle. It's registered to Vicsorgó Farkas. But his nephew's been its keeper ever since Uncle Veech was arrested last year."

Gracie felt her eyes go wide. "Zach Farkas? *That's* who tried to kill you?"

"Well, I suppose he *might've* let somebody borrow the bike, but my money's on Zach, though he never mentioned anything about it in his communications with Veech or anyone else. I know that because I've been scrupulous about tracking the activity on both of their smartphones." Pirin rubbed her forehead. "Even so, I should've anticipated this."

"How?"

"By paying enough attention to Veech's deets to notice that he turns forty this coming weekend."

"Oh shit," Gracie groaned. "So Zach's birthday present for his Uncle Veech was gonna be smoking *you?*"

"Woulda been quite the happy surprise, don'tcha think? 'Woman Shot Dead In Home Invasion.' Sure as hell explains why Zach kept his mouth shut. And why at this very moment his smartphone's location is his dorm in Worcester. Which suggests he didn't want to be trackable."

"Do you think *anyone* knew what he was gonna do?"

"Got my doubts—but who can say? I suppose he could've been communicating with someone during his 'mission,' though obviously not by smartphone. For what it's worth, I didn't hear him speaking as he went by me. And after he took his shot—"

"From what I saw through Dragonfly's cam, he looked damned distracted. And I tried to keep him that way."

Pirin nodded. "With spectacular success, Gracie."

"So if he's somehow survived the river—"

"My guess: He'll be too humiliated to admit anything." Pirin took hold of Gracie's hands. "And if he's dead, it looks like he lost control on a wet, slippery road in the middle of the night. Which is true enough."

"Regardless, there'll be plenty of questions."

"No accident, though, that you flew the tricopter last night minus ID transponder and nav lights, huh?"

"I just—I, uh…"

"You calculated the risks fucking brilliantly, Grace Gwyllt Olwyn. Low likelihood of witnesses at three in the morning. Since the tri's comms are military-grade encrypted, eavesdropping's close to impossible. Best I can tell, no one anywhere saw or recorded anything." Pirin quirked an eyebrow. "Although a UFO *was* sited about thirty miles north of here. Good odds those questions you're worried about will be directed elsewhere. Because you and I are the only ones who truly know anything."

"You and I and Zach Farkas."

"It'll all be obvious soon enough." Pirin gently squeezed Gracie's hands. "A few days. Maybe a week."

"Or I could just, y'know, give myself up right now."

Pirin leaned in close, squinting as she examined Gracie's face, Gracie's eyes. "Do you think you did something wrong?"

Ah, the crux.

Gracie responded with a shrug.

"So tell me what you'd have done differently."

"I…" Gracie shut her eyes and tried to breathe. "Nothing," she finally acknowledged. "I-I'd do it again. All of it. Even though I keep thinking I should feel bad—remorse, regret, self-loathing. I *am* scared of prison, but besides that all I feel is relief, the lightness of relief…"

Gracie opened her eyes to meet Pirin's gaze. "I thought he *killed* you. For this horrifying moment I believed you were *dead*, Pir. And then, when I realized he failed and was bolting, I thought: If that shit-prick gets away, he'll try again and keep on trying till he succeeds. And the whole time we'd be *so freaked*, perpetually verging on panic—you, me, your fam never safe, forever spooked, exhausted, even driven into hiding—and he has *no right* to do that and the fact that such an *outrage* is even possible just—just…"

"So you went after him."

"I wanted to eliminate any possibility of a next time. If that meant he'd end up dead—well, that's on him." Gracie curled in on herself, spooked by how little she remembered of Utterly Other Gracie's piloting and the game of chicken she played with a hit man. "Am I a monster that I kinda *do* hope he's dead so he can't come after you or me or anyone else ever again? Even if he turns out to be a teenage fool, I-I just don't feel bad about it." Gracie shook her head. "*Why* don't I feel bad about it?"

"Maybe because you didn't do anything wrong." Pirin leaned in and kissed Gracie's forehead.

"A judge in a courtroom may beg to differ."

"Courtroom." Pirin snorted her contempt. "That hallowed bastion of male privilege where less than one percent of men brought to trial for sexual assault get a prison sentence, not least because fewer than one in four sexually-assaulted women have enough trust in that other hallowed male bastion—the police—to even report the crime, since only about twenty percent of those reports leads to an arrest, while way too often the assaulted woman gets charged with 'false reporting' after some asshole redpilled cop conjures a sluthate excuse not to believe her."

"But what happened last night wasn't about sexual assault."

"No, *last night* was about, first of all, preventing a murder that was attempted to impress a man who's in prison for domestic violence and—oh, the irony!—attempted murder," sneered Pirin. "And second, it was about reducing the odds of future attacks just like the one last night. And if we can duck the fallout, we damn well should."

"I know that, legally speaking, I shouldn't have chased him, but—but *he* was trying to kill *you!*"

"Which, legally speaking, means tough fucking luck for me. I'm on my own if—when—Zach tries again, just like I'm on my own when his uncle Veech takes a crack at me," said Pirin. "As for you, there's no legal defense except maybe insanity, temporary or otherwise.

"And even if you *did* have a legal self-defense claim, without incontrovertible proof on your side—like that video you recorded in the park the day we met—you'd be suspected and impugned. Odds are the cops you'd encounter would doubt you, disrespect you, accuse you, interrogate you, lie to you, force you to spend thousands of dollars on an attorney you shouldn't need, upend your life for months even if they don't arrest you, and turn you into a target for every misogynist trolling social media."

Whoa. If Pirin meant to rebalance Gracie's perspective, it may have worked. "Sounds like the voice of experience."

"Almost. My run-in pre-dates the current social media delirium, thank you, Alama. But the rest? Oh yeah."

"What happened?"

"Summer before my junior year in college, Jessica and I were up in Portland visiting some of her school friends, and one night the two of us got jumped outside a bar. Three dudes." Pirin snickered. "Heh. We took 'em all down. I wanted to leave 'em lying there and just walk away, but Jess insisted on calling the cops, who decided we'd 'overdone it' cuz alpha dude's daddy was connected and alpha and beta were hurt pretty bad—serious brain damage and permanent paralysis. Never mind that they were huge and alpha was waving a combat knife."

"'Hurt pretty bad'?" Gracie couldn't help but smile. "That was you, huh?"

"Oh, Jess did plenty. She can be ferocious when she wants. Has a mean snap kick. Eloquent, too—she almost singlehandedly stopped the Portland cops from coming after me for felony battery. Did a way better job than the lawyer her mother hired. But the whole thing with the so-called justice system was really unpleasant and scary. Right up there with the assault itself. Which is why I don't want any cops coming after you just because you were protecting me."

"Do you think I'll eventually regret what I did last night?"

"I hope not." Pirin sighed. "It's sad, but I no longer believe that men who benefit from their own violence can be fixed. They do have to be stopped, though. By whatever means necessary. And by whatever means necessary women with the courage to stop violent men have to shield themselves from the perverse lack of justice built into 'the law.' Which is why I've never regretted what *I've* done."

At last, Gracie thought. "What've you done?"

"Started when Ayesha was killed."

"Ayesha was...*killed?*" Gracie startled upright on the lounge chair. "What happened, Pir?"

"Our senior year of high school. We'd been—" Pirin's voice cracked. "—Been together for almost two years, keeping it *very* closeted because Ayesha's family was repulsively reactionary. When they started pushing an arranged marriage to this rich guy who was an assistant district attorney and promised to get her brother a job after law school, she resisted. But she was trying to stay at home till she turned eighteen and could leave without legal hassles. Basandere, Gracie, I begged her. *Begged* her to get the hell outta there..."

Tears slipped down Pirin's cheeks and she barely contained a sob when Gracie reached out to touch her. "Th-That night," she continued, "the night before the night before Christmas, Ayesha finally agreed to leave, so we made a plan for her to stay here hiding for a month till her birthday. We were gonna meet at the edge of her backyard, then come back here, but—but..."

Gracie wrapped her arms around Pirin, who sank into Gracie's embrace crying uncontrollably. And Gracie knew—just *knew* that Pirin had never before recounted these moments to anyone, never before wept for Ayesha in another human being's presence.

"I waited an' waited." Pirin voice rasped as she calmed down. "I waited too long." A low, groaning growl rumbled within her. "Dumb shit that I was, I was still waiting when instead of Ayesha, these two clearly agitated dudes came out of the house, whispering and pacing, circling each other, coming closer and closer to the shrub I was hiding behind. Close enough that I worried about them seeing the mist of my breath in the cold air.

"One of 'em started raising his voice, and suddenly he got really belligerent. I'll never forget what he said: 'Your fuckin' kutiya sister asked for it! Calling me zina biljabar karne wala! How *dare* she say that after your father *promised* her to me! That meant she was already mine, Hassan. *Mine!*'

"I recognized that phrase—zina biljabar karne wala—so I knew Ayesha had stood up for herself. She'd called him a rapist. An' I realized this was the arranged-marriage dude—Rashid. Basandere, Gracie, till then I'd never seen such malice. It contorted his face, burst out of his eyes, curdled his voice. He enraged me. But the sight of him also terrified me. And paralyzed me.

"Then the other guy—obviously Ayesha's brother Hassan—tried to speak up, though it came out like a whimper. 'We coulda worked it out, Rashid. Ayesha would never disobey...'

"But Rashid had lost it. He yelled 'Ayesha disobeyed *me*, asshole! She *hit* me in the *nuts!*' Then he pulled out a pistol, shoved it against Hassan's chin, and I'll never forget his words—'Of *course* I fuckin' threw her down the stairs! She's the one who said she'd rather be dead than be with me! So have it your way, cunt! And then *you* want help with CPR? Ha! Lucky the bitch was already dead, cuz otherwise I'd have blown her fuckin' head off.' Then he rubbed the gun along Hassan's cheek. 'Like maybe I should blow you away right the fuck now.'"

"Omigod, Pir," gasped Gracie, "Omi*god!*"

"I figured he'd shoot Hassan right then like he said, but he didn't. Instead he insulted Ayesha's parents and threatened Hassan again. 'I'm leaving now,' he said. 'You will count to ten before you call the cops. You will tell them Ayesha fell down the stairs. An accident. And I was never here. When they ask about the bruises on her arms, you will tell them you tried to stop her fall but you couldn't hold on. And you will be grateful that I'll owe you one. Even though I've been royally ripped off and *you* oughta goddamn owe *me*.'

"Then he drove away in his slick black Porsche, and as Hassan scuttled back inside I thought, what if Ayesha's *not* dead, injured maybe, but alive?

"So I ran to the side of the house, to the living room window with a view to the foyer and the stairway. And there she was, lying at the bottom of the stairs, her head twisted way too far 'round, blood from her nose and mouth pooled on the floor, her eyes vacant—but she was staring right at me, and I stared back hoping pleading begging: Move, Ayesha, c'mon move, blink, just one blink, *please*, Ayesha…

"But Ayesha didn't move, didn't blink…an'…an' I don't remember much after that. I mighta screamed, but I also saw the cops' blue lights, coming closer. I don't remember running off, but I must have. I'd kinda snuck outta the etche earlier, planned to come back with Ayesha like, y'know, a surprise, like 'We gotta help my friend,' an' my parents woulda heard Ayesha's story an' agreed, I knew that. But when I came back alone, I didn't say anything to anyone about any of it."

"*Nothing?*" Gracie shuddered at the thought of Pirin's shock, the agony of Pirin's unspoken grief for the unspoken love now lost forever. "Nothing to your ama? To your amatchi?"

Pirin's head shifted slowly back and forth. "So many times when we were together I wanted to reveal our secret, to shout it out, celebrate it. But Ayesha begged me not to. 'Not till I'm eighteen,' she always said. 'They own me till I'm eighteen, and if they find out before then, my life will be *over*.'

"So I never said a word, not even to Jessica, who suspected, I think, but understood and kept our secret. After Ayesha died, I turned that silence into a weapon. I decided the secrecy Ayesha had needed in order to experience love would now serve another purpose.

"Took me about five minutes to get back home." Pirin spoke in a low, soft voice, gaze glued to the floor. "By then I'd formed a plan. Complete, detailed. Every move laid out. And I executed it without a single hitch. Like it was meant to be."

"And you never told anyone."

"Not till right now." Pirin's dark eyes rose to meet Gracie's. "I knew Hassan would say exactly what Rashid told him to say and Ayesha's death would be declared accidental and Rashid would get away with murder."

Quite suddenly, Gracie was floating. Her head felt heavy but in reverse, because gravity was pulling her from above, lifting her higher and higher. And one more time, she knew, *she just knew* what Pirin would tell her next.

CHAPTER TWENTY-SEVEN: THAT KIND OF NERVE

G racie couldn't imagine how Pirin managed to remain so calm as she described what had unquestionably been *the* critical moment of her life. Yeah, okay, it was half a lifetime ago, but even so...

"One of our secrets—Ayesha and me—was that I'd go over to see her on Thursday evenings when she'd be the only person at home," Pirin explained. "The house had no cameras or alarms, and there was this pergola over the deck right below the windows in Ayesha's room, so I'd shinny up a post, sneak in through one of those windows, and we'd hang out, make love, and talk and talk and talk.

"In those last few months, when her father and brother were trying to shove Rashid down her throat while her mother wimped and whined, Ayesha figured the best way to duck him was to find out about his schedule—mostly from Hassan, who fawned all over him—then make sure she was busy whenever he wasn't. To keep track, she wrote it all down in a little secret calendar she kept.

"About a week after she died, there was this memorial thing that her family went to, which meant the house would be empty. So I went over there, snuck into her room the usual way cuz she never ever locked that window, and collected what I knew I'd need, starting with her secret calendar. Some of Hassan's stuff, too—jacket, sweatshirt, baseball hat, leather gloves, sneakers, a used towel from his bathroom, and especially the handgun Ayesha told me he kept loaded in a bedside drawer.

"I'd also started stalking Rashid, which would've been problematic except that Amatchi always went to bed early, Ama was working nights, Esti had long since tuned out her older dyke sister, and my dad was all drugged up on painkillers after smashing the hell out of his femur. So I had use of a car whenever I wanted, and after dinner, nobody ever noticed anything I did.

"I found out Rashid was quite OCD, always parked in the same spot at his apartment complex, always went whoring after work on Thursdays before coming home about ten at night. So on one of those Thursday nights I drove to Rashid's neighborhood again."

Pirin paused before continuing in a shaky monotone. "I-I'd put on Hassan's baseball hat over a tight surgical cap, had Hassan's sweatshirt under the jacket I took out of his closet, wore his leather gloves over a layer of nitrile I'd rubbed on his used towel. I crouched behind a car near Rashid's parking spot, and while I waited I used Hassan's sneakers to make a false trail through a muddy puddle away from my escape route. Since Hassan's right-handed, I put the gun in my right hand all wrapped in his towel." Pirin exhaled. "I was ready."

Gracie cringed; here it comes...

"Soon as Rashid stepped out of his car," Pirin said with preternatural serenity, "I shot him from maybe six, eight feet away. Right between the eyes.

"I dropped what was in my right hand—the gun plus Hassan's right-hand glove wrapped together in the towel, which was smoldering—and took off back to my dad's car on the other side of some railroad tracks. Drove home, ran straight to Ayesha's house, stuffed Hassan's jacket and his left-hand glove into one of their garbage cans and tossed his sneakers into some bushes. Lights were on in the house, but no one noticed me.

"The etche was quiet when I came in. Everyone was asleep, even Esti—and thank god, cuz that's when I started shaking. Not out of guilt but cuz I was afraid I'd made all kinds of mistakes and would end up caught by morning—even though I'd tried to anticipate, well, everything. But I couldn't stop worrying. The questions just kept on coming..."

"But no regrets?"

As Pirin turned to peer at Gracie, she looked like she always did, lean and strong and inexplicably handsome, and now her dark, dark eyes almost smiled. "No regrets," she replied evenly. "That man had no right to live in this world after he took Ayesha from it. He needed to be put down like the rabid monster he was."

Gracie nodded. "Yeah," she said. She wanted to say more. But she couldn't; she'd become flattened and numb all over again.

"Gotta admit, though—" Pirin shook her head. "That night was… *endless*. When morning came and my world was still normal, I tried to be normal, too. Went to school, even to a basketball game that night, just waiting to be found out. The news of Rashid's murder was a big friggin' deal, headlines everywhere, and the cops were on a tear. But damn, they bought the evidence I'd planted—all of it—and within about two weeks they arrested Hassan, charged him, and locked him up, no bail.

"Of course, he pled not guilty. Months later, though—*long* months—on the second day of his trial, he changed his plea. To guilty of first degree murder. Life sentence, no parole. He told the judge he shot Rashid to avenge his sister, described what Rashid did the night Ayesha died, even described their conversation in the backyard exactly as I'd seen and heard it.

"A year or so later, in this TV interview he did from prison, sure as hell he looked and sounded like he truly believed he killed Rashid. And I think he *does* believe it. One way to take responsibility for not stopping that fiend from throwing his little sister down the stairs."

The words that had streamed out of Pirin now halted. She briefly scrunched her shoulders, exhaled, and folded into repose, staring at her hands in her lap. There was more, much more. Gracie *knew* that, perceived it as one of the universe's elemental truths. And yes, she wanted to hear all of it.

First, however, you need to *say* something, Grace Gwyllt Olwyn.

But no. Nada. Silence.

Too much silence.

When at last Pirin gave up waiting, her voice quivered. "Y-You okay, Gracie? Have I scared you into packing your bags an'—?"

"No, Pir. You haven't scared me. But I guess I'm—yeah, I *am*. I'm in awe. Again."

Head lowered, Pirin reached for Gracie's hand while her almost-smile reappeared. "I understand. Because I'm in awe of *you*."

Before Gracie could reply, Pirin's phone pinged: a work text. "My two o'clock interview just canceled," she said, thumbing a reply, "which means I can blow off work today and try to get some sleep. How 'bout you?"

"Nothing I can't rearrange," teased Gracie before turning serious. "I do have a question, though, which you don't have to answer if you— if it makes you uncomfortable."

"Try me."

"How many other people have you killed?"

Pirin's eyes flared. "Oh."

Then her eyes closed, and Gracie realized...omigod...she's *counting*.

"Worst was this dude who I overheard threatening to shoot Roz Marin. I wasn't *trying* to kill him; but I did want to, y'know, effectively interrupt him. So when I clocked him retrieving a gun from his truck to use on Roz, I managed to clip him from behind with a baseball bat." Pirin offered a small crooked smile. "Just dumbshit luck there were no cams, no witnesses. I bolted immediately, heard later that 'they' figure he got up pretty quick, gun in hand, then collapsed and died a few minutes later. Brain hemorrhage. Dumbshit luck there were no witnesses, no cams.

"Roz doesn't know it, but that asshole was the reason I pulled back from her when I did. I just couldn't get her to understand she needed serious security because too many of the men she deals with are really dangerous. That night was the third time I'd intervened in less than two years. Also the only time I've ever acted on impulse without planning ahead and protecting myself. No regrets since it was clear the dude would've probably killed her if I hadn't done *something*. But I was too reckless. I knew if I kept it up sooner or later up I *would* have regrets."

"What about the people who, uh, weren't 'worst'?"

"There've been...a few. Most were carrying, a few stalked me. All of 'em rabid like Rashid. Conveyed how much they'd get off on raping, torturing, killing 'the cunt.' I always went for 'permanent offset,' y'know?—enough damage so they'd never pose a threat again. And some were unlucky, which is on them." Pirin shrugged. "Eliminate the threat—that's *my* principle of self-defense. Sticking to those phallocentric legalities about duty-to-retreat and 'proportionality' can be fatal when you're a female targeted by someone who'll keep trying till he doesn't fail."

"Yeah," Gracie muttered. "I-I'm learning that."

"Mmm, my education about it began in college. Kept having these run-ins with asshole men. I finally understood that something about the look in my eye—or maybe that I wouldn't be intimidated into looking away, into submitting—it hiked their testosterone levels all the way to toxic. I'm proud to say I didn't give a shit. Their problem, not mine. Got a bit better later because the asshole men at work had to restrain themselves. They couldn't risk making it physical, since either they were fellow employees or they were hoping I'd be generous in assessing their claim.

"But Basandere, asshole men are *every*-fucking-where, and generally three or four times a year, when something gets egregious enough—as in I've witnessed, or someone I deeply trust has witnessed his abusive crap—that's when I do what I call a recycle.

"Means I gather information about him, or occasionally them, then find an anonymous way to use it against him—them—in the most devastating way possible. Amazing how the right information delivered at the right time from the right source will inspire a friend to become an enemy. And people do sometimes kill their enemies."

"Did that happen? Somebody getting killed off one of your recycle things, I mean."

Pirin's shoulders hunched again. "Can't be certain—but yeah, at least twice I think."

"When did you first, um, 'recycle' someone?"

"Hmm...senior year of college, I guess. Roz and I were just starting out. I came by her work to drive her to the airport for this conference in Chicago before staying at her place to take care of her dog. And there was this creep at her office who swore right in front of us that he was gonna kill her. First of too many, it turned out. Anyway, I believed him. So I wheedled his name out of Roz on the way to the airport. Back at her place, I used her credentials—she had access to all kinds of databases—to find out what I could about him, including a few possible enemies."

"And then you played this guy and his enemies against each other."

"Bet," Pirin acknowledged with a sly little smile. "The files I found included lots of background info and phone numbers on a whole cast of characters. So I sent anonymous texts from a couple burner phones to the people who I suspected had 'issues' with the creep. All about how he'd be at this seedy bar at a certain time. Next I burner-texted *him* the same about *his*, uh, foes. My hope was that they'd all show up at the appointed time and place—and find themselves facing off in a circular firing squad that would distract the creep from even thinking about Roz."

"So did the circular firing squad actually happen?"

"Not quite. Turned out somebody *else*—god knows who—heard about it all. Whoever this was came early, snuck into the restroom through the bar's back entrance, and shot the creep dead. Bullet to the back of his head while he was pissing into a urinal."

"I can see why you try to keep your 'recycles' anonymous."

"Always. Anonymity and invisibility—the secret sauce."

"Could you stop if you wanted to?"

The question seemed to bring Pirin up short. Seconds and more seconds passed before she replied. "I could stop if I *had* to. But I'd feel the loss. Because it's become more than a 'hobby.'"

"So it's your true avocation. And here I was thinking that the little server farm you've squirreled away in the closet next to your desk was for perimeter cam video storage along with your pentesting and drone stuff."

At this Pirin laughed, her relief apparent. "About sixty-forty, I'd say."

One of Gracie's eyebrows poked upward. "And that 'sixty' is dedicated to recycling?"

"For now, mostly because the Bonecrusher-Whiting recycle is really data-intensive. Otherwise the proportions would be inverted *and* there'd be plenty of unused storage." Pirin nearly smiled. "Till now my recycles have been modest. Onesies, usually. Dudes into hurting women, the occasional local child porn hustler, like I thought Bonecrusher would turn out to be. But Bonecrusher *and* the Whitings? It's huge, a whole other order of magnitude."

Something in Pirin's voice made Gracie squint at her. "Are you—? Damn, I do believe you're nervous about this one."

"Oh yeah."

"But you've got a plan percolating…"

"Sort of. Next moves depend on what the river spits out over the next week or so."

"Zach, you mean."

Pirin nodded before once more studying her hands. "Are you okay not calling the cops?"

"I—" Gracie met Pirin's gaze. "Maybe someday I'll feel like I did something wrong—that I overreacted. But right now… Right now I'm okay with it. The guy who came here with a gun intending to murder you, maybe murder all of us, even Alaia and Astiri—he should *not* be allowed to fuck up our lives. And if I ever change my mind about that, I won't involve you. *I* took up Dragonfly, not you—and I did it without your permission. *I* used Dragonfly to force that scumbag into the river, not you. Hell, Pirin, you didn't know anything about it till it was over."

"I know keeping this to ourselves is hard," murmured Pirin, "So… thank you."

"You do realize that 'keeping this to ourselves' means *you* are committing a crime; 'accessory after the fact' I think it's called."

Pirin nodded.

"Which means I should be thanking you." After a long moment during which Pirin mutely stared at her, Utterly Other Gracie stood. "How 'bout we get naked in that wonderful bed of yours? I need cuddles. And… And I *so* wanna go down on you…"

Pirin took Gracie's hand, anxiety still in her eyes. "You're okay with this?"

"Not a hundred percent yet," Gracie admitted. "But mostly. The further I get from the moment when I made Dragonfly force that prick off the road, the safer I feel, the more liberated I feel. And I *like* feeling liberated."

"I was worried you'd freak when I told you about, y'know…"

"Early on, I knew there was *something* you wanted to say—major enough that you worried it might scare me away. So I watched you. Tried to imagine the worst. To see how my perception of you would change."

"Did it? Change, I mean…"

They had reached the bedroom. "I think it's more accurate to say it became part of my nascent impression of you."

"Which was—?"

"That within your hard-ass cocoon of impeccability almost anything's possible—but your impeccability holds." Gracie smiled. "Your impeccability is a constant. Which means that no matter what I've imagined, I can trust you. And love you. So I waited for you to feel safe enough with me to reveal yourself. When you finally did, I was shocked not shocked because I'd already—"

"—Imagined it."

"Here and there, more or less. Dreamed it, too. Which didn't alter my perception of you so much as deepen it. And I realized I wanted that kind of nerve."

"Oh, Gracie, I've seen the videos. You have that kind of nerve in abundance."

CHAPTER TWENTY-EIGHT:
WHENEVER YOU HAPPEN UPON SPIRALS

Two days.

That's how long it took Zach Farkas's body to be found by an aghast riverside homeowner who discovered it snagged on his dock some five miles downstream. Because Zach carried no phone, no ID, at first the body couldn't be identified. While that soon changed, how a leather-clad nineteen-year-old ended up in the river without anyone noticing remained a mystery.

"So—identified via his fingerprints…" muttered a subdued Gracie when Pirin showed her the news report. "That's it, then. The hit man really was Zach Farkas. And he really is dead."

Pirin waited for Gracie to say more. And waited. "You okay?" she asked finally.

"I guess. He was a dumb kid who got suckered by his asshole uncle and truth is, I feel sorry for him." At her desk pretending to work, Gracie tried to appear calm as she slowly exhaled. "But no, I don't feel remorse or guilt." Then she asked a question of her own. "Do you think the cops'll figure out what he was up to once they find the motorcycle?"

"Well, the Ducati's GPS can be linked to a smartphone app, which Zach has used," Pirin mused. "But not for this. If he *had* recorded anything, it'd be on his phone or stashed in the Ducati account or both—but I didn't find anything anywhere. Not even from earlier, when he came around here scouting. Also, he didn't use his smartphone or laptop to tell anyone about his plans. Looks to me like he didn't want a trail of incriminating evidence."

"Sooner or later, though, that motorcycle will be found, right?" Gracie was frowning. "Five miles upstream from his body. Half a mile from here. Think maybe the cops or his father might see significance in that and recall how close Zach was to his uncle? And how much his uncle wants you dead?"

"Good reason to, um, persuade their attentions elsewhere."

"So you have a plan now." Gracie leaned back in her chair. "Ready to tell me?"

❖

Somewhere in the night, way too wide awake, listening enviously for way too long to the steady rhythm of Pirin's slow, deep breathing, Gracie slipped out of bed to brew some chamomile tea and amble around the living room sipping it till she wore herself out.

As she plodded into the kitchen, however, she encountered a surprise—Eletun was already pouring boiling water into two mugs.

"Chamomile, yes?" Eletun asked, dangling a tea bag.

"Uh...yes." Gracie murmured, noticing Eletun's new clothing: undyed silk probably, elegantly, envelopingly long and flowing.

"Shall we sit?" Eletun suggested, handing one of the mugs to Gracie, who followed her to the bistro table. "Quite nice, this," she noted while she settled into a chair and looked around the space and outside too, where morning sun sent dappled light through leafed trees. "You've got a solid three or four generations to go here, though it might be wise to consider a move to higher ground ahead of the crowd."

"I can't imagine Pirin moving. She loves this place."

"Understandable. But it's barely more than a hundred feet above sea level. She'll come 'round in about ten or fifteen years. You'll see."

"Will I?" Gracie smiled politely. "So I'll have time later to fret about it. Right now, though—"

"Ah yes, you're worried about Pirin's plan."

"Is there anything you *don't* know?"

Eletun threw back her head and laughed, a belly-deep guffaw.

"*Shhh!* You'll wake—"

Oh, Gracie realized at last: I'm dreaming. She peered at Eletun, who'd quieted but couldn't seem to quell a broad grin. This *is* a dream, right?

"Pirin's plan," Eletun resumed, still grinning. "This recycle is a three-step, correct?" A rhetorical question apparently, since she kept on talking. "But you're stuck on step one—how to neutralize the threat Veech poses. I rather like Pirin's idea—to reveal his betrayal of Billy Whiting by disclosing his arrangement with TJ in a text to Billy's Norfolk prison bossman. That should keep your snarling wolf both isolated and quite distracted."

"Trouble is, somehow we have to stay not only anonymous but also invisible." Gracie slumped as she recalled those dispiriting, dead-end debates with Pirin. "Ideally, Pirin would spoof a text from one of TJ's disgruntled minions that would include damning evidence of Veech betraying Billy's interests. Except we have no inroads into TJ's operations. No smartphone access, no computer access."

"Oh dear." Eletun gazed at Gracie. "You two are *dangerously* tired. You need some genuine rest." Then she asked, "What about Zelda's?"

"Zelda's?"

"That sports bar where, at least by Pirin's reckoning, Veech regularly met TJ. It's still there, complete with phone number and email address, no? Just a quick targeted wardrive away..."

"Yes!" Gracie bounced to her feet. "What a great idea! An anonymous someone spoofs a text to a Whiting minion from the bar's phone—a text with Pirin's recording of that conversation between Veech and TJ..."

Eletun nodded approvingly. "You might want to omit the end, when Veech mentions Pirin by name, but you'll certainly want to include TJ's comment." Eletun cleared her throat and proceeded to mimic TJ's baritone with eerie, otherworldly precision: "'Not like before, boy. Now the *only* thing y'got t'trade is whatcha can tell me 'bout Billy Whiting's hustles. T'do that y'gotta be useful t'his lockup crew. Y'be our mole inside, Veech, we help ya out here.'"

Not until Eletun reached up and delicately placed a finger under her chin to encourage it upward did Gracie grasp that her jaw had dropped. "No," Gracie said to Eletun's now benign smile. "I will *not* ask how you did that."

"Good. Explaining it would take forever. So what's the problem with steps two and three?"

"According to Pirin, nothing. The covert gateways she planted in Bonecrusher's home systems last March gave her access to his company stuff, too—including the money laundering he does for the Whitings. She plans to use the gateways to sneak in and convert all liquid Whiting assets into cryptocurrencies, then stuff 'em into Bonecrusher crypto wallets." Gracie was pacing around the table now. "But Pirin figures Bonecrusher would move the crypto *again*—into anonymous wallets— before converting *that* into dollars to be donated to charities."

"Ah, for credibility's sake, Pirin wants to replicate what she thinks Bonecrusher would do. But these days truly anonymous crypto wallets are more complex to pull off, especially when converting crypto to fiat currency. As opposed to anonymous donations directly from either Whiting or Bonecrusher crypto wallets, which could save critical amounts of time. Mmm, credibility versus time…" Eletun paused to sip her tea. "Small reminder: Once completed and accepted, blockchain cryptocurrency transactions cannot be undone. No matter what."

Now it was Gracie's turn to smile. "Yeah, I think Pirin will bite on that. If we time it right, we won't need to mess with converting crypto to dollars because the Whitings won't realize they've been robbed till after the effects of step three kick in."

"You mean Bonecrusher's spectacularly irrational, world-shattering pang of conscience?"

Gracie's smile widened. "Yep. Bonecrusher will have a divine revelation and suddenly see his craving for underage girls as wretched depravity. Desperate for redemption, he'll shoot confessional messages to the feds, state LEOs, several media outlets, and some child exploitation NGOs—with attached files that lay bare the Whitings' sex trafficking operations. Everything related to Billy Whiting's chief pedophile-pimp Ryle, including terabytes of customer data. Plus the complete Whiting org chart in all its lurid detail."

"The Lotus Man brought down at last." Eletun winked. "How appropriate."

"Say what?" Confused, Gracie sat down again. "I don't get it."

"Oh? You didn't know? Bonecrusher's name—Andreas Nelumbo—means 'Lotus Man.' Actually 'Man Lotus,' to be literal." Once more, Eletun cleared her throat, whereupon a very familiar child's voice whispered "I am hiding from the Lotus Man, who wants to hurt me. But he cannot see you, so if you hold my hand he will not be able to see me either and I can escape him. And someday we will meet again."

At first, Gracie blanked, her mind reeling with *What the fuck?* Then...

"Omigod, *yes!*" Gracie gulped a breath. "Kaldi said that. When she and Analergin were very young." Gracie stared at Eletun. "And *you*...You haven't told me what happened to them."

"Ah, about that." What was it about the expression on Eletun's face as she slowly rose from the table? Suddenly Gracie suspected their time together was nearly over. "Let's move to the office so we don't disturb Pirin."

"Um...okay." She followed Eletun, who sat at Pirin's desk while she took the nearby lounge chair.

"I know you have many questions," Eletun said, her words cadencing into that gently hypnotic rhythm of hers. "Some of them I've answered, but you don't remember. Most of them I cannot answer. But I *can* show you a culmination that will become a beginning, and eventually you will arrive where you started 'and know the place for the first time.'" Eletun laughed softly. "Ah, time. So much of this is about the irreversible flow of time, perhaps better understood as the flow of entanglement, also irreversible. So close your eyes now, child, and go with the whirl."

Gracie obeyed, and soon Eletun's words transmuted into visions as immediate, as powerful, as *real* as any lived experience...

"Okay," said Pirin the instant Gracie's eyes blinked open to the sight of her a few feet away standing akimbo—and exquisitely, deliciously naked. "I have two questions."

Gracie blinked again. *So* much was wrong with this picture: She'd just woken not in bed but in the office lounge chair wrapped in her robe, Pirin was scrutinizing her with that you're-scaring-me-now bemusement usually reserved for her moments of especially overzealous drone flying, and—

And wait, where's Eletun?

Time, perhaps, to deflect: "Good morning," Gracie said, glancing around the office. "It *is* morning, right?"

"Oh yeah."

"What would you like to know?"

"Why are you sleeping in here? Do I snore now? And why are there *two* mugs with used tea bags on the bistro table? Were you entertaining?"

"That's four questions."

Still standing gloriously strip-akimbo, Pirin went slitty-eyed. "Corollaries don't count."

Beneath her robe, Gracie undulated to the rhythm of her impetuous arousal. "I love looking at you in the buff, Basamendi."

Nice try—but Pirin remained slitty-eyed and Eletun remained vanished. So Gracie rolled out of the lounge chair to approach a now furrow-browed Pirin. Time for the truth, even though Gracie wasn't quite sure what counted as true and what counted as…something else. "Couldn't sleep, so I decided to have some tea, but—" She cringed at the words she was about to say. "—But Eletun was, um, already pouring…"

"You had tea with Eletun," said Pirin, suddenly stolid. "In the middle of last night."

"We sat at the table and talked about ways to handle Veech and Bonecrusher and the Whitings and—"

"Really." Pirin face stayed blank but incredulity inflected her words. "And how'd *that* go?"

"Zelda's."

"What?"

"Eletun's idea. 'Just a quick targeted wardrive away—'"

"God*damn!*" Pirin whooped, her face transformed by a shit-eating grin. "That's fucking *perfect!*" She paused. "And I feel like an idiot for not thinking of it myself a long time ago."

"There's more." Gracie moved closer to twirl a finger around Pirin's left areola. "I'll tell you the rest…" Her finger slid across Pirin's chest into a come-hither gesture. "In bed."

And so she did. In detail. From between Pirin's magnificently muscled legs.

❖

"I wish Eletun would visit *my* dreams to have tea with me in the middle of the night," said Pirin after Gracie had slithered back up her body to burrow into her shoulder. "I have *so many* questions…"

"Maybe she will. Maybe it's your turn." Immersed in intoxicating Pirin-scent, Gracie nibbled Pirin's neck, Pirin's jaw, Pirin's warm, almost-smiling lips. "Anyway, just a feeling, but I'm not sure *I'll* see her again."

"Why?"

"I vaguely recall her reminding me to voice-record what I keep sensing is the last of her story, at least the part she wanted to tell me. But just like when she first showed up after lightning touched the ohskal, I have no memory of doing it. The last I saw of Eletun, I was sitting on the office lounge chair. She leaned over me, kissed my forehead, and whispered, 'As I've told you before, Gracie, pay attention whenever you happen upon spirals.' And then I closed my eyes because it felt like her goodbye."

"So there's another ohskal dream voice recording? On your phone?"

"Dunno. Maybe."

Pirin threw back the bedcovers. "Let's find out." She returned a couple of minutes later holding Gracie's phone. "It was on my desk." And yes, there was a new recording:

⚡ The women had reached this new Sea at the beginning of low-Sun season, and their chilled journey across it claimed several Mooncycles as they sailed westward whenever the volatile weather permitted, first to one island, then another and another. Throughout this time, Bele and her family glided overhead, perching nearby when the people aboard Bisiberria took shelter from low-Sun storms and angry Lightning.

They paused longest on the third island, through the worst of the tempestuous low-Sun weather. Here they repaired Bisiberria's bedraggled birdwings sail as best they could, though Analergin understood the implications of the outrigger's poor condition: Soon, too soon, this vessel that had so reliably sustained their journey would no longer be Seaworthy.

At least they were able to learn the ways of surviving in these new Lands so much farther north than they had ever been before, receiving much-needed help from the Gentles, a big-boned, fair-haired people willing to share not only their food but also their intimate knowledge of the Land and Sea around them.

And indeed, the women had much to learn—about the sort of raiment capable of keeping them warm, about what was edible and where to find it and how to make it safe to eat, about which animals to befriend, which to fear and how to defend against them.

Analergin was particularly interested in the Gentles' dugout canoes, which were smaller than Bisiberria and had no sails; instead they were paddled in nearshore waters and on Rivers. Analergin eagerly helped build these vessels and, with Kaldi, Jarrai, Honsoli, and Mardul, learned how to maneuver them upstream on fast-flowing Rivers without capsizing, a necessary skill for reaching the New Motherworld.

And when a group of Gentles trekked northward to gather blackglass from the surrounds of a long-sleeping Firemountain, Analergin persuaded them to allow her and two others from Bisiberria to accompany them. The three Bisiberria women returned with as much blackglass as they could carry—enough to make many blades and arrowheads and scrapers and spearheads while leaving plenty for gifting or exchange.

The women sought to reciprocate the Gentles' kindness and generosity by sharing Kaldi's knowledge of bowhunting and flatbow-making as well as Analergin's midwifery and Healing. During these long low-Sun Mooncycles, both she and Sineusi aided a number of Gentle women through difficult birthings of their offspring.

The pregnant Bastegaleki woman also gave birth. Meanwhile, the young Bastegaleki male's seed was taken by several Bisiberria women, including Jarrai, whose womb nurtured the seed. Meanwhile, the womb of another Bisiberria woman, Alaba, successfully cultivated Gentle male-seed.

With low-Sun season at last receding, Analergin was eager to follow the pull of the New Motherworld, now stronger in her than ever. So she offered the Gentles' leader a parting gift of one of her crystal firestarters. Then, as Bele flew overhead, she took to Sea yet again, sailing Bisiberria westward.

By this time, the outrigger carried just eleven souls. The Bastegaleki woman who had given birth did not want to return to Sea, so she stayed with her Gentle friends. And the other two from Bastegaleki, mother and son, had been lost to fatal falls from a cliff when one slipped and the other futilely attempted a save.

A further four chose to make home with the Gentles, too. "We have traveled far enough to be safe from Privation, and we are sick of being made sick by the Sea," one explained. "So we will birth our children here."

Over the generations since that moment, many have asked why Analergin, Kaldi, and the others did not also stay on the blackglass island with the Gentles rather than face the risks of further journey to unknown places.

Once, just once, Analergin provided hint in words she is known to have spoken to Kaldi: "I hear this New Motherworld sometimes, at night usually—a Resonance coming from within me yet from outside me, too. She beckons, always in Rhythm, always magnificent past description. And I *must* follow."

While we may understand how love alone kept Kaldi and Sineusi with her, we are justified in wondering why those eight others joined them. We may only surmise that the others also felt the pull of the New Motherworld's Rhythm. And, of course, they trusted Analergin with their lives.

At last came a cloudy morning bearing a strong southeast Wind that found Bisiberria off a richly green coast that fronted craggy, misted hills hundreds of reaches high. The northeast edge of an immense Seastorm was approaching, Analergin knew—a storm likely to destroy Bisiberria and everyone aboard if it caught them at Sea. And no matter which way they went, it would overtake them in two or three days.

When Bele swooped low before veering rightward toward the wide flatland of a River delta, Analergin followed. Sublime Perception had shown her that soon the River would angle northward, putting the intensifying southeast Wind nearly at their back.

She steered Bisiberria into what appeared to be the River's widest channel, past a small band of male fish-foragers who stared dumbfounded at the outrigger canoe sailing past them. Tempted though Analergin was to stop and engage them, she did not; they might well exhibit the same Privation-like aggression the women had faced from occasional bands of males during their low-Sun season journey.

More importantly, Analergin also knew she must bring Bisiberria as far upstream as possible as fast as possible and find shelter there before the Seastorm caught them. So she kept Bisiberria close to the River's edges, where, thanks to the same Wind that would soon endanger them, she exploited countercurrent eddies to defy the River's downstream flow.

Thus by late afternoon Bisiberria had covered a significant distance. When Kaldi pointed to what appeared to be a cave opening near the top of a limestone cliff along the River's east bank, Analergin steered the outrigger toward it, mourning that this likely would be Bisiberria's final harbor.

Soon Bisiberria's eleven women stood upon a small sandy beach at the bottom of the cliff pondering whether any other people might be nearby. Gazing at each other, Analergin and Kaldi raptly listened to this new place.

No, they simultaneously concluded—no other people anywhere close, nor any worrisome predators.

Soon Kaldi and Mardul had searched out a path up the cliff, examined the cave, and reported it to be both habitable and empty of predators. "The most recent occupants have been hyenas," Kaldi said. "People have been there, too—hunters rather than fishers. I judge we have time—a Mooncycle or more, before they return. So we are safe here for now."

To fend off nonhuman predators, the women built a robust fire on the rock ledge at the cave entrance, where Analergin watched Lightning illuminate the storm clouds to their south and understood: Not only would the storm soon be upon them, it would continue northward across high Mountains, its substantial rains filling this River's tributaries.

A few days after that, the overflowing River would rampage. Analergin could only hope the cave where they sheltered would remain above the floodwaters.

The women prepared by carrying all they could from Bisiberria up to the cave and tying down the outrigger to strong trees along the Riverbank. Those expert at fishing, hunting, and gathering collected what they could to sustain all eleven of them through the impending tempest.

Shortly after the rain and Lightning and Wind moved on, a freezing cold descended and had not yet abated when the River began to swell. Soon the River's flow was rolling breaking churning past the cave faster and faster, rising, rising, quickly inundating the Riverbanks, tearing trees from the cliffside—and ripping Bisiberria from its tethers to forever disappear downstream.

Watching the outrigger fracture in the River's madness, Kaldi's arm wrapped round her, Analergin thanked Bisiberria, tears in her eyes, grief in her heart.

Safe at the cave opening above the rushing water but shocked and shivering, the women watched it all—a seething jumble of debris that included at least one empty dugout canoe and several bodies, animal and human.

"I miss the warmth of Sundaselai," one woman muttered forlornly.

"But not, I wager, the rapists who condemned you to Ilchullo when you dared to resist them," Mardul scowled. "I would rather be cold and free than hot and enslaved. And hot or cold, we will need a canoe. Even if only to cross the River."

When Analergin suggested they craft two smaller, lighter canoes rather than one larger, less maneuverable vessel, and continue upstream, the others concurred. Even before the flooding receded, Bele and Analergin selected two trees. Thanks to the women's experience and their blackglass handaxes, both canoes (and thirteen paddles) were completed in slightly more than a Mooncycle.

Paddling their canoes upstream against the River's current was not easy, but most of the women had learned how from the Gentles on the blackglass island, so neither canoe capsized as they became accustomed to the River and its countercurrent eddies—though the farther upstream they journeyed, the faster the main current flowed against them.

Jarrai soon became expert at exploiting the eddies near the Riverbanks, mastering how to cross the main current to take advantage of an eddy spotted on the opposite bank. She did this with little or no downstream backsliding—a worthwhile endeavor because some eddies were quite lengthy. For Jarrai, this was "fun" and she enjoyed teaching her techniques to all the others, even Analergin.

Whenever the River lacked eddies, the women employed other means to journey upstream, grabbing rocks or branches along the banks to pull the canoes hand over hand or using axes to clear obstructive undergrowth before taking turns hauling the vessels by rope as they trudged along the bank.

Especially during these periods of slower upstream travel, Kaldi and Mardul or Honsoli ventured away from the River into an increasingly rugged landscape to bowhunt small creatures and occasionally a deer, search for signs of people, and pick out places where the women could safely pull the canoes ashore and rest.

Their first encounter with other humans occurred along an extended stretch of mild downstream current where the River passed through a wide valley. They came upon a small group of Gentles fishing at the River's confluence with a tributary, made friends, and remained long enough to learn much about what this higher terrain offered—including several types of mushrooms and legumes previously unknown to them.

These Gentles were adept at Taming, having collected a few diminutive, shaggy grazers for milk and meat. Upon noticing the little grazers sluffing off thick coats of low-Sun season hair, Sineusi realized she could spin it with her fingers into thread and, grateful for the knowledge and the male-seed the Gentles had so willingly shared, showed them how she accomplished this.

Just before they departed, Analergin gave the Gentles' leader two blackglass handaxes; in return, the eleven were gifted with a pair of Tamed grazers—a pregnant female and a male—which would provide milk, hair, offspring, and eventually meat. This thrilled Sineusi, who became the creatures' caretaker and somehow, when the women returned to the River, managed to keep them calm while floating along in a canoe full of humans.

Fortunately, the women enjoyed a protracted period of easy travel from countercurrent eddy to countercurrent eddy. Only when Analergin led the two dugouts onto one northerly tributary, then another, did the main current become more challenging before forcing them to a Riverside shelter to avoid another storm-induced flood.

While they waited for the high water to subside, they rescued two people clinging to tree debris—a mother and a child who clutched a wolf pup no more than a Mooncycle old. Some of the women wanted to drown the pup—"That is a *wolf!*" one screeched—but Sineusi defended the tiny, whimpering creature, declaring it Tameable and saying she would assume responsibility for it.

This garnered the deep loyalty of the rescued child, a boy of about ten or eleven Suncycles. "I did not realize you were such an adept Tamer," Analergin said to her later, "though I should have, since you Tamed me."

Before they returned to the River, Analergin told the women "Our upstream journey is nearly finished." Soon, she explained, they would sink their canoes to preserve them for possible future use, then journey across low Mountains to the headwaters of a new River.

"On foot?" asked a frowning Jarrai.

"Yes, but only for a few days," Analergin said. "To keep us from any injury, we will move slowly and carefully. And we will meet no crocodiles."

Mardul laughed. "A worthwhile trade—cold for crocodiles."

"So," Jarrai responded, rubbing her visibly pregnant belly, "we are close."

"Oh yes," Analergin replied. "When we reach the headwaters of the new River, we stand at the threshold of the New Motherworld. There we will find shelter and take time to craft new dugouts for the final part of our journey, which will deliver us to the shores of the Sea Beyond."

"Downstream all the way to the Sea Beyond?" asked Honsoli.

"Downstream all the way," Analergin assured her.

And finally Jarrai smiled...

As high-Sun season began to wane, they at last glimpsed the Sea Beyond ahead of them, misted blue behind thickly forested Land that rose many reaches on either side of the River. When their view of the Sea widened, Analergin pointed up to a long, high ridge looming on their left. "There," she said to Kaldi. "I want to see with my own eyes what this world looks like from up there."

While the others rested on the Riverbank, Analergin and Kaldi walked up the ridge to its highest point. Soon Kaldi found and explored a large, unoccupied southeast-facing cave with a view that encompassed both the River on which they had traveled and its confluence with another flowing from the west.

Here she and Analergin signaled the others, then waited to be joined by Sineusi and the two women who would shortly become the first Mothers in their New Motherworld. When they arrived, Analergin turned to Jarrai and Alaba. "Yes?" she asked.

Jarrai answered with tears, then a nod as she gripped her swollen belly.

"Yes," concurred Alaba.

One arm around Jarrai, the other around Alaba, Analergin scanned the Mountains lifting out of the mists to their east, their south, their west, then turned to gaze at the pristine streams flowing northward down to the Sea Beyond.

Knowing they would be safe here for all their lives and for many, many generations to come, Analergin smiled at Kaldi, at Sineusi, at Bele spiraling above them...*Thank you, Alama...*

"We are home, then," she affirmed. "Our children shall hail from here."

CHAPTER TWENTY-NINE: ALL THE WAY

Six twenty in the morning, still mostly dark outside, and, of course, Gracie was still asleep.

Already out of bed and imbibing coffee, Pirin headed to the office to check her two monitoring apps—Spotter and her homemade version of news-alert software originally designed for journalists that she used to track the effects of what Gracie had dubbed the VBW Recycle.

Those apps, now focused on B and W, were silent on this morning, like too many mornings before it. Frustrating, given how remarkably well—and fast—V had played out.

Way back in December, Pirin had resisted an urge to get fancy and instead, as Eletun suggested, spoofed a text from the nonexistent "Zelda" herself using the bar's actual IP address. The message went to Billy Whiting's chief thug incarcerated at Norfolk Correctional—a one-liner that read "We don't want your trash no more" and came with an MP3 of the audio revealing Veech's collusion with TJ Sunty that Pirin had recorded with her zero-click exploit, the same clip Gracie heard Eletun so uncannily mimic.

Result: Veech was in *deeep* shit, afraid to leave his cell after getting cold-cocked and nearly shivved on the tier a couple of weeks after "Zelda" sent her text, whining hysterically to his mother and his brother about having been greenlit by Billy's crew and begging for help.

Just before she deleted the zero-click exploit she'd put on Veech's phone, it recorded Ezra: "You stupid donkey *bastard!*" he'd screamed. "What the fuck is *wrong* with you? Billy is family! You betrayed *family!* An' Zach! My son ended up in the fuckin' Merrimack River cuz you wouldn't stop bitchin' about that dyke you hate so much. *My son is dead BECAUSE OF YOU!* I don't *ever* wanna hear your voice again."

From LEO sources, Pirin learned that within a week of that conversation Norfolk Correctional's screws "discovered" Veech's smartphone, which they confiscated before dragging him off to the prison's restrictive housing unit, where'd he'd been ever since. Not perfect, but not bad either.

Gracie had lobbied against following up too quickly with B and W. For the sake of invisibility, she'd argued, the surprise reveal of Veech's treachery must not be linked in any way to what would follow.

And even though Pirin knew Gracie was right—damn, it was *hard*. No amount of impatient scowling got Gracie to relent. "Not yet," she kept repeating.

So instead Pirin planned. And planned. How to make Bonecrusher's unlikely come-to-Jesus moment believable. Choosing which LEOs and NGOs and media were uncorrupted enough to entrust with what had become extensive evidence of Whiting dirty dealings. Best ways to ensure that chief pedophile-pimp Ryle and his customers didn't slink away unscathed. Honing the timing for a single sudden, disorienting B&W takedown. And, most especially, keeping it all not merely anonymous but invisible.

At last, in late February Gracie said it: "Yes. Now."

And after all that buildup, the whole thing went down in the wee hours of a Sunday morning like the fucking Kentucky Derby.

Blink and you missed it.

Heh.

Once into Bonecrusher's laptop and using his credentials, Pirin shifted every cent of the Whiting cash to which Bonecrusher had access—as well as a hundred million dollars' worth of other Whiting liquid assets, stocks and bonds mostly—into already fat Whiting crypto wallets. Then she moved all the Whiting crypto into Bonecrusher's personal crypto wallets. Upwards of eighty percent of this was immediately donated to nonprofits focused on child exploitation, sex trafficking, and violence against women.

Next came Bonecrusher's divine-revelation email, a confession drenched in narcissistic, blamecasting hyper-religiosity sent (to the FBI, the IRS, the DHS, the state attorney general, plus several human trafficking and violence-against-women NGOs as well as several major media outlets) from his business email address, along with an abundance of incriminating audio, video, and annotated Whiting organization data carefully curated to cement the impression that Bonecrusher had compiled it.

To give Bonecrusher time—and sufficient motivation—to grasp that denying authorship of the divine-revelation epistle and its accompanying evidence would be far worse than running to the feds for what protection he could get, Pirin had his email account send copies of his confession, with all the attachments, to every Nelumbo family personal email account.

Finally, she deleted her presence on every device linked to everyone Bonecrusher- and Whiting-related—the covert gateways, the assorted surveillance apps, the zero-click phone exploit, *everything*. Though this would radically reduce future listening and data gathering opportunities and leave Pirin (sometimes uncomfortably) clueless, it was the price of a nearly invisible hand.

All in all, the entire B&W Kentucky Derby took about two hours.

Pirin didn't expect to hear much for a few days anyway, not least because her information sources had been reduced to LEOs, the usual commercial databases, and the media.

The Whitings, she reckoned, would be bouncing between shock, rage, and panic. They'd try to keep their quite significant losses secret for as long as possible while they chased down who took how much and what happened to it.

Nor were any LEOs likely to acknowledge squat as two opposing forces within their ranks clashed: The ambitious would launch investigations to validate the Bonecrusher documentation and turn it into evidence, while those on the Whiting payroll would work hard to discredit it. The media people, meanwhile, would also hesitate, seeking confirmation from somebody somewhere—until, at last unable to resist, somebody somewhere would blab, and voilà!—a leak.

But damn, the B&W Kentucky Derby was *seventeen days* ago. Though Gracie remained sanguine—"Hey, no cops at our door yet, so let's take that as a good sign"—Pirin was getting antsy. What the *hell!* After seventeen days there should be hints, ripples of LEO agitation at the very least.

Which was why Pirin couldn't stop pacing like a caged animal.

Nine thirteen in the morning now, a sunny day, and, of course, Gracie still sleeping ("one of the meager privileges of the semi-furloughed," she'd said). As Pirin attempted to sip rather than gulp her third cup of coffee, her homemade news-alerter beeped. Then it beeped again. And again…

Finally all hell was breaking loose.

And yes, waking Gracie to share *this* news was definitely worth it: The feds had just announced with suits-before-the-microphones brouhaha that…

Whiting-affiliated chief pedophile-pimp Ryle and several of his best customers had been arrested, and more arrests were "pending."

Both the Whiting organization and Brian Whiting's hedge fund faced multiple federal investigations, all their financial assets frozen or seized.

Billy Whiting, "a person of interest in these matters," was nowhere to be found.

Meanwhile, in other news, Cleary Whiting had been hospitalized; something about his heart. And Congressman Whiting was disavowing everything and everyone.

Minutes later, Spotter reported internal LEO chatter about Bonecrusher: He was now a material witness in federal custody. His family was hiding. Spotter also picked up a Norfolk Correctional staff memo noting that the investigation of a death ten days earlier in the facility's restrictive housing unit concluded that the inmate, Vicsorgó Farkas, had committed suicide.

Gracie said simply: "Wow."

"Wish I could listen in like before," Pirin grumbled.

"Price of success, sweetums. Pretty damn effective, this invisible hand stuff." Gracie's words exuded her vast relief, as did the kiss she bestowed on Pirin's pursed lips, a kiss that lingered until Pirin's lips found their appetite.

❖

They made love slowly, savoring every scent, every taste, every soft laugh. When at last they pulled up the covers and curled under them into a contentedly undulating head-to-foot hug, Pirin spoke first. "I meant to ask you—any dreams last night?"

"Nope." Gracie exhaled slowly. "Gotta admit I kinda miss Eletun."

"So you really think her story's ended and she's gone?"

"Maybe..." Gracie's shoulders bobbed beneath Pirin's encircling arm. "Analergin, Kaldi, Sineusi, and the others got to their New Motherworld. That qualifies as an ending."

"A happy ending, I'd say. Especially if they're my forebears."

"From forty thousand years ago."

"Everybody has forebears from forty thousand years ago. Why couldn't these be mine? Even setting aside any connection between lightning touching Amatchi's 'lightning stone' right in front of you and this dream journey Eletun took you on—even besides all that, *so much fits*. The words, the language. The old tales."

Gracie's voice grew wistful. "Gotta say, I'd love to experience Analergin's New Motherworld, so undamaged, so pristine. Those women had to struggle really hard, but they found genuine freedom. So different from now. Nowhere left to run anymore..."

Pirin drew Gracie closer. "Which is why we make a stand for *our* freedom right here, where we are, in whatever way we can for as long as we can."

"Like your recycling."

"Mmm. Gotta do *something* when all the world's legal systems are rigged against anyone female. My recycles—hit-and-run hacks using those same legal systems to ruin our abusers—have been my tiny contribution to fighting rape culture." Pirin paused, stomach tensing. "Does that freak you out?"

"Truth?" Gracie lifted herself off Pirin's shoulder and their eyes locked. "Early on, as I kinda figured out some of what you were doing, I found it breathtaking. But really scary, too. Like, what if you got caught? And *then*, when that fucked up kid tried to kill you..." Gracie blinked back tears. "I'm not scared anymore, Pirin. I'm with you all the way. All the way."

Gently pulling Gracie in close, Pirin shivered as she exhaled into her future. Thank you, Alama, thank you thank you thank you... "You know what day it is, right?"

"March sixteen. We get our first vaccines this afternoon."

"Also, we met exactly a year ago, in the park where you gave me back the ohskal."

"The ohskal..." Gracie snugged into Pirin's shoulder. "Y'know, I've touched it only twice—first time for a few seconds when I took it from its box and held it up to the sunlight. Don't remember putting it down, but it was on the windowsill when the blue lightning tapped it. Then I touched it again later, when I returned it to its box as fast as I could. Haven't seen it since." She paused. "Certainly seems longer than a year..."

"Is that good or bad?"

"Oh, it's *good*." Gracie grinned. "I'm the happiest I've ever been. Ever."

"Well then, *happy* anniversary." Pirin nuzzled into a slow hotmelt of a kiss that kept on melting.

Half an hour later, she rolled onto her back feeling lighter than—well, than she had in half a lifetime.

"Hey, wanna take a look at it?" she dared to ask. "At the ohskal?"

Pirin wasn't entirely surprised to see Gracie hesitate. Right from the day they met, it was clear she wanted nothing to do with ohskal. And when she moved in, she acted as though the ohskal didn't exist. Now Pirin waited, unable to guess what Gracie would decide.

"Yeah, it's time," Gracie said, yanking the bedcovers aside and donning a robe she didn't bother to tie. "Show me."

Pirin led the way into the living room, retrieved the little wooden box from the cabinet beneath the TV, and handed it to Gracie, who opened it and gazed at its contents for a full minute. "May I?" she asked Pirin.

"Of course."

Gracie handed the box back to Pirin, delicately reached in with both hands, and lifted the stone into the springtime sunshine cascading through the room's high east windows, angling the ohskal's starburst of clear quartz crystal spears so bright spectra of sunlight twirled across walls and ceiling.

"Mmm," she murmured, "in a somewhat gentler mood this time, are we?" Then, as she turned the stone over, her eyes went wide with genuine shock. "I never looked at the other side. I-I can't believe this..."

"The ammonite fossil, you mean?" Pirin smiled. "Basamendi sorginak will tell you that once upon a time lightning struck it and the quartz starburst instantly popped out, but Jess's favorite geochemist thinks the ammonite fossilized into pyrite and then quartz crystals slowly grew off the side of it…once upon a time…"

"I—" Gracie's voice caught as her finger traced the fossil's meticulously proportioned, red-brown ribbed curves. She pulled in a breath before hoarsely whispering "I never knew the ohskal *spirals*."

Pirin sat down on the sofa. "Oh yeah—you can actually see the spiral's Fibonacci sequence." But why, she wondered, get so rattled by—

And then she remembered Eletun's words to Gracie: "Pay attention whenever you happen upon spirals…"

Gracie's eyebrows jittered. "What do you think it means, Pir?"

"Wish I knew."

"Seems like it means *something* though, huh?"

"Can't say it's not possible." Pirin winked. "Guess you'll just have to do what Eletun always told you."

They both laughed as they recited in unison: "'*Pay attention*, Gracie.'"

About the Author

With her fifth novel, *Dreams Entangled*, Sophia Kell Hagin continues exploring crossgenre speculative fiction, this time combining action/cyber thriller elements with magical realism and mythopoeia. *Dreams Entangled* follows *Not All A Dream*, which won a 2022 Golden Crown Literary Society Award in General Fiction. Sophia's first novel, *Whatever Gods May Be*, also won a Golden Crown Literary Society Award (in 2011, for Dramatic General Fiction) as well as several other awards. Two more novels about the protagonist of *Whatever Gods May Be*, Jamie Gwynmorgan, ensued: *Shadows of Something Real* and *Omnipotence Enough*.

Website: https://www.SophiaKellHagin.com/

Books Available from Bold Strokes Books

Anywhere with You by Margo Glynn. On a road trip through the Great American Southwest, two friends discover nature, hope, and each other. (978-1-63679-907-0)

Burning Bridges by Lesley Davis. Can Clancy and Jude crack the case of nine missing women—and the secrets of their own hearts? (978-1-63679-872-1)

Dreams Entangled by Sophia Kell Hagin. Amid self-doubt, secrets, a pandemic, fear of attack and attempted murder, Pirin and Gracie's attraction turns to love and their lives will never be the same. (978-1-63679-892-9)

Echoes of Love by Catherine Lane. As Hazel's and Jo's paths intertwine, they're swept up in a whirlwind of long-buried secrets, sizzling chemistry, and memories that won't be denied. (978-1-63679-835-6)

Moonlight Obsession by Sheri Lewis Wohl. All it takes to stop a clever killer is moonlight, love, and a silver bullet. (978-1-63679-831-8)

My Boyfriend's Wife by Joy Argento. Amid betrayal and heartbreak, can two women discover a love that could heal their pasts and rewrite their futures? (978-1-63679-866-0)

Tapout by Nicole Disney. A struggling MMA fighter finds her edge in an underground ring, but as she falls for the magnetic and ambitious promoter behind the matches, their dangerous world threatens to destroy everything they've fought to rebuild. (978-1-63679-924-7)

The Fame Game by Ronica Black. Wild child Hollywood actress Luna Kirkman begins dating Hollywood's leading man, only to fall for his straitlaced sister instead. (978-1-63679-858-5)

An Extraordinary Passion by Kit Meredith. An autistic podcaster must decide whether to take a chance on her polyamorous guest and indulge their shared passion, despite her history. (978-1-63679-679-6)

That's Amore! by Georgia Beers. The romantic city of Rome should inspire Lily's passion for writing, if she can look away from Marina Troiani, her witty, smart, and unassumingly beautiful Italian tour guide. (978-1-63679-841-7)

The Unexpected Heiress by Cassidy Crane. When a cynical opportunist meets a shy but spirited heiress, the last thing she plans is for her heart to get involved. (978-1-63679-833-2)

Through Sky and Stars by Tessa Croft. Can Val and Nicole's love cross space and time to change the fate of humanity? (978-1-63679-862-2)

Uncomplicate It by Kel McCord. When an office attraction threatens her career, Hollis Reed's carefully laid plans demand revision. (978-1-63679-864-6)

Vanguard by Gun Brooke. Beth Wild, Subterranean freedom fighter, is in the crosshairs when she fights for her people and risks her heart for loving the exacting Celestial dissident leader, LaSierra Delmonte. (978-1-63679-818-9)

Wild Night Rising by Barbara Ann Wright. Riding Harleys instead of horses, the Wild Hunt of myth is once again unleashed upon the world. Their ousted leader and a fey cop must join forces to rein in the ride of terror. (978-1-63679-749-6)

Heart's Appraisal by Jo Hemmingwood. Andy and Hazel can't deny their attraction, but they'll never agree on the place they call home. (978-1-63679-856-1)

Behold My Heart by Ronica Black. Alora Anders is a highly successful artist who's losing her vision. Devastated, she hires Bodie Banks, a young struggling sculptor as a live-in assistant. Can Alora open her mind and her heart to accept Bodie into her life? (978-1-63679-810-3)

Fearless Hearts by Radclyffe. One wounded woman, one determined to protect her—and a summertime of risk, danger, and desire. (978-1-63679-837-0)

Forever Family by L.M. Rose. Two friends come together after tragedy to raise a baby, finding love along the way. (978-1-63679-868-4)

Stranger in the Sand by Renee Roman. Grace Langley is haunted by guilt. Fagan Shaw wishes she could remember her past. Will finding each other bring the closure they're looking for in order to have a brighter future? (978-1-63679-802-8)

The Nursing Home Hoax by Shelley Thrasher and Ann Faulkner. In this fresh take for grown-ups on the classic Nancy Drew series, crime-solving duo Taylor and Marilee investigate suspicious activity at a small East Texas nursing home. (978-1-63679-806-6)

The Rise and Fall of Conner Cody by Chelsey Lynford. A successful yet lonely Hollywood starlet must decide if she can let go of old wounds and accept a chance at family, friendship, and the love of a lifetime. (978-1-63679-739-7)

A Conflict of Interest by Morgan Adams. Tensions rise when a one-night stand becomes a major conflict of interest between an up-and-coming senior associate and a dedicated cardiac surgeon. (978-1-63679-870-7)

A Magnificent Disturbance by Lee Lynch. These everyday dykes and their friends will stop at nothing to see the women's clinic thrive and, in the process, their ideals, their wounds, and a steadfast allegiance to one another make them heroes. (978-1-63679-031-2)

A Marvelous Murder by David S. Pederson. When a hated director is found dead in his locked study, movie star Victor Marvel, his boyfriend Griff, and friend Eve seek to uncover what really happened to Orland Orcott. (978-1-63679-798-4)

Big Corpse on Campus by Karis Walsh. When University Police Officer Cappy Flannery investigates what looks like a clear-cut suicide, she discovers that the case—and her feelings for librarian Jazz—are more complicated than she expected. (978-1-63679-852-3)

Charity Case by Jean Copeland. Bad girl Lindsay Chase came home to Connecticut for a fresh start, but an old, risky habit provides the chance to save the day for her new love, Ellie. (978-1-63679-593-5)

Moments to Treasure by Ali Vali. Levi Montbard and Yasmine Hassani have found a vast Templar treasure, but there is much more to the story—and what is left to be found. (978-1-63679-473-0)

The Stolen Girl by Cari Hunter. Detective Inspector Jo Shaw is determined to prove she's fit for work after an injury that almost killed her, but a new case brings her up against people who will do anything to preserve their own interests, putting Jo—and those closest to her—directly in the line of fire. (978-1-63679-822-6)